About the author

As a young child, Golnaz Hashemzadeh (Iran) fled with her parents to Sweden. She graduated from the Stockholm School of Economics, where she was the eighth woman in the school's history, and the first with a foreign background, to be elected President of the Student Association. She was named one of 50 Goldman Sachs Global Leaders in 2005 before founding the non-profit organization Inkludera Invest. Her debut novel, *She Is Not Me* (*Hon är inte jag*), was published in Sweden in 2012 to great critical acclaim. She lives in Stockholm.

About the translator

Katarina Tucker was born in the United States and raised bilingually with English and Swedish. She holds a doctorate in Scandinavian literature from the University of Wisconsin-Madison. In 2003 she won the American-Scandinavian Foundation's Translation Prize for her translation of Sven Delblanc's *Jerusalem's Night*. Her previous translations include Monika Fagerholm's *The American Girl* and *The Glitter Scene* as well as Maria Sveland's *Bitter Bitch*.

She Is Not Me

Golnaz Hashemzadeh

She Is Not Me

Translated from the Swedish
by Katarina Tucker

World Editions

Published in Great Britain in 2015 by World Editions Ltd., London

www.worldeditions.org

Copyright © Golnaz Hashemzadeh, 2012
English translation copyright © Katarina Tucker and
World Editions, 2015
Cover design Multitude
Image credit © Silveri/Plainpicture/Hollandse Hoogte

The moral rights of the author and translator have been asserted in
accordance with the Copyright, Designs and Patents Act 1988

First published as *Hon är inte jag* in Sweden by
Wahlström & Widstrand, 2012
Published by agreement with Ahlander Agency

British Library Cataloguing-in-Publication Data
A catalogue record for this book is available on request from
the British Library

ISBN 978-94-6238-031-8

Typeset in Minion Pro

The cost of this translation was defrayed by a subsidy from
the Swedish Arts Council, gratefully acknowledged

Distribution Europe (except the Netherlands and Belgium):
Turnaround Publishers Services, London
Distribution the Netherlands and Belgium: Centraal Boekhuis,
Culemborg, the Netherlands

For our beloved father
1960 - 2012

Every body perseveres in its state of rest, or of uniform motion in a right line, unless it is compelled to change that state by forces impressed thereon.

The alteration of motion is ever proportional to the motive force impressed; and is made in the direction of the right line in which that force is impressed.

To every action there is always opposed an equal reaction: or the mutual actions of two bodies upon each other are always equal, and directed to contrary parts.

Newton's Laws of Motion

FACTORY TOWN

It deserved stillness, this place.

The Girl knew they had done something big. She had felt it in Mama's shaking hand as the soldier studied their passports and cast coal-black glances at her face, comparing it to the photo.

'What's your name?'

'Setareh,' Mama had answered.

She had wanted to protest, but Mama's nails were digging deeply into the palm of her hand. Pomegranate-red drops pushed out through her skin and burnt her fingers, tearing her eyes away from the soldier's darkness.

'Can't she speak for herself?'

'She's tired; it's early.'

She knew they had done something big. She had felt it in the pit of her stomach as the plane was taking off, and Mama was sometimes shaking with laughter, sometimes shaking with tears, or was it something else entirely? But most of all she had seen it in Grandpa's eyes when he released his tight grasp on her and handed her to Mama. Grandpa, the biggest and strongest person she knew. Who hated tears.

She had felt the unknown, ungraspable plan so strongly that she had felt called upon to do her part when the plane touched down and they were met by the police again. Police officers who said no. Police officers who opened the door to a small room. She had pulled away, screamed. She had tried running out to Papa. Wasn't that his voice she heard on the other side of the thin wall? They couldn't be stopped now, not when they were so close, had come so far. Where were they going?

She had been caught and gave up. She lay down on a cold stone bench, and with her eyes half-closed she followed the police officer's writing hand, as it filled in one sheet after another. Mama's voice churned on, a mixture of words she understood and something else. The Girl could see in the police officer's hesitating hand that she didn't understand all of Mama's words either, but there were stacks of paper with questions that needed to be answered.

She didn't understand the police officer, and she didn't understand Mama. She didn't understand how the police officer could be a woman, a woman with such thin, such fair-coloured hair.

'Tell them your name,' Mama said now, and stroked her back. She hesitated. What did they want to hear?

'Setareh,' she heard herself answer. She was trying to support the plan, but it must have been the wrong answer because the policewoman stopped writing. Mama froze.

'No, your real name!' Mama's nails dug into her skin again.

The policewoman stood up, and shouted out into the corridor. She closed her eyes completely, hoping to make herself invisible until the plan had been carried out. It was probably too big for her.

The small room was smaller than all of the flats they had lived in over there. She knew because she had measured by taking long strides from one end to another. But this room felt bigger, it felt endless. She curled up in the window. The white ground stretched as far as the eye could see, and then those tall trees took over. The window made all the difference. They had never had windows before. Back there they had hung large sheets along the walls; it was the first thing they did every time they moved in someplace new. Dark sheets that sometimes allowed blinking police lights to slip through, making Mama's hand search for hers, and Papa's hand reach for the pack of cigarettes. Back there, the world had ended at the wall. Here, it was at the wall, at the window, that the world began. She stretched out on the windowsill, rested her ear against her upper arm. There was no movement outside. She was used to outside meaning that she had to hold Mama's hand tightly and struggle against the flood of people who wanted to pull her along with them. She was used to seeing the women's black *chadors* dragging in the dust from the street. She was used to everyone looking like Mama. And to the fear that one day she would look up and discover that she was holding the wrong hand.

She was used to new smells at every street corner: saffron on newly steamed rice, raw lamb, man-sweat, and heated oil. She was used to Mama's eyes opening wide every time they left the house. Used to focusing her own gaze up, toward Mama's face. She was watching over Mama's eyes.

She was used to the crushing sound of car tyres against uneven asphalt, the street seller's songs, the sirens that screamed the second before a sea of people dressed in black streamed toward open cellar doors in search of protection. She was used to the loud beats of Mama's heart drowning out the ear-splitting sound of the sirens. The beats that never grew silent, not even when they were lying next to each other at night.

Here, *outside* was something else. It was quiet outside. She had never heard such a silence. It was so quiet it was deafening. If she lay in the window long enough someone would race by. Someone in bright, colourful clothes. Someone who held two sticks in his hands and glided over the white. Someone just as soundless as the trees. The colourful one reminded her of the white rabbit that leads the way to Wonderland, the rabbit that is in a terrible hurry. She wanted to run after the colourful figure to see if he had fallen into a hole when he changed from a ball of colour to a dot to nothing. She had tried once. She had run out into the snow in just her socks, but there was nothing there. Nothing but the silence. She had fallen to her knees and felt the tracks in the snow with her bare hands to reassure herself that something had actually passed by. There was something unnatural about the movement, the speed. This place was made for silence. She breathed in the scentless cold. Treading carefully, she tried retracing her steps back to the window.

It deserved stillness, this place.

*

The Girl chose to lie with her back to the room and to Mama and Papa, her gaze focused outside. She didn't need to look to know that Papa was resting his head in one hand and holding a cigarette in the other. Or that Mama was standing by the simmering teapot on the stove. They were waiting. In the same place. With the same expression on their faces every day.

'*They* decide if we're allowed to stay,' Papa had explained.

She had only nodded in reply. She didn't need to ask who *they* were. As long as she could remember, *they* had decided everything. *They* had taken Amo Taghi, Papa's best friend. *They* had taken the red car. *They* had forced Mama to wear a heavy, black *chador*. It was time to move again, because of *them*. And now *they* would decide: between sheet-covered walls or the white endlessness. She thought that the big plan was to get away from *them*, to make Mama stop arching her eyebrows, to keep her eyes from becoming wide and filled with fear. To make Mama's heart stop pounding when they were lying close together in the large bed, all three of them. Make it so that she wouldn't have to feel the beats echoing inside of her.

*

Sometimes she felt something in the air change and Mama and Papa would go into a kind of trance. Papa's wide Cheshire grin stretched out bright and shining, and Mama's laughter raced like pearls between the walls. Papa slapped *oddkollon* against his newly shaven cheeks and pulled her in so close that the aftershave made her eyes water, and Mama drew black lines around her eyes and looked at Papa, blushing.

'We did it, *dokhtaram*, Mama and Papa did it!' Papa would shout then, while Mama stood at the stove and carefully spread *esfand* over the warm burner. The burnt seeds would make sure that the good luck didn't end here. It would travel through the cosmos and make sure *they* made the right decisions. 'We're in Sweden! Do you know how many people there are back in Iran who want the same thing?'

She had no idea how many people were left in Iran, but she knew how much Mama and Papa had wanted this. How much they had whispered, how often they had made phone calls at night, how many times they had packed and later repacked.

'Do you understand what's different, *dokhtaram*?' Papa looked at her with hope in his eyes. She wanted to point out the window. She wanted to discuss the stillness, the endlessness, dots of colour gliding over untouched snow, rabbits and holes. But she let him answer the question. The plan was his, after all.

'Here, you're free! You are free *dokhtaram*! You can do whatever you want. You have rights. There are laws and rules that say you have to be treated like a person. No one is allowed to force you to think and believe what they think and believe. No one is allowed to kill you. Do you know what that means?'

She nodded, shook her head. Looked deep into his honey eyes, so many shades lighter than hers. Papa's honey look was so pure. She wondered if it knew what his hands seemed to know. His hands that shook and fumbled for the pack of cigarettes when his honey gaze disappeared and was replaced by something she still didn't understand.

'Everything we've been hiding from, all of the terrible things that could have happened, are gone. As soon as we get the right papers from *them* we'll get a new home, a home no one can make us leave. You'll get your own room with your own toys that will be yours forever. Then you'll learn Swedish, and do your homework, and get the highest marks, and do you know what the best thing is? Then you can become whatever you want. You can become a doctor, an engineer, a cabinet minister, a lawyer, anything! There are *emkanat* here, *dokhtaram*. Opportunities.

She recognized that voice. Papa had used the same voice during his *jaleseh*: meetings with strangers who arrived by motorbike; they would put on blindfolds and sit in a circle on the floor and never stop talking. She wondered where all of the words came from. Wondered who had taught these strangers all the thoughts and ideas that kept the sentences alive. Circle after circle of grown-ups with covered eyes who never stopped talking. They picked their noses and scratched their groins, convinced that no one saw. That was the whole point: the words could never be connected to a face. No one ever tried to look, to cheat. No one except her. She couldn't resist.

She recognized the voice and suspected that things hadn't turned out the way Papa had hoped the last time he had spoken that way. She hoped that he didn't remember, that he wouldn't be reminded. That this time was the time the plan would work.

In these moments, Mama didn't say much. Her red lips cast pearl laughter against the walls, but her eyes were blank between the lines of kohl. If you looked carefully, you could see that Mama sometimes let her guard down, that she tried to imitate Papa's happiness, but sometimes she forgot why. The Girl nodded to herself. *That's the way it is.* She looked at the empty air between Mama and Papa. There was no tension. They hadn't noticed that Mama wasn't really participating. The Girl chewed on the inside of her bottom lip and wondered how long it would take for them to notice, and if she could deceive them, mount blinders alongside their bright eyes, and absorb their sight into her own dark gaze.

She could read their every thought. In her, they only met silence.

It's hard to explain. If only you were here and could see for yourselves. I wish I was there with you and that things hadn't ended up like this, but we can't turn back time. Both of us have understood that. We talk about it a lot. What if we had done this, what if that had worked, what if we had come up with a different plan. But we understand that there were no other options. No, I'm lying when I write that. I haven't understood. But he says that I have to, so I'm trying.

This is a strange place. I was prepared for the cold; that's not a problem. There are many different types of clothing to wear. A ski-suit for her that's made of plastic and feathers. Pants and jacket-in-one. Like baby clothes, only thicker. He thinks we should get some for ourselves too. It's important not to get sick, he says. We need all our energy to understand this. He says that all the time. That we need to do our best to understand. He wrinkles his brow and rubs his chin as he did when we were writing speeches and planning travel routes. Do you think this is a maths problem? I say to him then. Do you think we can sit and philosophize and suddenly, eureka, there's the solution? We'll never understand because we won't be here long enough to understand; that's what I say to him. Then it becomes quiet, and he turns his back to me.

Spring came outside the window and they were still waiting. They walked back and forth and around each other at
the asylum centre. In the afternoons, the Girl would stretch
out on the windowsill, dozing in the weak rays of sunlight that burnt through the windowpane. Mama sat at the
kitchen table, writing letter after letter to her sisters. She
looked up sometimes, but not to look at anything. Just to
find the words. Papa wasn't there. Papa left the tiny room
as often as he could, and was gone until bedtime. He sat in
the common room and talked to the people who worked at
the asylum centre.

'Do you think you'll get to stay if the Swedes like you?'
Mama had said with her arms crossed, the first time he
wound the scarf around his face five times in order to take
the ten steps over to the main building. She gave him that
look that made him crumble and look away.

'They are uneducated, untrained prison guards. Your
new friends have no say in this.'

'I'd rather be there than sit here with your sour expression. I'm learning something about the future,' he had replied. He had slammed the door and stayed away for several hours.

The Girl had sneaked after him once when Mama wasn't
looking, and seen him sitting among the thin-haired
blonde women drinking coffee from a small porcelain cup
with blue flowers on the sides. The cup drowned in his large
hands, that is how small it was. The women couldn't take
their eyes off him. They were looking at Papa the same way
Mama did when she drew black lines around her eyes and

enhanced the redness of her lips. And Papa talked, went on and on. What did he have to say to them, and why did they giggle when it was impossible for them to understand him?

'He's sitting alone,' she assured Mama later.

'What else? Who would want to talk to him?'

*

Papa was sitting talking with the fair-haired women and Mama was sitting whispering over her stationery, her pen making scratching noises as she wrote, when a sharp ring cut through the silence.

'Why don't you get it?' Mama didn't look up from the words she was writing; she was staring down as though someone was looking back at her through the thin sheet of paper.

The Girl got up from her spot at the window and ran to the door. No one had come to their Swedish door before. She associated the sound of a doorbell so strongly with grown men playing blind man's buff that she hadn't expected anything else when she opened the door.

Two men in uniform. She saw right away that it was *them*. *They* were the ones who had rung the bell. Papa and Mama had carried out the big plan so they would never have *them* at the door again, she knew that much. And here *they* were standing, and looking at her, as if *they* weren't the ones Mama and Papa were most afraid of, the ones they hated the most. Something warm and wet ran down her legs, but she hardly noticed. *They* were here. Mama was sitting there unsuspecting, writing to the aunts who in turn were convinced that something good had come out of the distance, that they were safe. Papa was probably on his way home, maybe whistling. Probably mumbling the new words he had learnt today: butter cookies, Eurovision, light beer. He was mumbling his way right into the trap! She was standing there with all the information but there was nothing she could do. *They* stepped in, walked past her, and she was powerless. She ran. She ran as fast as she could in her wet pants, all the way over to the woods, in among the trees, and didn't look back.

*

It was Papa who found her. When she heard him shouting she thought she was dreaming, that she was mistaken, that *they* were trying to catch her. But no, it was Papa's over-excited Cheshire-grin voice. She could never mistake that voice. She got up carefully, wrinkling her nose at the sour smell of dried urine. The white envelope in Papa's hand was shining as white as his teeth.

'They've made the decision! We get to stay! We're staying here! *Dokhtaram*, did you hear that? Freedom, *dokhtaram*, freedom! Everything starts now, everything starts today!'

LETTERS HOME

Everything is sorted now. The residence permit came last week. It's a strange feeling. We've been talking about it and yearning for it for so long. We had put our lives at the feet of this decision. And then it comes, in a white envelope, and is so ordinary. You can scrunch it up or burn it, just like any old piece of paper. He says that I'm being silly; that I know it's the kind of letter that exists regardless of what I do with the paper. He says that I have a bad memory; that I've forgotten what it's like to walk around and hide every day, with the smell of death tickling my nose. He has the audacity to say that I've forgotten.

But I have to admit, no matter how much we've planned and sacrificed for that damned residence permit, I had in some way hoped we wouldn't receive it. If they had said no, we would be forced to go back. Then we could comfort ourselves by saying that we had tried this escape, and understood that it doesn't work. And we would come back to handle the situation while in our own country, among our own people. He thinks I'm selfish for thinking like that. We have to think about her, he says. What will happen to her if they take us, execute us?

To be honest, and I can only say this to you, I lie awake at night thinking. Yes, my heart pounds just as loudly as it used to. I've tried the herbs mother sent, but they don't help, I lie awake night after night, my heart pounding. Sometimes it feels like my girl's heart is pounding just as loudly as mine, but maybe it's just the echo of my own body that I hear.

In any case, I can lie and think, okay. If it were to happen, okay. It's simply the consequence of our own actions, right? Who are we to run away? Think that we can get away with it? Who are we? With this shame something will always be lost inside me.

My girl was the one who opened when the letter came, completely unaffected. She just ran past them, two uniformed men, out into the woods to play. If only we could be as unaware and innocent as she.

It didn't take long for them to pack their things, and after only a few days a yellow delivery van pulled up outside the door.

'That's a mail van,' Papa explained. 'They're smart; no wastefulness here. The mail van will bring us to our new home!'

Our home. He said it with the same tone of voice he used when saying *dokhtaram*. With the same facial expression he had had when he put together the ping-pong table in the house with the large basement, the house where they hadn't stayed for more than a few weeks. The house over there.

'Our home,' Mama shook her head. 'Just like that?'

He pulled Mama close, gave her a wet kiss on the forehead.

'Not even you can make me feel homeless today.'

She sat on Papa's lap and listened to the story about our home while the yellow van drove between the motorway and the small cities with red houses and green mailboxes. In and out. The trip in the mail van was long. It almost felt longer than the plane trip from over there.

'It's a factory town. All of the porcelain in Sweden is made in Factory Town. It's an important Swedish city. You know those delicate cups in the common room at the asylum centre? They're from Factory Town. And the toilets! Only Swedes live in Factory Town, so you're going to have Swedish friends, and eat Swedish food, and play Swedish games. You're going to speak Swedish right away, then Papa's smart girl will have to help Mama and Papa learn.

You'll learn much faster than us! Oh look, maybe this one.'

Every time the van turned off the motorway, Papa would sit up straighter. He got ready to get out in front of every house with white eaves and overhangs. He would sit quietly for a moment when the sliding doors remained closed, before continuing with his story.

'Do you know why it's a good thing we're moving to Factory Town? There are other places where Iranians and people from other countries live, and if we were to move to one of those cities it would take much longer for us to learn everything about Sweden. It's important to learn; this is our future.'

Mama shook her head and held the Girl's hand tightly.

'He has such high expectations. He's going to be disappointed. You'll have to help him then. I've said everything I can say.'

Papa pretended not to hear.

'Sometimes, *dokhtaram*, you have a dream and then you wake up. You can become sad, especially if it was a really nice dream, like the one Mama and I had. But just because you've woken up doesn't mean it's time to stop dreaming. Then you have to close your eyes and find a new dream, start working hard for that one instead. Those are the two most important things in life: dreaming and working hard.'

He looked out at the greenish-yellow fields and weighed his thoughts on a precise scale, squinted to make sure he was reading off the correct weight.

'The most important thing is to work hard. Dreams come and go, but if you work hard you'll win in the end.'

Mama looked up.

'Oh, really? What happened to the idealist? Who lived

for his dream? Has he given up? Didn't it take more than some fundamentalist illiterates with turbans and machine guns to turn him 180 degrees?'

Papa kept his gaze focused on the fields.

'Dreams are fleeting. You don't have control over them. Other people can destroy the dreams. People can wake you up; do you understand? But if you're able to work hard, then you'll always have something to fall back on. Then you can always have new dreams. It's important to have new dreams. Otherwise you wake up and just lie there and think about what could have been. That's when you stand still. You shouldn't stand still. You should look forward.'

Mama clenched her hands and turned to look in the other direction. The Girl could see Mama's jaws quivering, she knew that Mama was trying to remain silent. Mama was trying to remember why it was best just to emulate Papa, why it was best to push her own voice aside. But it didn't work, Mama couldn't remember.

'That's how a real fighter talks! A real warrior! What kind of man are you? You long for your new home in a dirty toilet city, think it's so good because it's Swedish. If we had decided to live in one of the places we were told about we could have been closer to our friends. We could have gotten the news quickly, continued the debate, held meetings, planned ...'

'We didn't come here to plan the past, *Baba*, stop. We're here to start a new life.'

'You should hear yourself. You sound like a deserter. Like all those we've despised over the years. You make it sound like it's over. It's called a *fight* because you don't stop fighting. I'm not thinking about giving up. What's wrong with you, *tarsoo*? It'll turn around. Maybe not tomorrow, maybe not this year, but it will turn around.'

Papa didn't answer Mama. He wasn't listening. He pulled his daughter's head toward his and buried his cold nose in her locks.

'It'll be okay, *dokhtaram*; it'll be okay.'

*

When the driver finally spoke it was already dark outside the van's windows. Mama and Papa were sleeping deeply. The Girl leaned forward toward the driver's seat, as if she would understand if only she heard the words. He was driving up a long hill. 'Nelson's Hill,' he said. She whispered, imitating his syllables. Brown blocks of flats with orange-coloured balconies stretched along both sides of the street and broke through the darkening spring night. They were identical, those buildings on Nelson's Hill. And there were more than she could count. She expected a small red house with a white picket fence to pop up off to the side of the massive buildings. Preferably with its windows facing the woods and the endlessness. She was chewing on the inside of her bottom lip when the van stopped in front of a grey metal door. She hoped Papa hadn't been expecting the same home she had.

They followed the driver up the stairs in silence. He unlocked the door to the flat and handed the keys to Papa, who received them with cupped hands.

'Home,' Papa determined proudly. The fifth Swedish expression he had learnt, after *hi*, *thank you*, *excuse me*, and *my girl*.

The postal worker looked surprised. It was hard to tell if it was because of the Swedish word or Papa's ceremonial pride.

'Welcome,' he replied and then pulled his cap down over his eyes and disappeared, his heels sounding against the concrete.

'Welcome,' Papa repeated to himself as he hurried to place their suitcases on the soft linoleum inside the door, as if to mark off his territory before anyone closed the door.

'*Residim!*' We have arrived.

LETTERS HOME

We've gotten our flat now. It's small and dark. The ceiling isn't that far above our heads; sometimes it feels like it's inside me.

We have nothing! We've spread the blankets over the floor, so it won't echo as much. I'm so happy we could bring the blankets! I lie on them for hours, with my eyes closed, inhaling the scent of parsley and dried lime. Sometimes, when I'm lying in that sleeping-awake state, I forget everything that has happened the last ten years. I'm sixteen years old again, slumbering after lunch, hearing your breath next to me. I get angry at my girl sometimes when she makes noise and brings me back to the present, to where everything is lost. I yell at her often. I don't like that I do it, but how can I stop?

She lies next to that red merry-go-round, just like she always did at home. It seems like it doesn't matter to her that everything has been turned upside down, that we're entirely alone. It is as if she might as well be lying here, or back there, as if it were the same merry-go-round. It may be the same piece of plastic, but it's not the same merry-go-round. Every single piece has been replaced!

If she understood my pain she wouldn't give me such a scorching look with those black, black uncomprehending eyes. Her beautiful eyes. Beautiful untainted eyes.

And him. He runs around all day. I don't really know what he's doing. I'm building our future, he says. He waves papers under my nose, wants signatures, wants a smile, wants joy. Where is your joy? he says. What should I say?

HI

The Girl sneaked out when no one noticed. It wasn't that difficult. Mama was usually sleeping with her head buried in the blankets, and Papa left early and didn't come home until evening with his arms filled with papers and books and the kind of food the blonde women at the asylum centre had talked about.

'The future has no horns and no tail—it's endless,' he explained. 'It tastes, it talks, it reads.'

Sometimes he let the future trot along outside without him, that is when he sat with his Swedish-Persian dictionary and read official correspondence, maps, tables of contents. Mama spent her waking moments bent over stationery, in anxious conversation with her sisters. Both of them were too busy to notice how busy they were. So she filled her pockets with uncooked grains of rice and slipped away.

It really was endless, the hill with the brown buildings. She carefully marked the path with the grains of rice every time she went out, memorizing the differences between the identical trees. You must work hard for the future, Papa had said, and she wasn't planning on being second best. She had been to four playgrounds so far, and different children played at each and every one. They had light-coloured hair: light brown, light red, or simply no colour at all. They were dressed in something that looked a lot like pyjama fabric. They were snot-nosed, and they shouted at each other. Dug in the sand with their bare hands. She had followed the same route several times now, and tried to evaluate which group looked the most welcoming. They had started recognizing her; it showed. Did she dare? Papa's words in her head: don't get comfortable. Finally she ran over and jumped up into an empty swing.

'Hi,' the girl in the swing next to hers said and then stuck her tongue out and cleaned the green snot from her upper lip in a skilled movement.

'Hi,' she replied. Hard work wasn't harder than this.

LETTERS HOME

He has gone crazy! Yesterday he came home with pig's blood! Pig's blood! He came home with pig's blood, a knife and a frying pan, and he cooked pig's blood on my stove! Set it in front of us. I'm not eating that, I said right away. What do you mean—should we throw out food? he replied. Food? FOOD? That's not food. Get out your dictionary. I said. Read what it says. What IS that? That's not food. He listened for once, opened that book he carries around wherever he goes. Stuffed a big piece in his mouth before he started reading, just to quarrel with me. Then he threw his beloved book on the floor, ran out to the bathroom and threw up. Pig's blood! I had to laugh. Him and his future!

She's crazy too, just like her father. She sneaks out when she thinks I'm sleeping. Stays away for hours. A mother never sleeps! I sneak after her, check on her several times. She doesn't notice. Do you know why? Because she's sitting among the swings TALKING to those dirty children who run around outside after dark. Which language is she speaking? What does she have to say to them? I don't understand. The first time I wanted to run over, grab her, crawl under a blanket with her and never let her go. Hold her in my arms forever. But his words have had an effect. I don't know if this is the future, but it is our today. My little girl is brave, braver than her mother who hides all day.

IN-BETWEEN WORLD

Every Saturday morning Mama dressed the Girl in layer upon layer of wool and thermoplastic and braided her own long hair into two stiff braids that fell down over her breasts. Mama rolled up the past week's notes and placed the bundle of paper under her arm in a skilled and secure fashion. Then they travelled hand-in-hand, the Girl and Mama, first on the red bus from Factory Town and then on the subway's blue line to another world: Raspberry Hills. They marched into a circle of beret-wearing men and women without make-up who were dutifully gathered in the Community Centre awaiting their arrival. Mama unrolled her papers and changed her tone of voice. Spoke in a pitch that would have cut through the traffic noise of Tehran like a hot knife through cold butter, but which in the mid-morning desolation of the suburbs mainly clung to the walls, searching for openings leading to very distant places.

She sat in the middle of the circle and watched. The circle of people and their never-ceasing words opened the tap to a rippling flood of fear that travelled from her throat down to her big toe. She never understood what it was she was so afraid of. It was as if a hazy reflection of clear, everyday situations lived inside her. As if some of these images resonated in memories she couldn't access. Like patrolling police officers or the emergency siren that was tested on the first Monday of every month. Those types of things made the forgotten memories whisper inside of her.

After the meetings they strolled about in Raspberry Hills' selection of Iran: bookstore, bakery, rugs and the delicatessen. Mama and the women without make-up browsed music tapes and movies from the Iran they had revolted against, the Iran that was the only homeland they wanted to be associated with. She waited at the escalators, rode them up and down in the grizzled mall of Raspberry Hills. It was a mystery to her how a place so deprived of air and light could bear such a promising and inviting name.

As soon as they came home to the archipelago-framed Factory Town, Mama put on a scratchy cassette tape and lost herself again. Mama would sit on the thick blankets for hours and write long letters to every single one of her six sisters, filling the letters with details of the everyday, repeating time and again her most vivid memories from childhood. She would ask if they remembered how they used to sit in a circle and braid each other's hair while they debated who was the cutest boy in the world, the neighbour on the left or the neighbour on the right? She wondered what had happened to the boys—had they been sent to war? Had they come home safe and sound? She wondered what it had been for, the whole revolution, and wished she could change what had happened. In letter after letter she asked her youngest sister for forgiveness, wished that she had been the one to have taken the lashings, wished that she could slice off her unscarred feet and hand them over to her sister. Those letters were returned every time, the text crossed out with a thick, black felt-tip pen. Mama wrote the same words over and over again, hoping they would eventually slip through the censorship machine.

The Girl would lie next to her with her chin in her hand and watch Mama's hand as it wrote. The hand with a glowing cigarette constantly positioned between its fingers. She always smiled when Mama looked up. Mama always smiled back.

They lay there in a longing togetherness, and the Girl spun a picture of Iran for herself. The fairyland where you were never alone. Where men with deep, yearning voices couldn't live without their pure, innocent princesses. Where the air was filled with the sweetness of the flowering trees. But when darkness fell outside their still curtainless windows and Papa threw open the front door, the picture vanished into a thousand vaporized drops. There was a chill in the air every time he came in and found Mama lying there on the floor among the cassette tapes and cigarette butts. He would stand next to Mama for a long time without saying anything, before he started yelling. Always the same words.

'You're wasting everything! We could have lain on these blankets in Tehran and cried over everything having gone to hell. We didn't need to come here for that. Pull yourself together.'

She always stood at attention at these moments. Alert, ready to serve everyone.

'I'll cry as much as I want to! You don't care. Run around and become Swedish if it's that easy. I'm going to lie here.'

Papa shook his head, closed the door to the bedroom and hid behind his adult education books. The Girl was stuck in between. She learnt Swedish words through Papa's textbooks and teaching aids, and Persian melancholy from Mama's cassette tapes.

They lived in that ice-bound silence for a long time.

LETTERS HOME

I watch these people and I know that I never want to become like them. They drink all the time. Not only on Thursday nights, at home, among friends. No, they are drunk all day, every day. Grown men who walk around with liquor bottles in their hands, swaying back and forth, collapsing, screaming, wetting themselves, throwing-up among the swings. Should I let my daughter watch them through the window, play in their shards of glass? Should I let their stench force its way into her life? And all those single mothers. There are too many to count. They have three, four small children, all with different men, and yet you see them outside the pizzeria on the weekends. They're hanging onto some new tramp every time. Do I want my daughter to turn out like that?

No one seems to keep an eye on the children. Sometimes a parent stands out on a balcony and shouts a name louder and louder, then goes in and closes the door when there's no answer, tries again half an hour later. What is that? I know that we fought for freedom, and I understand that this is freedom. They can do whatever they want and no one judges them: not the law, not their upbringing, not their neighbours. Well, no one except me. But what happened to dignity? To class? To style? We've come to one of the world's most democratic places, freest places, most just places. But they lack all feeling for culture and character. How is that possible? How do I make sure we aren't affected, aren't leached, don't end up like them? How do I do that when all he does is think about how we can solve their riddle as quickly as possible, learn from them, emulate them?

The worst, the very worst, is that I see in their eyes that they *are* looking down at me! I want to scream, Are you joking? I'm *educated*! I've been carrying out an intellectual fight against dictatorships since the moment I learnt to think! I've toppled a Shah! But they wouldn't understand half of the words, even if I knew them in Swedish. They call us sand niggers here. There aren't many of us, just one other woman. I can tell from the sorrow of her steps that she's Iranian too. We're the only ones. There are people from Finland, but they are fair-haired. And they're exactly like the Swedes, even worse. They're the ones who drink the most, the Finnish men. And then there are Italians and Greeks. But they came here a long time ago and they've become a part of this world. They came here to work in the factory. What do they know about our past? It doesn't matter because we're the ones they call sand niggers. I think they believe we came here for no reason,

without the factory needing us. That we came to take some-
thing that is theirs. I don't want anything! I wanted their
freedom, but I'm starting to have my doubts. They snicker
when we walk by, look angry, look away. As if I were a dirty
Afghan. You know nothing about me, I want to scream. But
I see in their eyes that they think they know everything they
need to know.

THE TORN SUNBEAM

One Saturday afternoon when they were on their way
home from Raspberry Hills Mama caught sight of the
lonely woman again, the woman with the sorrowful stride.

'Catch up with her, that woman there!' Mama gave her a
push on her back. 'Run!'

That day's meeting had been extra long. Extra-long and
without the ice-cream break that was the whole point of
the trip to Raspberry Hills. There had been talk of the third
way, nagging about resistance, shouting about revolution.
Mama had been the one shouting, it seemed as though the
rest didn't agree. That was nothing unusual these days. In
any case the meeting had been extra long and it had made
her restless, so she dashed off as fast as she could, elbows
dancing along her sides, her mouth in a wide-open attack
against the unmoving July air. The woman heard her steps,
stopped and glanced down at her with forest-green eyes.
The woman ran her hands through the Girl's frizzy locks
once the Girl had stopped running, out of breath, as if it was
a matter of course that a small girl would run up to her long
skirt and pull at it with sticky hands. As if she was expected.

She pointed at Mama who was drawing closer, looking relieved in the way she always did when they found something Iranian on the street. Mama was the adult world's Hansel and Gretel, picking up breadcrumbs from the ground and hoping that they were the tracks that would lead her home. The woman straightened out her long skirt, stood up straight and took Mama's tiny hand in her own strong ones. They stood like that for a while, ignoring the difference between the woman's covered legs and Mama's bare ones, searched each other's eyes, and found what was missing.

*

In the beginning, the Torn Sunbeam had lived in Raspberry Hills, drawn to the fragments of Iran. If it smells like home, tastes like home, sounds like home, and if the people look like the ones who filled the streets back home, then it should be home, shouldn't it? That's what she had thought.

But no. For months the Torn Sunbeam had wandered around between the concrete walls of Raspberry Hills with echoing steps, becoming more and more certain of her conviction. No, it wasn't like that. Decorating the set with props from the old world doesn't change time or space. This wasn't home. The promising Raspberry Hills didn't have the ability to rewrite history. The Torn Sunbeam had wandered around and looked at the old men wearing traditional hats, sitting outside the café in the mall drinking tea in the afternoons. Men who sat in separate groups, divided by geographic origin, and who had no common language with which to communicate across their distinct boundaries. She had sat with the young mothers at the beauty parlour, listened to their discussions about the right way to make *khoreshte bademjon*, the comments about nasty mother-in-laws who ruled with an iron fist all the way from Iran, and about how it was impossible to find tomatoes in this country, tomatoes that tasted like tomatoes. She had listened and then, out of the corner of her eye, she had seen how time was standing completely still, like a soldier at attention, confused about how everything kept going even though it was over. *We won't get anywhere from here*, the Torn Sunbeam had said to the still time. No. She had realized that days could pass without her hearing anyone speak Swedish. She felt how it became harder and harder to go anywhere, how it was much easier to stay where she was. She had caught herself whispering *racist* to herself every time a blonde person threw her a tired look on the subway, which didn't happen very often anymore because she rode the subway less and less. She had met time again at the beauty parlour and realized that she was standing just as still. No. The Torn Sunbeam had understood that it wasn't possible to separate the tree from the earth it is nourished by. That the roots must force their way deep down into the soil in order for the tree to grow. The Torn Sunbeam had nodded at her reflection when she finally took off her headscarf and folded it routinely. Then she turned on her heel, opened the door and threw the scarf down the trash chute.

*

When she moved her suitcases to Factory Town, the Torn Sunbeam decided to never look back, to never again talk about what had happened before the eternal winter twilight. Many people thought they could heal by talking. Heal by sharing their story, discussing, arguing. They acted like the fight was still going on, as if admitting that it was over meant admitting defeat. She made it clear that she was on their side, that she had done her homework, that she had done her part. But she didn't share her story. Instead of reading political publications or listening to nostalgic music in the evenings, she sat with her *Swedish For Immigrants* books until her eyes teared up, and finished her courses in half the time. She covered the black-sooted history with Swedish things: rag-rugs and daisy-patterned wallpaper, and filled her emptiness with the raspberry filling from Linzer cookies.

But when the strange girl pulled at her skirt and looked up at her with those dark bottomless eyes, the dam broke. The Torn Sunbeam fell into the arms of the woman who was holding out her hand, spoiled herself by putting words to her pain. Just this once.

*

One winter night in the middle of the revolution. The creaking from the street door told her that it was him coming in. He had been in the field for forty-eight hours, her heart had been pounding in her throat for forty-nine. She never counted on him coming home. They always said farewell when they parted, sometimes several goodbyes in one day. They tore her pounding heart to pieces, those goodbyes.

The Torn Sunbeam had become tied to the home, to her daughter. Her contribution to the fight hadn't become less as a result, just the opposite. She was the one who weighed their words in her hands day after day, wrote the texts he printed manually in the cellar under the canned goods factory and later handed out to their friends, who then in turn went out to the workers' neighbourhoods and stuffed leaflets under hundreds, thousands of doors. Her words.

He was tired that night. The dark circles under his eyes had spread toward his cheekbones and he had become thin. He forgot to eat, sleep, and go to the bathroom during those expeditions. The fight met all of his needs. He only hoped that change would come soon because the worry that everything was for nothing had started creeping in, and if it gained ground everything would be lost. The purpose of everything.

The Torn Sunbeam saw it in his posture, his fear of doubt. She lay awake next to his shrinking body, wanting to fill him with hope, nourishment and faith. But there wasn't much she could say, not much that would have an effect, not much that was true. She lay awake and watched him on her right side, and the little one on her left side. She wanted to do everything for them, but had so little to offer. It became impossible for her to lie still, idle, powerless. She got out of bed carefully, and pulled a coat over her thin nightgown. In the hour before dawn his favourite meal could be bought at the market: salt-boiled lamb's head. She wanted to set something in front of him that he wouldn't be able to resist, something that would divert his thoughts, if even for just a moment. She was bending down to buckle the worn walking shoes when the little one caught her gaze.

'Take me with you,' she stated with a two-year old's stubbornness.

'Go to sleep! I'll be back soon.'

She had tried pulling the covers over the girl, tried to get her to lie back down.

'Noo,' the girl screamed in reply and gripped the coat firmly with her damp hands. 'Take me with you.'

He had started moving restlessly in his sleep, and she pulled the girl into her arms.

'Sch, bashe bia.' Okay, then. Come.

With a large pot under one arm and the child on the other she hurried away in the darkness, in the last hour of the night.

Fifteen minutes after they left the house the door was knocked down by the police. He was brought out with his hands over his head, placed with his legs spread apart against the wall, and was then hit with a baton in his lower back until he collapsed convulsively in a heap. Five minutes before the Torn Sunbeam rounded the street corner with the pot filled with the lamb's head and an extra large tongue, he was taken away in a van that would be filled with beaten men before the sun had risen in the sky.

The dust from the screeching tyres had settled, but the Torn Sunbeam took notice of the tyre tracks on the gravel road before her eyes saw them. She looked for warning signs on autopilot, didn't need to look up at the door in order to know that it had been knocked down. She fell to her knees, the pot fell from her hands and the lamb's head rolled along the street, the dark eye sockets glowing. The cry got caught in her throat, she couldn't risk uttering her newly burgeoning loss. The wall was marked with a large red X, which meant they would be coming back. So the Torn Sunbeam lifted the little one in her arms, turned her back and ran. Behind her the life she had known floated together into a salty pool of dust and liquid. A swollen tongue lay in the middle of the soggy mess, howling at everything they had been up until that moment.

The Girl and Mama followed the Torn Sunbeam home that afternoon. The name suited the unknown woman so well, something so beautiful that looked so worn out. Torn apart. They sat down at the kitchen table. The raspberry Linzer cookies were waiting and the dark black tea was simmering on the stove. She wondered whom the table was set for, wondered if the Torn Sunbeam had been expecting them. She dropped cube after cube of sugar into her narrow tea glass until there was no room to stir with the spoon. She didn't look up at the two women. She had learnt that there was no comfort for what they were talking about. That they weren't sad, sooner sorrowful, and that those were two very different things. Sorrow doesn't disappear when the tears have dried.

So she kept her gaze on the white sugar cubes instead. Followed the warm tea's path deep inside them, watched how they were dissolved against their will. She felt a bit guilty for forcing the perfect cubes to take on a shape different from the one they were meant to have.

The Torn Sunbeam turned toward her after a while, carefully stroked her hair, pulled her close.

'My girl is the same age as you. And has the same crow's-wing-coloured hair. You could be sisters. She'll be back soon, very soon.'

The Torn Sunbeam took her hand and led her to the adjacent bedroom. She forced herself not to protest, felt the warmth in the Sunbeam's hands, and understood that she wanted to protect her from the conversation. That the Torn Sunbeam didn't understand that she already knew everything.

'Play in here. I'll come in with ice cream in a bit. Stay here and play.'

The Torn Sunbeam closed the door and the Girl turned her gaze to the stuffy room. Ten porcelain dolls were lined up in a row on the tightly made-up bed, their heads on the pillow. On the nightstand a colouring book was leaning against the night-light, and there was an unopened box of crayons next to it. She carefully sat down on the taut bedspread, didn't dare mess up the lines, destroy the order. She wanted to run out of the room, but didn't want to anger the stranger who appeared to have been expecting them.

Then it happened. A large head popped out from under the bed, with locks just as tangled and bushy as her own. The Girl pulled up her knees and backed up across the bed, but the deep black eyes that met hers were impossible to escape. A girl towered flaming yellow in front of her, glaring from behind her eye-glasses and holding her fists clenched at her sides. The girl wasn't moving, but still looked like a running cheetah, frozen in mid-leap.

'Don't wake my children!'

*

They clicked immediately, the girl and her. Dearest Sister and her. They peered at each other with eyes the same

44

black colour of liquorice pastilles, to work out in which direction they would grow, and with which force they would break out. That is what they would end up becoming: tree roots tightly wound around each other rising toward the sky, to later spread apart in branches, pointing in different directions, the trunk connecting them.

Dearest Sister knew from the beginning that she deserved her place on earth. Dearest Sister combined their money for sweets on Saturdays and bought a joint bag, then she locked herself in the bathroom and ate all of it herself. Dearest Sister ignored the Iranian courtesy codes, took cookies from serving plates even though they had both been taught to say no thank you even if they were offered. Dearest Sister turned on her heel and went home when she got bored, refused to open the door when the Girl ran after. Sat with her back to the window and pretended the Girl didn't exist.

The Girl never took offense. She knew that at the core they were the same thing, Dearest Sister and her. Two branches from the same trunk.

MAMA, PAPA AND THE CLASH

It happens so soundlessly, those few drastic events that really change everything. They are so deeply ingrained into everything that happens later that they don't stand out.

That escape, a hazy adventure that might as well have been a dream.

Arriving in Sweden, arriving home.

A unit as action-packed and silent as the skier outside

the asylum centre. Escape and arrival. Past and present.

It would turn out that the wild card was the clash between Mama and Papa. That the abyss between their broken dreams and hopes for the future was the alarm that cut through the pine trees.

*

Between the trips to Raspberry Hills and the conversations with the recently found Sunbeam, Mama lay on the blankets. They were like a magnet, those blankets. When Papa was in a good mood he would pull Mama to her feet, and hold her in his arms and glide around on the living room floor. Mama allowed herself to be lifted, allowed herself to be dragged, allowed herself to disappear in his powerful arms.

Sometimes, when Papa came in through the door with that puppy-dog look that screamed *someone is standing on my tail*, he was the one who lay down next to Mama, closed his eyes and burrowed his head into her warm breasts. Mama held his head between her hands, lowered her lips to his ears and whispered words no one else would ever understand.

But most of the time they just watched each other from a distance. Allowed the ice-bound silence to roll along undisturbed. She had a hard time deciding what their looks wanted to say. Did they despise each other's method, or did they both secretly wish they had chosen the other's way?

The evening when the monster came to life inside Papa, the Girl could hear already in the way the key entered the lock that something was different. Papa closed the door carefully, calmer than ever before. He remained standing at first, then he bellowed like a stuck lamb, only louder. He howled and threw his book bag against the wall of mirrors, as hard as he could. The eight mirrors broke into thirty-two pieces, then fell heavily to the ground to be crushed into sixty-four. Everything stopped. Three pairs of eyes stared emptily into space. Passive observers. The monster was born then and there to its own life, beyond them, beyond their control. A glowing creature with an unwieldy sweeping tail. They had been awaiting its arrival, they realized this as they silently waited for the beast's next move. All three of them were hoping that one of the others would get hold of the horns, bring the creature in.

The monster didn't always stick around for very long, but for its debut it came filled with compressed air. It dragged Papa across the hall floor, took hold of his arms and raised them above Mama who was sitting on her blankets, knocked her over with a roar. Then the monster took hold of the cassette tapes, broke them in half and stomped on them with the heel of his dirty shoes. When there was nothing left to shatter it looked up, snorting and hissing. The Girl rushed forward before it decided to destroy Mama. She took the monster's hands in her small, determined ones, and captured its honey eyes with her coal black ones, searched until she found.

'Salam, Baba.'

She picked up the driver's hat that had been stomped on and wrinkled during the monster's rampage. After his adult education classes Papa was going to evening school to become a bus driver for SL City Buses. It was a big thing that Papa would have his very own bus to drive. He was so big in her eyes. He looked down at her now, shoulders sagging, such a small big man.

'What should I do, eh? What else can I do?'

'There are potato chips. We bought chips, do you want some?' That was her short-sighted answer to an endless question mark.

*

The birth of the monster did something to Mama. It made her get up from the floor and claim a spot for herself on the red velvet sofa. Papa had pushed the sofa through the front door several months earlier, maybe it had even been years. It was the same day he had cooked pig's blood on her stove. Mama had ignored the sofa up until then. Instead she chose to remain on the blankets with her back to the smell of warehouse and plastic and a world that should have been very far away but which suddenly made claims at being their reality. Mama had a stepmother's relationship with Sweden, and the monster pushed her from avoidance to aggression. Mama was going to prove that she could do it if she wanted to. And if things didn't work out, she could always put it down to a lack of will instead of ability. She would show all of them. And the change happened quickly: before she had become stubbornly resigned to sadness, she had been stubbornly eager; the difference was subtle. Now notebooks replaced the stationery and adult education books filled her corner of the sofa. She stopped going to Raspberry Hills on Saturdays, stayed behind in Factory Town instead where her braids were replaced with a tight bun, her beret with glasses. They were in competition, Mama and Papa. Papa's study time decreased when he started driving the bus at night, but they still went to school together in the morning. Mama and Papa. Two brooding strangers who supported each other.

Hey, you there!

I'm gonna show you, I'm really gonna show you, please can't you show me?

*

Mama cleaned houses along the coast after the adult education classes and then picked the Girl up from preschool on the way home. She waited at the window, sensed when Mama was about to round the corner. She watched over Mama's steps, waved until their eyes met, then rushed to meet her at the door.

'What would I do without you?' Mama whispered, bent over the Girl's shoelaces.

She ran her hand over Mama's soft hair, grabbed hold of the ever-more chapped hands and held them tightly all the way home. They sneaked into the kitchen together and were quiet so that Papa could rest for the night, quiet so as not to wake the monster. Mama cooked dinner with the books open on the counter, set a plate next to the Girl on the floor where she was lying with a colouring book. But Mama remained standing, poring over the course literature. Couldn't afford to let any more time go to waste; they had already lost so much.

After a few hours Papa came out into the kitchen, picked the Girl up from the floor and kissed her forehead. Then he pulled at her shirt and took a good look at it. A relentless honey gaze directed at Mama's back.

'Her clothes are dirty.'

Mama didn't look up.

'Wash them, then.'

Papa picked up the Girl's empty plate and raised it above his head. She closed her eyes. She always closed her eyes when the blow was coming, then quickly got to her feet and came to the rescue.

*

Papa would sit down next to her at breakfast in the breaks between the night shift and his studies. His driver's cap was balanced on the top of his head; it was far too small for his wide head. He took it off and pulled it down over her eyes.

'Papa is tired now, *dokhtaram*; *kheyli* tired.'

Liquorice pastilles against honey eyes, liquorice pastilles that wanted nothing more than to suck Papa's tiredness into her own body.

'But that's how it is *dokhtaram*. You have to work hard. You have to start at *A* in order to get to *B*. You know, like in the alphabet. If I drive the bus at night, we can go to the Tivoli in the summer. If I study during the day, then we can go to the Tivoli every summer, maybe several times. If Papa stays in bed, you'll have to keep to the playground.'

Mama came into the kitchen, half-dressed.

'Isn't she going to have eggs for breakfast?' Papa nodded at the box of cornflakes that had been set out on the table.

'Not today.'

'Why not? Because you're too lazy!'

'Boil the eggs yourself if you want her to eat them.'

'Shut your mouth! Shame on you! Don't walk around without clothes like a whore!'

She followed all of their short, harsh conversations with wide-open expectant eyes, like an inexperienced spectator at the US Open final who can't decide which strike is a match ball, but recognizes a decisive move when she sees it. She closed her eyes tightly when it was time, and Mama always fell to the floor after the first blow. When she heard the thud of Mama's body against the linoleum she opened her eyes again, ran forward, and stood between them. Sometimes the thud came before the sound of the blow. Sometimes she wondered if it was another force that brought Mama down. Wondered if Papa's blows had nothing to do with Mama falling. But when she laid Mama's head on her lap and pressed a cold apple from the refrigerator against the red marks on Mama's neck, every single one of them an impression of Papa's familiar fingertips, she knew that it didn't matter what made Mama fall. That it didn't matter what made the monster hit.

DOCTOR

One early evening when summer was in the air and the promise of the Tivoli reigned in the tree-tops, Mama walked in to the preschool with large strides and her Raspberry Hills' sway.

'I have good news, *dokhtaram*,' she said. 'Mama is going to become a doctor.'

Doctor. That was big, she understood that right away. Grandma, Grandpa, the ice-cream man back there, they had always told the Girl this was the best you could become: *May you become doctor*, dokhtaram; *may you become doctor.*

She nodded. The news wasn't just big; this was bigger than the plan.

She and Mama passed the department store on the way home. Mama allowed her pearl laughter to fill the seats on the bus and she stared up at Mama with hungry eyes, hungrily swallowing every drop of the untainted happiness. She was so unaccustomed to it that she became intoxicated after the first gulp, and she couldn't stop staring, stop swallowing. She wanted to fill herself with what was coming out of Mama, wanted to show Papa, wanted to hold on to it forever.

They walked up and down the aisles, placing marzipan pastries and barbecue chips in the basket. Mama hummed a familiar melody, picked out a red lipstick, and held out lip balm that smelt like bubble gum. When they got home, Mama dug around in the drawers for joyful Persian songs, then carefully painted her lips and danced around in the smells coming from the simmering pots. The bag with schoolbooks rested on the hat rack. The crayons were picked up from the floor.

'Tonight is a good night, *dokhtare azizam*.' My beloved daughter. 'This is what we've dreamt about.'

Papa came into the kitchen, heavy with sleep. The Girl searched his face for signs of anger over them having woken him. But his lips spread into the ever more seldom Cheshire grin. The honey eyes couldn't tear themselves away from Mama. Papa looked like he was in love. Going from latent fury to glittering love in no time at all.

'What's going on here? Why are we having a party?' He stepped up and pulled Mama close.

'I've been accepted! Medicine! Uppsala University! The letter came today!'

Mama grabbed a white envelope from the side of the stove, pressed it into Papa's hand. Happiness mixed with worry. Papa took out the white sheet of paper, read the letter with trembling hands. The warm air in the small kitchen with the turquoise cabinets was still. She went to stand in the door opening and prepared herself to run away. Knew that she would never leave them.

But Papa was beaming. Papa had the future in his sight, dreams and opportunities. Papa looked at Mama as if she was showing him something he had decided to believe in, but wasn't sure existed. Papa touched Mama's cheek and helped set the table. He watched Mama during the entire meal, so many emotions were alive in his eyes that Mama looked away, embarrassed. Papa held Mama in his arms for a long time before he left. He would rather have stayed. Mama probably hadn't counted on that: warmth and Cheshire happiness. Mama gave him a wait-and-see look, awaiting the next phase of his reaction.

*

They all gathered around the telephone the following evening to call around and share the good news. The comforting smell of *esfand* rose from the stovetop. The burnt seeds that would ward off the evil eye, push back the powers of jealousy and convince the cosmos that nothing in this house was taken for granted. She didn't understand why

Mama and Papa were in such a hurry to tell all their friends and relatives the good news when they were also afraid of the evil eye. She didn't trust the crackling seeds to ward off bad luck. She didn't think they understood the severity, the importance of their task.

Mama called her sisters first, her voice relieved at being able to share good news. The shouts of joy travelled through the phone lines and Papa chuckled with pleasure. He got up humming and quickly changed to his uniform behind the kitchen door. Then he hurried back, took the receiver and shouted to Grandma.

'See, I didn't destroy your daughter's life. Just the opposite!'

Mama smiled, a real smile. Real pearl laughter.

'We'll call your friends before you go,' Mama suggested when the conversation had ended. It was the first time Mama had ended a phone call to Iran without guilt in her lowered gaze.

Papa dialled a number, and spoke to his friend on the other end with childish enthusiasm.

'Good for her. Is that why you went to Sweden? To become a housewife?'

The muffled man's voice echoed through the receiver. The Cheshire grin vanished on the spot. Papa hung up the phone, kneeled down to tie his shoes. He wasn't looking at them, not at Mama and not at the Girl.

'Put her to bed on time! And cook proper food tomorrow. Leftovers are for dogs.' The front door closed with a slam. The air filled with the melancholy of the most joyous Persian songs.

Alberto and Lelle lived on the other side of the yard. Mama pointed out that they looked like Laurel and Hardy when they were walking next to each other. The Girl remembered the black-and-white TV show that was so well-suited to being watched with the sound muted—the way she had always been forced to watch TV in that sheet-covered world far away. But she still couldn't see the likeness. Laurel and Hardy were cheerful souls. Those two looked like Grumpy and Grumpier. They didn't walk next to each very often, either. Most days Lelle sat near the benches at the very bottom of the hill, the ones that were located closest to the store and the pizzeria. He held the bottles in his arms and muttered softly in the mornings, howling in tune with the departing seagulls at dusk. Alberto kept to the playground at the top, closest to the woods where the swings were the best.

It was at the playground that he blended into their world. She was lying on her back in an unmoving swing, counting the fluffy white clouds. Observed that they must be connected to snow. There hadn't been any white clouds in the Iranian sky, had there? She couldn't even remember having seen an Iranian sky. She wondered if Iran was located behind the blue sky beyond the clouds? Or rather on the other side of the sand under the swings? Dearest Sister whizzed through the air next to her and snorted at her questions.

'Who cares?'

That was the latest expression they had learnt.

'Look at that fatty instead. He's crawling around like a

hungry cat. Look. He's always staring at us. Doesn't he have anyone to play with?'

She sat up in her swing, and peered in the direction of the jungle gym. Alberto was perched on it, what looked like milk-chocolate-brown skin was stretched over his chubby belly.

'Is he naked? He looks naked,' her sister determined. 'Naked fatty!'

They turned away giggling, but Alberto didn't react to their words. His look was brimming with an intense lack of expression. He almost looked like he had been painted there. A runaway spot of colour against the sky. Static props on Nelson's Hill. Dearest Sister shrugged her shoulders, jumped off the swing and ran into the woods. The Girl stepped down into the sand carefully and glanced furtively over her shoulder at the motionless boy before running after her.

*

The next day the Girl went to the playground without stopping at the Torn Sunbeam's first. The boy was lying on his back at the top of the jungle gym. She sighed with relief at the sight of his small, red terry-cloth shorts; he hadn't been naked after all. She climbed up in her swing and got it going with a few powerful kicks. The boy slowly turned his head, looked up with blue eyes behind a golden-brown fringe. She mustered her courage.

'Hi.'

Silence.

'Is that your father—him with the bottles? Lelle?'

Alberto shook his head.

'Where's your father, then?'

He shrugged his shoulders.

'Your mother?'

He turned away.

'Do you live with him—Lelle?'

He nodded.

'Is he nice?'

The boy remained sitting with his head turned away. He seemed to be wondering more about whether the question deserved an answer rather than what the answer actually was. After a long silence he heaved himself down toward the sand, landed like a cat on all fours and stomped off with heavy steps. He almost crashed into Dearest Sister who was rushing over with her fist raised in the air.

'You went off without me! You'd rather play with that fatty than me?' Her sister banged her fists against the swing.

The Girl stared at the furious liquorice-pastille eyes and tried not to look away. It was the hardest thing she knew. Then she ran after the boy, took his hand and led him back. Her sister remained standing, fist raised in the air, staring them straight in the eye, waiting for the Girl to look away. She refused.

'He's with us now.'

*

They took Alberto under their wings. Dearest Sister didn't like it. She stared at Alberto from behind her tangled locks and he glared back through the golden fringe that was constantly hanging between him and the world around him.

Dearest Sister ran as fast as she could, knowing that Alberto didn't have a chance of keeping up. Alberto tackled Dearest Sister to the ground and knew that she couldn't hit back. The Girl was stuck in the middle, calming and intervening. She laughed at Alberto's trite jokes and listened seriously to her sister's endless expounding about how they should protect themselves from the dark forces in the woods.

'I've seen it in the movies. You fall down on your knees, like this. And then raise your arms up and say, *Ghool boro, ghool boro*, then you're safe. I've seen it.'

'What do you mean, "*jool boro*"? Why would anyone care if you said "*jool boro*"? And what's this about the woods? There aren't any monsters there, just the drunks, I know that. Lelle sleeps there sometimes, when he can't make it up the stairs.'

Alberto sneered at them and Dearest Sister bit her cheek and took all of the candy. Punished the Girl in all possible ways for having dragged the fatty into their friendship. Alberto retreated into sullenness as soon as her sister drew near, whispered that they should go home and play doctor in the closet instead, just the two of them. Lelle was lying under the large pine tree, sleeping. He wouldn't notice. They were unpleasant, those games and the sour smell at Lelle and Alberto's place. The brown stains in the bathroom that no one bothered to clean. Papa had explained many times.

'Lelle was probably a good person when he was a child like you. But Lelle isn't Lelle anymore. Lelle is that bottle he's always holding in his hand, you know? It's the alcohol that's in control, not Lelle. Lelle can't be trusted; he could do something stupid. So it's best if you don't play with Alberto.'

'It's best?'

'Yes, it's best. You are NOT allowed to play with that boy. I don't want to see you in the vicinity of those two, understand? They are trash!' Mama pulled her close into that embrace that made it feel like the two of them were one, her and Mama. As if nothing else affected them, no matter how loud the rest of the world was screaming.

'That man calls me things every time I walk by. I may not understand all of the words, but I understand the tone. I don't care if it's the alcohol or Santa Claus who's talking, you don't get close to a man like that. Not my daughter.'

She listened. Wondered if it would make things better or worse if she pulled Alberto into the hall and showed them the circular burns in his armpits, and the fiery red sores on his bare back that were hidden from the world by the appearance of his red terry-cloth uniform. She concluded that they would become even more aggressively disposed to everything he stood for. She showed her sister instead; explained. The Girl ran her hand over the constantly fiery hot lines on Alberto's bare skin, patted him on the arm when his face twisted in pain. Her sister bit her bottom lip. Nodded. Stopped glaring. Even held out the bag of sweets for Alberto, but only once. Enough's enough.

POO

It turned out that Alberto was a year older than the girls. He walked toward Factory Town's school while she and her sister watched him disappear from the security of the pre-school window.

'No one would have guessed,' Dearest Sister said, smacking her lips and wiping her mouth with the back of her hand. Then Dearest Sister glanced over her shoulder and handed over the chocolate rooster they had found at the back of the Torn Sunbeam's pantry and cleverly sneaked with them. The Girl took a big bite and chewed noisily.

'I hope he remembers the bit about not eating his snot …'

Startled, Dearest Sister snatched the rooster back.

'Not so much—are you stupid? That's my rooster. We stole it from MY pantry.'

She didn't answer, was too busy chewing the enormous piece of chocolate and worrying about what they would do to Alberto, over there in the school building.

'*Shekamo*, you stupid pig,' her sister muttered, then stuffed the rooster inside the elastic waistband of her track-suit pants and disappeared.

*

The weeks of autumn passed and Alberto became grumpier with every leaf that fell to the ground. His bottomless blue eyes explained that it was best she kept her distance and she did, but with a watchful eye on the schoolboys who never left him alone. Alberto always stayed a few steps behind them, but somehow he still managed to be in the way—that much was clear even at a distance. He knew that she was keeping watch. He looked in the direction of the preschool window, her lookout on to the world, even though he had no way of seeing her. She thought about

Mama's words: *I need you here at home so that I can look up at you and know that I'm not alone.*

She hoped that she conveyed exactly the same thing to Alberto—that he wasn't alone.

*

The Girl was lying on her back in the swing at the pre-school, wondering about the white clouds. Out of the corner of her eye she could see her sister floating to the sky and back. They weren't saying anything; they already shared every thought. At the sound of raised voices they stopped swinging, both at the same time as if on command. The schoolboys had gathered in a circle on the other side of the fence. They were tossing something around: red terry-cloth. It was Alberto's shorts. He was running between the boys panting, naked and covered in snot, his look desperate for dignity. But the boys couldn't stop. Testosterone was in charge now. It had unexpectedly exploded in their hormone systems, test-driving their masculinity. Dearest Sister sat down in her swing. The Girl stood up in hers.

'Stop!' The Girl wanted to run over and pull at them. She wanted to pull Alberto under her shirt, hide him in the pit of her stomach, shield him with her ribs.

'Quiet!' her sister hissed. 'Stay out of it!'

The schoolboys turned toward them with surprised looks, searched their repertoire for an appropriate response. Alberto saw his chance, threw his backpack down and ran in between the swings with rage in his eyes. He ran straight toward her and pushed his body against her swing with all the force he could muster.

'Piece of poo,' he screamed as he pushed. 'You piece of poo!' She responded by holding on tight. Alberto pushed and pushed. Her swing flew higher and higher.

The schoolboys had lined up appreciatively below.

'Poo! Poo! Piece of poo,' they chanted. 'Come on Alberto, higher, faster!'

Adrenaline was pouring from Alberto's eyes.

'Been rolling around in poo, have you? Ever looked at yourself in the mirror? You're brown like poo.'

She flew higher and higher in the air. The pendulum movement became rougher and rougher. The swing set was shaking, and the palms of her hands were becoming chafed and small red drops were forcing their way through her skin, staining the dirty grey chains.

'Dirty brown poo!' Alberto screamed.

'Dirty brown poo!' the boys repeated.

Dirty brown poo, she thought the second before she lost her grip on the swing and flew through the air in the direction of the fence. She hit her head against the fencepost.

*

Papa was shaking with rage that night. She didn't tell him the bit about the poo, it felt like a bigger mockery of him than her. She hadn't wanted to say anything at all, but by the time she had woken up in the nurse's room it was too late. The teachers had pounced on the telephone and shouted accident a long time ago.

'These things happen when kids play,' Mama said.

'These things don't happen,' Papa said. He pushed the living room furniture back against the wall and forced her to get out of bed. 'I'm going to teach you to fight back. You should always fight back.'

He held a pillow in front of his stomach, and they practised: punches to the face, fists, kicks, punches and then fists again.

'What do you do when someone hits you?'

'Hit back!'

'How hard?'

'As hard as I can!'

'How often?'

'Every time!'

LETTERS HOME

He's here now. It makes me think of when she was born. How all of us gathered weeks before the birth. How I lay there and listened to you breathing while I longed for her breaths. How I convinced him to continue going out with the flyers at night; didn't want to stop fighting. We wanted her to become a part of us, of you, of totality.

And now he's here, this angel with his enormous eyes. They're even larger than hers, I didn't think that was possible. He comes from nowhere, into nothing. There is no totality, no history. You aren't here. It's strange because his large questioning eyes almost make me wish you'll never get to see him. That Iran will be a place he has heard of, but doesn't know. Like a distant relative. Like a deceased relative. He's a seed, my beautiful little mountain peak. He'll get to blossom in fertile ground, grow into anything, something completely different. He's that freedom we've all been going on about

63

since we learnt to think. The future. Maybe this little one is our path there. He's so pure. Maybe he'll be allowed to be the product of the opportunities we've created, instead of the mistakes we've made.

OUR MOUNTAIN PEAK

'This is your little brother.' Papa placed the chocolate-brown blob in the Girl's arms and brought her hand to the blob's neck. 'You have to support his head. He can't hold it up himself yet. We have to help him.'

She held him tightly, tried to absorb her Little Brother's nut-brown gaze with her black one, but couldn't. His gaze was slippery—it slipped away. She nodded respectfully. He was his own person.

In that moment Little Brother became the only thing that mattered. She would place herself like a shield between him and the world, rather let everything topple her than allow even a breeze to touch him. Little Brother's birth made her understand the plan, understand what *the future* meant.

'Just think—this is his country. We'll get to follow him, in his country. He's our guide, our mountain peak.'

Papa fluttered femininely with his long eyelashes. He was in love. She ran her fingers along the rolls on Little Brother's arms. He was so soft and so dark, darker than her and her parents combined. *Poo*, she thought. Then shook her head. *My own chocolate rooster.*

Papa and Little Brother were waiting on the sofa when she stepped out of the bedroom. She hardly saw them. First she looked at her reflection in the repaired wall of mirrors, then in the blind-covered windows. Her cheeks were flushed from nervousness.

'*Khoshkele baba*.' Papa's beautiful girl. Papa pointed at her and Little Brother, who could now lift and hold his head. He laughed delightedly at her neon-pink velvet dress. Papa was wearing his mustard-yellow blazer over a brown-patterned button-down shirt. The newly purchased dress pants were so wide they hid the tassels on his loafers. Little Brother was dressed up too, in a white shirt with a black bow tie that was already covered in his drool. Papa picked up the camera, directed her in a purposeful way.

'Put your hand at your waist, there, and look away, in that direction. Look like you're thinking about something important! It's the first day of school; you're a student now. We want to see that in the picture.'

She straightened out her skirt and ran her hand over her hair that was stiff from the mousse Mama had instructed her to use.

'We should go now; we don't want to be late.' Papa put Little Brother on his hip, unconsciously took off the damp bow tie while he patted a bit more *oddkollon* on his newly shaven stubble, for good measure. The Girl was already standing outside where Dearest Sister was waiting.

'What a lucky girl you are, with a grandma who thinks about you and sends you beautiful dresses.' The Torn Sunbeam touched the Girl's cheek, reached out for Little

Brother and greeted Papa with a handshake.

'Are we ready for school?'

They walked hand-in-hand, the Girl and Dearest Sister and the Torn Sunbeam with Little Brother in her arms. Papa ran ahead of them taking pictures from all possible angles until beads of sweat threatened to soil his newly ironed shirt collar. They had all walked this road many times before. Ever since they had started becoming familiar with Factory Town, the school had stood like a monument for all of those opportunities, that future.

The school was housed in three turn-of-the-century villas set up in a semi-circle facing the factory chimneys in the valley and the glittering harbour.

'That's the future,' Papa determined and pointed at the villas. 'That is going backward,' he continued, pointing at the factory. 'This,' he went on and pointed back at the colourful houses: yellow, green, pink, 'will keep you far away from that.'

The factory wasn't allotted anymore finger pointing. It was clear from the tone what Papa meant, and what kind of distance he expected her to keep from the smoke-filled valley.

The Girl and Dearest Sister knew the story as well as the path by heart. It was their responsibility to help themselves to all of it, to everything that was too big, remote and impossible for the nameless girls who were growing up underground, in hiding in Tehran's working-class district. It was obvious, even though it had never been said out loud, that it was their responsibility to compensate for all the dreams that had already been lost. They had to balance the budget, add weight to the other side of the scale. They had to make sure that the returns on the path that had been chosen became larger than the losses their parents wanted to forget, the losses that were constantly padding around, sweeping through their nightmares at night. Floated in black fingerprints hidden under turtleneck sweaters. It was up to her and her sister to make everything worth it. Now they were finally standing there, in bright colours, silk and velvet, ready to roll up their sleeves and get to work.

'We're standing at the doors to the future now.' Papa's voice faltered from all the enthusiasm. 'The doors to the future … Stand there, up there on the porch. Excuse me, excuse me—can you move?' He shushed away people wearing airy cotton fabrics with flower prints. 'Look at the camera! Smile; you're standing at the door to the future.'

*

'They're lazy,' Papa explained to Mama that night. He was crumbling saffron into a bowl with a few drops of warm water in deep concentration. He added a spoon of steamed rice and stirred. Then he spread the golden grains over the white rice on the serving dish.

Mama was sitting at the dinner table with a steady grip on her glass of tea, sucking on a sugar cube, and focusing a longing look on Little Brother. Little Brother was rocking back and forth in his high chair, loudly discussing the day with himself, dressing it in his very own words that no one understood. Mama had gotten up earlier than the rest of the family that day, just like every other day. Heavy with sleep, she had gotten on the train heading to Uppsala and medical school, after yet another sleepless night because of Little Brother's feverish new teeth. Mama usually came home when dinner was already on the table, and she was never hungry. She had the habit of sitting with her glass of tea in a steady grip, watching them with an ever-increasing sleepy look, waiting to be allowed to clear off the table. Then she would sit in the bedroom with the breast pump and the empty plastic baby bottles that had been used that day. Usually she fell asleep like that, half-reclining with the breast pump in her hand.

'I tried asking questions about what she was expected to know, how many hours of homework she's supposed to do every night, how quickly they progress through the maths book. But no answers. They talked about gym clothes, lunch breaks, school trips … What kind of education is that? They showed me the maths book. It's so thin! The whole book is the sort of thing we learnt the first week in Iran! And this book is for the whole term.'

'Calm down,' Mama replied. 'They know what they're doing. This society functions better than ours ever did, despite the fact that we wrote out homework until our fingers became deformed. You don't need to take responsibility for her education. There are many people who can do a much better job than you.'

Adrenaline was racing through Papa's system. He set the rice dish down on the table with a bang and pulled the lemon chicken out of the oven. The Girl was standing quietly, with the knife in a steady grip, absorbed in the challenge of trying to slice as thin and symmetric slices of tomato as possible.

'*Deeh*, hurry up!' Papa hissed and pulled the knife from her hands. 'Sit down and eat.' He dumped the cutting board and the carefully sliced vegetables in the sink then slammed his fist on the metal counter. He paused for a moment in the face of his anger, then hurried out of the kitchen.

'Did you look pretty in your dress?' Mama asked quietly and stroked her stiff locks of hair. 'I wish I could have been there.'

'It doesn't matter. We took pictures,' she said and climbed up into Mama's lap. 'The teacher called me "the girl with the hair," because she couldn't say my name.'

'The girl with the beautiful, beautiful hair,' Mama whispered. 'My girl with her beautiful, beautiful hair.'

She touched Mama back. Mama's hair wasn't bushy and rough like hers. It was straight and soft under her touch.

'Can't you go to bed?' she whispered to the tiredness in Mama's voice. She dried Mama's cheeks with her shirt-sleeve. Mama shook her head without saying anything, slurped her tea with the sugar cube between her teeth. They both sat up straight when the bathroom door opened and Papa came back into the kitchen.

'Sit in your own chair,' he said to the Girl in a voice as soft as Mama's hair. He picked up Little Brother and let the little head with the heavy eyelids rest against his neck. He dished up rice and chicken on three plates, then cut up the tender meat in front of her before he turned to his own plate.

'I need to study a few hours tonight.' Mama had gotten up to pour herself yet another cup of dark red tea.

'No,' Papa answered.

'I have to. We have an exam next week.'

'No. You know the rules. You don't touch the books when you're at home.'

Mama laughed, picked up her heavy bag from the floor

and walked out of the kitchen. Papa carefully placed Little Brother in the Girl's arms and ran after. She buried her head in Little Brother's elbow, tried to lose herself in the scent of his innocence, in the stories that rested on his clean slate.

'Are you laughing at me? You won't laugh at me! Who the hell do you think you are? You're no one; do you hear that? You're not even a woman. What kind of woman leaves her baby all day, every day? You're trash, do you hear that? Just because you're becoming a doctor doesn't make you any less trash. You're trash.'

She closed her eyes instinctively before the blow came.

TURNING THE OTHER CHEEK

The teacher was the most elegant person the Girl had ever seen.

She didn't remember the steamy beauty parlours in the sheet-covered country. She didn't remember the enormous eyes framed in kohl, yard after yard of silk fabric, copper-coloured bosoms. Pink lips that curved into the eternal question: *Koshkel shodam?* Do I look pretty?

She didn't remember how black shawls were thrown over well-formed strands of hair; how dark coats were hung over voluptuous, brilliantly coloured bodies.

She had forgotten.

Her teacher wore starched blouses with ruffles and white underskirts that slipped out from behind the tightly fitting hem. The grizzled hair was always newly done up and there was a waft of strong perfume that made your nose tickle. The teacher was the most elegant person she had ever seen.

The teacher called Dearest Sister and her to the front after the first day.

'We'll have to make the best of this difficult situation together. It's important that we cooperate. Can you do that?'

The Girl smiled widely, nodded. Papa had been clear about the fact that everything the teacher said was right. She would listen to the teacher.

'It's been decided that it's in the best interest of the class if you receive help outside of the classroom. So that time and resources aren't taken from the other children.' The teacher blew her nose in a piece of cloth with lace edges and pushed the handkerchief into the sleeve of her blouse. The Girl felt her sister's disgusted look without needing to turn her head. The teacher's snot was reminiscent of Alberto, of fighting, red terry-cloth shorts, and brown stains.

'Starting tomorrow you'll be picked up here by another teacher. You'll get some help until you can understand our language. Is that clear? Do you understand?'

'We already know Swedish!' Dearest Sister shouted in a shrill tone of voice. The Girl reached out for her sister's clenched fists.

'We understand!'

The boys were waiting outside the classroom. They were hanging on the coat racks, kicking the rows of shoes, pulling each other's hair and hitting each other. When the door opened they lined up in a row, identical sneers on their lips. She let go of her sister's hand and clamped her own hands together instead, instinctively warmed up her knuckles.

'Watch out, the monkeys are escaping from their cage!' The row of sneers giggled.

'But boys, really,' said the teacher.

'Watch out, it's burning! Damn soot-head, go home and wash your hair!'

The teacher folded her hands over her stomach and tilted her head at an angle.

'Oh, boys, boys. Go outside and play together now.'

The teacher disappeared in the direction of the staffroom. Dearest Sister sneaked into the lavatory. The Girl remained standing there. Now it was her turn to clench her fists.

*

Alberto had broken the cap off a shaken bottle that afternoon at the swings, and no version of her good-natured smiles was enough to gather up the bubbling streams and force them back inside the bottle again. She was different, and it was becoming ever clearer.

Once she had learnt to defend herself it was much easier to stay and fight than to turn and walk away. Soon enough, it became a ritual. The bell rang for the break, she went out onto the playground, and the boys pulled at her rough hair.

'Now you're gonna get it, you damned broom!'

'No, *you're* gonna get it!' she yelled back. She rehearsed sequences of moves in her head, and focused on not showing that she was scared or weak.

She thought the boys would stop if she showed enough resistance, thought they might think that she was one of them, that the similarities were bigger than the differences. But she quickly distinguished herself even more: a girl who fought. A beaten one who didn't know her place.

Sometimes, the teacher would stand and watch from behind the curtains in the staffroom, holding a coffee cup in her hand. It was one of those white ones with blue flowers, the kind that used to disappear in Papa's hand at the asylum centre. The teacher used to stand and watch and sometimes their eyes would meet and she would think: now the teacher is going to say something. She'll say what's right! But the teacher never moved.

She didn't tell Papa about the fights, blamed the torn clothes on football games. Papa liked sports. Sports were dreams and hard work. Discipline. But they still continued practising fight sequences. It became their way of arming themselves, those evenings on the mattress-covered floor. Papa taught her everything he remembered from angry boys' punch-ups on childhood streets so far away. She absorbed every move, ready to defend herself in all the ways Factory Town might ask for.

Then there she was, standing in the middle of the ring: in a grove in the woods, in the boys' bathroom, the last one in the dressing room after gym class. She elbowed them, kicked at them, pushed with her fists. There were more of them and they were stronger, but she still stood her ground. It was part of her daily routine just as it was to tickle Little Brother under his chin, or put all of her schoolbooks in her backpack even though they never had any homework. She stood there in the ring, regardless of who was being attacked—her or someone else.

Dearest Sister hated it. She thought the Girl had started everything when she had gotten involved that day at the swings. Thought that they could have avoided all of this if the Girl had left the fatty to his fate from the beginning. Dearest Sister cast angry looks at her every time it started, as if she was the one who had come up with the words:

sand nigger, *blatte*, poo, Paki.

'You should turn the other cheek,' was her sister's response when the Girl suggested they could achieve much more if they fought together, and offered to teach her sister some moves. 'That's what my mother says.'

The Torn Sunbeam was the most sensible person she knew, but turning the other cheek sounded like asking for more. She continued fighting, defending. Her sister continued turning the other cheek, walking away.

SWEDISH FOR TWO

Maja was the name of the teacher who was supposed to make sure that the Girl and her sister didn't take time and resources away from the others. Maja discreetly knocked on the door to the classroom every morning, just as everyone had settled down. She looked apologetically at the head teacher, who paused impatiently from reading aloud while Maja read her version of their names from the well-thumbed note she kept in her breast pocket. The Girl and Dearest Sister had already stood up at this point. They were already on their way out.

"My name is Maja," the extra-resource teacher had slowly explained that first day as she led them to the cubicle next to the classroom. 'Together we are going to learn Swedish. Swedish 2 is what we are going to learn. *Swedish For Immigrants.*'

The Girl answered before her sister had time to clench her hands in protest.

'We already know Swedish,' she explained, pronouncing

the words just as slowly in response.

Maja lined up the picture books in front of them.

'Let's not be difficult now.'

And then their education began. Maja held up picture after picture and articulated in a pedagogic manner.

'This is a train. Say "train". 'Traain'.

'Train,' She and Dearest Sister replied. They tried not to giggle. Fiddled with each other's hair.

'She doesn't know more than we do, you can hear that in her voice.' Her sister declared during a rainy walk in the woods. 'She can stand there and pronounce our names wrong all she wants. I think we should stay in the classroom tomorrow.'

She had seen the way Maja looked at the head teacher, the looks of admiration. How Maja aspired to look like the head teacher with her knee-length skirts and ruffled blouses. The short haircut that Maja insistently ran her fingers through in order to conceal the bald spot on the top of her head. The fingertips that groped up toward her chapped lips and in between her teeth when Maja became nervous.

'I don't think Maja is the one who decides.'

*

The Swedish 2 lessons continued.

'Ch-aai-r. Chair. Chair … Yes, chair.'

It was a particularly slow day. Maja pointed time and again at a black-and-white picture of two rickety Windsor-style chairs and articulated carefully. Dearest Sister was struggling to keep her eyes open, and yawned audibly in response, then finally rested her straggly locks against the desktop.

'Goodness! That's not okay. We do not behave like that.'

'Aren't we supposed to learn something at school?' Dearest Sister asked, suddenly wide awake. 'We can bring our library books if you want—if you don't have any real books here.'

Maja took off her glasses. Red blotches were spreading across her cheeks and she tried to drum her fingernails against the desk, but no sound came. Maja searched for loose pieces of nail with her teeth, but found nothing to bite on. So Maja put the glasses back on her nose and picked up the picture book again.

'That's nonsense, we still have a lot of words left to learn.'

But Dearest Sister had had enough. She stood up and threw her backpack over her shoulder.

'Her father said,' Dearest Sister put her hand on the Girl's shoulder, 'that we came here to work hard.' The Girl felt Dearest Sister's hand shaking against her skin, felt her own liquorice pastilles flicker at Maja who had made Dearest Sister sad. The Girl got up and opened the door, let Dearest Sister walk out and then followed.

'We already know it; we've told you that.' The Girl didn't wait for Maja's reply, she just left. Led the way to the swings where she and Dearest Sister lay down to look at the clouds and think the same thoughts without saying a word.

*

The next day Maja had two workbooks with her.

'These are the books your classmates have started working on.' She set the books ceremonially in front of them. '*Apple* is the name of the first book. Then it continues, *Pap-*

ple, Pear. But we shouldn't get too eager. Let's just start at the beginning and see how it goes.'

That night she and Dearest Sister sat together on the Torn Sunbeam's bed, and completed the *Apple* book with sharpened pencils and wrinkled brows.

'You're doing such a good job,' the Torn Sunbeam observed from the doorpost.

'What have you done?' Maja exclaimed in alarm, when they handed over the completed pages. 'These books actually cost money, you can't just scribble in them like that! You'll have to spend the whole day erasing.'

'Sorry,' she answered for both of them.

'Aren't you going to check them first?' Dearest Sister said and straightened her glasses.

*

Maja looked more relaxed after that day. She stepped into the classroom and threw a collegial look in the direction of the head teacher. Maja no longer needed to call out any names, everyone knew who she was there to get. Maja unlocked the door to the cubicle and lined the workbooks up in front of them, confirmed chuckling to herself, 'things are going so well,' and then she left. When it was lunchtime she came back, smelling of coffee and with a women's magazine tucked under her arm.

'Did we work hard today?'

Soon there weren't any workbooks left. She and Dearest Sister had worked their way through everything in the textbooks and teaching aids' storage. They had searched again together with Maja, but there was nothing left to practise with.

'Now we're finished here,' Dearest Sister observed determinedly. 'Tomorrow we're staying in the classroom.'

They were standing next to Maja when, in a shrill voice, she explained to the head teacher that the girls had done so well. They had even done exercises from year three! She explained that it was time for them to sit with the other children.

The teacher flipped through their books, her brow wrinkled. Then she looked up and pursed her pink lips.

'Well then. All right, I suppose we won't be needing any extra resources then.' The teacher nodded at Maja. 'You don't need to come tomorrow. We'll be fine on our own.'

The next day it was the head teacher herself who led them out of the classroom and unlocked the door to the cubicle. Then they sat there, Dearest Sister and she. Without exercises, without Maja. They brought their own library books in order to pass the time. They rocked back and forth impatiently with their heads bent over the pages, bumped into each other restlessly, and rested their dark locks against each other now and then. Waited.

They saw Maja in the corridors sometimes. Maja never made eye contact, just fumbled at the bald spot with her hands, mumbled something, nodded.

SHOPPING FOR CHRISTMAS

She noticed the scent of his *oddkollon* before his Cheshire grin broke through the evening darkness and Papa took shape in the hazy beams of the streetlights. He was standing at the gate to the rec centre, wearing his long, black woollen coat and holding Little Brother's hand in his. The coat and the strong seaman's smell emphasized that it was a special event. She wondered if he was going to become a doctor too. She hoped so; maybe then Mama and Papa would stop straining the air between them like a bow ready to snap.

'We're going shopping for Christmas!' Papa said and acted like it was the most natural thing to do, considering that Christmas regularly showed up year after year, tucking them into its safe light without them really understanding what was embracing them.

But the porcupine still crept out in her stomach, the one that always appeared when the Girl was out in Factory Town with Papa at her side. Factory Town's Swedishness was so self-evident to her. It was real and it was everywhere in contrast to the Persian that was no more than bits of music and stories about everything she should know, everything she should feel. Swedishness was something completely different for Papa. It was like a soap bubble he wanted to pop, the matador's red flag he needed to bite into, a secret club he wanted to join. He put on the Cheshire grin and approached the Swedishness as if it were a continuation of the revolution, as if it were possible to fight your way to it. But what he was trying to capture was perhaps out of his reach. If not, then the Swedishness was playing hard to get—very hard to get.

It wasn't Papa's enthusiasm that coaxed out the porcupine in her stomach. It was the contrast between his enthusiasm and the looks it received out in Factory Town. She couldn't really read them, didn't know what the sender wanted to communicate or achieve. She tried to see him through their eyes. Tried to understand what they saw beyond the Cheshire grin and honey eyes. Maybe he looked scared, did he, her big strong Papa?

'Never let a dog see that you're afraid,' he instructed her when she backed up at the sight of Factory Town's free-roaming German Shepherds. 'It's the smell of your fear that makes them bark and bite.' She wondered if the same applied to Factory Town's people.

The porcupine crawled out like Pavlov's most good-natured dog at the scent of *oddkollon*, the sight of the black coat and Cheshire grin model *extra large*, in the presence of all the expectation Papa was dripping with. The porcupine pricked, because Papa's pain was her pain, and she felt the pain even when it seemed to pass him by unnoticed.

Now she took Little Brother's hand in hers, squeezed his soft skin so hard that his wide-open eyes blinked and he turned toward her with unspoken questions.

'Great!' she shouted at the little blob who was hopping along beside her so full of blindness. *You'll never have porcupines crawling in your stomach. Never. I'll gobble up every single one that comes your way,* her heart whispered to the tassel on his hat, which was bobbing up and down, steering their steps to the white Volvo 240.

*

Rush-hour traffic filled the city centre of Factory Town, and the aisles at the department store were filled with families doing their Christmas shopping. Children's shouts filled the air, and the floor was covered in slush. There was no smile bigger than Papa's Cheshire grin, no steps more careful than hers.

'What are we going to buy? You two get to decide! I'll get the biggest tree, then you decide what we're going to hang on it.' Papa lifted down the heavy box with the plastic tree and placed it next to the still-empty shopping cart.

'This goes in the window, right?' he continued. 'We can put a white one in the kitchen and a red one in your room.' He carefully set the advent lights in the cart. She followed his expression with her eyes: copy, open your mouth, paste. Cheshire-grin junior.

'What do you want, *pesaram*?' Papa crouched down next to Little Brother, who was dragging a floorball stick behind him with mitten-covered hands.

'We can hang that one in the window. You two get to choose, you get to decide. It's your Christmas,' he laughed and looked up at her.

The porcupine pulled his quills along her intestines and she stood still as beseechingly as she could, as if to keep the quills from tearing something, setting off a flood, a bleed, and turning the evening into a scar. She laughed along, but with watchful eyes around her. Vigilant, still, beseeching, appealing eyes, which she hoped would work like a wall around them. Let Papa remain a hardworking man who, dressed in his black coat and smelling of *oddkollon*, had taken his children by the hand to enthusiastically take part in the play that was going on around him.

She picked out silver balls and glitter, red elves; that was enough. They had enough now. They really didn't need any more.

'Ice cream!' Little Brother came to the rescue. She took his hand and Papa nodded.

'We're finished, we're going home now.' He picked up the

cardboard box with the plastic tree and carried it under his arm, and she helped Little Brother push the cart. They took a spot in the queue, each of them firing off a Cheshire grin at the cashier when it was their turn: first Papa and then the Girl in his wake.

'Is it time for the Christmas decorations?' The woman smiled back and ran her hand over her nicely done-up white fluff, pink lips pouting, and eyelashes fluttering. Papa still had that effect.

'Yes,' Papa nodded. 'We've been shopping for Christmas.'

'How nice!' the woman giggled and ran her fingers along her necklace. 'I'm going to buy wings with my money,' Little Brother hummed and played air guitar using the floorball stick, 'Hii!' Dearest Sister shouted and came running over from the entrance to the store. 'Let's see,' Papa mumbled and dug around in his pocket for his wallet. '*Smash*,' he had bumped the cardboard box with the Christmas tree with his elbow and it hit the floor. 'What the hell are you doing?' the man behind them in line shouted. Everyone froze: the flirting woman with the 100-kronor bills in her hand, Little Brother holding the floorball stick in the air, her sister running, Papa with the Cheshire grin.

'No harm done, it's all right.' Papa bent down and picked up the narrow box. 'No problem,' Papa said and nodded at the man.

'Are you crazy? Hang on to your things would you! Here in Sweden we don't throw things around; haven't you figured that out? You make trouble left and right, try and understand that this is civilization. I'm so damned tired of all of you sand niggers. Take your dirty kids and go back to where you came from.'

'Hey, that's enough!' Dearest Sister had stepped forward and was now standing in front of Papa, who was shaking and staring the man straight in the eye with a dark look.

'Which banana peel did you come sliding in on? Don't get involved in things that aren't your business.' The man grabbed Dearest Sister by the arm and threw her against the gumball machine, then pushed Papa's chest hard. 'Are you just gonna stand there? Cat got your tongue? Aren't people like you used to shouting and fighting?'

Little Brother started screaming, the woman at the cash register called for security and Papa raised his arm and struck the man above his wide-open bloodshot eyes with his fist. The man fell to the ground and the security guards ran over and took a firm hold on the sleeve of Papa's coat, tearing it off when he tried to break free.

'It wasn't his fault!' her sister shouted. 'It wasn't him.' Sobbing, Little Brother threw his arms around Papa's legs. The Girl pulled Little Brother toward her. She avoided making contact with Papa's honey eyes when the guards were relieved by a uniformed police officer who lead him to the exit. Instead she looked at the crowd in the queues. The crowd had stopped moving, was staring in their direction shaking their heads. *It wasn't him!* She wanted to shout. *It wasn't him.* Instead she looked down at the floor.

*

She and Little Brother stood next to the police car and stared at the police officer in the front passenger seat. They continued staring hard until Papa was allowed to get out.

'Do you have everything?' Papa asked. He was holding

the wrinkled piece of cloth that the coat sleeve had been transformed into tightly. She nodded. Papa lifted Little Brother into his arms and walked to the car with quick steps. She and the porcupine followed him loyally.

*

Long after bedtime she was sitting upright in bed holding that week's book so tightly her knuckles had turned white. *The Grapes of Wrath*. Papa had been clear about it being an important book, the kind everyone has to read, so she was reading obediently, line after line. She barely understood the words, much less what they wanted to say, and even if she had understood there wasn't room for anything but paralyzing silence that night. It was tearing at the walls, and beating against her eardrums. The silence was everywhere.

Hayedeh, the most sorrowful yet life-embracing of the Iranian singers, was singing on Papa's cassette player. The sound was low and scratchy. Papa had purchased the cassette player when he was sixteen years old, the same day he had moved away from home and left his small traditional hometown. It wasn't just a cassette player. She had always thought of it more like a teddy bear.

'This is freedom,' Papa had said and lifted the cassette player with his large hands. 'Freedom, *dokhtaram*.'

Now Hayedeh's voice was singing on the cassette player, and the pauses between Papa turning the pages of his book revealed that he was just as shaken up by the silence as she was. The Girl was waiting patiently. Papa's heavy breaths could be felt in the air all the way under her warm covers; he would fall asleep soon. His light snores finally cut through the music. She dropped the heavy book and sneaked out into the hall, carefully opened the door to her parents' bedroom and stuck her head in. As usual, Papa was lying on his side with his arms crossed, eyes squeezed tightly shut and his forehead in deep furrows. Vilhelm Moberg's *The Emigrants* was lying on the floor and the Iranian movie magazines he allowed himself as a break from his integration were lying on the nightstand. The spot next to him was empty. Mama was working an extra night shift.

She went out into the hall, picked the black coat up off the floor and dug the sleeve out of the rubbish bin. She sneaked back through the dark hall and carefully laid the pile of fabric on the patterned rug next to the double bed. She went out into the kitchen again, poured two glasses of milk, set ginger snaps out on a plate and carefully placed the dish next to the remains of Papa's black coat. In a final turn out into the hall she climbed up onto a stool and lifted down iron, needle and thread from the cupboard. Then she sat on Papa's rug, leaned against the side of the bed, placed the cassette player next to her and rewound the tape to the beginning. In the pale light of the reading lamp she ironed out the wrinkled piece of fabric and started sewing. She looked up at regular intervals and observed Papa's facial expression, tried to read what the dreams were telling him, what they were reminding him about. Morning approached before she managed to reattach the loose sleeve with the small cross-stitches they had practised during home economics. She knew that he would never use the coat again. It didn't look the same, and even if it had he wouldn't forget the scar that was hiding between the folds.

Then it came, right as she was laying her head on the rug and pulling the coat over herself. Papa's face twisted in his sleep, twisted into that horrible expression when his cheeks and mouth both scream fear even though his eyes are closed.

'*Mamaaaan!*' he screamed. '*Mamaaaaan!*'

That was what she had been waiting for: Papa's call for his mother that had cut through the darkness as long as she could remember.

'*Baba*, wake up, *Baba!*'

She got up quickly and shook his large body. Papa woke up with a start, sat straight up in bed and gasped for breath. He stared at her with wide-open eyes. She held out her hand and caught the sweat from his forehead.

'*Dokhtaram.* What are you doing?'

She held out the plate with cookies. He shook his head and was about to order her to go back to bed when he suddenly changed his mind and got up.

'Bring the cookies, we're going to make Christmas.'

*

The snow was falling softly early that Wednesday morning in December when she and Papa put the Astrid Lindgren classic, *The Children of Noisy Village* in the VCR, decorated the tree, put the advent lights in the window and ate ginger snaps and drank lukewarm milk for breakfast. When it was time for school, she walked backward toward the bus, couldn't tear her gaze from the kitchen window. For the first time it wasn't shining like a dark hole among the surrounding December lights.

Papa's frustration about the lack of education in her schooling increased with every day she came home without homework. She hadn't told him about the head teacher or the cubicle. She didn't want to reveal that Papa's plan probably wouldn't be realized via her schooling, or say that it wasn't quite that simple. She made up stories about what they learnt in the classroom, copied the atlases from the library and showed Papa. Learnt capital cities by heart and rattled them off while she set the table for dinner. She tried to avoid meeting Papa's honey gaze so that he wouldn't see what was swimming in her eyes: the knowledge that she was in the process of hindering Papa's dreams, that she was letting Papa's dreams be hindered.

It was on an ordinary Tuesday evening that she came up with the solution. Little Brother was lying on his stomach in his crib and Mama was lying on the floor next to him, their shared breathing was vibrating between the flowered wallpaper like the pulse to the new life that had suddenly replaced everything that could have been. She and Papa had pushed the coffee table aside in order to practise new kicks. Papa had changed into a white undershirt and short blue shorts. Drops of sweat ran along his broad, dark biceps as he demonstrated how the hands should always cover the face, the kicks should be preceded by a jump for increased power, the calves should be taut, and the kicks should be timed right. Papa's recording of the *Rocky* movie was playing on the VCR. The Girl was sitting on the rug with her legs crossed, also dressed in blue shorts but with no shirt. She was watching Papa intensely, sometimes casting a glance at the TV screen. The sound was off but she knew the melody by heart. It provided the rhythm for her breathing, just like the air that was travelling through Little Brother's soft body and the pounding of Mama's heart. Papa motioned for her to get up, held a pillow in front of his stomach and she held her hands in front of her face. Focused. Flexed calves and a small jump.

'What do you do when someone hits you?' Papa whispered.

'Hit back!'

'How hard?'

'As hard as I can!'

'How often?'

She stopped, thought about the teacher. Nodded.

'Every time!'

The following morning she didn't react when the head teacher called them to the cubicle. Dearest Sister got up, but she remained sitting. The Girl stared straight into the teacher's ice blue eyes, shook her head slightly. The teacher stared back, then walked over and grabbed hold of the Girl's arm. She wanted to say something but couldn't find the words. The teacher pressed her fingers into the Girl's skin, but then let go. She returned to the teacher's desk and lifted the chalk, hesitated for a moment, then started the day's Swedish lesson. Dearest Sister sank down in her chair again.

Hit back.

She and Dearest Sister never sat in the cubicle again.

*

But Papa wasn't satisfied. He knew nothing of the rescue she had made, and his whole frame of reference told him that this wasn't enough. It must be possible to do more. He met her at the door to the rec centre every afternoon with the same question: *Do we have homework?* And in the evenings he sighed over his deep red tea in disappointment over the fact that the day the future would start hadn't come yet. In the end he decided to take matters into his own hands.

'Tonight we're going to do homework. We're going to do homework all night.'

'But we don't have any homework.'

'Now we do. I don't care what the other kids are doing; you're going to do homework.'

A notepad filled with neatly printed maths sums was waiting on the kitchen table at home.

'I have divided it into different chapters,' he explained proudly.

'Addition, subtraction, division, multiplication, algebra. I have made a multiplication table at the back, see? We'll start with this. One hour of maths every night.'

He lifted the library bag off the floor and built a tower out of thick binders.

'You'll read four books a week and then write a page about every book: what it's about, what you thought about it, what you think the author of the book is trying to convey.'

She glanced out through the kitchen window. Dearest Sister was whizzing through the air on the swing, sending an extra-dark, liquorice-pastille look in her direction. The Girl could see the blackness in her gaze even though the early winter dusk had settled over the sky long ago.

'Sit with your back to the window,' Papa lowered the blinds and lifted a shiny reading lamp from the department store bag. He turned it on and took a step back, nodding at the picture: the books, the sharpened pencils, the main character, or was it the extra?

She sat at that kitchen table. In the beginning she didn't understand anything, but Papa's honey eyes persistently followed every pencil stroke, every one of her thoughts, and for their sake she made sure to derive x even though she didn't really understand how the unknown could be revealed with just a few simple strokes of a pen. Papa sat across from her during those hours of homework, correcting assignments, reading her texts. He flipped through the old adult education books to find inspiration for new maths exercises and reading comprehension exercises. Her homework made room for Mama's, and soon all three of them were sitting around that kitchen table. Mama lost in her medical books, she in abstract maths exercises that made her eyes hurt and Papa in producing teaching material. Little Brother first learnt to crawl and then to walk around their future-making island.

CONTINUING

The years passed. The past refused to disappear, the future couldn't be hurried.

They didn't live on Nelson's Hill anymore. They lived in a newly built flat where they were surrounded by red-brown bricks instead of grey concrete with endless fiery yellow balconies. They were surrounded by glassed-in entrances now, instead of the smell of urine and beer in the tunnel leading from the store.

Little Brother was older now than the Girl had been that night when she and Mama had left their false identities behind to meet Papa in freedom. Mama wasn't going to become a doctor anymore; she was a nurse. They never dug deeper into why, but everyone knew the monster was to blame.

'Being a nurse is a good profession,' Mama reminded them. Mama reminded them over and over again.

She understood that much. But you couldn't replace doctor with a profession, could you?

Papa's Cheshire grin about the future and the opportunities had been transformed into a wrinkled brow and discipline. He had butted his head against one immovable wall after another now, Papa. Those walls showed up everywhere, and the Cheshire grin wasn't able to force its way through. It bounced back instead, hissed at him with bared fangs. His power was met by resistance. Papa was in the middle of a duel, and all he could do was work harder. He saw no other way. Maybe the resistance would have eased off if he had reduced the pressure instead. Maybe his dreams and the resistance would have been able to live in coexistence, if he hadn't pushed so hard. But Papa wasn't willing to take any risks, the plan was too important. Everything that had to be achieved. Everything that had been lost and needed to be compensated for. The plan was all they had left, maybe the only thing they had ever had.

So Papa worked harder. He put up a noticeboard on the wall of her bedroom where he attached rules and schedules, built the plan with yellow Post-it notes. They were placed in straight lines, those notes, they didn't flutter at the edges. He decided that the hours she spent on homework weren't enough. He decided that it must be possible to do more, that it was best to do more, to reassure himself that they had done everything they possibly could. Or even more, to have a buffer.

One evening he brought home a former concert pianist in exile. Together they sat and reminisced over old classics. Papa hummed and the pianist wrote the notes. She and Little Brother lay on the rug and listened.

The following morning Papa attached a new Post-it note to the notice board.

'You're going to play piano for one hour every day. I'll keep track, and I'll decide when you're finished. He's going to teach you all the classics and you'll learn them by heart.'

Handball was already on the noticeboard. Sports were dreams and hard work.

'Hit harder!' Papa shouted from the sidelines. 'Come on, work now, run faster. *Deeh*, don't pass, shoot! Shoot!'

She ran, she countered, she made goal after goal after goal, became player of the match, organized penalties, made penalties, a wall of defence, a shark on a feeding frenzy.

'You aren't jumping high enough.'

One afternoon she found a jump rope lying on her bed, and yet another note on the noticeboard.

"Thirty minutes every day. You'll be faster, better, can jump higher."

She listened. She knew that he had a plan; she had always known that. She wouldn't stand in its way. But sometimes she didn't understand what the rules had to do with the plan, like when a new note determined that she wasn't allowed to open the door to the refrigerator. She was to eat what was served, when it was served.

'We're building character,' was Papa's answer to her unspoken questions. 'You aren't allowed to go out and play,' Papa said. 'Put the phone down,' Papa said. 'You aren't going anywhere!' Papa said. 'Score harder, run faster, rest less often,' Papa said. The noticeboard was filled with notes, plans, rules. 'What is it you don't understand?'

Sometimes she became tired. She said that to Papa once and the monster replied.

'Do you think you can quit because you're tired?' the monster screamed. The monster screamed his lungs out. 'Do you think I'd be standing here in front of you now if I had stopped when I was tired? All of this is for your damn sake, and you're telling me that you're tired? Don't you dare tell me that you're tired! Never dare quit something because you're tired—do you hear me?'

Papa kissed her forehead.

'Finish that now.'

She finished it, and never became tired again.

*

She stopped going out to the swings in the evenings; there was no time. Stopped fighting as well; it achieved nothing. She stayed inside during the breaks instead, locking the door to the classroom when everyone else had gone out. Then she read her books, did Papa's homework. She glanced at the door sometimes to let in Dearest Sister who came to check on her, but not to stay.

'I think you need that homework more than you need me.' Her sister got the sound of the pencil sharpener in response.

'Opportunities, *dokhtaram*! My dear girl. Don't forget. You should make use of every opportunity.' Papa's voice singing in her ears.

She never forgot. She would never forget how lucky she was, how everything could have turned out differently. It was an abstract thought, yet the clearest image she had in her mind.

THE TEACHER FROM SALTSJÖBADEN

The junior high teacher came from Saltsjöbaden. After only a few weeks, the students knew everything about Saltsjöbaden. Everyone in Saltsjöbaden lived in houses, had a view of the water, ate fillet of beef for Sunday dinner and drove down to Germany to buy big cars. After about a year the class understood that Saltsjöbaden's Coeducational School was one of those *good* schools. Where you got *good* grades, a *good* education and the ability to earn enough money to live in a house in Saltsjöbaden, look out over the water and eat fillet of beef while you drove your new car home from Germany.

When the schools in Stockholm were being compared the teacher from Saltsjöbaden brought in the newspaper, pointed out The Coeducational School at the top, and the Factory Town's school at the bottom. When it was time for the national exams, the teacher looked out across the harbour below the classroom window, and held her hands behind her back.

'Now you have the chance to show what you're made of. Now you can prove that you aren't more stupid than the kids in Saltsjöbaden just because you were born on this side of the water.'

The class giggled, turned their faces toward the window and the water. Then they took another three-second pause to think about it. It was the kind of three-second pause that takes hold in your mind and knocks now and again, even far in the future. Did the teacher mean that they were stupid? Or that they weren't stupid? And if they actually were stupid, what did the tranquil sea have to do with it?

PARENT-TEACHER MEETING

Papa always put on the mustard-yellow blazer when it was time for the parent-teacher meeting. He had a deep, Persian and unshakeable respect for teachers and the educational system. He shook hands with a firm handshake and showed off the Cheshire grin. Sat with his back straight and his hands folded on the table, tense and waiting to hear what else they could do.

The porcupine crept out in her stomach for those fifteen minutes. It wasn't out of fear for the collision between Papa and the Swedishness, or out of fear of disappointing Papa. No, the porcupine crept out in the hopes of being more than anyone had expected, exceeding Papa's expectations, and showing the teacher from Saltsjöbaden that she didn't belong in a cubicle, that she had never belonged in one.

Of course it had started out as Papa's plan, the future and the opportunities, but his plan was her plan. Without it she had no plan. She had to be good; she knew that. Better than that, she had to be the best.

The teacher from Saltsjöbaden met them at the door. She observed Papa over the rims of her glasses, fingered her pearl necklace.

'Shall we let you interpret?' The teacher nodded at the Girl.

'That won't be necessary.' Papa's Cheshire grin. 'We've lived in Sweden for eight years.'

'Yes, well. That doesn't have to mean anything.'

The Cheshire grin refused to make room for any worry lines. Papa wasn't there to discuss assimilation politics.

'How's my girl doing?'

'Well, there isn't that much to say really. She works hard, does her homework, scores well on the exams, but you know that already.'

Papa nodded, patted her on the back.

'We do a lot of homework together. But what can she improve on? Can we do anything else?'

The teacher leaned back in her chair, had Saltsjöbaden in her eyes.

'There really isn't anything else you can do. But soon it will be time for real exams, and marks, and things will become harder and harder. And you should be prepared, her handicap will become more and more obvious.'

The Cheshire grin froze. Papa looked at the Girl, not understanding. She avoided his gaze. They had developed a routine where she translated voice tone and gestures that hadn't found a footing in Papa's communication storage yet. But even she didn't understand this one. She suspected, but didn't understand.

'My daughter doesn't have any handicaps. She's strong. She plays handball and football. She scores a lot and runs quickly. What do you mean?'

The teacher gathered her papers together, pushed them into a bundle with smooth edges. She clenched her fists until her knuckles turned white.

'I think we all know what I'm talking about. In the real world a homework assignment here or there doesn't make a difference. There is an order that can't be played with. Everyone has their place.'

Papa was sitting tensely in his chair. The Girl caught the scent of monster, she placed a hand on his, smiled at the teacher who stood up. 'Well, these fifteen minutes are over. Nice to see you; now it's the next student's turn.'

Papa ignored the hand that was offered. He just turned around and left. She took the teacher's hand in his place.

'Thank you. See you tomorrow.'

The teacher pursed her lips.

'Tell your father that kind of behaviour isn't appropriate. That's just not done!'

She walked through the fight sequences in her head. Sharp elbows, strong knuckles, lashing ankles. The Girl saw burning houses and bloody Sunday roasts in front of her eyes.

'Sorry,' she said on their behalf.

I'll show you my place, said a new voice in her head. *You'll be eating my place. It will get stuck in your throat, and you'll be choked by my place. My place will force itself down so deeply you will stop breathing. You'll see so much of my place you'll wish you were deaf and blind.*

97

On the last August day of the fifth year the door to the classroom was opened by a girl with golden hair. Her hair wasn't blonde and it wasn't just light. No, it shone like gold, like an angel's halo, a princess's crown. It got the whole class to stare. The new girl smiled from the door opening and greeted them with a hand gesture. She managed to be both warm and cool in one fell swoop.

She was a princess—Evelina. The kind of girl who doesn't sweat no matter how hard she runs. The new girl in the class took over without even trying, as if she was born to rule. *It's not like I want to lead the way, have everyone emulating me, following in my footsteps wherever I go, but it's my responsibility, my role in life—what can I do?* she said without a word.

Everyone wanted to be like Evelina—even the boys. And everyone wanted to hang out with Evelina, boys and girls alike. She kept a small notebook in her desk where she planned in afternoons and weekends at terrific speed. Girls from the other school buildings made the pilgrimage in the hopes of laying claim to one of the small blocks of time that Evelina had carefully drawn in with a ruler.

She and Dearest Sister watched the princess from a distance. They laughed at the queue that formed in front of her at every break, were embarrassed by the warmth in her mother of pearl-coloured lips.

'She reminds me of that girl in the story about the bears. You know which one I mean.'

'Hm, Goldilocks.'

'Hm.'

'Look at how stuck-up she is.'

'Hm.'

'Who would want to hang out with someone like that?'

'Hm.'

*

She and Mama had the habit of meeting behind the kiosk in the mall after school, between Mama's day and evening shifts. Mama was always on her way between shifts. But when they shared a chocolate milk behind the kiosk in the afternoons, Mama let herself go for a moment. She leaned against the wall with one knee bent and the sole of her foot resting against the wooden wall. The years that had passed disappeared, the ones that had brought her further and further away from the street riots and the Molotov cocktails in her hand. She dreamt herself back to smoking mopeds and cigarettes in the corner of her mouth. Mama looked just as at home behind the kiosk as the secret smokers, the bikers and the transient neo-Nazis. They kept their distance. If they came too close they were met with a look that said it was armed with a box knife in its pocket.

Mama had a lot of youth to catch up on. Her daughter didn't understand that, didn't understand that that was why they were hanging out behind the kiosk in the afternoons. The Girl still knew nothing about time that passes without having existed, time that later returns and claims its right.

Mama let herself go sometimes and the forgetting was just as nourishing as ice-cold chocolate milk.

*

The Girl was on her way to Mama and the kiosk when she heard footsteps running behind her, crushing the dry leaves. She instinctively balled her hands into fists and repeated fight sequences in her head. She was waiting for a shove to her back or a pull to her hair. At the very least, a travelling rock. Instead she was struck with the scent of flowers and princess shimmer.

'Hey! Wait!' Evelina called determinedly and grabbed hold of the Girl's denim jacket. 'Wait.' Evelina searched her face during a moment of silence. 'You're the best student in class, aren't you? You must be.' Evelina was waiting for an answer, but she only got silence in return. 'I need help with maths. Can we go to my place and do our homework together?'

The Girl hesitated, glanced around discreetly to make sure that this wasn't a set-up. That taunts wouldn't be heard coming from the bushes if, for even a moment, she got it into her head that the princess really had asked for her company.

Evelina took her hand and started walking. She didn't dare squeeze back, just allowed her fingers to rest in Evelina's. She held her breath so that she wouldn't say something that would make the princess release her grip. Finally, she explained that she was expected behind the kiosk, then let Evelina lead the way.

*

The Girl and Evelina were only a few steps away when Mama noticed them and without the slightest hiccup switched from street revolutionary to Factory Town mother. She put both feet on the ground and zipped up her open jacket while she observed Evelina from head to toe with curiosity.

'What a beautiful girl!' Mama embraced Evelina's hands in a long handshake. 'Are you my daughter's friend?'

The Girl held her breath, didn't dare look at Mama or Evelina.

'Yes,' Evelina nodded. 'Can she come to my house? I thought we could help each other—with homework and stuff.'

Mama nodded back, just as captivated by the princess's steady look and sunny lips as everyone else.

'Of course, go. More chocolate milk for me.'

She and Evelina started walking again. Mama remained standing, leaned back against the wall of the kiosk again and drank from the bottle carefully, as if to buy some time, or in any case make the time move forward less quickly. Despite the intense look or maybe because of it, Mama looked so lost as her little one disappeared with a fairy-tale figure and left her behind, alone. At home on foreign soil.

FAIRY-TALE CASTLE

No one had ever been better than Evelina in school before. She made that clear right away.

'But I'm not jealous,' Evelina continued. 'I think it's cool.'

And with that the after-school routine moved from the kiosk of Factory Town to the house in the archipelago, where she and Evelina each sat on a leather chair and did their homework.

'The smartest girl in class,' is what the princess's parents had said when they introduced the Girl to their friends. She had nodded grandly: that was her.

Soon she started taking Papa's extra homework assignments with her and spread them across the desk that was at least twice as big as the kitchen table at home. She was so small behind the thick oak top, but with the pen in her hand and Evelina at her side she grew. Inch by inch she grew, like Alice when she entered Wonderland. The Princess was the secret brew.

The Girl would sneak off when Evelina disappeared into Papa's equations, and lose herself in the shimmering green garden that stretched all the way down to the sea. She imagined singing frogs and talking squirrels that couldn't possibly exist. Sometimes, when she was feeling really brave, she set out on an exploration of the princess's fairy castle. The kitchen smelt of freshly baked bread and full fruit bowls and the white floor tiles were so shiny she could see her reflection in them. She didn't dare walk on them, so she just stuck her head in, drew in the scent, avoided seeing her reflection and then continued. The bedrooms were pink: pink lace, pink velvet. The curtains, bedcovers, pillows and stuffed animals were all pink. Everything was in its place. Everything ethereal and fragile. She was afraid to touch anything. One time she went down the creaking stairs to the basement, and leaned against the ping-pong table for a while. It felt like home and familiar in some way, but she didn't know why. Then she caught sight of what must have looked like a gigantic glass box and she rushed over to throw open the lid. A deer stared back at her; a frozen deer with wide-open eyes. She ran away, slipping over the floor in her knee socks and then sank down into the chair next to Evelina again. Safe beside her leader.

After doing their homework they hung out together in the fairy-tale castle, the princess and the Girl. They put on so much make-up they were unrecognizable, lip synched to 'Sleeping in my Car' in front of the rolling film camera, lay in front of the TV watching *Beverly Hills 90210* and eating ice cream with caramel sauce right from the jar: Evelina ate a few spoonfuls; she ate the rest. She glanced nervously at the clock the whole afternoon, wanting time to stand still. She never wanted to leave.

It was warm and comfortable in Evelina's aura. Nasty words, spits and blows didn't belong around the princess. It was so obvious, a rule that didn't need to be clarified. Factory Town looked at her differently when she found herself in that aura. Evelina was a princess and the Girl was the little troll who was standing next to her, covered with the remains of the princess's starlight.

*

Dearest Sister fired her liquorice-pastille eyes at hers from the other side of the classroom when she left the books to stand next to the princess during the breaks. She couldn't avoid those dark spots, but she pretended they weren't there. In time her sister stopped looking. She stopped knocking on the door, stopped throwing gravel against her window-pane. Soon Dearest Sister wasn't there at all. It was like she had never existed.

Papa was the one most captivated by the arrival of the princess. He saw the future in those golden locks and the plan in Evelina's determined eyes. He assigned even more homework now, corrected Evelina's assignments with the same enthusiasm with which he played floorball with Little Brother in the hall.

'You're good for each other,' Papa said contentedly one afternoon after they had dropped the princess off outside the fairy-tale castle. 'It's good to have a friend who wants the same thing as you. You're helping each other. It's good; very good!'

Her spine tingled with pride. *You're good for her.* She had something to give the princess. *That's good; very good.* She was supporting the plan.

Soon Papa started talking with Evelina's parents. He thought that Factory Town wasn't good enough, that the girls should spread their wings somewhere else, in a place where the runway answered their engine power. She nodded at Papa's side. Her dangling roots couldn't take root in Factory Town's grainy soil. There must be richer soil, richer soil must be waiting somewhere. No plans would be realized in Factory Town.

It took a while to convince Evelina. Her roots were deeply anchored, had never fluttered; why should she run away? 'You aren't the best until you're the best among the best.' She repeated Papa's words.

Evelina tossed her soft hair, the angel's halo.

'Do you have to be the best? Can't you just be good?'

The Girl put her pencil on the notepad, stretched out her

hand and carefully touched the tips of Evelina's hair. Understood that Evelina didn't need to be the best, Evelina hardly needed to be good. Evelina saw the insight in the Girl's eyes. She couldn't interpret it completely, but enough to give in.

'Okay, we'll try it! If it's too hard we'll move back.'

'Okay,' she answered quickly. 'But it won't be, I promise.'

Hard work. Nothing was too difficult.

Evelina held out her hand, a nervous glimpse in her sky blue eyes. She shook Evelina's hand excitedly.

They walked up to the desk the following morning to tell the teacher from Saltsjöbaden about their decision. They would start at Saltsjöbaden's Coeducational School and get a *good* education. The Girl, because she was determined not to hinder the plan, not to fail. Glittering with the princess shimmer at her side. Evelina, because it didn't matter much. She was unaware of princesses and trolls.

The teacher listened. She got up, stepped forward and put her arm around Evelina's shoulders.

'Wonderful! What a wonderful decision.'

The Girl stood next to them, beaming Cheshire grin. They were on their way! But no, she made eye contact with the teacher. The teacher's eyes were saying something else. She slowly took off her glasses, looked the Girl over from head to toe. Handicap.

'But you, well you know …' the teacher cleared her throat. 'You know that not everyone fits in at Saltsjöbaden.'

In the corner of her eye, she saw Evelina flinch. She saw Evelina look down and pull away from the teacher. Saw Evelina open her mouth to provide an answer, but that she wasn't sure if the teacher had asked a question. She saw

Evelina close her mouth again. The Girl remained standing still, didn't move a muscle.

What do you do when someone hits you?

Hit back!

How hard?

As hard as you can!

How often?

Every time!

Not this time. The Girl smiled at the teacher. The teacher was right. She turned on her heel and walked out into the schoolyard. She tried to look like she hadn't understood, like she hadn't heard. As if she was unmoved, as if the words had nothing to do with her. But she knew that the teacher was right.

MAMA, PAPA AND THE LAST CLASH

It was a sunny Sunday in May, and an enormous trampoline had appeared in Evelina's garden. The trampoline was a world of its own; did they need any other? They were flying up and down toward the sky and back on the trampoline, like two small rockets. The princess was ready to take flight, the troll was waiting on the runway. Evelina's golden locks hung tousled in front of her eyes. Her shirt arm was torn and bits of snot were glittering in her nostrils. Evelina looked like she could fart at any moment. The troll stared with large eyes and felt the happiness creeping around in her stomach. If the princess could jump and become a troll, the troll should be able … to become something else. It was the first time the idea had struck her, the idea of transformation. The Girl lay down on her back on the trampoline, bounced along with Evelina's jumps, and in the spring sun she suddenly saw a vivid image: a skinny girl in new clothes with shiny, flat hair hanging all the way down to her waist. The girl up there arched her thin eyebrows and smiled coolly, as if saying, *just wait.*

'Isn't that your dad?' Evelina shouted.

The girl in the sky went up in smoke. It couldn't be Papa, she was supposed to stay here for several more hours. But it was Papa's 240 that was pulling up the driveway. The tyres were tearing at the gravel far too quickly. She could see Little Brother in the front passenger's seat, his small chocolate face twisted. Evelina fell down next to her, her cheeks were flushed and her eyes were glittering from the cold.

'I have to go,' she didn't dare look Evelina in the eye. She just hopped down into the grass.

'But we were going to play the whole day.' The troll princess was lying on her stomach, there was a greenish-brown grass stain on the backside of the stonewashed Levi's.

'I know … I don't know. I'm sorry.' She wanted to hurry off before Papa got out and revealed more than she wanted Evelina to know. She knew exactly what was going on and needed to keep it separate from the princess world, protect that world from her trollish reality.

*

The Girl ran over to the Volvo with Evelina's disappointed look bouncing against her back.

'Your mother is at it again. She wants to leave. She wants to leave us and go.' Papa was standing inside the car door, leaning against it, searching for something that could carry him.

She walked past him, got in the backseat and made sure that all of the windows were rolled up. Her body was as tense as the rubber from the trampoline. Everything that came at her had to bounce away. There was no space left inside her.

Little Brother was sitting in the front seat sobbing. At the first red light she unbuckled his seat belt and pulled him close, held his warm body tightly in her arms, his damp head leaning against her neck. She watched in silence as the view changed from that of the sea to the countryside and then to spotted grey asphalt. She knew what was waiting. It was the same drama that was always waiting. The play they never managed to carry off on their own, the one they were constantly asking her to join: as a walk-on, audience, props, weight-bearing pillar. Her eyes like a mirror for things they couldn't see.

The reason was the same every time: nothing. Folded laundry that was still a bit damp. A hello that hadn't sounded welcoming. A cooked chicken that had become dry. Maybe a flower that had withered. The slightest disappointment was enough to set off a conditioned response. It was enough to get them to crush all the opportunities they had longed for with the memories they cast around themselves. Enough to destroy that plan they had come up with. They destroyed it several times a week, sometimes several times a day.

And the Girl always came running, placed herself between them. She cooled off the fresh bruises, hugged hyperventilating lungs. She never understood the script, but she played her part. It was never enough. She was never enough.

*

With Little Brother still in her arms, she stepped into the flat several steps ahead of Papa. She knew that Mama would be lying in some corner, and there she was, lying between the stove and the refrigerator. She turned on her heel, and put Little Brother on his bed, then got out the Walkman and put on Little Brother's only and favourite cassette tape—Orup, the pop singer, on maximum volume. Relieved, Little Brother crawled under the covers, leaned against the pillows and closed his eyes. She wanted to do the same; she wanted to hide. But the silence told her that they were waiting for her. They had paused the play while waiting for an audience, taken half-time while waiting for a referee.

She locked Little Brother in the room and walked back out to them, placing herself in the space between them. Mama was lying, shaking in her corner. Papa was sitting at the kitchen table with a cigarette in one hand, his forehead in the other. *Strike the pose.* The actors had taken up their positions.

'What does she want from me, huh? Can you ask her that? Why does she have to torture me like this?' Papa's honey eyes were like suction cups against her skin. Mama looked up, her eyes flashing with contempt.

'I'm torturing you, huh? Who are you trying to fool? She has seen everything, she knows everything. She knows who is torturing whom. You are a monster and you don't

109

even realize it. A monster!' Mama screamed with all her might, and the Girl sat down next to her to calm her down. It wasn't so much for Mama's sake but for Little Brother under the blanket.

'Ask her what she wants from me,' Papa repeated. 'I'm tired now, I'm tired of all of this. What does she want?' Papa stands up. Ash from his cigarette falls on the kitchen rug, lands in fresh tea stains that are still damp. Props in position.

'I want to leave, *dokhtaram*. I don't want to stay here any longer; let me go.' Now even Mama's eyes are on her.

They are standing in a triangle of *help me!* Of *I hate you. Of oh, how I know this script by heart, haven't we rehearsed the same scene, the same film, too many times before? Of how in the hell did it end up like this? This wasn't part of the plan.*

'You aren't going anywhere, do you understand? You're staying here. You're going to stop being a lazy idiot of a woman and stay here.'

Papa comes closer. His body is shaking. His voice is shaking. The Girl follows the path of anger from the pit of his stomach up to his eyes and out to his fists, sees that it bypasses the brain, wonders if she can knock and explain that the shortest route is the longest of all detours. But the rage is crawling in his arms, exploding in his fingers. She places herself in between them, calls out to him calmly.

'Baba. Baba. Baba.' She tries to pull him back to the present, but he is already wound up. He is already back there. In his eyes she sees the shadow of a bullet, it brushes his right ear, and the contours of a blood drenched T-shirt grow, then she sees the lifeless body of his comrade, running feet, now the sounds of the boots of armed pursuers. The Girl is standing between them, Mama is lying curled up on the floor, and the memories are spinning, fingers are exploding, take number who cares?

*

Cut. It's time for dinner. Papa is stirring the pan on the stove, turns the heat up again. She is setting the table, glancing in their direction, doesn't feel comfortable about leaving the air between them.

'You stay where you are. We don't need you at the dinner table. You can sit there with your threats and your dirty tears.'

Papa hisses at the floor. Mama doesn't react. She wonders if Mama can hear him, if his tone can reach the place where she is. She wonders where Mama actually goes. She can't tell based on her expression, but knows that even Mama must be somewhere else, somewhere far away, in a place even stranger than Papa's. Why would she stay here otherwise?

'Go get your brother.' He turns toward her.

'No.'

'I said go get your brother.'

'No.'

The Girl doesn't look up. Doesn't want to see him. She wants to have as little of him inside her as possible. Sees in the corner of her eye that he is coming at her holding the spatula in the air. She continues setting the table: spoon and fork, spoon and fork, straight lines. Shimmering straight lines.

'You'll do as I say.'

He is standing right next to her. She looks up, looks him as deeply in the eye as she is able, and tries to sneak past the phantoms that are still swimming in his glazed eyes. The Girl tries to find Papa behind them. He turns around, throws the spatula at Mama with force. Mama screams, the spaghetti sauce burns her bare legs.

It's enough now. Something snaps inside her and she tears the plates, the utensils, the straight lines from the table. Shards of china swim to meet the cigarette ash in the puddles of tea.

'Weren't you going to leave?' She screams and stomps over to Mama.

'Go then! Why are you still sitting there? Disappear! Gooo!'

The boiling kitchen is now completely still. Adult eyes are fished up from two worlds far away, and are staring in disbelief at the eleven-year-old girl who is deafening them with a voice they have never heard before, with a rage they didn't know she possessed. They look like they've been interrupted during a game they hadn't realized had gone too far. They look like they've been caught red-handed, but don't know they've done something wrong.

She starts shoving Mama, shoving her along on the floor in front of her toward the door. Papa is sitting on a kitchen chair again with a cigarette in his hand. For a moment he looks like he is staring at them, but his tense posture tells her that he has lost himself in some nightmare again. His forehead is resting in his hand. *Strike the pose.*

She gets Mama out onto the rug in the hall. The Girl sits down in front of her, wants to slap her across the face, make her stop crying. Do something!

'If you don't go, I'll go. Do you hear? I'll go.'

The Girl runs to the doormat where she had thrown her denim jacket, puts it on and sticks her feet in her sandals.

'I'll go. You'll never see me again and then you'll regret that you stayed.'

This wasn't part of the plan. It wasn't part of anyone's plan. Little Brother was lying under the covers. She would never leave him; never leave without him. She runs over to Mama again.

'You have to go. Do you hear me?'

Mama nods. Finally she makes contact. The Girl pulls a suitcase out of the closet. Pulls on Mama and gets her up from the coarse rug. The burns on Mama's skin are already starting to turn yellow.

'Come! Hurry!'

She throws Mama's clothes in the suitcase, everything she can get her hands on. There is little time. She needs to hurry before the monster wakes up in his chair, before Little Brother starts pulling on the door handle, before Mama disappears somewhere far away again. Mama gets to her feet, pulls out dresser drawers and empties them into the bags. Mama has also understood that they don't have much time, that regret can strike at any moment, that the monster can decide to stop her. They help each other close the bags, the Girl and Mama. They freeze when they hear him push back the chair, it scrapes across the damp rug. He is coming, he comes in with tired steps. He isn't interested in them, just opens the bags, digs through the contents. He takes out the small oak box, the most valuable remains of Iran. It is filled with gold jewellery, traditional wedding presents. He puts the box under his arm, grabs the Girl's wrist firmly without looking at Mama.

'You aren't going anywhere.'

He turns away, goes back to the kitchen chair. Mama grabs her suitcases and drags them behind herself over the rug in the hall, but stops outside the locked bedroom door. The Girl rushes forward, pushes Mama away. She is ashamed of hitting the wounded body, but Little Brother is more important, most important.

'No! He's sleeping.' She throws open the front door and presses the button for the elevator. Sets the suitcases inside. Then she shoos Mama inside with her gaze.

Finally the elevator goes down. She listens through the closed sliding doors until the movement of the elevator stops and Mama's steps can be heard echoing in the corridor at the very bottom. She hears Mama open the door to the building, then hears it slam shut. The Girl stays there for a moment, on guard. She is afraid Mama will come back so she calls the elevator back up, and keeps it on the fourth floor. Mama would not be strong enough to drag the suitcases up the stairs. The minutes pass, maybe it becomes an hour. Mama doesn't come back. She leaves her station.

The stink of cigarettes billows forth from the kitchen. She thinks for a moment, then decides to forget about searching for Papa in the smoke. Instead she unlocks the door to her room, closes it and locks it again from the inside. Little Brother has created a hide-out for himself under the covers. He has stuck his head under the pillow and fallen asleep with his soft hands over the headphones. He is sleeping deeply, eyes squeezed tightly shut. She sets the alarm clock for seven and puts her arms around his ginger-snap-coloured body. Hopes he senses that she will never disappear, that he is eternally safe.

Something rustles a bit right before sleep forces its way through the evening's scenes. Surprised, she pulls a new leaf from her hair. She remembers the May sun and the trampoline. The image of a girl smiling down from the clouds. She hangs her thoughts on the princess hook, on the other one she will become. It keeps her mind off the evening's unpleasant footage.

*

There was a knock on her bedroom door before the alarm clock rang. The Girl got up and looked at Little Brother. She briefly searched for the source of the pain in her chest, then remembered with more force than she would have liked.

When she opened the door Papa was standing outside with honey-brown eyes and a Cheshire grin that was trying to force its way through his tired, chapped skin. The ghosts and the zombielike posture were gone.

'Good morning, *dokhtaram*. Did you sleep well?' He pulled her close with one arm and picked up Little Brother with the other, rocked him back and forth and showered his newly awakened face with his wet kisses.

She nodded and played along.

Act Two.

Nothing has changed.

After that last fight, Mama sought refuge under the calm wings of the Torn Sunbeam, and with Mama's disappearance came the monster's retreat. It was as if two family members had left them: one detested and feared, the other whose sweet scent was missed between every breath.

Papa sat on the rug in the living room in the evenings, with his back against the sofa, his legs crossed and the raspy cassette player placed next to him. He was flipping through photo albums. He flipped through slowly, got lost in every picture as if a film was playing on the photo. He told the story out loud sometimes. Little Brother lay next to him on his stomach, with his elbows on the rug and his chin in his hand, absorbing the words with his deep black gaze. She sat at the kitchen table with her homework, but put the pen down every time Papa started talking.

Papa talked about life before everything had turned out the way it had, and the Girl and Little Brother needed to hear this. They needed to hear it so much that they played the film in their own minds, allowed scenes they had never actually seen play in front of them. How Papa had worked so hard to be accepted at the leading university, gotten as far from his small traditional hometown as he could get. How Mama had been the first thing he had seen, the first thing he remembered of the big city. How she had been standing in the middle of a crowd of people wearing a red beret over her thick braids, shouting words he had only read in books before then. How her pearl laughter had echoed between the tall buildings of the capital, despite the noisy demonstrations. That Papa had known, the first time their eyes met, that they would come to share dreams and a future. He had just known.

Papa talked about how everyone became far too occupied with trying to group together to be able to focus on their studies: Leftists, Islamists, Independents. Leninist, Maoist, Cuba-inspired. Militant, reformist, pacifist. He talked about how he and Mama had shared opinions, created their own group. How they had nourished each other's arguments. He talked about how bewitched he became by her tireless discussion and angry verbal attacks of those who didn't agree with her. About how her eyes glowed with the strength he hoped to find again in his own eyes. About what a contrast she was to the women who had surrounded him during his childhood and adolescence. There had been sisters and cousins with headscarves who mainly kept to the kitchen, and had had nothing much to say about the world outside of the family. He said his love for Mama was a part of his revolution.

Papa talks about how something that is so right can turn out so wrong. Explains how a blank surface obscures scratches that don't reveal themselves until the light shines from a different direction. He hesitates there, wonders if the scratches have always been there, or if they were created by the rays from the new light. He doesn't know, he doesn't know which answer would provide the most comfort.

Papa says that Mama is still the most beautiful thing he has ever seen. That none of them will ever see anything more beautiful than Mama. Then he rewinds the cassette back to the beginning, picks up the first photo album again and starts over. She lifts her pen and returns to her homework. Little Brother is still lying on the floor, chin resting in his hand, his deep black eyes trained on Papa's full lips.

*

She still met Mama behind the kiosk in the afternoons. They no longer stood among the teenagers, instead they sat in the front seat of the used rust-red Honda, each of them holding a chocolate milk in their laps. Mama asked about Little Brother, wanted to know what he ate for breakfast, if he was restless at night. She didn't tell her about Little Brother's nightmares, or that they now slept in the same bed. She put him next to the wall, and she slept next to him, watching over him. She also didn't mention that the monster was gone, or that Papa had told them all of the stories and showed them all of the pictures. She didn't want to tempt Mama to come back, not with the worry and not with the memories of a home. The monster had disappeared and calm had taken over. And that is how it had to stay.

Usually the Girl and Mama didn't speak at all. They looked out silently over the mall in Factory Town, while she held Mama's hand tightly and Mama sobbed and moaned. Mama wailed sometimes, as if someone had stabbed her in the spine with ten screwdrivers. The Girl didn't say anything, just held the delicate hand tightly in her own. When Mama was shaking the most she even grabbed hold of the other hand, held Mama's hands in hers, tried to envelop them. She sat there and embraced Mama in complete silence.

She was always forced to let go in the end, allow Mama to drive away to the evening shift. She watched the small red car until every molecule from the cloud of exhaust had evaporated and become one with the oxygen she was inhaling. Then she went up to Papa and Little Brother who were waiting on the rug, and the schoolbooks that were waiting on the kitchen table. She sat down next to her sharpened pencils, turned to look out the window searching with her gaze, and realized that the monster wasn't gone after all. Realized that it was still moving around inside Mama. The monster was sticking screwdrivers in Mama's spine, and fluttering under Mama's eyelids at night. No one was standing between the monster and Mama anymore. The Girl was supposed to protect her. Someone had to protect Mama.

FAMILY COURT

The calm broke when the custody battle started. Sture and Maria, the administrative officials at the family court, were going to conduct an investigation and make a decision. Shared custody wasn't an option, Mama and Papa couldn't share anything any longer.

Sture and Maria explained that they just wanted to talk, to get to know her. They wanted what was best for her; they wanted what was best for Little Brother. They explained that she had a lot of say in this.

'The system is set up in such a way that you have a lot of say in this. Because you're twelve years old. As long as everything looks to be in order then it's up to you to decide where you're going to live. In other words, you decide.'

Sture and Maria smiled wide, as if this freedom was good news. Maybe it was; she had a hard time deciding.

There was a lot the family court wanted to know. She had to cancel piano lessons and scheduled homework hours in order to go there. Sometimes she went with Little Brother, sometimes with Papa or Mama but for the most part she sat there alone in front of Sture and Maria, rocking back and forth so that the creaking from the wooden chair would drown out her silence. Sture and Maria leaned forward, their tone becoming increasingly brusque. They chewed on their pens in the anticipation that she would say something worth writing down. But she was looking out the window behind them, had her liquorice pastilles trained on the snow-covered woods outside the window. The snow-covered endlessness. She had nothing to say. Who did they think they were, strangers who were going to figure out what was best? It wasn't their plan, their opportunities, their future. But she caught herself glancing at Sture's white beard now and again. There was something familiar about him. Yes, Sture's white beard reminded her of Grandpa. Grandpa. Grandpa would have known what was best, of course he would. She allowed her liquorice pastilles to search Sture's foggy blue eyes. Someone had to step in and know what was best.

*

When the custody battle started, Papa stopped sitting on the rug in the evenings. He hardly sat down at all. Instead he hung a cleaning schedule on the refrigerator and divided chores. They were going to scrub the skirting boards, polish Little Brother's floorball clubs, organize the books alphabetically. Every time Papa stepped out onto the balcony for a cigarette break, Little Brother threw himself down on the rug to lie with his chin resting in his hand. She sat down next to him, her cheek leaning against his cropped head. Evening after evening they scrubbed, polished and sorted. Two weeks into the schedule Little Brother looked up at her from his spot on the rug and threw his arm out.

'What's the problem? Everything is already clean! What are we doing?' She buried her head in his soft back. She didn't have an answer.

*

Mama picked her up at the kiosk like before, but was too restless to stay put. So around and around they drove in the rust-red Honda, she with her hands in her lap, Mama with a tight grip on the steering wheel. She looked away every time they passed the red-chequered brick building of the Social Welfare Office, and Mama pulled her head close.

'Everything will be fine, *dokhtaram*, don't worry. This isn't a matter for children. Don't worry, it will be fine,' Mama smiled tensely, lines of mascara were running down her cheeks. 'I don't want to give us false hope, but everything will be fine.'

VERDICT

The investigation drew to a close far too quickly. It was time for the last home visit, high time to make a decision.

Papa baked pound cake and served tea, showed the notice board and the piano.

'Your father is so committed,' Sture and Maria said. 'You're lucky.'

Mama served coffee at the kitchen counter in the temporary flat the council had arranged. Offered hot cross buns on a plate, and sent pearl laughter racing between the walls.

'Your mother is so beautiful and kind. You're so lucky!'

'I want to live with Papa,' she said at the table in Papa's kitchen.

'I want to live with Mama,' she said at the counter in Mama's flat.

Sture and Maria looked at each other confused, wrote in their notebooks and then called her to yet another meeting in the brick building.

'You know, you can't choose both of them. Now when sole custody has been insisted upon we have to choose one or the other. And this is what we're thinking …'

Maria glanced at Sture who nodded calmly.

'You already have a home at your father's, wouldn't it be easier to stay there? There's no reason to uproot you, is there? Do you understand our reasoning? Should we say that then? Say that you'll live with your father?'

She looked at Sture and Maria in their swivel chairs waiting for her to nod so that they could transcribe the verdict, put the future on paper. What did she know? Why were they asking her? This wasn't her plan, why didn't anyone ever remember that? Stay at Papa's. She couldn't leave Papa, could she? But what would happen to Mama? Who would watch over Mama, and protect her from the monster who was still tearing and pulling on her body?

'Dear child. You must give us an answer. Don't you think it's best if you stay at your father's?'

Maria drummed with her nails against the coffee cup, one of those white ones with flowers again. *Blue flower* is what they're called, she knew that now. She remembered the asylum centre. How the delicate cup had disappeared in Papa's large hands. Papa. Papa, who had a plan with the noticeboard. Papa, who was waiting behind the thin office door. She nodded.

'Okay?' Sture asked.

'Okay,' she replied.

*

She was the one who had nightmares that night and Little Brother's warm, soft arms tried to provide comfort. She dreamt that a monster was crawling around inside Mama's body, chewing on Mama from the inside. She dreamt about soldiers who stopped them at the border, took Mama away and left her alone with nothing more than the false name. Setareh. Who was Setareh? She heard Mama crying. What were they doing to her? She dreamt that Mama was wearing a clean, white doctor's coat, and she had a stethoscope around her neck. But then a red stain started spreading across Mama's stomach. It became larger and larger until the entire coat was dripping with blood. Mama was laughing her laughter of pearls, and her eyelids were heavy with eyeliner, but there were black holes instead of eye white and pupils. She heard Mama call her name. She was in the woods, in the classroom, at Evelina's house, but she heard it everywhere. Mama was screaming her name.

*

The next day she sneaked through the woods back to the Social Welfare Office. She sneaked, leaning forward, held her big hair down with her hands and tried to sink through the moss, make herself invisible.

She knocked on Sture and Maria's shared door. She explained that it wouldn't work, the decision they had made yesterday. She understood that it was the easiest and maybe the best, what did she know. But it wouldn't work. She needed to be with Mama. She didn't say that Mama needed her, or that she needed to watch over Mama. She didn't say anything about the monster. She didn't even mention the plan, or that this was their journey, so to speak, hers and Mama's. Or that they had fled together a long time ago. That they were going to be free together.

Sture and Maria weren't happy.

'This complicates things,' Maria determined.

'Yes, what do we do now?' Sture sighed.

They exchanged a look. Sture wrote something on a note, handed it over to Maria. Maria nodded. Sture leaned forward.

'This is what we're going to do. You can live with your mother if you want to, we won't object. But we see no reason to move your little brother. He will stay with your father. Do you understand? Do you still want to move to your mother's? And leave your little brother?'

She flinched so hard that the wooden chair screamed. It felt like a lizard had jumped into her mouth, slid down her throat and raced toward her stomach until its head hit her diaphragm. Leave Little Brother? She was supposed to protect Little Brother. They were a pair, Little Brother and she, they were two halves of a whole. She couldn't leave Little Brother. They had to understand that. Who would lie between him and the open air at night? Who would count his breaths, cover his ears when the world screamed? She can't leave Little Brother. She can't be the one who leaves Little Brother.

'Dear child, you'll have to give us an answer now. We don't have all the time in the world to spend on your case. The resources are limited. What do you want to do? And this time it will have to be a final decision, we can't have this conversation again tomorrow, you need to understand that.'

Little Brother with his elbows on the rug, chin in his hand. Mama's delicate hand, shaking in the driver's seat. Papa with the raspy cassette player. She can't leave, and most of all she needs to protect, and the monster is hunting all of them. There is no time. She has to interfere with the plan but there is no time to think, no time to ask anyone. Who would she have asked?

'Okay,' she answers Sture.

'Okay? So we move you to your mother's and your little brother will stay with your father. Will that be okay?'

Okay? She shook her head, but her mouth said something else.

'Okay.'

'Okay?'

'Okay.'

*

She couldn't feel her legs when she left the family court and walked out into the winter night. She put one foot in front of the other but couldn't feel her legs. The lizard had bitten off the threads, caused a short circuit in her system. It must be the lizard.

She met Papa outside the department store. They were going to pick out a new floorball stick for Little Brother and new knee-pads for her. Papa knelt down in front of the shelves, read the packages carefully.

'It's important to get the right size, *dokhtaram*. Otherwise the knee pads won't be very good.'

Their heads were at the same level, and Papa turned his honey eyes to meet her liquorice pastilles. She looked in his eyes and felt the lizard hit her stomach again when she saw that he understood. He didn't say anything, but they both knew he had understood, they both knew that she knew that he had understood.

Then they walked home in silence, the Girl and Papa. They walked in the kind of silence that preferably lasts as long as possible, not because it is pleasant, but because you know that what follows is worse. That silence had been occurring more and more often between her and Papa, since she had sent Mama away.

PAPA

The day the family court's ruling was going to drop down on the doormat, she stayed at the sports hall after practice. She sneaked back onto the field when the team had finished showering and gone home. The Girl inhaled the comforting smell of ingrained sweat and worn rubber. She scored goal after goal, aiming at the point right next to the left goal post, eight inches above the ground. It was the blind spot, few goalies blocked that type of ball. She scored goal after goal, until the yellow lines melted together with the green field and her fingers couldn't feel the ball any longer, were flying through the air like flimsy flyswatters instead. The ticking of the minute hand was deafening, something that normally only happened when the team was down by one point and there was a minute left and she knew that she could get two balls in that spot next to the left goal post if only the rest of the field would move with her. She usually managed. Nothing put wings on her knees and rubber in her arms like a minute left in the game and two goals that needed to be scored.

Now it was approaching closing time, the minute hand and the two perfect balls in an empty goal wouldn't help anyone. She thought about crawling under the training mat in the corner, being locked in by the janitor and not needing to go home for at least another twelve hours. But the janitor was sitting on the bleachers watching, a plastic cup in his hand, fingers in his beard, waving the *Evening News* at her.

'That looks good. Good kid, good. You're a fighter, you are.'

She waved back. He pointed at the clock. She dropped the ball reluctantly, pulled Papa's tracksuit pants over her shorts, lifted her bag over her shoulder and walked out into the November rain.

'Do you need a ride, kid? You're tired tonight, I can see that.' She chewed on the inside of her lip, thought about crawling down under the tarp on the back of the janitor's truck, following him to wherever he was going in that endless wood and never coming back. No. She backed up toward the red metal door.

'Okay, kid, but don't stand here in the rain and chill your muscles. Your father will be worried, you know that.'

The janitor wasn't stupid. The longer she waited, the worse it would be. The fluorescently-lit darkness outside closed in around her. In the city centre there were fewer and fewer car engines heading in the direction of home, and her skin was already damp. Her stomach started rumbling and she turned her bag inside out, emptying out boots, a dry towel and deodorant onto the asphalt. But no coins, no apple. It quickly became eerily quiet. The wind was howling up on the hill and through the woods where she had hidden, playing guerrilla soldier on her way to the family court. She wasn't in a hurry. She sat down on the empty bag, stretched out her legs in the puddles of water, then leaned back and observed the small dot of Factory Town that was stretching out in front of her. She observed it carefully as if the wet gravel and the red buildings were the most bewitching of gallery paintings.

Then Papa's quick footsteps cut through the canvas. Her first thought was to hurry back to the guerrilla woods. Her next one was to gather up the pieces of the good girl that were lying around her, squish them back into the bag and go and meet him. But he was a part of the canvas, right? And she was just a particularly captivated observer.

'Get your things,' said the robust man who had been painted in a deep-grey oil paint. The rough stubble of his beard had been dotted in place with the thinnest of brushes. A careful stroke with the nail of a little finger had accentuated the shadows under his eyes.

She stood up, a small creature in the big pants, her hair a still-life of a Brillo pad. You couldn't make out the facial features—was it a girl, a boy, or maybe even a troll? She actually wasn't more than the hair. At first glance nothing more than a spot of bad weather. She stood up and they started walking side by side, the man and the troll, a taut string between them. If you touch it with your fingertips you'll realize that it's the thinnest piece of a steel wire. They are stuck to each other, the beard stubble man and the girl troll.

LITTLE BROTHER

After the family court's decision, silence took over: not calm but silence. The kind of silence that beats in your ears. Papa was sitting on the rug again, sorting photos in chronological order. Little Brother was lying on her bed, watching without really being able to understand. She was packing, taking apart the desk, and stacking books in the banana boxes she had asked for at the grocery store. She folded every piece of clothing carefully. Finally she sat down next to Little Brother, and explained the decision the investigation had resulted in, that she was going to move and he would be staying there, but nothing would change. The bed would stay there, he would continue sleeping in it and she wouldn't be sleeping that far away.

A look of understanding appeared in Little Brother's pupils. He grabbed the floorball club and banged it hard against the wooden trim. In the living room, Papa screamed in response. She threw her arms around Little Brother and he held her tightly, locking his fingers around her neck.

'We're on the same team. We're a team, aren't we? You can't move. There won't be any team left if you move.'

Little Brother's sobbing words made her gasp for air. She fell forward but was held up by his embrace.

'I don't want to move,' she tried to explain, defend herself. 'I don't want to … of course we're a team, we'll always be a team. I just need to do this now, but we'll always be a team, okay? I'll always be on your team.'

A car honked down on the street, and they both knew that it was Mama in the red Honda. Little Brother pushed her away and lay down on the bed with his head hidden in his soft arms. She tried to move them, make contact with his deep black intensity but he waved her away, turned away, his elbows wet with tears and his body shaking. She got up, knowing that there was no explanation and no defence. She knew that everything would change.

She pushed her boxes toward the elevator and slowly closed the door. Silence was the last thing she heard. The silence, and Little Brother who was calling her name.

MAMA

The boxes barely fit in the red Honda, but it didn't matter. Mama left the trunk open, pushed the gas pedal to the floor, and started driving without saying a word. The silence kept them company in the car. The silence, and the thought of Little Brother the mountain peak. The chocolate body who wasn't in the backseat.

Mama stopped behind the kiosk. She let the engine run, sank back in the seat and grabbed the Girl's hand over the handbrake. Mama's long fingers around her short stubby ones. She sat close to Mama, as stiff as a frozen windshield wiper. She was afraid she would destroy the system if she so much as took a deep breath, afraid she had upset too much already.

The engine was running and Mama was sitting there like a sack of potatoes, no air left. They sat like that for a long time before Mama slammed her fist against the steering wheel, rolled down the window, lit a cigarette and then backed out again. They drove through the centre of Factory Town, with the many round eyes of the library as their audience, swerved around red buses and then out among the green fields. The Girl sat still, frozen, until the distance between the houses widened and the fog was rolling thick and unhindered over the ground. Then a shock travelled through her body. It travelled through her whole body, as if she had stumbled during a dream, been woken by the fall. She blinked a few times. Little Brother. She glanced at Mama who was sitting, leaning forward and chewing gum with her lips closed. Little Brother.

Cloud-covered fields became grey foggy sea and Mama braked suddenly, at the very end of the dock leading to the car ferry. The waves slammed against the cliffs like sulking children who think they deserve so much more. Children who are planning on screaming until someone listens.

*

131

When they finally pulled into the foggy parking lot she was lying in the car half-asleep, the air around her was stuffy. Mama fished for the red lipstick, pouted and then smacked her lips. She looked at her reflection, liked what she saw.

'Wake up, *dokhtaram*. We're home now.'

They left the boxes in the car, and walked hand-in-hand into the new stairwell. The flat Mama had gotten from the council had been completely renovated, the scent of drying paint and plaster still hung in the air.

'She smoked a lot, the woman who lived here before. The wallpaper was yellow from the cigarette smoke the first time I saw the flat. But they've fixed it up so nicely.' Mama ran her hands over the white walls. 'It isn't bad, this flat. And the area isn't bad either. It's better than Nelson's Hill anyway; they assured me of that.'

The flat felt eerily empty, empty except for the two bags she had forced Mama to pack that last night with the monster. They were still standing next to each other, under the hat rack.

She carefully padded inside, knee socks over light-brown linoleum floors. There were two narrow mattresses in the bedroom. She threw herself down on one and opened one of the three *Kinder* eggs that were lying on the covers. Mama had covered the window with a sheet. Seeing the sheet gave her a stomach-ache, or maybe it was the *Kinder* egg. Perhaps it was best to eat one more.

'This flat is like a blank page in your diary,' Mama stroked her hair. 'We're going to decide what you write.'

She didn't really know what that meant. She thought about the plan, the future. It was given, wasn't it? She thought about Little Brother, the mountain peak, that it was all for his sake and now she had left him. Her stomach-ache became worse. Best to eat the last *Kinder* egg as well.

'I'm so happy you're here; do you understand that? I'm so happy you're here.'

Mama sank down on the empty floor, which had been scrubbed clean, curled up with her knees bent against her chest and stuck her head between them. She got up, closed her body protectively around Mama's, the radar in her neck was searching for its coordinates, the signal threads suddenly made contact: it isn't here. The monster isn't here.

They lay down on their backs next to each other on the mattress. She glanced at Mama's face, at the red lips that were always pouting. Mama's eyes were closed, her eyelashes resting against her cheeks. The Girl could see the calm through the eyelids. She touched Mama's smooth cheek, and her hair that was spread out over the pillow like a peacock's feathers. The Girl pulled her fingers through Mama's locks of hair until her head fell to the side and the twitching of her eyelids indicated that she was sleeping and dreaming. She got up and carefully closed the bedroom door, as if to protect them from everything outside and make sure that nothing sneaked into the room and into Mama's dreams. She curled up close to Mama, then pressed the whole of the warmth of her body against Mama's back.

BLATTE-LAND

One doesn't become more Swedish than this.
You won't become more Swedish than this.

In the beginning Mama and the Girl were joined at the hip. She sat on the toilet seat while Mama showered in the mornings. Mama sat on the floor next to the desk with her strong tea while the Girl did her schoolwork. They changed together when it was time for the nightshift at the nursing home. Mama changed into her nurse's uniform, the Girl into her pyjamas. Mama made up a bed for her on the sofa in the nursing home's common room, always with several layers of sheets to make sure the urine stains wouldn't force their way through and up into the Girl's sleeping skin. She followed Mama during rounds, sat on a chair in the corridor while Mama went to the residents, while Mama handed out medicine and changed diapers, and while Mama stroked the elderly over their heads and chatted, especially with those who no longer seemed to hear, or understand.

Sometime around midnight the Girl went back to the sofa, curled up in a ball, closed her eyes and kept watch with alert ears. She lay there like a cat and listened for Mama's footsteps, for burglars at the rose buses outside. She didn't fall asleep until she felt Mama's breaths in the room. They were safe, or at least together. She was standing between the monster and Mama.

But the cocoon didn't last for long. Mama became too restless. The Girl's companionship wasn't enough to keep the monster at bay; she had never been enough. She hadn't been able to prevent black eyes, bloody teeth, dislocated arms. Mama needed something stronger, something that wouldn't slide away across the rug when strength and firmness were needed. Mama needed something more.

Mama stopped bringing her along to the night shift, said that the Girl needed to sleep in her own bed. Mama stopped coming home to eat breakfast with her in the morning. Instead Mama washed her face with cold water and went straight to the day shift at the next nursing home, and then on to the evening shift when it became late afternoon, always with the red lipstick in her breast pocket. Her legs on autopilot, she returned to the night shift in the hours after dusk, dipped a candy bar in extremely strong black tea, licked the chocolate off her fingers and added warmth to the nurses' debriefing with her clanging laughter.

'Someone's slept well today,' the ladies observed.

'Yes! I always sleep well,' Mama shouted delightedly in reply before she went on her first rounds, her footsteps echoing in the corridor.

When Mama stopped at home she usually stood in front of the bathroom mirror, brushing her hair a hundred times, and looked at herself. She had layer upon layer of red lipstick on her lips, but her gaze was focused higher up, searching her eyes. *Who are you, when did I disappear, who took me? Was it Them, was it him, maybe it was her?*

Mama never found the answer in her own gaze, she just tied her shoes again and drove off in the red Honda.

Yes, Mama was doing what Papa had said you should do in the mail van that had driven them to Factory Town. Mama had closed her eyes and found a new dream. She was working hard for the new dream instead.

When high school started she stayed in Factory Town while Evelina disappeared to the other side of the water. She never explained to Papa why she didn't go. She didn't repeat the teacher's words, didn't talk about how some people don't fit in, would never fit in. She suspected that Papa didn't know that yet. That he thought it was possible to fix, that you could fix it.

In response to Papa's arguments and uncomprehending looks she said that commuting back and forth every day seemed like too much work. She would rather stay where she was, said it was more convenient. Papa was disappointed by her laziness, and her failing courage. He was disappointed by her not having understood the bit about opportunities, the bit about dreams and hard work, and by her not understanding how to create the future.

Papa thought he had raised a different kind of daughter. And he wondered for a moment if the teacher had been right. If his girl had a handicap after all, one you couldn't see with the naked eye.

*

With the princess on the other side of the water, Dearest Sister and the Girl were reunited at the boulders in the yard.

'Did you notice that I'd disappeared?' Dearest's liquorice pastilles were as sharp as Turkish pepper.

'Of course.' The Girl didn't meet the burning gaze.

'You're lying.'

'No, I'm not.'

'Don't lie. I know you.'

The Girl shoved her hands in her pockets, stopped protesting. Dearest Sister looked up at her with burning liquorice pastilles and kicked at a rock with her worn boots. The Girl followed the quick movement with her eyes and was just about to explain about the difference between princesses and trolls. Explain that the two of them would become something else—that they had to become something else. But before she could utter a word a familiar fist came flying toward her, and knocked her down on the ground. Dearest Sister was standing over her, one leg on each side of her torso. She bent down and hissed between her teeth, 'Don't you dare disappear again, you hear me?'

The Girl wiped her mouth with her hand and her shirtsleeve turned red. She wanted to say that they would disappear together, that they couldn't stay behind.

THE DREAM ABOUT ALLY

Disappearing. High school was about disappearing. That was all it was about.

The Girl minimized the opportunities for social contact. She stacked books around herself and took shelter behind them. She stopped existing. The Girl moved her existence further into the future, so far that it was actually invisible, but still more real to her than reality. Sometimes she glanced up from behind her fringe, to make sure that other people were keeping their distance. But she made sure that it wasn't obvious that she was peering out because she really wasn't there. She wasn't there.

She was located so far in the future that the only sign of her was a small flickering flame, a star whose light was shimmering before it started burning. Twinkle, little star. She twinkled away at her desk while the teachers walked around collecting snuffboxes and fruitlessly tried to get the class to learn.

'You don't need to come to class,' the maths teacher had said. 'There aren't any resources for extra tutoring. Your classmates need to pass first, you know. I can't do anything for you, there isn't any time. Take a break.'

So she sat at the very front and twinkled, twinkled and dreamt about Ally McBeal, with a leather briefcase, blazer and a short, short skirt. A desk far away, working days that never ended. Her own flat on a rainy city street. Dearest Sister and her. There were no looks and no jeers in her world. She had tied colourful balloons to her house, rise and she was gone. Who was left? She didn't need to know who had made out with whom, or who had been caught shoplifting, or who had lost their virginity in the locker room. She didn't need to stand and smoke in secret, become one with the smoke from the factory chimneys.

*

A system grew and laid itself over them like a grid. Yes, high school was a continuous rerun of the system that had developed over the course of previous generations. The others were absorbed in the process of repeating what life had always been like in Factory Town. She was hiding behind the books, invisible, somewhere else. She was never meant to be there. She should have been somewhere else, in a place she didn't know.

Sometimes she could be struck by the vacuum that surrounded her space in this system. The bang was so intense that kicks and punches weren't enough of a defence. Like when her Swedish teacher took her out into the corridor and explained that it didn't matter that she was sitting at the front of the class like a star, answering all of the questions. In the Swedish teacher's class, the Girl would never get an *A*, did she hear that? Not someone like her! Coming here, thinking she was somebody. The Swedish teacher became angrier and angrier as time went on. The teacher kept the Girl after school one day, picked out the short story she had handed in right before Christmas and asked her to tear it in half.

'You didn't write that yourself!'

She went home to Papa with deep creases in her forehead that afternoon. The teacher. All teachers. They knew the system. They knew that everything had already been determined. But none of them knew about the plan. They knew nothing about hard work and dreams. They didn't know that there was something else that was just as determined. Just as determined.

'There must be more we can do,' she said to Papa. 'We won't get anywhere from here.'

He searched for her hidden handicap. The honey eyes answered: *No, that's what I said.*

Dearest Sister wasn't someone who accepted the invisibility. They were there for crying out loud; everybody could see that. Dearest ran back and forth between the groups in the cafeteria. Eavesdropped, collected stories and gossip and dumped them in the Girl's lap. Dearest would stubbornly argue about whose side they should take.

'Who wants us on their side?' the Girl answered without looking up from the books.

'What do you mean?'

'I mean, do you see anyone who wants to talk to you?'

'Shit, aren't you being nasty.'

'It's true.'

'Damn nerd! Bookworm. Douche!'

The Girl turned away, leaned over the lab report, the history book, the story book that was still unwritten. Dearest walked around the cafeteria again, then plopped back down on the bench. She tapped the Girl on the shoulder when she wasn't paid any attention.

'Hey.'

She shook her head.

'Don't you have any other clothes? People are asking. You've worn that shirt three times this week, and those pants, haven't you had those for years? At least that's what people are saying.'

She looked down at the red-and-blue chequered flannel shirt and the white jeans. Who had noticed her?

'And then the hair, I mean, it's sticking out in all directions. Haven't you noticed? No wonder people are laughing, you could hide a porcupine in your hair.'

The Girl ran her hand through her frizzy locks. When were they laughing at her?

'And, like, your eyebrows. Can you even see anything? Is that why you're sitting with those books every day, because you can't see what you're reading?'

Furious liquorice pastilles in an air duel.

'Super cool. Have you looked at yourself in the mirror lately?'

'Yes, I saw a monkey who looks like you!'

The Girl turned away and waved with her hand. Waved away, gone and away. *Disappear, let me disappear, leave me alone and let me disappear.*

*

Dearest Sister didn't accept things as they were. She took measurements with her eyes, tested colour charts in her mind, tore ads out of the *Weekly Review* and studied them for night-time reading. Dearest sneaked around the department store for several hours and stuffed their new life into the sleeve of her jacket, and inside the waistband of her pants. She slipped invisibly past the guards. Finally she had everything they needed.

'You're coming over to my place before school tomorrow! Do you hear? Early!'

She didn't look up from the books, but they both knew she would obey.

*

The Torn Sunbeam met her at the door the next morning.

'My how you've grown.'

She looked down at the floor, didn't dare meet the forest green gaze.

'I'm glad you're back,' said the Torn Sunbeam.

She looked down at the floor, stared at the shoe stand.

'Is she here?'

'Of course she is. Where else would she be?' The Torn Sunbeam pushed the bedroom door open, then hesitated ever so slightly before stepping aside.

*

'What do we have that no one else has?' Dearest Sister declared proudly as she quickly shut out the Torn Sunbeam's questioning eyes. She pointed at a ready buffet, a colour cavalcade on the bed: bits of fabric, cans, bottles, torn-off price tags.

Puzzled, the Girl held up a neon green push-up bra with a matching thong between her fingers.

'This?'

'But you do understand?' Dearest persisted and knowingly unbuttoned the top buttons of the Girl's chequered shirt. She looked down embarrassed: *yes, I understand*. She kept picking. Raspberry scented lip gloss. She squeezed a bit out on the tip of her tongue, smacked while she pushed away the purple eyeshadow, it reminded her of black eyes.

Dearest stepped forward, focused liquorice pastilles six inches away from hers, shiny metal in Dearest's hand. The Girl pulled her head back.

'What are you doing?'

'Sit still!'

Then she felt a cold hand on her chin, and strong fingers with nails as shiny as the neon clothes that were lying on the bed. She felt sharp tweezers against her soft skin.

'Are you crazy?' She screamed.

'Sit still and be quiet.'

'It hurts like hell.'

'So? We need to do this.' The hand was like a vice on her chin. She capitulated, bit the inside of her lip until the taste of blood overpowered the scent of raspberries. Dearest stuck her tongue out between her teeth, pulled with the tweezers until her fingertips turned white. The Girl closed her eyes and let Dearest have her way, tried to think about something else instead.

'You can look now,' her sister said after a numbing period of time. A completely naked face was waiting for her in the mirror. Her eyebrows had been transformed into thin lines, albeit varying lengths. The carpet on her upper lip was gone. She tried to hide, covered her face with her hands and closed her eyes, then opened them again. Yup, she was naked.

Dearest Sister assessed the situation from a distance, and rummaged through the items on the bed, then hopped over and pulled the Girl's shirt off so roughly the buttons popped off and she was left sitting on the linoleum floor even more naked than before. Before the Girl had time to react a neon-green bra was being strapped on her. Her sister pushed her forward, cupped her hands under the Girl's breasts and pulled them forward as far as they would go. That was how the Torn Sunbeam did it; they had witnessed it on countless mornings. But the Torn Sunbeam always wore a thick turtleneck sweater. Her bosom was there but it didn't make a fuss. In the tight camisole her sister pulled over her head, her breasts were playing the lead role, the diva, the star that was drawing all of the stares. She hadn't realized that they had grown so much, and was forced to investigate. Yup, they were hers. Two soft hillocks that were pushing against the fabric. She touched them again. Was she supposed to walk around like this? She blushed but couldn't tear her gaze from the reflection in the mirror. The image that was staring back wasn't beautiful. No. The red dots of blood that were appearing in place of the strands of hair gossiped assault. Her face was an exploding pool of colour in the morning haze. Her hair was pulled back tightly, stiff from water and hair spray.

But she liked the transformation anyway. The Girl twisted and turned. Yes, she was different. She was changeable, not constant. She could become something else; she would become something else. The Girl nodded to herself, collected evidence. Everything would become something else.

'We're going now,' said her sister, who was wearing chequered knee-high socks, tight shorts, and was a head and six inches of heel taller than usual. The Girl tried to tear her gaze from the mirror so she could glare angrily, protest a little. Talk about how calm and comfortable it was to be invisible. Explain that there was a system, a system they couldn't break simply by changing costumes. But the expression on her face didn't want to listen, it licked its lips instead, like a filthy man at a valley girl party. She wanted more.

*

They were late to the first lesson. She who was never late. Dearest Sister had staggered up the long hill with the smallest of steps, and the Girl hadn't had the heart to walk ahead or even ask her to take off the damned shoes. What kind of power did she think lay in a pair of high heels?

Alberto was the first to see them when they finally came into the classroom. His radar picked up the movement. The ball had been thrown too perfectly; he couldn't miss the smash. His thin body stiffened and he stood up, parted his lips. The air molecules in front of his face started vibrating, but he couldn't find any words. He tried and tried but couldn't find any words. She made eye contact with him and maintained it until she got to her desk. This was her sister's plan and she was a protector of visions. She ran with the torch when the torch bearer got a cramp in his calf. *Get out of the way—here comes our passion!* Her liquorice pastilles found the boy in the red terry-cloth shorts, the one who had to repeat a grade, the one who would come to repeat most of life's lessons. She sent the message that this wasn't the right time, definitely not the right time. Alberto sat down again. He threw an eraser at Ebba who was sitting in front of him, shouted, 'Damn whore!' to nobody in particular, then turned to look out at the schoolyard again.

WHO THE HELL DO YOU THINK YOU ARE?

Dearest Sister experimented to new heights of tight, short and impossible to ignore. She hurried to the cafeteria after every lesson, leaned against the ping-pong table, pouted with her lips, pulled in her stomach and pushed out her chest. Dearest looked around with expectant eyes and attacked every person who passed by with that look, challenged them to study her up and down. Most obeyed, it was hard not to.

Their looks said: *Who the hell do you think you are?* That wasn't the kind of look she had hoped for. Dearest wanted to stand out, but only enough to be allowed to join in. What else would she do with the plan? They looked, but Dearest wasn't satisfied.

The Girl didn't understand Dearest's plan. She lent her face and body to the experiments, stood by loyally and pouted her lips in order to avoid a telling-off. But she didn't understand.

But we don't want to stay here and become one of them. That can't be what we want? If that's what we want, we don't need a plan. A plan doesn't keep you here, a plan leads you away. Only people without plans stand still. We can't stand still. We're already gone. I'm not here.

KAWA

'You have the sickest eyes.'

She didn't answer.

'Hey, anybody home?'

She turned her head in his direction, but kept her eyes focused at the end of the street. She didn't dare look straight at him.

'Who, me?'

'No, your mama! Of course you. Irani?'

She looked at his shoes. Strange shoes. They were like

trainers but with really thick soles.

'Eh. Me?'

'You joking?' He tapped her right shoulder lightly with his fingertips. 'You can tell by the eyes. Iranians, they have the most beautiful eyes.'

The Girl looked up at him with big eyes, the biggest eyes. She looked behind her, in front of her, next to her for anyone who was more deserving of his words and attention, but he was talking to her. Of all the people who were filing past, she was the one he was talking to.

Dearest Sister had declared that they needed to travel beyond Factory Town's department store to acquire everything they needed to be seen, to be seen in the right way. Dearest had said this and then pointed decidedly at the bus to Stockholm. The Girl had wanted to protest, say that this had gone far enough, tell her that the line between invisible and impossible to ignore was so thin, they were almost the same, they could slip back to the right side. But Dearest walked to the bus and she followed to later stand outside the shops and wait, staring at the ground and hunching up her shoulders in order to hide her face. Disappear in the moving crowd of people, become an invisible particle, a part of the whole.

And now this stranger was standing next to her as if that was exactly where he was supposed to stand. He was standing next to her, talking. He was talking to her, looking at her, with a look that made her bite her bottom lip. He was looking her over slowly, from the high heels she had just started getting used to, up her legs in those really tight pants that revealed every line of her handball muscles, to her breasts that were pressing against the tight camisole.

She resisted covering herself with her hands, and his look continued, past her lips that tasted like raspberries up to her fluttering eyelashes, which were heavy with clumpy mascara. Short, tight, high, and glittery had become her sister's motto. Through his eyes she started suspecting why.

She looked away with her liquorice pastilles when his eyes tried to find them. She didn't want him to see the troll under the layer of pretend princess. He grinned, as if he understood what she wanted to hide. He grinned and held out his hand, took hers in his large, steady one. It reminded her of Papa's hands, despite this boy being so much younger.

'Kawa,' he said. 'My name is Kawa.'

She nodded in reply.

'And you? Don't you have a name?'

She was tongue-tied.

'Okay, okay. Damn, you playing hard to get.'

He was going to leave now, she was completely convinced of it. He would turn around and walk away and take his gaze with him.

'What's happening?' he asked.

She closed her eyes, then forced them open again. He was still there.

'Now?'

'No, yesterday. Course I mean now.'

'Uh, nothing. I'm waiting.'

'For who, the boyfriend?'

'Naa.'

'Your brother?'

'Naa. My sister.'

'Ah, she pretty as you?'

'Prettier.'

'Impossible!'

She looked behind him, looked at the end of the street. Someone must have been messing with her: Candid Camera, Alberto on a city tour.

'You're really blushing. Don't people usually say you pretty? What do you mean you don't know? Of course you know. I think people usually say that; you just playing hard to get. Or you hanging out with the wrong kind of people.'

Out of the corner of her eye she saw Dearest Sister rushing out of the H&M shop, her jacket sleeves were stuffed and her forehead was sweaty.

'I have to go now!' She tried to walk toward her sister but her feet wouldn't move.

'What do you mean go, go where?'

Dearest Sister had caught sight of them and was walking toward them carefully. One eye was studying the boy from head to toe; there was a glimmer of hope in her eyes. The other eye was filled with confusion. *What's happening? He's happening. Who is he, happening to us?*

'I've never seen you,' he continued. 'That's crazy. I know everybody. Where you from? No, I mean, where in Stockholm? Not Märsta, I never seen you in Märsta. Husby, Kista? All Iranians live in Husby, Kista. No? Raspberry Hills? Where? Never heard of it. The archipelago, what, the countryside? You hillbillies? Who you hang out with? What do you mean no one, you guys not popular? Shit, course you are. What are you doing then, where you going? Don't know? Okay, you coming with me. Cig?'

*

152

Dearest Sister and the Girl stumbled after him, each with a limp cigarette between their fingers. They wanted the cigarettes to burn out as quickly as possible so they could throw them away. Absolutely didn't want them to burn out, so they had something to do with their hands, something that kept them from grabbing hold of Kawa's jacket and asking him if he knew that he was the one they had been waiting for. The one they had been looking for. They had neither guesses nor expectations about where his path would lead, but they followed him. They would follow his hypnotically swaying figure to the end of the world if only he would let them.

Kawa seemed to understand exactly that. He hadn't wasted any more words, just grinned again and indicated their direction with a movement of his chin before he started walking down the street as if it were a corridor built for his advance. He nodded, shook hands and pounded people on the back. There were suddenly so many guys, everywhere, guys like Kawa. She had never seen anything like it. It was like they had a world of their own here in the big city away from Factory Town. They all looked like him. Not in appearance, but in the way they tilted their heads back, their chins held high, like *I'm about to fall over backward but it's worth it as long as you take note of the fact that no one is looking down at me, you understand, I'm the one looking down.* She imitated them without thinking, held her chin high until there was a pop at the base of her skull.

*

Kawa led them to a dark alley.

'Are we going to follow him?' Dearest Sister suddenly hesitated and tried to slow down without it being obvious. She pretended to glance at the shop next door, where there would turn out to always be a sale on nylon tops and plastic bags.

'It's the middle of the day. What could happen?'

'We don't know him.'

'That's the best thing about it. He doesn't know us.'

Kawa held the door open to the café next door, Café Claudia.

'What's happening, you coming?'

They quickly stumbled over and he put them on a red plush sofa.

'I'll be back. Don't go anywhere.' Kawa walked off between the tables with a swaying gait.

She nodded at his disappearing figure and heard a bright voice singing on the upper floor, singing with emphasis. There was a tingle along her spine. She recognized the song from Mama's crackly cassette tape, the find from Raspberry Hills.

'Ei, girls, how you doing?' A guy leaned over from the table next to theirs, his black hair combed back with wax. His nose was hawk-like, his eyebrows prominent. He looked like a sculpture, something someone had made up.

Her sister squirmed nervously and coughed from the cloud of smoke.

'I mean, we didn't come alone. We came with that guy over there.'

'Ah, you here with somebody.'

'Yes, I mean, it wasn't like we came alone.'

'Okay, okay, it's chill.' He raised his hand and turned his chair away.

Dearest Sister turned around and hissed in her ear.

'What are we doing here? We should go. This is crazy. We don't fit in.'

She pinched her sister in the thigh. *Stop. What do you mean* fit in—*who fits in where?* Kawa came back now. He set a tray down in front of them with three glasses of saffron-red tea.

'You don't smoke, right?'

'Yes we do!' Her sister shouted in their defence.

'It's cool. It's better not to smoke. They're *kef*, these cigarettes.'

Kawa smiled crookedly. Small lines formed around his eyes.

Kawa had a gaze with no colour, a gaze that couldn't be met. He made eye contact with her, but he wasn't there. She nodded to herself in understanding. She saw them from three feet away: the colourful balloons that were carrying his house. Kawa was far away. He wasn't here.

BLATTE-LAND

'Ei, what you doing tonight? There's a party; come along.' Kawa put out his cigarette, lit a new one, pulled his mobile out of his pocket, put it back again.

They were sitting at Café Claudia again. Only a few weeks had passed since he had found her in the crowd, but it didn't feel that way. It felt like he was the one she should have been with from the beginning. As if this was what

155

the system would have proclaimed if only it had a voice to speak with. She was sitting across from Kawa, shoulders relaxed, listening to music she knew from crackly cassette tapes. She didn't need to fight or disappear.

Kawa had led them straight into *Blatte*-land. Introduced them to people who didn't need any introduction. People who recognized them, even though they had never met.

'Irani,' *Blatte*-land had observed with a sneer, and that seemed to be enough of a description, a definition. They nodded, agreed. Irani, what else? *Blatte*-land seemed to have been expecting them.

Kawa didn't wait for them to accept the invitation. He just pushed the pack of cigarettes across the table toward her. He raised an eyebrow when she placed the cigarette in her mouth with a skilled movement, and let him light it. He smiled at her expression.

'Yeah, course you coming. You with me.' He leaned back in his chair and slammed his hand against a passing fist.

You with me. She gulped, nodded. *I'm with you.*

*

They met outside the large department store that same night. He was leaning against the illuminated glass walls of the store. He was by himself but not alone. There were small groups of people around him; they looked like him. They were dressed in short bomber jackets, most of them military green, some black and a few brilliant white: Alpha jackets, tight jeans and leather belts. They were wearing thick-soled shoes that looked like a mix of trainers and boots: Buffalo boots. They were cloned groups, identical.

Their likeness signified brotherhood, togetherness. It was brotherhood that characterized *Blatte*-land.

When Dearest Sister and the Girl came closer the groups peered up from behind wax-laden hairdos. Black, green, colourless eyes drew them in from head to toe. They all had the same look Kawa had had that first day. She could feel her nipples harden under the tight-fitting camisole, tried to hide her satisfaction. She knew everything about not being seen. This was the exact opposite.

Kawa let them stand there being stared at for a while before he pulled himself away from the wall and walked toward them. No, he wasn't walking—he was gliding, floating above the ground. She drew him in, hypnotized. His left hand made a gesture she didn't understand. The crews shifted their gaze: black, green, colourless.

You with me.

*

Islands of dirty grey concrete and illuminated balconies rushed past the window of the commuter train. They reminded her of the false Raspberry Hills: hazy images of Mama wearing a beret, circles of people in heated debate. She remembered that the scent in Raspberry Hills had been familiar, but couldn't remember the exact smell. She wondered if she would recognize it, if she ever encountered it again.

Kawa was staring out at the passing buildings as if he was seeing them for the first time. Or rather as if he wasn't seeing them, wasn't seeing anything. She tried to find his gaze in the window, but his colourless eyes had no reflection.

Sometimes he was dragged back into the car by a passing fist that wanted to strike his firmly.

'Bro.'

'Bro.'

His gaze returned to staring outside. It fascinated her. The brotherhood that had no root or explanation, conversations that started and stopped hand against hand, brother against brother. Uniformity, belonging, solidarity. She realized that it was enough: uniformity, belonging, solidarity.

*

Kawa suddenly held out his hand, grabbed hold of hers. There was a blue shadow in his colourless eyes. His full lips broke into the warmest, most crooked grin.

'We're getting off here.'

The party was happening in one of those concrete buildings. Kawa pulled open an orange exterior door and motioned for them to go inside. The sound hit her like a shock wave. It sounded like a sports hall during a handball tournament. People were leaning against the walls, sitting in the hall with their knees pulled up, lying on their stomachs on the double bed. All of the guys looked like the ones in the crews, every single one. The girls fell into two categories: high, tight, glittery, their own style in volume. And then those in Alpha jackets, Buffalo boots and with their heads tilted at an angle, the guys' style. She looked at the latter category carefully. They looked like the room's rightful owners; she was nothing more than a trespasser. Dearest sensed her conclusion and poked her with an elbow, nodded at the sofas in the middle of the flat. Five pairs of piercing eyes had zoomed in on them. Thick lines of kohl were arched in distrust, and tense lips indicated self-defence. Five pairs of piercing eyes claiming three square feet each were holding the rest of the room at a distance with their sharpness. In the centre a girl with impossibly long legs, a sweeping mane of hair, a birthmark under her high cheekbone, eyes you couldn't see into.

Her sister was quick about going around the room in search of information.

'We need to be careful. That girl there lost her virginity to Kawa. He is, like, hers. You need to stay away!'

Her, big-eyed, starry-eyed. Her sister making yet another round around the room.

'Be careful, for real. They say she has a knife, and she deep-sixes you in the bathroom.'

Her eyes wide-open, cross-eyed. She had so much to learn.

*

They followed Kawa anyway, Dearest and her, but at a respectable distance. They didn't have anything else to do, and couldn't really identify with the image of a drawn knife. After a few rounds her sister got held up by a guy with a hawk-like nose. The Girl waved goodbye and continued, was pulled along in the whirling currents in Kawa's wake. They walked through room after room, first Kawa and then her close behind. They slid slowly through the never-ceasing flow of brothers, of hands in the air, of the heartiest laughter that flowed without being preceded by any joke. She laughed along. Hands were held out to her and she shook them firmly: up-down, up-down. Kawa didn't say anything to her. He looked for her now and then with his eyes, as if saying that he remembered she was there even though he didn't want to make a big deal out of it. It was enough for her; she was preoccupied with scanning the new world. Highlighting, copying, pasting.

During about the eighth round through the kitchen she stopped abruptly. Familiar tones were coming from scratchy cassette tapes again. They were coming from a corner. Yes, three guys were sitting in the back corner drumming on the table top with their knuckles and palms of their hands. Two girls were standing next to them: version high, tight, glittery. They were leaning listlessly against the kitchen counter, with their eyes closed and lips embracing Mama's songs. She stared as though bewitched, Cheshire grin shining across her face. She saw an image of Mama's red lips and the thick Iranian blankets. There was a shiver in the pit of her heart. She sang along for herself: *khanom gol'ay khanom gol*, forgot everything named Kawa, *baram sakhte tahamol*, the boys changed rhythm now, a new song. Her hips started moving entirely on their own.

'*Deeh*, I don't know this.' The girls at the counter became roused and lost interest. The guys continued, their knuckles and palms of their hands against the tabletop, resonance in her flesh. *Gole sangam, gole sangam, chi begam az deleh tangam*. She jumped at her own voice, it had risen, was singing along, sinking in.

The guys laughed appreciatively, waved her over. She took a careful step toward them, then a big step, took up position at the kitchen counter where the girls had been standing and what came, came all on its own. It wasn't

in her hands but holed up somewhere in her gut. *Blatte-*
land had found its way in and caused a leak and now it
was streaming out, what she was without having known
it. She disappeared in her song and her hips and suddenly
remembered what it had smelt like, that familiar scent in
Raspberry Hills. She sang until the song flowed over into
the next one and then she saw that the kitchen was filled
with people, that she was surrounded by a crowd. People
who were snapping their fingers. People who were singing along, singing the same songs. Kawa leaned toward her
from behind, shouted in her ear: 'So you're Iranian after
all.'

A shudder in the pit of her heart. That was what she was,
and this was where she was going to stay.

HE UNDERSTANDS

The Girl studied her reflection in the grimy windows of
the red bus on the way home. The darkness outside rested
heavily over the woods that framed the motorway between
Factory Town and the city. The light of the moon rebound-
ed against the surface of the water when the bus crossed
the bridges. It shone right into her wide-open eyes, and
glittered in her piercing liquorice pastilles. But she didn't
see the moon and the calm lakes; her gaze was occupied
with itself. She inhaled deeply, held her stomach in. It made
her breasts swell, and rub against the camisole, threaten to
rush over. She tilted her head to the side, the tamed tresses sneaked into the cleft between her breasts, caressing her
skin along the way. She unconsciously brought an index

finger up toward her lips, let it slide into her mouth, just a few millimetres. She bit down, wide-open eyes. She saw Kawa's gaze in front of her, how he had looked at her from across the kitchen. How his eyes had climbed over her body, starting at her feet in the high heels, to her waist that could be glimpsed under the tight cotton fabric, then up the cleft in order to caress her face. The caress had almost felt physical, she had almost closed her eyes and waited for more. Now her lower abdomen and legs shuddered at the memory. It had shuddered then too, but she had squeezed her legs together, looked away. And later she had seen that Kawa's gaze wasn't the only one that was climbing over her, the room was filled with climbing eyes and they were travelling over her like a fireworks show. She was one of the ones they were climbing on.

She glanced at Dearest Sister who was sleeping heavily with her head resting on the Girl's shoulder. The Girl wanted to ask if her sister had seen it, if she had felt her own body changing in the presence of those looks. Felt her body become something located outside itself, something she could observe and touch. Become something the Girl could shape, a power that could control what they were seeing, those who had been staring so intensely. But she didn't dare say it out loud, not even to her sister. The Girl didn't want to hear that she had imagined it, that those looks hadn't existed. That she hadn't taken on a new shape at all, that everything was the same as it had always been.

She carefully kicked off her heels and pulled her bare foot along her calf, saw Kawa's face again. Everything shuddered a second time, and with flushed cheeks she turned to stare at the invisible forest and her own reflection again.

She studied her face; her eyes were enormous. They were dark, smoky with make-up, enormous. She lifted her hand and ran her fingers over the straight bridge of her nose, captured the blob in her hand and squeezed it. Her nose was too big; there was too much flesh in the middle of her face. She bit the inside of her bottom lip, wondered if Kawa had been thinking the same thing. Kawa. She brought her index finger to her mouth again, ran the tip of her finger along the contours of her lips. Her lips were thick, just like Papa's lips. She had a feeling that that was where Kawa's caresses had stopped, that her lips had stopped his eyes. The others' eyes had never reached her face. She bit her lip, and felt a shudder in the pit of her stomach. She wanted to go back. She wanted more.

She saw the headlights of the 240 when the bus turned into Factory Town's city centre. Papa. Her hand reached instinctively for her chest, up over the cleft and the new, soft hillocks. She looked for something to cover herself with, something to wash her face with, but knew there was nothing. She would have to stand in front of Papa naked, naked and with her face hidden under a layer of colour. No, that couldn't happen. She sank down in her seat as far as possible, but her head was still sticking up over the edge of the window. She nudged Dearest Sister.

"Wake up! Wake up dammit, Papa is in the city centre."

Dearest Sister grunted in response, then turned her head and fell back asleep. The Girl glanced at her watch, it was 3.34 a.m.. She wondered who was waiting in the parking lot: Papa or the monster. Wondered what Papa was doing here; how he had known that she wasn't asleep in the new flat.

*

The family court had sent home a schedule about the time she had stopped forgetting and walking in the wrong direction after school. About the time she had started understanding that she and Mama were supposed to create a home within the newly painted walls they had started filling with furniture: a sofa, a TV that was still sitting on the floor. There was a double bed to put the mattresses on, and a flowerbox on the balcony. Everything that was supposed to represent a home. Mama and her, without Papa and Little Brother. The Girl knew right away that it wouldn't work, knew that they needed more than IKEA furniture to create a home. The empty chairs at the kitchen table would always remind them that it was nothing more than the remnants of something that had been split in half, divided into four pieces.

The family court had decided that she and Little Brother would see each other every weekend, one at Mama's and the next one at Papa's. The Girl didn't stick to those weekends, she couldn't let that much time pass without checking on Little Brother. So she took her homework with her and went down to the sports hall. She sat on the bleachers during Little Brother's practices, cheered when he scored, ran over when he got hit in the stomach with a floorball stick. She made eye contact when he glanced up at her with his deep black eyes, as if to make sure that she was still sitting there, that she hadn't gone up in smoke.

She didn't stay after the practices, didn't really know what she was supposed to say to Little Brother, which words could put together what had been torn apart. She had the habit of waving at him when there were five minutes left of the practice session. She didn't know how to say goodbye and go to another home, different from his. She was afraid she wouldn't be able to do it, that she would start following him, stay with him. And what would happen to Mama then?

Little Brother always raised his floorball stick in response, then turned away so he wouldn't see her leave. He understands! She repeated silently the whole way home. He understands. She thought the words in a louder and louder tone of voice, tried to drown out all the voices that were echoing in her head that were screaming her name. He understands!

*

But this wasn't Papa's weekend! She sat slumped in the worn bus seat thinking through the hazy fog of vodka that was weighing down her synapses. It wasn't even the weekend. How did Papa know? Not even Mama knew. Mama was at work and thought that she was sleeping at the Torn Sunbeam's. Then the bus stopped in the city centre and the doors opened. Papa turned off the engine of the 240. Was he going to jump out of the car, tramp at the bus, grab hold of her upper arm? What would he scream? Would her clothes wake the monster? She swallowed thickly, tasted smoke and the sour aftertaste of liquor. No, her breath, her breath would give the monster oxygen. She would never get away. She grabbed her bag firmly. It wasn't going to be neglected homework or discarded opportunities that would rouse Papa's fury. The heavy bag contained her biology book and maths notebook. She was doing her part, more than enough. Papa knew that, he had to know that. Papa had nothing to worry about. She was the protector of visions, she ran with the torch when the torch-bearer got a cramp, automatically sped up the plan when needed. She wouldn't disappoint anyone. The breaths she had been holding in hissed out between her teeth. She leaned back in the seat, pulled her legs up toward her body and held them tightly, rocking herself to calm down. She wouldn't disappoint anyone. Papa knew that, Papa had to know that.

The red bus was standing still in the centre, waiting for the local bus with its doors open. The 240 was also sitting quietly with its doors closed. She turned her head carefully in the direction of the car, squinted. She was drawn into Papa's honey look in the light of the street lamps, became frozen inside it, didn't move. She was able to tear herself away when the bus started rumbling under her and the doors closed. Little Brother was sitting next to Papa in the front seat, sleeping deeply with his head resting against the taut seat belt. The bus started rolling and the engine of the 240 started up. She didn't need to turn around to know that Papa and Little Brother were driving behind them.

The car pulled up when she and Dearest Sister got out at the bus stop and stumbled toward the Torn Sunbeam's building with aching feet. Her heart was pounding and she thought about stopping, about walking over to the car and getting in the backseat. Thought about going with Papa without saying a word; never saying anything again. Her heart was pounding, but the car rolled on quietly without catching up to the bus. Papa's gaze burnt into her back without the monster bellowing. She held the front door open for Dearest Sister but stopped in the doorway. She was standing with her back to Papa's gaze, her heart pounding. The more time that passed without anyone shouting the louder her heart pounded. She stepped inside and let the door slam shut and heard the 240 glide away carefully so Little Brother wouldn't wake up. She heard the 240 disappear and she understood that it wouldn't be coming back, and that made her heart pound even more. It made her heart pound harder than it ever had before.

THE BUS TO THE CITY

Dearest Sister and the Girl had acquired a new scent. They smelt of Tommy Hilfiger, strawberry-flavoured chewing gum and Marlboro Lights. But most of all they smelt like something so rare in Factory Town: another world.

Their scent was the strongest on the outskirts of Factory Town's existence, among the girls who hadn't found their place in the system. Among the girls who loudly asserted that it was only a matter of time before they left Factory Town, left it to never come back.

They were drawn to her and Dearest Sister, and she and Dearest Sister embraced them. They blew pink bubbles, exhaled cigarette smoke through their noses, and talked about newly discovered hunting grounds. They talked about a system that allowed itself to be stretched, a system where everyone was a brother. Hand-to-hand, bro-to-bro. The Girl and Dearest pointed at the red bus and the girls followed hungrily after. They melted together into a hunting league.

The sisters Ebba and Klara with their long chestnut-coloured locks, cheeky chins held up high and a shrill tone of voice that cut through the buzz of the school cafeteria and received turned backs in response. The sisters completely lacked the subtle intuition required to dig your way into *multiculti*-land. They made out too much and in the wrong way, took cigarettes and drinks without saying thank you, cast glances at unavailable men and time and again plunged the Hunting League into a turn-tail situation, on the run from knife-carrying alpha females with quick heels. Delicate, sweet Lotta with her timid bearing and a southern-softness rolling over her tongue. She hated guys in Alpha jackets and Buffalo boots. Hated all the drama that went hand-in-hand with the restless roaming around. But most of all she hated the blindness of Factory Town. Then there was Carina, coarse and out of place in all situations. She was the noisy addition to their straggly crusade. The bus to the city was a bus away from an alcoholic mother and constantly hungry younger siblings. And Mirja in her white sweatpants and the plastic bottle in her handbag that was always filled with vodka. She was already a mattress queen in Factory Town and needed to spread her lust for life outside its boundaries. Filippa, the princess from the archipelago area who would come to scan the boys' gang for the cockiest Kurd with the longest rap sheet and take him home to her parents. Filippa's revolt became explosive and intense, and she could soon walk away.

And then there was Dearest and the Girl: engine and map-reader. They had learnt that the best way to get attention was to act like attention was the last thing you wanted. They understood the fine line between a good girl and a whore, and that in order to be on the right side of the line there needed to be plenty of distance from it. They learnt to read the shifts in the boys' looks when a fight was simmering in their fists and wove a rhythmic accent into their speech but knew to cast it off as soon as the bus spit them out in Factory Town. They caught the scent of knives and drugs at a distance, chose company with greater—though seldom perfect—precision. And they memorized faces and names, soon knew most of the crews, and could sort them into groups both ethnically and geographically.

*

Kawa's colourless eyes would cut through the crowd now and then: at house parties, in the suburb centres, through the windows of a silver-grey Mercedes that was mostly made up of scrap metal and had a star glued on the front. He came over sometimes, sat next to her half-smiling and hid his head behind her back as if he was a brother seeking protection from adults' demanding questions. The warmth from his forehead burnt through the layers of polyester clothing. The Girl rose from the table without balloons, left the new world that otherwise had her undivided attention. She felt him floating in the layer of fat right under her skin, impossible to distinguish from her own body.

But most of the time he just passed by. She caught the movement out of the corner of her eye without having looked for it, her eyes searched for his figure before he disappeared. It was his gait that made him stick out, from his position at the front of the group. He swayed in a rhythm different from the rest. The stable bass in a straggling jazz melody.

Kawa was like a river that always flows in the same place but in reality has already passed.

YOU HAVE GOTTEN SO MUCH MORE

The Torn Sunbeam was sitting across from them at the kitchen table. She set out a plate with raspberry Linzer cookies and poured a glass of milk for each of them, wrinkled her nose when they asked for coffee instead. She made eye contact with their identical liquorice pastille eyes and tried to explain.

'You're wasting your time in the city. *Ba on bacheha.*' With those kids. 'You won't get anywhere from there, do you understand? Time stands still there!'

Two sets of liquorice pastilles in self-defence.

'Shit, this is where nothing's happening. This is where everything is dead.' A pink bubble, a pop and a persistent chewing in response.

They were chewing with their mouths open. Mouths open! The Torn Sunbeam felt a strange sensation in her hand, she wanted to lift it and slap their cud-chewing mouths, strike their eyes that were covered in blue eye shadow. Was this the result? Everything they had done, everything they had given up, was this the result?

The Torn Sunbeam sat on her hands and started again.

'They live in isolation—do you understand what that means? They live outside this society. They are outsiders.

To share being an outsider doesn't mean you are on the inside, do you understand?'

Cud-chewing mouths.

'What do you mean? This is where we're outsiders.'

The Torn Sunbeam pressed her buttocks against her hands and turned her forest-green eyes toward the newly budding birch trees outside the window. She wanted to talk about trees, about roots that need to force their way deep into the soil in order for the tree to be able to grow. That without roots forcing their way into the earth everything will fall in the end. She wanted to explain that that was what they were, a tree, a little tree. A little tree that absolutely must grow to be tall, that mustn't fall. But they wouldn't understand. She saw that in their retreating looks. Their identical, burnt-black looks. Retreating liquorice pastilles that didn't want to listen. If only she could tell them everything she knew, everything she had seen. Protect them from all of the mistakes that had already been made. But she knew that it was outside her power. So she got up and left, walked with heavy steps over the soft rug in the hall.

'You're Swedes, don't you understand? One doesn't become more Swedish than this. You won't become more Swedish than this. It's best if you both understand that.'

The Torn Sunbeam slammed the front door, leaving them alone.

*

Mama came home unexpectedly between the night shift and the morning shift and found the Girl standing in front of the mirror wearing lacy underwear and holding the rouge brush in her hand. She quickly hid the pack of cigarettes on the floor with her foot. They both ignored the movement.

'What are you doing? Where did you get those clothes?'

Mama picked up a slip from the bed. It had lace along the low neck; the price tag was still on.

'Have you borrowed this from someone?'

She nodded. Mama nodded back.

'Do the girls at school look like this? Wear this much make-up?'

She nodded.

'How did your biology test go?'

'No mistakes.'

Mama nodded, then stood there and stared at her. *She looks like a woman*, Mama thought. She was close to saying it, then was struck by the next thought. *She's a child.*

'Good. You did well! I'm very proud.' Mama stroked the Girl's hair and made eye contact with her in the mirror. They both looked away. Mama turned on her heel, walked toward the front door, turning off the radio on the way.

Let me lick you up and down till you say stop. Let me play with your body, baby, make you real hot.

'I know what you're doing out there.' Mama hesitated; she really had no idea. 'But I haven't raised a daughter to run around with Turks and Arabs. Do you understand? I expect more of you.'

She nodded in response.

'Return that slip; it isn't yours!' Mama stopped at the front door, wanted to say something else—anything. But no words came.

*

It wasn't that she didn't see the faults in *Blatte*-land. The Girl saw how Kawa and the crews took their frustration out on well-off Swedish boys. That they hurt them in order to tear apart something they thought had been taken from them. The Girl saw. She saw that they weren't stealing for a winter coat or a mobile phone, that it was about something bigger, something worse than that. They thought they had no place in the real world that populated the streets out there, and they assumed they never would. Those attacks were their way of showing that they existed. It was their way of showing that they made a difference, that they couldn't be ignored.

She knew that the accent was often a personal choice. Maybe she didn't see that it put heavy locks on the doors to the city, but she saw how people listened, and then looked away. How people looked at *Blatte*-land, and then looked away. She came to understand that the roaming through the city streets and city centres wasn't a weekend thing or for fun. That it wasn't anything more than a repetitive unchanging routine. Every day, every hour of every day, in a world where everything else had been judged to be too difficult.

The constant loafing was nothing new; it also characterized Factory Town. It ran from the desks along the back of the classroom, past the kiosk to the mall to the pizzeria next to Nelson's Hill. But in some ways it wasn't the same thing. Maybe it was the will that was lacking in Factory Town, while it was the conviction that nothing else was possible that characterized *Blatte*-land.

She hadn't forgotten about the plan, hadn't stopped just because Papa had pushed pause on the dreams. Her homework schedule was printed on the inside of her brain; hard work pulsed stronger than her blood. She studied on the subway to Akalla, on the commuter train to Märsta and on the benches at the Metro Station when she missed the night bus back to Factory Town. She still sat at the front of the classroom and hid behind her books during the lunch breaks. The Hunting League prowled around her table in a group, discussing text messages and looking out over the cafeteria, with their thin, arched eyebrows. They kept Factory Town at a distance with their arms crossed, chins in the air, strengthened by the knowledge that they weren't there. They were somewhere else, far away.

She still sat at the front of the classroom, twinkling without being there. But the repulsion toward Factory Town and the open arms of *Blatte*-land had raised questions about the plan. Maybe she had been on her way to *Blatte*-land from the very beginning. Maybe that was what the system was proclaiming, and that was the only place she fit in. Perhaps some things really were predetermined, things that had nothing to do with dreams, hard work or handicaps. Maybe that was what the teachers knew, those who were always right.

Maybe Papa had misinterpreted, misunderstood. Perhaps he had made a mistake there in the mail van so long ago when he had so proudly announced that they were going to a Swedish Factory Town, a Factory Town where she would become Swedish.

Maybe that's not how it works, Papa. Maybe I'll be the one to show you the way home.

The Swedish teacher retired and the new teacher's name was Nina. Nina was younger than all of the other teachers and wore her soft, dark hair pulled back in a ponytail. Nina's slanted eyes were just as black as the Girl's.

'Ching chong!' Alberto shouted when Nina explained that she had been adopted from South Korea. Nina didn't respond. She just searched for his constantly shifting gaze, caught it and held it there. The class watched and waited for Alberto's response, but nothing happened. Nina drew him in and Alberto never raised his voice in Nina's presence again.

About a month into term Nina picked up a stack of bound A4 sheets and pulled her chair around to the front of her desk.

'I'm going to read a story that a student handed in last week.' Nina looked out over the class, waiting for the room to become quiet. 'For me, this story is about tolerance, or understanding, or empathy as it's called. I think the writer wants to say that when people behave poorly, it's because someone has treated them poorly. I also think the writer wants to say that we should forgive, but I'll let you decide for yourselves.'

Nina cleared her throat and started reading. She used a soft tone of voice that rolled over the consonants without pressing too much. There was something soothing about Nina's voice, something comforting. The Girl lowered her shoulders and started sliding down in her chair. She had turned off her thoughts and was in the process of floating away when she suddenly jumped in her chair. Those were her words being read out loud in the classroom! They sounded completely natural, like words from someone who is sure of herself, someone who has never experienced self-doubt. Ebba and Mirja were whispering and giggling, but quieted down when they saw her sitting on the edge of her chair, her back straight. She knotted her hands, placed them in a frozen lump on the top of her desk. This was serious. This was the step away from Swedish for two, away from handicaps. Nina was reading her words, her words were the words the class got to hear. This was dreams and hard work, this was about breaking the system.

Alberto was sitting just as upright as she was, listening intently with his arms hanging at his sides. When the story ended he turned his head and looked straight at her. He understood that it was about him. She tried to make eye contact with him, but he turned away and got up clumsily. Pulled the Adidas-pants up over the yellow waistband of his underwear and shuffled out, with his back still straight. She stayed in her seat, stared at his desk as the classroom emptied, then remained sitting until only she and Nina were left.

'I'm impressed! It's obvious that you work hard, but it's more than that. You're smart, young lady.' Nina smiled. 'Keep up the good work!'

Nina closed her folders and stood up.

'I'll see you tomorrow.'

The Girl nodded in response, remained sitting at the desk at the very front, twinkling twinkling. She felt something inside start glowing, a small ember. Maybe it was the beginning of a fire, of a burning star. The Girl remained sitting, twinkling. She twinkled away.

*

The term drew to a close and it was time to set the marks. Nina asked if they could talk and she resisted the urge to say no, claim that she had already heard everything Nina had to say. Instead she stood up, steady on six inches of stiletto heel, and followed Nina out into the corridor. The Girl was several heads taller than Nina, but she still felt small in the presence of Nina's proud bearing. So she tried to make herself even taller, her chin held high in the air. Nina closed the door to the classroom and turned toward her with a serious expression on her face.

'There is no mark higher than A, so that will be your mark for Swedish. But that probably doesn't come as a surprise.'

The words spilled softly from Nina's mouth without meeting any resistance, but they slammed against the Girl's eardrums. She clenched her fists tightly to keep them from shaking and revealing that it actually was a surprise. The Girl didn't say anything. Nina's expression revealed that there was more. She expected a sneer and handicap. Nina continued.

'We don't need to talk about your school results anymore, everything is crystal clear. But there's something else …' Nina's normally steady gaze faltered. 'I just want to say…Well, I hear the language you use … When you're talking with the girls. And I understand that you hang out in Stockholm a lot, and … And I see the way you dress. I'm from the other side of the city you know—I know what those clothes signify. I just want to say that it's easy to make a mistake … I know that you think you're in control and you are, absolutely. But …'

Nina was searching for the right words.

'Sometimes you just get pulled along by the people around you or by life I guess, there isn't always someone to blame … I see what you're up to and I see that you're on the verge of being pulled into some shit you should stay away from. So I just want to ask you to, well, not to take what you have for granted. What you're capable of. Don't throw it away.'

She felt something rise in her gaze, something with sharp teeth that wanted to dig deeply into Nina's soft cheeks. Something with more power than she could control. Nina saw it too, and held out her hand in order to calm, but found nothing to hold on to.

'I'm not accusing you of anything, it isn't like you've done something wrong. I just want to ask you to be careful, you know. So that it doesn't turn out badly. I don't want things to turn out badly for you.'

The Girl was surprised by the force of what was rising in her throat. She tried to hold it back, but couldn't.

'Why would things turn out badly for me? Why would there be more risk for things turning out badly for me than for someone else? I don't understand what the problem is. You said yourself that I'm smart and that I work hard and all of that. It should be the other way around then; it should go brilliantly. You should be standing there telling me that it's going to be great! Why are you warning me when the whole class is filled with idiots who are never going to get anywhere, who barely pass the maths tests?'

Her voice was shaking as much as her hands. Nina's

warm eyes narrowed, squinted in order to see her better. The Girl caught her breath, tried to stop what was bubbling out of her, but couldn't.

'I'm so damned tired of this kind of shit. This is the kind of crap that makes you tired; do you get that? If I get tired one day and make a mistake, then it's because of this kind of crap.'

She focused her gaze on the tile wall and managed to catch what was leaking out of her, pushed it down again. She glanced at Nina's feet, steady boots on the stone floor. Nina remained standing, listening; she wasn't going anywhere. The Girl wanted to explain to Nina. She wanted to explain why she was screaming, but she didn't have the energy, and wasn't sure she understood it herself. The Girl just turned on her heel and left, to hell with the rest of the classes. She waited for the bus to the city and sat in the seat at the very front, alone, without Dearest, without the Hunting League. She watched the motorway that stretched endlessly in front of her there where she was sitting on the first row. She bit her top lip hard, wished that Nina had been the last Swedish teacher, or the teacher from Saltsjöbaden, or her first teacher, the one with Swedish for two. That one of them had read her short story out loud to the class, or that she had raised her voice to one of them. That one of them had taken the blow, now when she had finally shouted back.

The next evening she was sitting at the corner table at Café Claudia. Ebba was calling around for information about a house party in Tensta and Klara was holding their glasses of Coca-Cola under the table, filling them one after the other with vodka from a plastic bottle.

'Malik is outside, he's going to drive us!' Ebba got up quickly and downed her glass in four large gulps. Klara had already had time to finish several glasses. She scraped her chair across the stone floor and stumbled in the process. The Girl followed them to the door and got into the car, not really caring who Malik was, or how they were getting there, or where they were going. Thought she was already there, wondered if it was time to disappear.

The sisters soon disappeared behind closed doors while she remained sitting on the kitchen floor with her legs crossed, comfortable among familiar strangers. She leaned her head against the wall and swayed in time with the music without noticing it herself. The rhythm was so familiar; it was part of her heartbeat. She wasn't paying attention to the conversation; she wasn't there to talk. The Girl just sat quietly on the coarse rug with her legs crossed, the rhythm integrating with her heartbeat and she felt like she recognized the room more than she had recognized any room before.

'Cig?' A tall, tawny guy leaned forward and held out a newly-rolled cigarette.

'Berkan,' he introduced himself with a nod and smiled, he had a thin layer of down on his upper lip. She held out her hand, the expression on her face was friendly but not inviting. She was starting to get good at that expression, had practised it in front of the mirror. Her sister went for a look filled with contempt and rejection; she believed that it was the only language guys understood. But the Girl didn't want to make any enemies.

A large guy stepped over and grabbed hold of the flimsy cig before her hand was able to grab it. Hakim. She had heard the room calling for Hakim the whole night. It was Hakim's flat. He didn't live there, but he owned it. The Girl didn't protest, she let him have it, backed off with a friendly but not inviting expression on her face.

But Hakim wasn't finished. He crouched down as he took the lighter from her open handbag, lit up and put the lighter in his back pocket.

'I've seen you. I know who you are.'

She felt that shudder along her spine. He had seen her. She had been seen.

'Why are you just hanging out with *Svenne*-whores? Do you think it makes you better? You think you're Swedish, better than us?'

Hakim was waving his index finger back and forth in the air. She followed the movement with her eyes, tried to become hypnotized, avoid hearing what he was saying. Who was *svenne*? What was *svenne*? Why did he have to show up now, and destroy the rhythm, start talking different and difference. There were no differences; didn't he see how well she blended in? That she was part of the pattern on the rug, the flower petals on the wallpaper?

'You walk around with your Swedish friends and think you are something, don't you think I see! Playing hard to get. Don't think you're special, never fucking think you're special! You a whore, just like them, and you a *blatte*, just like us.'

His scent stung her nose: subtle *oddkollon* mixed with the sweet-sour smell of sweat and bitter vodka fumes.

'*Ei len* stop, she's just sitting there.' Berkan got up and put a hand on his arm, but Hakim knocked him over with a quick motion. The conversation in the room stopped. Everyone was looking at them. At Hakim, at Berkan and at her. The volume on the stereo was turned down. She didn't notice, because the rhythm was integrated in her heartbeat.

'You come here and hang out and laugh and then go home to your real life. Maybe that dog is stupid,' he pointed at Berkan who was swaying vigilantly behind him, 'But I get it.'

She didn't have an answer. She hadn't seen the division, hadn't understood that you had to choose sides; that the borderland was forbidden.

'What's happening—now you can't talk? Huh? The pretty girl with her pretty Swedish can't come up with any pretty words?'

She pulled her handbag toward her. The tones inside her were drowning out his words. She had barely heard his questions, that is how it was. But it was time to go. Her spot had suddenly become occupied, something was calling from outside, oh how she was in a hurry.

She walked toward the door on steady legs, was surprised at her own steadiness. Maybe she had actually known about it, about different sides and borderland and things. Maybe she had known that it was only a matter of time before someone called her bluff, lifted the mask, shouted out that she wasn't one of them. Had that happened now—was it over? She glanced over her shoulder. Hakim was standing with his feet apart and his head leaning forward. He was waiting to see what she did. Berkan, dog eyes, was standing between them like a human shield, maybe that is why she wasn't shaking. He followed her to the front door.

'*Ei*, it's cool. I'll keep an eye out.'

But Berkan hit the floor when Hakim thundered out of the kitchen, his eyes bloodshot, steaming with something more than vodka. Hakim grabbed hold of her arm and pushed her against the wall, his forearm against her throat.

'You don't turn your back and walk away when I'm talking to you—get that?' His other arm moved down. Looking over Hakim's shoulder, she made eye contact with Berkan; his ashamed dog eyes turned away, and he walked into the kitchen and closed the door. She and Hakim were alone in the hall. The silence was waiting.

'You can't look like a whore and think you a good girl at the same time, get that? You can't like having guys look at you without spreading your legs.'

Hakim tore her fly open, she tried pushing him away using her body weight but his forearm was pushing against her throat. She got nowhere. He grinned, placed his knee against her thighs and pushed.

'I never want to see you playing good girl again, you hear? I can fuck you when I want. You'll never be better than me.'

He pushed his forearm against her throat again.

'Don't walk around thinking you Swedish. You'll never be Swedish. It's no damn hobby being a damn sand nigger, you ain't the one who decides if you *blatte* or not.' He threw her toward the front door and she slid over the rough hallway rug. She lay there with her knees burning and thought about Mama and Papa and her place in between. She wasn't in a hurry to go anywhere. Hakim went into the kitchen.

'I'm gonna take that damn whore's virginity!'

She didn't hear the room's response, didn't hear anything. After a while she got up and left the flat. Her head was just dead weight for her feet, all thoughts turned off. She walked down concrete stairs after concrete stairs and further across the parking lot with her eyes trained on the pointy toes of her shoes. She walked all the way until the edge of the woods, then she stopped. The space between her legs was not tickling but pounding, like someone was standing there hitting her. Like someone was pounding on her. She stood at the edge of the woods and wanted to go home, but didn't know where she had ended up, or how to get away from here.

Diagonally across the parking lot a pair of headlights suddenly came on, two curious wide-open eyes that were digging through the darkness. The car drove up slowly and was almost past her when the window was rolled down. Kawa looked out with a naturalness in his colourless eyes, as if they had agreed to meet in just this place, at exactly this time, and that he had arrived early in order to watch her entrance without being interrupted.

'Everything okay?' he asked.

She nodded.

'What the hell you doing? You know a girl shouldn't be running around here in the middle of the night.'

She nodded.

He smiled that smile and moved his gaze across the darkness of the woods.

'You staying here or you getting in?'

*

He didn't ask where she wanted to go, and she didn't ask
where he was going. She tried to conceal her torn fly with
her handbag and he tried to avoid looking at it. She was on
nails out of fear that he would say something about whores
and good girls. Or about *blatte* and Swedes. Or about pretending, most of all she was afraid he would say something
about pretending because damned if she knew what was
fake and what was supposed to be reality. *Blatte*-land had
declared *Irani* and Factory Town had never claimed anything else.

Kawa drove in silence. His gaze trained on that spot in
the distance that was only lit for his eyes, a star that was
shimmering even before it started burning. *Twinkle little
star, please don't stop twinkling.* She saw it. She had her own
star, even though she forgot about it every time she arrived
in *Blatte*-land. She lost herself in the memory: leather briefcase, nights at the office, rainy streets far away. The dream
about Ally. She jumped when he suddenly spoke to her.

'Do you know what you doing here? Like for real, do you
know why you hanging out here? With those dirty Turks,
hell, with *me*? I don't think you know. You think this is
where you belong or something, but you just fooling yourself.'

Silence.

'That day when I met you, I thought you were a nice
Irani girl, like all the others. I took you to Café Claudia, to
parties; it was no big deal. We hang out, we have fun. But
now I had my eye on you for a while. You not supposed

to be here. You think you like everyone else here, but you ain't. Got it? You something else.'

The Girl turned toward him. She felt like she was five years old, like she was back on Nelson's Hill. Like her sister had locked herself in the bathroom with all their sweets.

'What's the difference between us?'

'Shit, you messing with me? You don't get it; you don't get anything. I don't have time for this.'

He didn't have time for her. He was going to slam the door he had opened in her face. He would send her back to Factory Town where she would disappear again, not exist while waiting to become something else. Something with a system and a place. She stared toward the woods that she couldn't see because of all of the trees. *Opportunities. Dreams. Hard work.* What if there wasn't anything else? If there wasn't anything else.

Kawa put a cassette tape into the car stereo. *Emshab az on shabast ke man, delam mikhad dad bezanam.* The tones mixed together with the rhythm in her heartbeat, deafening the silence. *Too shahre in gharibeh ha dardamo faryad bezanam.*

'That Moein, you know. He makes grown men cry. The best Iranian. Kurds love him, you know?'

She nodded. That damned rhythm.

'Okay, I'm gonna explain.' Kawa lowered the volume and stuck a cigarette in the corner of his mouth. 'Everyone has to have a position, a platform. To live from, you know. Something you are. It's the platform that determines everything else. If you become rich or poor, if people have your back or not, if your mama smiles or shakes her head when she sees you. Hell, if you live or you die. You work to build up the platform. It's not like you get it for free, you shouldn't fool yourself.'

Silence.

'You need to know who you are, you know, where you come from. I kiss my mama's forehead every night when I leave home. I remember where I come from. But then, then you need to become something else. Something that don't have nothing to do with your mama, or with feelings and things. Something that's about how I want people to look at me. What I want them to see.'

Silence.

'I want respect, that's all. You can't get it from everyone, you know. I can't get the ugly lady cashier at the grocery store to stop wrinkling her forehead and look away when I come over. She knows nothing about me and she's already made up her mind. I can't control her. But what I can control…I want respect, that's all. And people don't just give respect, you have to take it, you have to force them. Your platform has to force people to respect you.'

He leaned forward and opened the glove compartment. The blade of the knife glimmered in the dark. She nodded to show that she had seen, that she understood. He continued.

'But the first person who respects you is you, understand? You can't get respect from anyone else unless you respect yourself. That's why you can't hang out with those Turks, like what kind of people is that? Do you know how they see you? You can only hang with them if you don't respect yourself.'

Silence.

'When you respect yourself, you can differentiate between what's me,' he pounded his chest, 'and what's somebody else's shit. Like those clothes you walk around in, like take them off, they ain't yours. All that damned make-up on your face. That is someone else's shit. And I've heard you trying to change your talk, imitate, you know. *Gitta, tagga, aboo, gus,* that accent you know. That's not you. You shouldn't change to be like this, get it?'

She was five years old and had been caught red-handed in Lelle and Alberto's closet, playing someone else's game. She was staring at the floor, filled with shame.

'It's chaos, in other words. You think there's something here for you. You think this is where you gonna to find your place, but you already have a platform—don't destroy it. You have your Swedish. I see you with your schoolbooks everywhere; you work hard. You're smart, you know, you have everything served on a plate. You don't trade in what you have for this, get it? This is like the Cola light you drink, a poor imitation.'

He turned up the volume to listen to the next verse. *Az in hame dar be dari, too ghalbe man ghiamate.*

'I don't want to see you around here anymore, get it? Be smart. Don't fail.'

PAPILLON

She was sitting on the sofa at Papa and Little Brother's watching *Papillon.* They had watched the film together so many times that Steve McQueen felt like one of Papa's many friends. Papillon and his eternal search for freedom. She was struck by a memory from the sheet-covered world that she otherwise remembered so little of. The memory of the small yellow chicks that were kept in cages and sold on the sidewalks. She and Papa had always stopped at the cages, and bought the weakest ones. They had stuffed them under their shirts to calm the chicks' racing hearts. They could fit three or four at a time under Papa's shirt. They fed the chicks breadcrumbs and kept them warm but the chicks still died within the course of a few days. *They were able to die free*, Papa had a habit of saying. *This is the most important thing, they were able to die free.*

Papillon is what they used to name the chickens. They named every single one Papillon.

Papa couldn't concentrate on the film this time. He glanced at her, looked at the worry lines on her forehead. He thought, her skin should be smooth. He thought the lines on her face weren't hers, that someone else had put them there. Later he thought that they actually were lines she had created herself, and that he shouldn't allow her to do that to herself. She had inherited enough wrinkles. He rubbed the spot where his moustache used to be, the skin was smooth now except for the faintest stubble.

'You know, now you might think it's easier, hanging with *on bacheha.*' Those kids. 'It might be easier than becoming friends with the kids here, or easier than going to school in Saltsjöbaden with Evelina.'

Pause. For a moment they both felt ashamed about her laziness, her handicap. Both honey look and liquorice pastilles were focused on the flickering TV screen. *Papillon* and freedom. Papa was also thinking about the chicks and how many times they had watched the movie together. Hadn't he taught her to fight, to work hard, and to never give up? Of course he had taught her. He looked at her face. A pool of colour in the winter haze. She wasn't allowed to become the person she suddenly looked like.

'Easy and difficult, *dokhtaram*, they aren't words with only one meaning. If you choose the easy path today, it will be difficult tomorrow. That's why you work hard, that's why you make sure you do the impossible. If you're hanging out with those kids because it's easy, then you're on the wrong path. Completely wrong.'

Little Brother put away his Game Boy, looked up from his spot on the rug and grinned at her.

'She hangs out with them because she has a better chance with them. There aren't any guys here who want her.'

She gave Little Brother a grateful look, let a sigh of relief slide through her lips.

'No one wants a chance with me, are you kidding?' She slid down from the sofa and grabbed Little Brother's chocolate-brown skin, tickled him until he shrieked with laughter. She felt his resistance, realized that he was stronger than her now, that he had become stronger without her realizing it. He had become stronger, but had chosen not to overpower her. He had chosen not to show it. She stopped and let him return to his game, buried her head deep in his back there where he was lying on his stomach on the rug. She looked up at Papa, whose eyes were focused on the TV screen again. He didn't expect an answer from her. There was only one answer; they both knew that. He was counting on her, and it was up to her not to let him down.

She stayed up late that night, her face covered in make-up and with the tight camisole pushing against her heart under the hooded sweatshirt. She had promised Dearest they would sneak out, but she was held back by the shared rhythm of Papa's and Little Brother's snores. She lifted out the old photo album while she thought about what she was going to do. She quickly forgot about the bus that would soon stop for the night as she flipped faster and faster through the pages. White holes met her where pictures of Mama used to be. Every picture of Mama had been torn out. In some photos showing her and Little Brother, Mama's features had been covered in black ink. Mama sat like a dark shadow with an arm around her at the Tivoli, Mama was a ghost behind the swing in Nelson's Hill. There was Little Brother at the maternity ward, in the arms of a navy-blue blob—the black felt-tip pen must have run out. She took out one of the pictures. She was sitting in the middle, the navy-blue blob on one side and the shining Evelina on the other. Evelina who had disappeared to Saltsjö-baden in order to realize Papa's dreams. A lost dream. She understood that that was what all of these destroyed pictures meant: a lost dream. Papa was starting to get used to dreaming and losing. It struck her that it was dreaming and losing that Papa was counting on, not on her. That was why he hadn't waited for an answer, that is why he hadn't said anything else, hadn't protested more. That was why he stayed in the car all of those nights when he was watching over her path from the bus to the door and didn't say anything. Papa wasn't counting on her; Papa wasn't counting on anyone. She slammed the photo albums shut and put them back in order, hoped Papa wouldn't notice that she had touched them, that she had witnessed his losses. She pulled off her clothes, unhooked the push-up bra and pulled on one of Little Brother's football shirts. It fit her perfectly. She breathed in the familiar scent of laundry detergent. Soon Little Brother's clothes would be too big for her. When had the time passed and could it be turned back? Could everything be put right? There was a click and the warm light of the night light started flooding out from under Papa's bedroom door. He was awake! She jumped into the bathroom and quickly locked the door, caught her breath sitting on the toilet seat for a while before she started washing her face, she had to wash several times in order to get rid of all of the make-up. When she finally looked up it was a child she saw in the mirror. A naked face, a clean slate filled with history. She looked at her features, Papa's features. She wasn't going to be the one who burst Papa's dreams. She wasn't going to let him down.

She crawled down in the bed that had been Little Brother's, he was sleeping in her old bed now. She ran her fingers along the side of the bed frame, it was lacerated with strikes from floorball sticks and tennis rackets. She felt like an intruder. This wasn't her home any more. She had sent Mama away, and then followed after. There was no home left. It was when sleep slowed her breathing and took hold of her heart's beating that the thought burst out from her chest, spread its wings like a delicate flower petal. It was too late; she had already failed Papa.

THE PASSING OF TIME

The red bus circled, in and out. From its concrete cave at the Metro Station, along the motorway, past the kiosk in the mall and out among the wide fields of the archipelago, all the way out to the furious waves. Then it came the whole way back.

You could count the passage of time with that red bus. That was what she did, now that she had decided to stop running out and jumping on it. She sat bent over her homework at the kitchen table and stared out through the window every fifteen minutes. In. Out. Stagnant movement.

Dearest Sister was the only one who saw the balloons lifting her house, watched her contours dissolve, felt her float away. Dearest grabbed hold of her collar.

'Don't you dare disappear again! You said you weren't going to disappear.'

Flashing liquorice pastilles against her receding reflection.

There is no me, there is no you, there is only us, she wanted to whisper back. But the words didn't come. She wasn't there.

Swedish Teacher Nina saw it as well, but Nina was seeing something else. Nina saw her pass by in flat-soled shoes, saw her hug the Hunting League in the morning but keep to the other side of the cafeteria. Nina saw Ebba and Klara look at the Girl with raised eyebrows and blow pink bubbles, before they shook their heads and turned their backs to her. Nina saw her walk home in the afternoons, while the Hunting League ran for the bus to the city. At first Nina didn't dare say anything to her, thought it was best to leave her alone, Nina was afraid that unasked for words would make her turn around again, go another way.

When it was time to set the definitive marks Nina finally said something. Nina slid down in the seat next to hers where she was sitting alone in the cafeteria. She spread butter on hard tack and tried to find the right words.

'How's it going?'

The Girl was pulled from her thoughts that were circling around chemical formulae and test results.

'Good. Thanks.'

Nina nodded and took a large bite of her sandwich, rough buttery crumbs got stuck in the pink lipstick. She stared at the drops of fat around Nina's mouth and felt a repugnance rising in her throat. She pushed her plate away. She didn't want the food, had mainly filled the plate because that is what you did.

'And how about you?'

Nina swallowed noisily, washed down the remains of her bite with a large gulp of low-fat milk, then wiped her mouth with her hand.

'I'm doing really well! Super!'

She nodded in response, then grabbed the tray and pushed her chair back.

'Wait.' Nina grabbed her arm. 'Sit down.' She hesitated at first, but then saw the Hunting League lumbering into the cafeteria. She sat down in order to avoid meeting them at the door.

'I've asked the other teachers and things … things are going really well for you. We were almost a bit shocked when we looked over everything, the results from the national tests and the homework and the class participation, and well, everyone knows that you work really hard, but no one thought … In any case. You're going to get the highest marks in every subject. Every single one!'

Nina took yet another gulp of low-fat milk, and looked at her with hopeful eyes. She looked back, but said nothing. Wondered if Nina could see the balloons pulling at her pupils.

Nina glanced at the Hunting League who were shouting to each other over the containers of fish stew, then she started talking again.

'I'm very happy that you listened to me. That you walked away from that and focused instead. You'll never regret it.'

The Girl tilted her head to the side, pushed back what was climbing up her throat, what wanted to spray over Nina's warm eyes, her friendly face. She smiled. People. She wondered why they all thought they were so damned important, why they pushed and shoved so anxiously, tried to find a place for her in their own play. She wanted to tell Nina that what she was saying was unimportant, that everything they thought and were so sure about was unimportant. She jumped. The smile froze. Only now did Nina's message take hold in her body, it spread through her pores like a grass fire. The highest marks, in every subject. The plan. Dreams, Papa who had stopped dreaming. She got up quickly.

'I have to call my father.'

*

In, out, the passing of time. The end of the school year. Junior high was over. Factory Town was over. Her marks honoured the dream about Ally and would lead her to a school in the city. A platform. Kawa. Gone gone, away.

The Hunting League showed up at her door that night. They came as a group and towered above her: Mirja and Carina in newly purchased white Buffalo boots, Ebba and

Klara in stilettos, Lotta in sandals. She tried to back away but Ebba arched her thin eyebrows while Klara tensed her deep red lips and Mirja took a firm grip on her forearm and pulled her out into the yard.

'We're going to have a party,' Klara instructed. 'At our place.'

She jumped. In Factory Town?

'It's cool. Everything's under control.' Ebba popped a bubble from her chewing gum, it became stuck on the tip of her nose, and she stuck out her tongue to sweep it into her mouth. 'We've fixed drinks, and like, invited everyone. Everyone's coming.'

'Like everyone.' Mirja leaned against the wall of the building and pulled a pack of cigarettes from her pocket. A small pocket-knife slipped out and fell against the pavement. Mirja picked it up and stuck it in the waistband of her pants.

'But Kawa will only come if you pick him up.'

Kawa.

'He, like, doesn't think you're gonna show up.' Carina let out her short hair, straightened it and put it back up again, a limp brush of bleached-out strands. 'Swear on your mama's life,' he said. 'So now you have to come. You want to see him, don't you?'

Kawa.

*

High, short, tight and glittery. The costume slid on without a problem. She got off the bus at the Metro Station and lit a cigarette with shaking hands, coughed at the first drag. She looked around, felt the thick scent of *oddkollon* before it appeared behind the glass doors of the subway. Kawa and his crew. They walked toward her with legs wide apart, steps long, shoulders thrown back, and then their heads: they were held so high they looked like they might fall over backward at any moment. She was standing completely still, hypnotized by their even movement. There was a story in their walk, in their scent, and in their skin that was already thick and furrowed. With every gesture they revealed a story that wasn't their own. It was like she was reading it for the first time.

Each of them greeted her with a nod of the head, first Kawa, the rest followed in a domino effect. She nodded back, pointed at the bus stop and let them walk ahead. She looked Kawa up and down, observed him carefully as he walked at the front. Suddenly she saw that he was standing still, that his movement had stopped. She saw that he was stuck between a story that wasn't his own and a future that should still be unknown. He was going nowhere, Kawa. He was nowhere else; there was nowhere else to go. She wished that it wasn't so obvious, wished that she hadn't seen it. She regretted having left the kitchen table. She should have stayed away, not come back.

Factory Town was standing around them at the bus stop, the queue with sleepy passengers looked up. They jumped, looked away, stared, looked away, stared, then shook their heads. She knew that Kawa and his crew looked out of place, that they shouldn't be here. She shifted between meeting the looks of dislike and looking down at the ground. Factory Town and she were dancing around each other, and Kawa and his crew were standing above that dance. It was too old, too tired for them, maybe barely noticeable. Instead they filled the back of the bus with a rumble. She wanted to ask them to quiet down, to walk with smaller steps, but what was so different about her bus and their commuter train? Who said that invisible is better than impossible to ignore? So she sat next to them and made herself non-existent, to in some way compensate for her crew filling the whole consciousness of the bus.

*

The house was crammed with people. The girls really had invited everyone, from West to North, Kurd and Turk, friends and enemies. She remained standing in the hall until Kawa's gang had disappeared into the crowd, and wondered for a moment if she shouldn't just turn around and go back to the kitchen table and the flat. But there were no books waiting for her tonight. Mama was working and she couldn't go home to Papa and Little Brother this late, not in these clothes. It would make Papa's eyebrows furrow, raise questions again. Questions he had never asked but that pounded like a little heart at his temples. No, she couldn't go home to Papa. And the Hunting League was here, Dearest was here, Kawa was here. She picked up a bottle of Absolute Vodka that was standing on the floor in the hallway and took five big gulps, then she lit a cigarette. Tonight this was where she belonged.

She pushed her way into the cloud of familiar scents: *oddkollon* and Marlboro Lights, Tommy Hilfiger and pink chewing gum, her own breath and vodka fumes. Somewhere she glimpsed her sister with her bare legs stretched out and yet another hawk's nose next to her. Hakim was sitting on the sofa. She continued through the room, slipping between the bodies with quick steps, stepped out onto the veranda. She inhaled through her nose and opened a can of beer, then lay on her back in the hammock and closed her eyes, let her breath hiss out between her lips. She heard Ebba and Klara shouting along with the music. She closed the doors when the Spice Girls started pounding through the roughhouse. She lay down again with her eyes closed, wished she had Little Brother's Walkman, headphones tight to her ears, Orup on the highest volume.

Someone sat down at her feet; she peered down. It was that Turk, Berkan, the one who should have stood between her and Hakim but fell at the first gust of wind. He said something, looked at her with his dog eyes, continued talking even though she didn't answer. He touched her knee awkwardly, and she allowed his hand to rest on her thigh. She closed her eyes again. She wasn't there. The vodka had blown extra wind into the colourful balloons, she was flying high, so high above everything, leather briefcase in her hand, rainy streets; she had never been anywhere else. The star had started twinkling even brighter, the glow would become a fire. This wasn't where she was supposed to be.

Suddenly Kawa's colourless eyes forced their way into her field of vision. She pulled her legs from Berkan's grip and the balloons popped one after the other, hung limply from her back when she tried to sit up.

'He hasn't done anything. It wasn't him,' she said with a nod of her head in Berkan's direction, but Kawa wasn't listening. It was too late.

'Outside, you fucking cocksucker,' Kawa hissed between

his teeth. He lifted Berkan by the upper arm and dragged him out behind him. She got to her feet, her senses suddenly crystal clear, nowhere else but here. Kawa dragged Berkan through the living room toward the front door, and she ran quickly after, tried to find the stop button or at least press pause. She saw the edge of the knife in Kawa's pocket. Platforms. She saw his gaze. It was black, blacker even than her liquorice pastilles.

The whole room froze at the site of Kawa's pounding temples. In one moment everyone was standing still, then someone shouted, 'Fight!' and it was as if the whole house had been waiting for the signal the entire night. The girls instinctively moved to the walls, arms across their chests in defence. The guys rolled up their shirtsleeves, grabbed lamps and porcelain figurines, dried beads of sweat from their foreheads and moved in a streamline formation in the direction of the fight. A floodwave of adrenaline and testosterone. The asphalted road that quietly floated through the roughhouse area during the day was transformed into a fully besieged warzone. Kawa against Berkan, West against North, Kurd against Turk. Everyone against no one.

The Hunting League gathered at the kitchen window and watched. They jumped when rocks crushed car windows, branches were torn from the birch trees, kicks bent traffic signs and blood streamed from broken noses.

'What the hell are we going to do?' Ebba screamed. Unbothered, Mirja made herself a cheese sandwich and washed the bites down with big gulps from the soda bottle. Carina opened the window a bit and shouted, 'Damn idiots,' in order to quickly shut it again. Dearest Sister was nowhere in sight.

Ebba grabbed hold of her hand.

'What the hell are we going to do? My mother is going to kill me, do you understand?'

A rock half the size of a human head flew through the window and into the china cabinet. There was shattered glass, shards everywhere.

'Run, dammit,' Klara shouted and they ran. They ran past overturned furniture in the living room, toward the patio at the other end of the house.

'We have to call someone! Someone has to help us!' Lotta was gasping with tears in her throat. 'Can't we call someone? We can call ChildLine!'

She stopped and laughed out loud, a shrill laugh, an unnatural laugh.

'ChildLine—are you an idiot? No one is going to feel sorry for you. No one is going to come and save you.' Her voice sounded more sarcastic than she had intended. She looked away, continued moving forward quickly to avoid seeing them, avoid seeing that they didn't understand. She was holding out her hand to open the patio door when a masked face popped up on the other side of the glass door. A masked face with a bat raised above his head. The girls screamed and turned around behind her, then ran. She didn't back away. She stood still, closed her eyes, and waited for the blow. It was clear that it would come, that the blow would come. A heavy stick would go through the glass pane and toward her pounding temples. It had been a matter of time, from the beginning it had been a matter of time. She closed her eyes and waited, but it didn't come. Instead she heard how the blows were aimed at tables and chairs, how the mask, roaring, shredded the hammock. She

peered outside, frozen in place. The small grassy area behind the mask was suddenly filled with a new type of gang,
wearing heavy boots with white laces placed firmly on the
ground and six-packs in their left hands reaching rhythmically up with the right hand over and over again. The
light from the living room reflected in their shaved heads
and the air was filled with their two-syllable declaration of
hate. She examined face after face, recognized every one of
them—from the Factory Town school, from the sports hall.

Now Kawa came running from behind. She felt his footsteps before he tore her from the door and shoved her into
a corner. The guys had heard the rhythmic chanting and
had united in the presence of a real enemy. They poured
through the patio door now in another flood wave. The
neo-Nazi rank quickly split and retreated, *Blatte*-land on
their heels. The Hunting League shouted from the floor of
the hallway. She carefully crawled toward the patio door.
The man with the mask was being held down against the
oiled wooden planks. To her relief it wasn't Kawa who was
holding him down, but a police officer, dammit. A big,
strong police officer. A woman who roughly pulled the
robber's hood from the masked face. She made eye contact
with Alberto's blue gaze, realized that it was just as colourless as Kawa's.

LIKE A RIVER

The police kept Kawa a long time that last night, asking
question after question, deliberating over the radio, whispering to each other. The Hunting League was lying in

the house sleeping, everyone but Dearest Sister who had followed Hawk-Nose into the city. The rest of the guests had disappeared within seconds of the sight of the police: rushed to the bus, into the woods, to waiting cars. Kawa was the only one who had stayed.

The June sun rose over the roughhouse neighbourhood while the police whispered with Kawa. The natural light seemed unnatural when it fell over bottles, kicked-over street signs and broken branches. Something had used violence on the gravel road and the blooming flowerbeds that framed it, assaulted the silence. She was sitting on a rock looking around. She looked at the nocturnal light, the assaulted system, at the sharp contrast between beauty and desolation. She stared intensely at the police car but tried to avoid looking straight at Kawa. She wanted to see as little of him as possible, keep the picture of him she had formed inside of herself intact. But she couldn't get up and leave either, leave him there to clean up the crumbs of someone else's gluttony. He ached in her eyes, ached in her whole body. She would never be the one who left. He would be the one to leave.

The police finally drove away and Kawa walked toward her. The broad legged gait and the head tilted back were gone. He was walking with his hands in his pockets, his back bent and his eyes on the gravel. She remained sitting on the rock, blinded.

'I've received my sentence.'

'Sentence?'

'Yes, sentence. My sentence—it came last week. I'm going to do time.'

'Time? What do you mean time? For what?'

203

'Shit. Time for shit.'

'What did you do?'

Now he looked up at her, straight at her. No, straight through her. He didn't see her. He was somewhere else again.

'Damn. It doesn't matter. It's my own fault, okay. Don't worry about it!'

He hesitated, kicked the gravel with the toes of his shoes. Pulled his hand through his hair that was heavy with wax, dried it on his jeans.

'I'm okay with doing the time, that's not the problem. The problem is that when it's over I have to come back to the same shit. That's the problem.'

She nodded, but didn't have an answer.

'When are you coming back?'

'That's none of your business. This has nothing to do with you! To you, it doesn't matter if I'm inside for a year or my whole life. You'll never see me again, okay? You have nothing to do with me.'

He shook his hands at her, stopped when he saw that she had jumped back. Now they were both standing still, looking each other in the eye, no one looked away. He raised his hand and placed it on her forehead. It was a light, brief touch.

Then the fog rolled in over his eyes again. He pulled his hand back.

'I need to go.'

And then he was gone. Gone even though he was still pounding inside her.

A whole new look grew forth in her eyes that summer: dark, steady, impassable. She jumped the first time she saw it in the mirror. It was a boiling kettle, that look. A kettle where everything had been thrown in, everything had been collected in order to be transformed into hard-pressed steam. Compressed air.

*

'Now, it counts,' Papa said on the last night of summer vacation and he nodded at the high school schedule she had set out in front of him on the chequered tablecloth of the kitchen table. She had just come home from a shift at Mc-Donald's and hadn't had the peace to sit down despite the exhaustion. Under the red-chequered button-down her heart was still beating in time with the clock on the cash register. The clock that timed every order and showed in a colourful diagram on the wall which cashiers were running the fastest. There was one column per red-chequered shirt. She took them seriously, those columns. She had developed a dependency on beating everyone, every time. Beating that ticking clock that always assumed it knew best. It moved inside her over the summer, that clock. Tapped her fingers against the kitchen table, heels against the floor, heart beating against her temples.

Papa sat calmly in his chair. He seasoned his *kabab kobide* with a thick layer of *somagh*, a sour, blood-red spice.

'This is where it gets decided, do you understand? This is when you decide if you're going to wear yourself out be-

205

hind the cash register the rest of your life for a shit salary, and then come home to a kitchen table like this,' He slammed his fist against the wax tablecloth.

'Look around. This is the best you've seen. If your life looks like this in twenty years, you haven't lost anything. If you just keep trucking along you can live like this, in a neighbourhood like this. You have no reason to struggle, understand?'

She understood. She threw every word in the kettle and stirred. The steam pressed against her temples.

'Those people you're competing against, their lowest level is up here.' He held his spoon above his head. 'Your lowest level is down here.' He lowered the fork to the stained kitchen rug.

'They won't be satisfied. Making it is their only alternative. For you it's a bonus. You can take the bus and the subway for an hour in rush hour in the morning and change into that shirt.'

He waved the fork and small grains of rice spilled over the chequered pattern.

'Run around in the smell of food all day long, take shit from bitter customers who look down on you, be kicked by the bosses who are angry at themselves for not having gotten away from there, and clean up after people who act like pigs. There is something inside of you that's okay with living like that.'

He chewed nervewrackingly on the tender meat, motioned to Little Brother to eat slower. The small drops of sweat showed that something had started boiling inside of him as well.

'Now you have the energy to take your lunch with you,

but you won't be doing that in five years. When you're finally allowed to clock out you'll be too tired to change into your cheap H&M shirt, so you'll sit on the bus with that smelly shirt on, like today, come home to a kitchen table like this, if you're lucky, throw something down that takes ten minutes to fix, yell at your children, if you have the energy, and then collapse on the sofa in front of the TV until you fall asleep and a new shit day starts. You'll have enough money for the rent, a bus card and cheap food on the table. Your children will always be unhappy because they won't get all of the things they want. You may go camping in the summer time, or take a last-minute to the Canaries every other year. You'll be happy if your boyfriend doesn't have a drinking problem.'

She laughed and Papa nodded. Lost dreams. From his side of life the matter was hysterically obvious.

'Mm, you're laughing now. Now you have the highest marks in everything, and you are the best of everyone you know. But it's easier to fall off the carousel than you think. And for you it's easier than others not to jump on again. Because you come from this.'

Papa's honey eyes were splashing with something pleading, forcing their way down to her boiling point.

'It's now or never. Everything we've talked about. Now is the time for hard work. You're the one who decides what you'll do with the opportunities and the future. You mustn't forget that.'

He pointed at the chair across from him.

'Please sit down now, your heart is beating so loudly it's giving me a headache.'

She plopped down in the chair, looked down at the

brown stick of ground beef in front of her and pushed the plate away. She had no appetite left. She just felt a completely unexpected longing to put her forehead in one hand and a cigarette in the other.

GRID

*It was masturbation without
the involvement of the flesh.*

The alarm clock sounded: 7.00 a.m.. Saturday morning. The Girl already had her eyes wide open and her stomach sucked in. She ran her fingertips along her hipbone that was rubbing against her skin, turned off the alarm with one hand and continued moving up her body with the other, then pressed her pinkie into the space between her ribs. She bit her lip from the pain. She continued pushing, pushed inside herself, could almost feel the contours of her organs. They were splashing around in there, unhindered, without eyes and ears, without compressed air, without plans. She wished she could trade places with them, become their mute, deaf, slimy limbs, put the spleen in the control room.

Her concave stomach rumbled loudly. She must have lost weight again, the hollow hadn't been that deep yesterday, had it? The hollow cramped in response: hunger. She hadn't eaten since lunch yesterday, two large apples. There was a small ripple along her spine, a millisecond of satisfaction.

She stepped in front of the mirror with her stomach still sucked in. Her thighs were too wide, nothing could be done about it; it was something about the shape, a thick clump of tendons that stuck out. She lost herself in the recurring fantasy: sharp knife blade against thin skin, fine cuts eliminating the excess, bloody scraps against the ground. What remained: straight legs, bones, edges. Clean. Pure. But it would be too simple, too weak, to get out the meat knife. The satisfaction lay in the castigation of the flesh, to carry on, carry out.

*

She understood early on that the reflection she saw in the mornings wasn't what people wanted to see. People pointed at undernourished when she felt rolls of fat. They screamed sick even though she had never been so healthy, whispered weak when she was the strongest. People turned around on the streets, gave her those looks.

'They're wondering what's wrong, don't you understand that?' Dearest Sister had asked. 'They think it's disgusting, that you look strange.'

She knew that people were wrong, they were ones who were disgusting. She was tired of them, didn't want to hear what they had to say. People and their opinions. What the hell did they have to do with her? People were distracting, they tried to steer the path. She didn't need them, didn't need any of them. The Girl wasn't planning on letting herself get distracted again. She would never let anyone distract her. People, she stood above them.

*

The first half of the morning's inspection was over. She sneaked into the bathroom, careful not to wake her mother. She wanted to empty her body as much as possible before weighing in, but nothing was happening. She remained sitting on the toilet and strained. There was no movement.

She ran her nails along the thin skin on the inside of her forearm, tore at the scabs leaving trails of pomegranate-red drops. The laxative had lost its effect. Her stomach was full of dead weight.

She stepped up onto the scale in the end, hesitated before looking down. The numbers would regulate everything. Everything was riding on those numbers: 40.2 kilos. There was a tingling in the thundercloud above her chest. She walked over to the desk and added the weight to the worn notepad, drew a small tail on the steeply falling graph: 800 grams less than yesterday. It was a roller coaster. She followed the graph with her fingertip and stopped at the top. It had started at 65 kilos, half a year earlier. She counted quickly in her head: roughly four kilos a month. It could have gone much faster, she could have done more. The chestcloud grew, pressed, changed position. Shit. Lazy, comfortable fatso. Damn lazy, comfortable fatso. Disgusting, saggy fatso.

*

It hadn't actually been the idea, to lose so much weight. It was more a side-effect, the consequence of that boiling gaze that had popped up in the mirror.

This is when it counts, it's fucking now or never, ruin this and you're stuck, ruin this and you'll never get anywhere. Ruin this and you're nothing.

The consequence of compressed air.

But once she had started losing weight the rush took over, the kick she got from resisting. She amused herself by staring at all the chewing mouths around her: the build-up of saliva, chocolate biscuit-crumbs falling from people's mouths, ketchup stains on frozen noses. Pleasure-seeking, she observed the stomachs of the girls in her class: they were doughy, protruding, hard lumps of deficient character. The girls shrank in front of her eyes. She saw them put their arms around their waists, strutting around, pulling in the fat as much as they could and looking away in shame.

She got a kick from resisting what no one else managed to resist. Masturbation without the involvement of the flesh.

*

The clock struck 7.20 a.m., it was time to prepare breakfast. The alarm would ring at 8.00 a.m. again, then the study schedule started. She spooned cottage cheese onto the baking scale: 100 grams, 90 calories. Four pieces of hard tack: 160 calories. That was 250 calories in total. Her stomach cramped again when she looked at the plate. 250 calories. The thundercloud shuddered. Her gaze followed the graph in the notebook, it wasn't dropping steeply enough. She pulled out the rubbish bin and threw in the sandwiches. The shimmering silverfish cawed in protest, they were flying in circles around her head like fateful crows, spotting her sight with their black wings. She asked them to shut up. Emptied a bottle of water in her stomach, and went to look at the Excel sheet that held the plan: 8.00–10.00 she would do chemistry, then a five-minute bathroom break. From 10.05–12.05, maths. At this point she would be really hungry; she knew that. Best to take something that didn't require as much concentration: 12.10–14.10 Swedish. Was it time to eat then? Food break from 14.10–14.40. Max 300 calories. 200 grams of peas. She typed in the box in the Excel sheet. 160 calories. Two pieces of hard tack: 80 calories. 50 grams of cottage cheese: 45 calories. It gave her a margin of 15 calories. Worried, she looked at the boxes. She counted, calculated, drank more water. On the last row the column's sums showed nine hours of studying, 2 hours of walking, and 1000 calories; 750 now that she had skipped the cottage cheese sandwiches. That was good, 750 would provide a good margin, if she had calculated something incorrectly.

*

She never calculated anything incorrectly. Damned if she didn't keep track of the numbers. She kept track of every number: from her weight to the time, from the physics textbook to the calorie table, from the decimals in her BMI to her average overall marks that never changed. She counted, calculated. She decided that she was in charge now, that she was the numbers. She allowed the numbers to decide what she should represent. Numbers don't lie, numbers say everything. What people think is unimportant, because people see incorrectly. People don't know what they're seeing.

*

The schedule had been checked, determined, was ever more fuzzy. More and more silverfish appeared. They were cutting at her ears, weighing down the power lines in her head. She squeezed her eyes shut, over and over again. She tried to scare them off, but they weren't going anywhere. They screamed louder, drowning out her thoughts. Suddenly they attacked her retina, like an attack by Hitchcock's birds. The world went from spotted to black. She ran to the kitchen and pulled out the rubbish bin, grabbed the bits of hard tack. She nibbled on small small pieces: a hungry squirrel with a mouth that was too small. The silverfish-fog lifted, the cawing subsided. Small small pieces, she made them last as long as possible. One final darkness, then clarity. It was 7.58 a.m.. Her tongue had licked the last of the cottage cheese. Her teeth mashed the dried tealeaves that had come along with the bread, trash from yesterday. Anxiety floated like frying fat through her heart. She tried shutting out the image of the food that was lapping around under her skin, the enzymes that were being broken down. The excess that was being transported to her thighs by men in bloody overalls, where the lumps of cottage cheese were being piled high forming a wall of fat she couldn't get at.

It was too late.

She had lost.

She wanted more.

it's none of your business

Papa was standing at the stove every time she visited, making favourite dish after favourite dish, tempting her with the smells of slow cooking. He looked pleased when she lifted the lid off the pan and drew in the steam of comforting dried herbs and tender lamb. He pulled his hand through her thinning hair when she so readily declined to eat in order to sit down at the books instead.

'Everything has its measure and limitations, *dokhtaram*. It's enough now. This is a marathon, *azizam*, not the hundred-yard dash. You still have a long way to go!'

She squinted, glimpsed honey streaks between the silverfish. What happened to 'the future has no head and no tail'? What happened to 'the future is now'? *This is the plan, Papa, the plan. I won't let you down, I won't let anyone down.*

*

Mama had tried putting a stop to it early on, poured oil in her food and thought she wouldn't notice. But she had seen them right away: the rings of fat on the surface of the water. They spread across the surface like dirty carnations. The broccoli and cauliflower were stained, ruined. Mama had sat at the kitchen table, peering up from behind her fringe. Mama had sat quietly, as if the silence would allow her betrayal to pass by unnoticed. The Girl had poured the inedible food into the sink. The chestcloud was suffocating her. She stomped away and collapsed on the hall floor, allowed something unknown to escape from her throat. An injured, dangerous animal had crawled out of her. Mama rushed over, tried to touch her, wondered what she could do. Mama would do anything.

'Go away!' She had screamed and Mama had backed away as far as she could. She had only screamed like that once before, right before she had packed Mama's bags and set them in the elevator. Neither of them would forget that moment.

'Are you trying to punish me?' Mama had asked from the doorpost.

It's none of your business was her response, but she didn't open her mouth to say the words. She saved her energy and went to sit at the desk instead. She was occupied with something more important. Something most important.

*

The goal was to maximize those opportunities, secure the best possible future. Dot the i's and cross the t's on the plan. She wanted to shield herself from the closed doors of Factory Town and the fenny ground of *Blatte*-land. Create her own milky way between the subway platform and the red buses, her own space in the traffic. Her very own place in the system. The goal was to walk with her chin held high without tipping over backward Kawa-style. Walk with her chin held high, supported by not just being strong but by being the strongest, not just as good but much better.

Platform.

To achieve this she drew a fixed grid and made sure the surface of her skin fit inside it. Every action became instrumental, everything that didn't lead toward the goal was discarded. She ate only so she could see the numbers in front of her. She slept so she didn't have to think about food. She spoke so that those who were stubbornly knocking, wouldn't start pounding, wouldn't intrude more than they already were.

The people disappeared quickly and lineally, one after

another. Even the ones who stuck around the longest were shaken off early, sometimes without them even noticing they had disappeared.

People are easily scared. Or she was good at scaring.

She let them disappear.

MAKING OUT WITH YOUR BEST FRIEND'S GUY

She always took the first bus to school in the morning. The bus was almost always empty, dozing. She was the only one disturbing the silence, chewing on her hard tack, flipping through her notebooks. She was always flipping through her notebooks. There was no time to waste, nothing to leave to chance.

The school building was empty when she arrived. The doors were unlocked for the cleaning personnel. She sneaked into the study room at the very end, closed the door tightly after her and didn't turn the light on. People, she avoided them, avoided all of them. She erased all traces after herself to minimize the risk that they would find her. Then she sat in the light coming from the streetlight outside the window and focused as intensely on the books as she could, with her toes on the floor and her heels raised until she developed cramps in her calves. She only got up for scheduled classes and bathroom breaks, and only packed up after the janitor shouted that it was time to put the alarm on, at 8.28 p.m.. He only shouted to her, no one else was there.

*

One day during lunch the door to her hidden study room was opened. It was Mariella, the physics teacher. She recognized the perfume, and didn't need to look up. She only tensed her calves, pressed her nails against the inside of her forearm. She hoped that Mariella would turn around and go if she pretended not to be there. Maybe Mariella couldn't see her in the dark.

Mariella turned on the lights.

'So this is where you hide out!'

She set two plastic containers on the table.

'I brought pasta salad! With chicken. It's healthy and delicious.'

The Girl didn't look up, just pointed at the freezer bag on the table, it contained ten carefully-counted rice cakes.

'That's not food. And it'll keep for a while, save it for tomorrow.'

The Girl shook her head. She focused on the last sentence she had read and tried to shut off her senses, keep them from allowing Mariella into the system, tried to maintain the order.

People, they're distracting.

'Come on! You can't just live on bread and water, you know.'

People, trying to steer the path.

The Girl shook her head again.

'Okay, I'm not going to nag. Eat your rice cakes. It's stupid to skip lunch. Maybe I can chat a bit while you eat. Would that be all right? You could close your books and listen for a bit.'

Mariella pulled out a chair and sat down.

'You know that you're really smart ... Probably the best

in the school! I understand that maybe that's what you want, but … You know it's not necessary right? You don't need to work so hard. Have such high standards … You can have a good life anyway, maybe even better … I was an average student, but I've got a great life.'

People, what do they have to do with her?

'Life isn't about marks and things like that. Not in the end. You need to do other things like eat lunch with your class in the cafeteria, start with that … Go to a party with your friends! Maybe watch a film with your mum in the evenings, you know. That's the kind of thing you remember later.'

People, they have so many opinions.

The strong light from the fluorescent lamps accentuated the pores in Mariella's budding double-chin, and lit up the thick, long hairs on her upper lip. A chewing, smacking upper lip.

People, they're the disgusting ones.

'And you know that you're very pretty … But you were actually prettier when you started here. You don't look healthy now. You're going to destroy your body if you aren't careful. Rice cakes and water … You're messing up the whole system. You can't have had your period for some time now, and it can affect your fertility in the future. Your breasts have probably stopped developing. Do you understand? You're going to have to deal with the consequences for a long time, and you have to think about whether it's all worth it.'

She wasn't listening, she was repeating physics formulae in her head. She tensed her calves.

Power.

She ran her finger along her concave stomach.

Resistance.

Touched her half-baked breasts unconsciously.

Gravity.

'These are your best years, you know. You should be having a smoke during the breaks … Getting drunk on the weekends. Hell, making out with your best friend's boyfriend!'

Mariella placed her hand on hers and laughed softly.

'Not everything needs to be so extreme, you know. You're good enough! You're fine the way you are. You're beautiful the way you are.'

The Girl smiled. The liquorice pastilles travelled over Mariella, filled to the brim with the same darkness that had climbed up her throat and poured over the Swedish teacher Nina there next to that tiled wall in Factory Town. But she held back, she liked Mariella. Mariella was tall and curvy and had big breasts; she wore tight T-shirts and skinny jeans and boots with studs. Mariella's hair was dyed black and pulled back into a thin ponytail. Most of her hair had probably fallen out, maybe due to too many chemical treatments; it was hard to say. But you saw in Mariella that she had set off on her own path, but had regretted it halfway, or at the end, and instead she was trying to make her life fit inside lesson plans and staff meetings.

Now Mariella was leaning back in the chair, popping fusilli in her mouth and feeling rather satisfied with her intervention, with her cheap clichés and generic lies. Who was Mariella to decide what was worth what? What did Mariella know about being good enough, being good enough as you are? She didn't need Mariella's damn help.

She was strong, stronger than Mariella had ever been. Mariella's small grin, thinking even for a second that she could save her. She hated Mariella.

What people think. Is unimportant.

MAGNUM ALMOND

It was different with Little Brother. He didn't say anything. He didn't say anything for a long time. He just looked at her with his nut-brown eyes. He looked deep inside, further than Mama's and Papa's eyes reached. Further than the eyes of people reached. Little Brother saw everything from his spot up there on the mountain peak.

Little Brother didn't say anything for a long time. He had said his bit when she had packed up her things to leave. *We're a team*, he had said. *There won't be a team left, if you leave.* He had said all that, and she had still left him. What was left to say?

But he knocked on her door in the end, chose a day during the summer holiday thinking she would feel less bothered, that he wouldn't be bothering her as much then. She didn't answer, so he stepped in. He stepped in and didn't really know where to rest his gaze while he collected himself, while he tried to find a tone of voice that wouldn't startle her.

The Girl was walking back and forth across the floor with quick steps, back and forth across the fifty square-foot surface of the bedroom floor. She had thick socks on her feet, had a shawl wrapped around her neck several times, and a woollen sweater over her body. She was walking back and forth with a book in her hand, holding it so close to her eyes that it was folded like blinders over her face. She didn't hear him at first. Finally she looked up, but it took a while before she actually saw him. Little Brother saw the dull layer covering her retinas. Her gaze looked like an emptiness, but Little Brother knew that it wasn't empty, that it was anything but empty.

'Do you want to come with me? Outside?' Little Brother asked.

A wave rippled across the glassy surface. Little Brother. Little Brother was back. She had abandoned him, split their team in half, but he was back. The wave transformed into a storm. She couldn't leave the room. In here she had everything organized: the schedule for the fall was on the screen, the weight curve and the day's calorie calculations were in the notebook, and carefully weighed carrot sticks were lying on a plate, waiting. The second hand was rattling in the clock that was timing her indoor walk. She had to keep going.

'I need help, with something.'

Little Brother knew that she couldn't say no to him, no matter how much she wanted to. She just couldn't. He was Little Brother and he was asking for help, and when had she helped him last? She only let people down.

So she nodded, stuffed the carrot sticks in the pocket of her jacket, and let the mountain peak lead the way.

*

Little Brother walked a few steps ahead of her on the gravel path leading toward the city centre. He kicked a rock now and then. They both followed the movement with their eyes, lowering their shoulders in disappointment when it was the friction not the power that won and everything became still again.

Little Brother didn't say anything. He wasn't like other people. He let her be, let her take care of her own business. Little Brother wasn't distracting. Lightning struck in the chestcloud: maybe she should let him distract her.

Little Brother stopped at the kiosk and bought something. They continued walking. Little Brother wasn't looking at her. She was bewitched by the golden-brown package in his hand: Magnum almond. She forgot about Little Brother, the ice cream interested her much more than anything else. She tore at her forearm with her fingernails, felt saliva run in her mouth. She wanted to tear off the paper, smell the ice cream. The Girl wanted to watch it melt, become goo between Little Brother's teeth. Teeth with resistance, weak teeth. Maybe she could take a bite herself and then spit it out right away, taste it without swallowing anything. Something shuddered in her lower stomach. Her chestcloud pulled together, thundered, rumbled.

Little Brother sat down on a park bench and started talking. She wasn't listening, couldn't see clearly. She sat down close to him and got ready to inhale the scent of chocolate almonds. There would be a small puff of air when he took off the wrapper.

Little Brother was talking, but she wasn't listening and suddenly something in his gaze changed. He hit her hard on her collarbone and she jumped as though she was coming out of a trance. Little Brother's fist pounded through her whole body, shit how it hurt.

'Are you listening to me? What's this?'

She backed up unintentionally and lost her grip on the notebook she was holding tightly against her body. She needed to look it up sometimes, to check if she had the right numbers in her head: 545 calories, 189 minute walk.

'It's your damned skeleton. Do you feel that? It's supposed to be on the inside of your body.'

Little Brother picked the notebook up off the ground, carelessly flipped through her careful documentation: the small, small symmetrical numbers and the carefully calculated sums. The steep graph: the rollercoaster. She wanted to take the notebook back and ask what business it was of his. She wanted to scream: you're the one who's disgusting, can't you see. But it didn't work of course. It was Little Brother.

Then she saw it. A shiver ran through her, it was as though she fell out of a trance when she saw it: Little Brother had tears in his eyes. Little Brother. She placed her hand on his bare thigh. There was nothing to worry about, she would protect him, he was safe with her. Little Brother pushed her hand away, it was dry and rough, covered in a thick mat of down and topped with blue, angular nails. Her hand was as cold as a gasping fish. She allowed her hand to fall, searched for Little Brother's gaze instead, but he was still staring at the symmetrical rows she had diligently filled in. That is when she understood. Little Brother was crying because of her. She had made Little Brother cry.

She tried to shake off her hand, but it just sat there.

*

Little Brother finally looked up, pushed the ice cream across the bench.

'Here. Eat it.'

She backed up.

'I'm not hungry.'

'Eat it anyway.'

Please don't do this, I don't want to ruin anything, but this is more important, I don't want to hurt you, but this is more important.

She shakes her head.

'I'm not hungry.'

'Eat the ice cream. For my sake.'

She collapses on the bench, disappears in between the wooden planks. She is so small next to Little Brother. He has grown, goodness how tall he is: shadowed cheeks, large hands. The mountain peak. That she had ever thought she could protect him.

'I can't.'

Little Brother looks up now and she sees it happen. She can really follow it with her eyes: how his pupils change. How those nut-brown eyes, which used to look up at her and then started to look right through her shift one more time. They are looking down. Little Brother is looking down at her.

Little Brother tears a page out of the notebook, draws a small square in the middle of the blank sheet of paper.

'Do you see this? You've put yourself inside it.'

With force he fills in the square until the pen pushes through the paper.

'You've boxed yourself up. You're locked in! You think you're in control, but you're not. You only know what's inside this square, what you write in this notebook. That's all you know.'

She rocks back and forth with her calves tensed, her chestcloud thunders. He'll understand some day, one day Little Brother will understand. She would make it worth it, everything would be worth it. He would understand.

*

The vanilla melted and seeped through the chocolate shell, it ran along her fingers as she followed Little Brother's disappearing figure. Little Brother walked just the way Grandpa had in her faded memories: his upper body leaning forward, head first.

She dropped the ice cream on the ground, dried her hands carefully on her shawl, and tied it tighter around her neck. She defied the winged insects that were cawing in front of her eyes and stood up, her gaze fixed on Little Brother's disappearing figure. She followed him at a safe, invisible distance. She let him lead the way, floated after him like a shadow: his shadow, her shadow, maybe the monster's shadow. He sensed her; she sensed that.

He didn't look back a single time. But he sensed her; she sensed that.

THE ELITE SCHOOL

*The hierarchy and the system had been blown over
and put right, so much had flowed under the bridges
that the water had been washed away.*

High school drew to a close. Her marks honoured the dream about Ally; she had the very highest marks. The scale showed 36.5, and her BMI was 14. Numbers don't lie. Numbers say everything. She was in the process of disappearing.

The winged insects on her retinas had transformed into a thick fog. She was too light-headed to go for her walks, she hadn't had her period in three years, and no amount of clothes were enough to keep her warm. The star was becoming fainter, her gaze was too clouded to see it. *You don't have control, you don't know anything*, Little Brother had said. *You've boxed yourself up; you're stuck. You only know what's inside this box.* Her head spun and confirmed Little Brother's words. This wasn't being in control. This wouldn't lead her away from here, all the way, as far as you could get.

*

Papa was the one who found the Elite School. He understood that elite meant taking advantage of opportunities, that elite was the result of dreams and hard work. Papa understood that she should become elite. He placed the pink business paper next to her physics books, circled photos and headlines.

'All of them attended the Elite School, *dokhtaram*. That's where you acquire power. People who want to become the boss study there, people who want to have a say in things.'

She looked at the newspaper photos. She saw neat suits, glimpsed briefcases in the background, saw rainy city streets and late nights at the office in front of her. *The dream about Ally*. Wondered anyway.

'Economics? What do I know about economics?'

'It doesn't matter!' Papa had done his homework. 'It doesn't matter what you study, what matters is that you're studying at the Elite School. It's a school that paves the way for opportunities.' Opportunities. Many opportunities. 'You can do whatever you want after graduation. Look, the average starting salary is listed here. That's more than your mother earns after ten years as a nurse.'

She took Papa's newspaper with her and showed Mama.

'Economics? What do we know about economics?' Mama shook her head. 'Your father and his ideas. You've worked so hard, why economics? You can become a doctor, *dokhtaram*. Why don't you want to become a doctor? There will always be sick people, you know. As long as you can save people's lives no one will care where you come from or who you are.'

Mama filled the tea glass, continued her train of thought.

'How will you impact the world if you know economics? Whose life will be affected, if you know economics?'

Mama pulled the newspaper toward her again, inspected the photos carefully.

'Bores. They look like horrible bores.'

She took Mama's questions with her to Papa.

'Your mother's thinking is old-fashioned! The future now isn't like the future when we were young. You live in a different world than we did. If you're going to succeed *dokhtaram*, you have to be on the inside. You have to be where things are happening, where the power is. You can never become anything without power, you know. You have to be somewhere where you can become someone, so that people can't ignore you, do you understand?'

Impossible to ignore. She understood and Papa saw that she understood. Papa turned his attention to the TV, pointed at it. The Champions' League final was on. Volley! Right in the goal. Papa stood up and shouted.

'Ziiidane!'

Zinedine Zidane. Real Madrid against Bayer Leverkusen. Elite against Elite. Papa remained standing, pointed at the TV again.

'You don't want to sit on the bench your whole life, you know. You don't want to be a reserve player either. You want to be a striker and score goals! You don't get any points for dribbling, or for passing to someone else. In the end, scoring goals is the only thing that matters! From the Elite School, you can make goals. From the Elite School you can make nice goals. Right in the net!'

*

So she ordered brochures about the Elite School and read about it, even though the decision had already been made. She mainly looked at the photos, saw princes and princesses with wide, bright smiles. Cheshire grins. She had no business there; that was clear. There would be no place for her in their system; it was obvious. They might look at her the first day and ask where she was from, maybe where she was on her way to. They would see her as a nomad, someone who had come and would move on, but who was never really there.

Like a river that had already passed.

They would see her for exactly what she was.

UP, UP

She applied to the Elite School, despite Mama's protests. She sent in her highest marks, and decided to create a space for herself in that system which couldn't possibly make room for her. A space among princes and princesses. She decided that that was exactly the place she wanted: the place that nobody thought could be hers, least of all herself.

'What difference will you make in the world if you educate yourself to count money, huh?' Mama asked that question over and over again. 'Counting someone else's money … Become a doctor! It's not too late to change your mind.' Dream and dream again. 'Save lives, what could be more important?'

She cut up her carrot sticks and allowed the sound of munching teeth to shut out Mama's voice. Small small pieces: a hungry squirrel with a mouth that was too small. Little Brother had looked down at her. No one looks down at a star, not at a star that is twinkling, twinkling before it has started burning. All she cared about was burning, burning so brightly that no one could stop staring. Burning so much that she would be impossible to ignore. Little Brother's gaze had to go up, he had to look up.

She still lay awake at night and thought about how she would avoid all of the stares. How she would instantly blend into the surroundings, become one with the wall. It would be so easy if she were allowed to disappear, continue disappearing.

'In the end scoring goals is all that matters,' Papa had said. 'Easy and difficult, *dokhtaram*. Those aren't words with just one meaning,' *If you do what's easy today, you'll have a hard time tomorrow.*

She closed her eyes tightly, ran her finger along her concave, cramping stomach. She wished she could crawl under the bed and hide, stop time and make it stand completely still, push the future forward to another day, maybe stop it from ever existing. But no. *You're too good to sit on the bench*, Papa had said. *Be a striker and score goals.*

The ball doesn't go in the net from an invisible side.

THE RED CARPET

The first day at the Elite School. She was waiting on the sidewalk wearing black pants and a black blouse, her hair in a bun. She tried to look like this was exactly where she was supposed be, exactly where she had always been on her way to. She tried to keep herself from turning around and walking away. Keep herself from hiding at the McDonald's restaurant she used to work at, which was located just a few hundred yards away. She saw the chequered shirt in front of her, smelt the frying fat. She heard Papa's voice.

Those people you're competing with—their lowest level is up here. Your lowest level is down here.

The silverfish cawed in front of her eyes, and she glanced at her watch. Her stomach growled. It had been eighteen hours since cottage cheese and an apple, eighteen hours of control. Her gaze was drawn to the sweets at the corner shop, she raked her nails along the scabs on the inside of her forearm and rocked back and forth on her stiletto heels. Focus. She resisted.

She watched the flow of layered blonde fringe, airy summer dresses and gold jewellery against sun-browned skin. She quickly observed that she should have come in flat-soled shoes, preferably with longer legs. She observed the parade of brands: Gucci, Louis Vuitton and Fendi. Observed that she wanted to throw her new, shiny bag from the department store to the morning drunks in Observatory Park.

She was waiting for Evelina. Evelina was also going to study at the Elite School. They hadn't seen each other since high school and the business with Saltsjöbaden's Coeducational School. Evelina had disappeared to the other side of the water, and the Girl had become invisible and then disappeared to *Blatte*-land. Evelina had called, suggested meeting for coffee, maybe some studying. Weren't they studying the same things even though they were on different sides of the water? The Girl had responded evasively at first, then not responded at all. Together Factory Town and *Blatte*-land had taught her that similarities are rewarded and differences are tolerated at most. She had understood how different they were, Evelina and her. That the differences between them were greater than the similarities.

Princess shimmer was the first thing she saw when Evelina was finally standing between Metro's sliding doors, as if she was being illuminated by spotlights. The Girl followed the shreds of confetti, watched how they became

236

stuck in the draft and whirled around Evelina's head like angels' hair. Felt them splash over her own neck when Evelina hugged her tightly, how she was strewn with extra starlight from the princess again. For the briefest of moments she became something else.

'I've missed this.' Evelina hooked arms with her and steered their steps in the direction of the Elite School's heavy oak doors.

I've missed it more, she thought. She didn't dare say the words out loud.

*

With Evelina at her side she became part of the crowd of people moving toward the Elite School. She floated into it, allowed her high heels to march in the same rhythm as the feet around her. Feet in loafers, everywhere feet in loafers. She followed their flat-soled rhythm, up on the red carpet that lay thrown over the stairs and past the orchestra playing music she didn't recognize.

Ten, broad, white smiles were lined up outside the oak doors. Cheshire grins. They were dressed in morning coats and silk dresses. Princes and princesses. They shook hands with everyone, welcoming them. She looked at them with big eyes. You could see at a distance that they were the ones who belonged here, that they were the ones who had always been on their way here. One was more tan than the other, they had white teeth, and thick hair with sun-bleached strands. She shook their hands lightly and let go almost immediately. She wanted them to understand that she knew that it was their system; she knew that she had no place in it. She kept her eyes trained on the carpet, didn't want them to be able to look in past her liquorice pastilles. Unconsciously she pulled a scab off, and routinely absorbed the dripping blood with her black shirt. She wanted to turn around and run down to the subway's underworld, kick off the high heels in the tunnels, crawl into the smallest little cave, and pull her knees to her chest, rocking back and forth. She wanted to disappear; she was almost gone. But Evelina grabbed her before she could slip through the cracks in the stone floor. She led the way and pulled the Girl toward the lecture hall.

An invisible star doesn't shine.

ORIENTATION

A man in a dark suit and sunglasses was standing at the front of the lecture hall. If you looked very carefully you could see that he wasn't more than a boy, a few years older than her. But she didn't look carefully, she just looked up, took her first impression at face value.

He was holding a staff in his hand, the man there at the front, a golden cane a head taller than he was. It was dead silent in all of the 300 seats in front of him. The entire crowd of people was staring at him expectantly. He lifted the staff and struck it against the wooden floor. It echoed even though the hall was full.

'Stand for the president of the student association!'

The crowd got up from the soft seats in the lecture hall. She remained sitting. She was sitting, staring up at the chandeliers, then straight into the red drapes. She drew in the smell of the polished wooden floors, read the small gold plates on the chairs in front of her. They bore the names of ministers and directors. She didn't know any of them.

Evelina pinched her arm.

'Stand up!'

She hurried to stand up. She stood up for the Elite School.

The doors to the lecture hall opened and they walked in in a line, the young men and women wearing morning coats and silk dresses, the ones who had greeted them on the steps. It was a stately row. A broad-shouldered young man was walking at the front. He was the tallest of them all, had shaken hands with the firmest handshake. He positioned himself behind the lectern at the very front. The rest stood behind him, with their backs straight.

A long silence followed. The Girl glanced at Evelina, she was looking straight ahead.

The staff struck the floor.

'Sit down!' It was the young man with the sunglasses again. The people sat down. She continued reading the names on the gold plates. The president cleared his throat.

'Starting today you are nothing!'

She looked up. Was he talking to her?

'You are used to being the best, the smartest and the most good-looking, but here you are nothing.'

No, he wasn't talking to her.

'Look around you. Everyone else is better. Everyone else is smarter. Everyone else is better looking.'

She looked around. Everyone else was looking around.

'You don't exist until you have earned it.'

The Girl nodded and glanced at Evelina—she looked displeased.

'There is a hierarchy here at the Elite School. We, the members of the student association, are at the top.'

He pointed at the morning coats and the silk dresses behind him.

'You are grovelling at the very bottom.'

Dramatic pause.

'You all want to be like us.'

Dramatic pause.

'Few of you will succeed.'

She sat with her back straight. There was a system. She hadn't expected anything else.

'Look around again. Look at the person to the right, the person to the left.'

She peered at Evelina, then at the young man sitting to her left. He had golden hair hanging in soft strands over the bluest eyes. He was dressed in a white, loose-fitting button-down shirt. Jonathan. He grinned at her dreamy look and she quickly faced forward again.

'You are each other's future. The people sitting next to you will determine what kind of job you get, what kind of parties you are invited to, what kind of holidays you will take. You are nothing without each other.'

The Girl glanced at Evelina again. She already seemed to know what he was talking about, that broad-shouldered president up there.

'So don't lock yourselves up with your books, don't go home early to study, don't think your marks will determine your future. Never say no to a party, help when someone asks for it; introduce yourselves to everyone. Network! The people are the ones who make the Elite School. The person who doesn't have a network doesn't exist.'

Dramatic pause.

'You are nothing without each other.'

She slid down in her chair. *People.* The ones who don't know what they're seeing. *People.* She might as well disappear.

*

The staff hit the floor and the crowd of people stood up immediately for the president, who was now leaving the room in his shiny shoes. The staff struck the floor one more time and the crowd of people sat down. She tensed her calf muscles, and struck her heels against the floor out of habit, grimaced when the muscles cramped. Jonathan in the chair next to her turned around and looked at her. He sneered again. Liquorice pastilles versus ice-blue eyes. Jonathan seemed to find the staff and the president's words amusing. He was amused by the fact that people actually stood up, that someone actually took all this seriously. That someone actually needed this in order to move up in the system. She looked at Jonathan and wondered if he had ever been on his way. He looked like he had always been at his destination.

Now a girl with blonde corkscrew curls stepped up to the lectern. She was wearing a blazer and button-down shirt that was buttoned all the way up to her neck, despite the fact that the August sun was blazing outside the high windows.

'My name is Isabella. I'm responsible for your orientation. I'm going to read out a group number and then call out the names of the people who belong to that group. Stand up when you hear your name called and remain standing until everyone in your group has been called. Look around carefully and remember who is standing up at the same time as you so that you can find each other later. The people who stand up at the same time as you will become your first friends here at the Elite School, and you will continue being friends for the rest of your lives.'

Pause.

'That is how it works.'

Isabella articulated every word loudly and clearly. She didn't stop to catch her breath. Sometimes she gesticulated in a determined way, otherwise she allowed her arms to rest on the lectern. Isabella was prepared, that was clear. Isabella knew the Elite School like the back of her hand. Now she was speaking loudly and clearly in order pass the Elite School on to them.

Her name was the first to be called out. Isabella pronounced it perfectly, with the same intonation Papa would have used. Still she hesitated a moment. To stand up alone in front of all those people, in front of their stares. *People, they see wrong.* Evelina pinched her thigh and she shot up on her heels, aimed Cheshire grin at everyone and no one. Her gaze was focused on the chandeliers. She was relieved when Evelina's name was called, nervous when even Jonathan stood up. Maryam, who had black hair and was ever so clearly Iranian. Sophia. Greta. Bengtsson and Gyllenstråle. Princes, princesses and trolls.

*

At the end of the day her new group gathered on the stairs. Together they were waiting for further instructions, holding their breath as the system's grid was slowly lowered over them. None of them reacted individually to anything as discrete as a particle any longer. Some of them waited until the group had chosen a course and then allowed themselves to be carried along. Others made the decisions, but only when they were sure the rest would follow them. Five hours had passed and they had already become a group—a group that moved in one harmonic wave-like movement.

Sophia was the one in charge; even the most untrained eyes could see this. Sophia didn't need any instructions; she had understood the rules early on. Sophia had highlights in her blonde hair and only a small touch of lip gloss on her lips. She wore white loafers with gold clasps and had a large brown bag covered with small *LV*'s hanging so naturally over her shoulder it looked like it was part of her anatomy.

'Do you know each other? You look like old friends.' Sophia pointed at her and Maryam.

Maryam, the Iranian girl, had been quick about sneaking in and pushing Evelina away. The Girl had tried backing away. Having Maryam so close by seemed to fill in the contours of the troll in a blacker colour, making them impossible to ignore. A lump of different. She tried backing away, but Maryam stubbornly remained at a distance of twelve inches, stood there with her enormous eyes wide-open. Every time the Girl backed away, Maryam followed after. Maryam's deer-like eyes made it clear how terrified she was, how intensely she longed to be somewhere else. It was clear Maryam had no idea what she was doing at the Elite School, that she knew she didn't belong here. The Girl wanted to lift her arms and push Maryam away, shove Maryam out of her field of vision. The Girl wanted to avoid seeing her reflection in Maryam's eyes.

Greta nodded affirmatively at Sophia's question.

'Yes, that's what I thought.'

Greta was trying to slip in close to Sophia the same way Maryam had done to her. As if Greta was trying to fill in her contours, become the same thing as Sophia and turn herself into someone who was impossible to ignore. Greta, with a small button nose and enormous sunglasses in her hair. Greta looked like a princess but was acting like a troll.

'No,' she replied. 'We don't know each other. But I know Evelina.' Evelina looked up from the other side of the crowd and smiled. Sophia and Greta looked at Evelina, then at each other. Finally they looked at her again. Stared. Nodded.

Now Philip was calling from the sidewalk. Philip was their sponsor, responsible for all future instructions. He straightened out his blue-and-white striped shirt over his light-coloured chinos and lifted a tray of shot glasses from the edge of the stairs. He sent them around the group, and every hand picked up its own plastic mug. They were sticky, pink plastic mugs: sugar and alcohol. She hoped Evelina would pass, but she downed it in one go. The tray was coming closer and closer. Sugar and alcohol. Alcohol in the middle of the day, calories she couldn't count. It wouldn't work, not for her. She was in control. She was the numbers. The tray reached her hand, she passed it on. The group reacted immediately, circled around her. Their attention was focused on only one thing. She didn't need to look over her shoulder to know that Maryam was standing right behind her, that even Maryam had turned down the drink.

'You don't drink?'

'No,' Maryam shook her head.

'Oh, is it because of religion?'

'Yes.' Maryam nodded. 'It is Islam.'

Religion, what religion? She avoided the insidious looks to glare at Maryam, to back away from Maryam, to get as far away from Maryam as the group would allow. But Maryam seemed to have become stuck in a magnetic field. Maryam came toward her even though the Girl tried to push her away. She saw in Maryam's eyes that she understood, that Maryam had taken note of the distance she was trying to put between them, but couldn't do anything about it. It was like a necessary involuntary movement.

*

When the conversation turned to the evening's hazing ritual the Girl cocked her ears. She would take part in everything. She would be hazed like nobody's business, be reborn, be scoured, be baptized. Damned if she wouldn't participate!

'Theme is *Pimps and Bitches*!' Philip explained and the group laughed. 'We're doing hip-hop: the girls will wear tight clothes and platform shoes.'

'God, who has platform shoes in their closet?' Sophia jumped in.

Platform shoes. Her voice was stirred to life.

'I do! How many are we? Eight girls. I have enough for all of us!'

The group roared. Sophia looked her in the eyes for the first time.

'Okay. Okay, cool. You sort the shoes.'

Instructions—the Girl accepted them gratefully. She

stood quietly during the rest of the conversation, listened carefully to the words in her head: *You don't want to sit on the bench the rest of your life.* This has to work. *You're too good to be a reserve player.* It would work! *Be a striker and score.* It was like an offensive strike in handball in slow motion. She saw the gap in the defence, saw the ball coming at her out of the corner of her eye, didn't know which steps would bring her eye to eye with the hopeless goalkeeper, or which corner the ball would be in, but she knew she had it in her to score. That all of the hours of training had prepared her for exactly this, even if she didn't know how.

*

She sat down on the red bus, headed back to Factory Town. She found Mama at the kitchen table, but she didn't know what to say, didn't know what Mama would understand. So she sat down across from Mama and made a big deal about taking a small piece of the ham quiche that was on the table. She broke off the crumbs with her fork and ate extra slowly, so that Mama would get a clear picture of her daughter eating. She offered this to Mama as compensation for not saving lives, or living Mama's dreams. She wondered if she should take the candy bar that Mama was holding out to her, as an apology for two having become one, for them having fallen apart, for her not having been enough to keep them together. But no. The butter in the quiche cut against the accumulated, corrosive stomach acid. The quiche came back up her throat and gathered in a sour pool in her mouth. She clamped her lips together and got up carefully. She walked to the bathroom on steady legs, turned on the tap and threw up the diligently chewed pieces of ham and rancid butter. She ran the tap, rinsed her mouth and then went back. She met Mama's questioning eyes with a steady look. Then she took a big gulp of tea and smiled wide—really wide.

'There's a party tonight. Initiation.'

Mama went from curious to surprised.

'Are you going?'

'Yes! Of course I'm going. It's important … to be part of the group.'

Mama got up and poured yet another cup of tea from the pot that was standing on the stove. She wanted to say something supportive, but was worried it wouldn't come out right. It seemed like something happened to Mama's words, with Mama's intentions, as her words travelled through the air toward the Girl's ears. So Mama didn't say very much anymore, said less and less.

'Have fun!' Mama smiled. Their eyes met for a moment and then they both looked away, each in their own direction.

*

She sat down on the red bus again heading into the city, wearing short tight shorts and large golden hoops in her ears. She had the highest platform shoes on her feet and the rest in a big bag over her shoulder, relics from *Blatte*-land. The reddest lips in the greatest expectation: excited girl on her first day of school.

The massive doors to the school were standing wide open, as if waiting to embrace the new groups of students who were swaying in the August sun. Fifteen open-bed trucks were waiting. Thundering music made the street vibrate, cans were being opened. Someone placed a can of cider in her hand. It was Sophia. Sophia emptied her can in ten large gulps, then belched loudly all the way from her stomach. The Girl stared popeyed, looked around. No one reacted. She brought the can to her lips while she handed out the shoes. The first sip burnt as it came in contact with her stomach acid, the rest flowed right through, filling up her hollow stomach. Someone lifted her onto the back of the truck, and yet another can was placed in her hand. The thundering truck began its journey through downtown Stockholm. The group rocked back and forth. Now and then someone stuck their head up, drowned out the music with a shout, then sat down again quickly, rejoining the rhythm.

The group drank ouzo and ate tzatziki in Vasa Park. Allowed a live goldfish to pass from mouth to mouth at Karla Square. They ate dog food and made out on command in Tessin Park. Her cider cans ran out before the sunlight turned to night. She ran across Stureplan, a popular meeting spot in the posh part of town, with a vodka bottle in her hand singing, *Rollin' down the street, smokin' indo, sippin' on gin and juice,* fell together in a laughing heap of bodies there. There were no ridiculing looks, only heels sticking up in the air, supported by sixteen unfamiliar legs that had already become a part of her, no, she had become a part of them—hadn't she always been? *Laid back (with my mind on my money and my money on my mind).*

*

As dawn approached she stumbled to the Metro Station, her eyes were fuzzy and her breath smelt strongly of dog food and other people's mouths. She sang for herself, completely new rhythms: *Rollin' down the street, smokin' indo, sippin' on gin and juice.* But then she tripped over her platform shoes, stopped. Alberto was standing next to the red bus. Alberto. She hadn't seen Alberto since that night on Ebba and Klara's veranda when he had been lying on his back and had his robber's mask pulled off.

On any other day she would have turned around, hidden behind the corner shop and taken the next bus. But no. *Rollin' down the street.* She walked straight toward him, swaying her hips unconsciously and sucking in her stomach under the tight top. He didn't recognize her at first, inspected her carefully from head to toe. She pouted her lips, expected shit, expected a bat, at least expected that he would turn away, not see her. But something else appeared in his eyes, something familiar, welcoming. Something that said, *Hey it's you, we're one of them, the two of us, one of us, Nelson's Hill, class 9A, do you remember?* She didn't know how to answer the look he was giving her, didn't know what he was seeing. The Girl wondered if he had really recognized her. Then it hit her: the hierarchy and the system had been knocked over and put right, so much had washed under the bridges that the water had been washed away. It was the princess who was standing in front of him, not her. The troll had disappeared with the first can of cider.

She had been reborn.

Lecture. It was happening now, it had started. She thought of Papa sitting at home at the kitchen table. It would be worth it soon, everything would be worth it soon. She was sitting in the carousel, searching for the stirrup. She wouldn't fall off, definitely wouldn't fall off.

She was sitting at the very front of the lecture hall. They were sitting next to her in a row: Evelina, Sophia, Greta, Jonathan. The whole group she had been assigned and now belonged to, the ones that the Elite School claimed would become her lifelong friends. She wasn't counting on that, not at all. Mainly she just watched and waited, allowed the Elite School's system to unfold. She peered at the seats at the end of the rows. Maryam had been sitting there during the first lectures, but she wasn't there today. She turned her head, looked discreetly along the remaining rows.

The lecture hall had quickly become a model for the system's grid, the system in a very physical form. On the right were those who saw the Elite School as being just as self-evident as the Alps and sailing in the summer. People who already knew each other from holidays and boarding schools. People who already had more networks than they could use during their lifetimes, who would be invited by the right people to the right places. They knew the people who would determine their future, and they didn't want to sully their group with anything from the outside. Maryam wouldn't be sitting on the right side.

The Girl didn't look for Maryam on the left. Only the boys, the interpreters, sat on the left. They had climbed up the military ladder, passing all the mere mortals, and been accepted to the military's elite education and excelled there. They had already defined elite, a very brilliant kind of elite. They had no interest in parties, in helping or in other people. They spent their time trying to get the highest marks from both universities. They didn't think they needed instructions. They were already everything they needed to be.

Sitting behind the interpreters were the save-the-world people. They had beards and wore knee-length skirts, no button-down shirts or designer bags. They asked questions that weren't related to the exam, would philosophize over what was right and what was wrong, and didn't accept given answers as true. They came to the parties, but stood against the wall, looking like they were discussing something they had read in a journal about international relations but in reality they were just standing there watching. Maryam wasn't there.

There was a large group of girls sitting in the centre rows. These were girls in pastel-coloured sweaters and wore headbands in their hair. Girls who got out their glasses and sat ready with their notebooks fifteen minutes before the lectures started. Girls who drank coffee with skimmed milk and carried around those hard, sour green apples in their bags, and chewed the apples down to the core. They were really good girls, the ones sitting in the centre of the centre rows. They wrote down all the instructions and learnt them by heart, but lacked the ability to apply them in real life. Or they never had time to put all of the knowledge they gained into practice. She searched carefully for Maryam among the good girls. Maryam could definitely have a place there. But no. Blonde and pale, mouse-coloured and light brown.

No black hair in the centre of the centre row.

She looked at the very back, at the group who always came late and stood leaning against the wall with their jackets on. Maryam wasn't there. Then she looked up. Maryam was sitting up in the gallery that was often empty. Maryam and a guy who was sleeping with his hood pulled over his eyes.

You don't want to sit on the bench your entire life, you know. You want to be a striker and score goals!

A system had been lowered down over them and Maryam was in the process of disappearing.

*

The professor was a short man with thick hair, who wore a tweed blazer and a bow tie. It was almost like the professor had been taken from a book. He was so small under the lecture hall's chandeliers, but he still filled her entire consciousness.

The professor cleared his throat in the microphone, then looked out through the high windows and decided that marketing theory could wait, that more important things needed to be taught.

'You're the ones who will run Sweden,' he proclaimed. 'You're going to run the finance market, you're going to run the big companies.'

You could hear a pin drop.

'You're sitting there dreaming about being one of the few who gets their first job at the Firm. That's all you want! You're prepared to work a hundred hours a week. You're dreaming about a bonus that is three times your annual salary. You're counting on having more money than you'll have time to spend.'

He looked from left to right, from the row at the front to the gallery at the back where Maryam was sitting.

'Maybe you don't know it yet, but that's what you want. That's how it will turn out.'

The professor took long, slow steps toward the overhead projector. He hesitated a moment before picking up the first slide.

'And how do you get everything you want, when you want to be the best, but everyone else is better?'

It was so still you could hear a pin drop. Eager pens were poised over waiting notebooks.

'You work harder! That's what you do. You work harder. When you think you're done with a task, you've only just begun. When you think you know what you need to do, you've missed half of it. You need to stand on point all the time. That's how it works. You need to start off at a sprint and never slow down! This may be a marathon,' the professor grew quiet, paused. 'But you start off at a sprint, run at a sprint and never slow down.'

The professor's words made her stomach growl. The system was sinking down over them, and it had a voice. The system was speaking clearly; it said that nothing was predetermined. *Late nights at the office, blazer and leather briefcase. The dream about Ally.* The system said that if you work hard you can earn a place. The system said that you could work your way to a position.

Her sponsor Philip grabbed hold of her as she was leaving the library late one afternoon. She had her book bag in a firm grasp and the bus card in her pocket.

'Hey! How are things going? Is everything okay? You aren't going home now are you? There's a business presentation, you can't miss that. Come on, we'll go together.' He took hold of her bag. 'If nothing else there's a free dinner! Free is good, you know.' He winked and led the way to the lecture hall. The companies had started coming to the Elite School from day one; the Elite School students were in demand. The companies introduced themselves, and treated the students to dinner and wine. The nicer the dinner and the wine the better the company, that was the rule. The Firm had distinguished itself immediately, treating them to a boat ride and shellfish, champagne and a three-course meal with a table setting. It was clear that the Firm only took the best of the best; that it was the Firm everyone wanted to work for. The Firm defined the elite.

The Girl had listened to the talk about the company presentations and had registered the information, but had never actually gone. It hadn't struck her that she could be someone the companies were looking for, that she could be in demand. She thought that she had to work hard first, that she wasn't welcome until she had worked hard.

Philip was holding her arm firmly now, pulling her behind him. She thought about the evening's study schedule, about the package of cottage cheese in her bag and that she didn't have time. But Philip's words drowned out her own thoughts. The system was speaking clearly and it was her job to listen, and figure out what it wanted her to do.

'I always go to the presentations.' Philip pushed through the crowd of people, filled a plate from the buffet and handed it to her. 'The food's good. You hang out, network. And then you learn what you need to do to get the best jobs.'

She accepted the food and quickly emptied the plate into a rubbish bin while Philip was saying hello to a passers-by. Princes and princesses. Princes and princesses and a troll. She stepped off to the side and listened carefully to the word choice, tone and stress of the speech in the room. She then automatically imitated it and whispered to herself, practised the sounds of the world around her.

'Your CV is the most important thing, you know. It's a whole damn science, how you're supposed to write a CV.' Philip had turned to face her again. He was chewing with his mouth half-open, wiped Dijon mustard away from the corner of his mouth with the back of his hand. 'It's about several different things: how much you do, what you do, and how you describe what you've done. You have to exaggerate; everyone exaggerates! If you don't exaggerate you'll disappear in the crowd.'

She absorbed the instructions: *Don't be invisible. Be impossible to ignore.*

'Your CV says who you are and what you'll become.' Philip moved in the direction of the buffet table again and she followed. 'You haven't studied finance yet, but you could say that your CV indicates the current value of your future. Get it? Your CV today says what you'll be worth in ten years. If you're going to be worth a lot in ten years, you're also worth a lot today. Or the other way around ... If you're worth a lot today, you'll be worth a lot in ten years ... Yeah, you get it.'

She understood. The CV was the essence of the system, the system was working toward the CV.

'And people like to keep an eye on each other's CVs. Everyone knows who is best, who is going to do well.' He held out a glass of wine to her but took it back when he saw the expression on her face. 'So your CV affects the way people look at you.' He waved his hand at the half-filled room. 'It determines who people think you are.'

She nodded. The CV was the platform. She would become her CV.

'It works out, you know, whether you want it to or not. It's the same process every year. It starts with a group of new students. They apply to the Elite School for different reasons; they want different things; they have different styles. I was a skater before. From Hägersten.' Philip grinned and pulled his fingers through his slicked-back hair.

'Just give it two months and everybody looks the same. Give it two years, and everybody wants the same job. Give it three years, and everyone will be acting the same way. After a few internships everyone will have the same body language.' He pointed at her stilettos. 'You won't be showing up here in those shoes a year from now. You just won't.'

She rocked on her heels while Philip swept invisible crumbs from his shirt, straightened out his shirt under his belt.

'Survival of the fittest, you know. You listen and adapt. It happens on its own. Quite simple really.'

She absorbed, registered. Listen and adapt. Copy and paste. Quite simple really.

The Girl notices the transformation in the window of the red bus. That is where she sees that the golden hoops from *Blatte*-land have been replaced with small white pearls. That is where she sees that her hair has been cut in a bob and re-laxed. Her hair hangs softly and perfectly straight. Straight, soft and flat hair that barely touches her shoulders. She sees flat-soled shoes, a cheaper version of Sophia's loafers, white with gold clips. She sees a baby-pink cardigan, a bag with the Gucci logo hanging over her shoulder, purchased on a side street. Her bag almost looks real, and people seem to think it's real. She's afraid that someone will notice that it's fake, that nothing on her is real, that all of her is fake.

She knows that she has a place next to Evelina, between Sophia and Greta. She knows that some of their princess-shimmer splashes over her, and keeps people from laughing, from hitting. Makes her exist. She wonders what would hap-pen if they disappeared, wonders if they wished she would disappear in the same way she wished Maryam would.

The Girl wonders if she imagined that it was possible to create a place in this system, their system. Wonders if she has made a mistake, if what she had interpreted as instruc-tions really were signs indicating private property. If all the Elite School has tried to tell her is that the ones who aren't already living by the rules don't need to bother. She won-ders if they are laughing behind her back, or if they even see her. Maybe she's simply invisible. Maybe she'll never be anything other than invisible, never really exist.

*

The more she sanded and sawed at her edges, the hazier Maryam became. The hopeful terrified deer-like eyes searched hers when they passed each other on the stairs. The Girl didn't see them. Maryam made unanswered night-time phone calls and left messages on the answering machine which she didn't hear. Maryam sat down in the seat next to hers in the library and opened her books with a bang without the Girl having pulled her earplugs out of her ears. Maryam followed her like a phantom, a presence that didn't exist.

Maryam finally stepped into her consciousness, tapped her on the shoulder while she was standing at the dairy section in the grocery store, picking out a package of cottage cheese. At first it was a light tap against the cotton fabric, easy to ignore. Then three taps with a fist.

'Hi.' Maryam's voice light, like an unripe peach. 'Do you have a second?'

Maryam didn't wait for an answer.

'Do you want to eat lunch with me today? I need to talk to someone, someone who understands.'

Maryam swallowed the last syllables. Maybe Maryam suspected that the Girl didn't understand, even though she looked like she should. Or even worse: that she did understand, but didn't want to.

She nodded in reply and led the way. She didn't want to be seen with Maryam, didn't want to be a part of what Maryam was. She wanted to erase the contours of the troll, not accentuate them.

They walked down the street, Maryam and her, their black tresses dancing in the autumn wind. Every lock was like a small dragon wishing to break free, fly away. The Girl stared at her feet, moving forward forward on the city concrete. She didn't look up even though she saw Maryam's tears shining out of the corner of her eye.

They reached the water's edge at the pier and sat down. Two small trolls: one with a package of cottage cheese pressed tightly against her concave stomach, the other holding a sandwich with the tips of her fingers, ready to drop it at the first call of a seagull.

'I don't want to complain or sound ungrateful, but I feel so isolated. And I just don't know what to do about it. I can't even really explain why I feel that way.'

Maryam's words hung in the air.

'It's not like anyone is being mean. No one says anything.'

The Girl followed the patterns of the calm waves with fascination, wondered what time it was, if it was almost time to go back. Then Maryam started talking again.

'Maybe that's what it is.' Maryam tapped her shoulder again. 'Do you understand? No one talks to me.'

The Girl bent down over her white shoes and rubbed at an invisible spot. She knew that she had become one of those who didn't talk to everyone. Someone who didn't talk to certain people, didn't talk to Maryam. One of those who was more interested in how their own contours reacted to the surroundings than anything else. Mostly she was interested in seamlessly blending in, becoming impossible to ignore.

'It's like I don't exist. I barely feel like I'm here, no wonder no else does. Do you understand what I mean?' That is when Maryam grew quiet, and looked at her. She looked at the Girl's fake bag and her beige painted nails. Looked at her buttoned shirt collar. The Girl was occupied with her package of cottage cheese: fishing up every lump, piece by piece, balancing with a small plastic spoon, trying to distinguish taste in tastelessness.

'Do you get it? Do you understand what I mean?'

What should she say to Maryam? That she understood? That Maryam wasn't alone? That not existing was completely normal, and that she felt the same way? Would that make Maryam feel better? Or should she say that it didn't need to be like that, and that reality has many sides, and that they only needed to take a few steps to the right, look at it from a different angle. The future has no head and no tail. You can twist and turn it at your every wish. A Rubik's cube with a thousand solutions.

'No.' She filled her mouth with two quick spoons of cottage cheese clumps. 'I don't.'

*

Maryam quit about a month later, disappeared from the Elite School. The Girl never found out where Maryam had gone. She made it a point not to know.

TO DREAM ANEW

She listens and adapts, copies and pastes, but she still ends up on the red bus. She studies her reflection in the dusty windows of the red bus every morning. That is where she asks herself if the reflection really is hers, and if she'll be allowed to keep it. Every afternoon on the way back to Factory Town she asks herself if the reflection has anything

to do with her. If you can really turn yourself into someone else, especially if you're constantly travelling back and
forth, constantly travelling back.

*

She took the red bus home on Friday nights and routinely
stepped over Björn, a father-of-two, who lay in the doorway. She made sure not to slip in his puke with her heel.
Björn was thrown out by his girlfriend, Pia, every weekend, and then he would lie in the stairwell like a guard dog
out of action. He was usually still lying in the same spot the
next morning when she steered away from Factory Town
again with her book bag over her shoulder. Sometimes
he had moved a few yards to the space under the stairs.
His subconscious knew that he could sober up in the cool
shadows, be shielded from the looks of passers-by, looks
that sprayed the contempt he didn't think he deserved.

She sat with her books on Sunday afternoons, learning
about the relationship between capitalized value and future yields when the chairs started flying past the kitchen
window. Tommie had woken up. Tommie, the ex-skinhead
who lived in the flat above. Ex largely because he didn't
have the presence of mind to shave his head these days, or
because he had stepped in so much mud that the white laces of his boots were the colour of shit, or because he was so
messed up in his head that his white power buddies didn't
want to put up with him anymore. Tommie often mixed
alcohol with some cheap mushroom, and it seemed like the
only way to get it out of his body was by throwing furniture
and knick-knacks at the rose hip bushes. He drank alcohol

and ate mushrooms until there wasn't anything left in his flat except a striped one-person mattress.

At one point in time Tommie had been so big and cool. He had thundered through the city centre at the head of the motorbike crew, and pounded her on the back after a handball match saying, 'Hey, good job. You were great. Not like the other sand niggers.'

He had lost a lot, Tommie. Sometimes she thought she would get it back for him. That she would lace his boots with brand new laces from the shop around the corner and shave off the sparse strands of hair with her Gillette razor. In a disguised voice, she would call and invite his soldiers to a party, set out some bowls with chips, and bring home so much alcohol that it would be impossible for him to down everything before the army stormed the flat. Platform. Everyone needs a platform.

*

One Monday night her mother called her name. Pia was screaming and Mama had called the Girl's name. Mama's shouting. She looked up from the pages of her book and stared straight ahead for a moment before getting up hastily. Mama didn't call out her name very often any more. Mama's shouting was so associated with the monster, her own name so associated with rescue, with rushing to defend.

Whereas Pia's voice could often be heard in the flat under theirs. It tended to start around this time, dinner time. It always started with the rising volume of a man's muffled voice. The sound was enough to make her and Mama choke on their food, make each of them sit in a room and lose themselves in shared memories.

'Should I call?' The Girl hurried into the kitchen with the cordless phone in her hand, 911 on speed dial.

Mama was sitting at the kitchen table with her hands in her lap, her grey T-shirt damp with drops from her newly washed hair, her face scrubbed clean.

'No, no, forget about it. Let's forget about them. Just come here and sit down. I have something important to say.'

The Girl obeyed. Mama didn't give her orders very often. Mama often didn't have anything to say, they both valued the silence too much to disturb it with words.

'I've saved enough now, enough for a flat.'

The Girl wrinkled her brow.

'Saved enough of what?'

'Saved enough money, *pas chi*?' What else. 'I'm going to buy a flat, far away from here. A flat in the city, on Öster-malm, a well-off area of town.'

Flutters in her chestcloud.

'Are you going to move?'

Mama was going to disappear; she was going to disappear even more. The Girl looks down at the tabletop, hears her nails tapping against each other. She pulls down her shirt sleeve, glances up to make sure Mama hasn't noticed the fresh sores.

Mama was busy with the files on the table, with the calculator and the letters from the bank. She hadn't seen anything.

'No, I'm going to buy a flat for you. You're going to get away from here.'

Mama looked up now, looked at her with a completely

new lustre in her tired eyes. The red lips were pouting un-consciously, and her face bore no make-up. Mama looked like a little girl, a blank slate. She pulled Mama's files to-ward her, went through the carefully calculated sums, the total amount of savings on the last row.

Plan, dreams, hard work.

'*Maman!* This is a hell of a lot of money. Where did you get so much money from? Do you have this much money?'

Mama nodded. She was as satisfied as a cat curled up on the windowsill.

'Yes. Even though he took all of my gold.'

*

Mama worked. Mama had worked since the move and the monster's retreat. Mama worked. Their cocoon hadn't lasted for very long, the Girl hadn't been enough. Mama had needed more in order to forget, more in order to feel protected. Mama had needed more than her to make it all worth it. To make it so that everything from the failed rev-olution up to the monster's clenched fists would be worth it.

Mama had left her in the flat and driven to shift after shift in the small red Honda. Mama had avoided coming home, didn't want to meet her own gaze in the bathroom mirror. Mama didn't want to see her own reflection in the Girl's liquorice pastilles that so openly displayed every-thing that had happened, the system that had ruled. She didn't want to have anything to do with what had been. Mama was looking to create something else.

Mama had closed her eyes tightly and found a new

dream. Mama had started dreaming about self-sufficiency instead, about becoming worth more than anyone had expected. Mama sat with her calculator during the coffee breaks, checked her current account, sometimes several times a day. She saw herself becoming something else.

Numbers don't lie. Numbers say everything.

Of course Mama had furnished that first one-bedroom flat quickly, traded in the Honda for a new car every other year, discovered that the smell of a new car was the best there was. Of course they had moved quite soon and each of them having their own bedroom was worth Björn's public naps, Tommie's bad trips and the echo of the fists against Pia's body. Of course they had taken a charter and drunk Sangria and she had gotten to hear about how Mama had once run faster than the fascists. How Mama had been able to lie her way out of a prison cell, dressed in a black beret with a red star on it.

She had certainly understood from all of Mama's stories that she was a lioness, that there was nothing Mama couldn't do. But she had never counted on life in Factory Town leading somewhere else, never dared believe that life in Factory Town could generate anything more than a repetition of itself.

*

'I want to buy a flat on Östermalm,' Mama said, and the Girl stuck her feet in flat-soled shoes and ran an open house marathon. She travelled at lightning speed, crisscrossing through the crowd of people, inexhaustible. She didn't know anything about city streets or plumbing maintenance, didn't care about balconies or tiled stoves. It just had to happen quickly, quicker than quick. She was going to leave, get as far away from Factory Town as possible.

Mama doubled her double-shift and they met next to the hotdog stand in the slot between evening and night in order to look at pictures and plan the bidding process. Mama was excited about everything being proven soon, she was like a diabetic child on the loose in Charlie's chocolate factory.

It didn't take long for them to sign a contract. They bought a flat with more ceiling height and air than any flat they had ever shared. A flat with large, curtainless windows and completely quiet neighbours, neighbours so quiet they both reacted to the silence more intensely than they tended to react to Pia's screams when the hitting began.

Mama dropped her off at the new front door. The Girl's luggage had fit in the trunk: a mattress and a few blankets, two suitcases filled with clothes and books, apples and packages of cottage cheese.

'We'll take care of the rest later, furniture and things. You'll be fine.'

Mama hurried out, she was late to the next shift. Mama turned around in the door and looked at the Girl standing there, holding onto the handle of the door to the new flat not knowing if she should go in or run away. *She looks like a child*, Mama thought and she was close to saying so, but then was struck by the next thought: *She's a woman.*

'You'll be fine! The most important thing is that you're here, not there.'

The entrance door closed and she slammed the front door with the same force. Echo. She collapsed in the bay window to the sound of Mama's car driving away on the otherwise quiet street. She was gone.

The most important thing is you're here, not there.

The Girl sat in the window and listened to the sound of the silence that was taking Mama's place out there on the quiet street. The snow struck the window pane, small flakes against newly washed glass. From the inside she traced the outline of the stars with her finger. She suddenly remembered the very first window, the one at the asylum centre, where she used to lie stretched out in the window sill so many years ago. She remembered how endless the white had seemed to her then, from her spot, the place between Mama and Papa. It struck her that she had actually had a position then, her own space in a perfectly self-evident system. It struck her that she had been the one who had torn that system apart. She looked out over the new flat, over all of the untouched cubic feet of air that suddenly surrounded her and wondered if it could become a home, if any flat could replace the home that had been lost.

SUPPLEMENTARY COURSE

More than a year had passed since the Elite School had rolled out its red carpet and thrown open its doors. A year since she had stepped into the Elite School's system and discovered that it had a voice. Discovered that there was a manual for someone who wants everything but is nothing, and instructions for someone who has dreams in her head and hard work instead of blood in her veins.

More than a year had passed since she had found her

way to the Elite School and it was impossible to look at her and suspect that she was someone without a position. She had the highest exam scores and handed out suggestions for answers. She polished away at her CV and led projects, pulled all-nighters with the same endurance as the finance guys, walked home through the park with a polka-dotted scarf around her neck and large sunglasses in her hair. In Verbiers she sailed down slopes rated red with the group powdering around her, imagined that the ski-debut was a childhood dream even though it had happened five days earlier.

*

It was after a Wednesday night at Stureplan that Evelina looked her in the eye. They were sitting at the 7-Eleven and Evelina was looking at her like it was the first time they were sitting across from each other.

'The elections are coming up you know.'

The Girl wasn't listening. Her head was spinning from the tequila, and she was busy making a rough estimate. She needed to know how many calories she would need to skip tomorrow to compensate for the evening's alcohol, while at the same time she was trying to resist the freshly baked saffron buns Evelina had placed on the table. Instead she soaked up the drink with a package of cottage cheese.

'What election?'

'Elections for the student association. For student president. I think you should run for president.'

Pearl laughter straight out in the air. Spraying pearls. Her laughter was light like Mama's.

'Me? Are you kidding?' She was wide-eyed, starry eyed, not understanding.

'I can't think of a better candidate than you. You're the smartest person I know. I've never met anyone smarter.' Evelina reached over and dipped her saffron bun in the cottage cheese.

'You mean, me? Do you want to embarrass me completely? No one would vote for me.' She was wide-eyed, cross-eyed, a bit too intoxicated, almost furious. What kind of a crazy suggestion was that? Evelina had been there when the teacher from Saltsjöbaden had said the words: 'Not everyone fits in.' Evelina had to understand that. 'Don't you understand? I'm fucking wrong in every way!'

Evelina stared back just as angrily, didn't seem to understand at all. How could the Girl explain? Where did the story about princesses and trolls start? Where was the line between invisible and 'you can't ignore me'?

'That's crap, then you don't see what I see.' Evelina grabbed the roll that lay untouched in front of her, took a big bite.

People, they don't see clearly.

'You're a perfect candidate, don't you get that? You're perfect, perfect in more ways than anyone else in the school has ever been!' Evelina raised her eyebrows meaningfully. 'You know what I mean.'

People, they don't know what they're seeing.

The Girl bit her bottom lip, and tried to hold on to the thought, stop it from taking on life. She was interrupted by a hand on her shoulder. She looked up and saw a guy wearing an Alpha jacket. He was searching her face for a hidden clue to a big question.

'Excuse me, but I have to ask … Are you kidding around?'

She wasn't listening, she just stared at his silhouette: his hair heavy with wax, the Buffalo boots, and his head tilted back, as far back as it could go. There was a smell of *odd-kollon*. Kawa. Was it Kawa? She tried to focus. Would she recognize Kawa if she saw him? Was he out now, Kawa? She calculated quickly in her head, five years had passed. He couldn't have done something that would have gotten him more than five years.

'I've never heard a *blatte* talking Snob-Swedish. Shit, you've got to be joking.'

She saw Evelina grow tense on the chair across from her. She understood that she should reply, defend herself, but she only had one thought on her mind: she wanted him to be Kawa.

A blonde guy got up from the table next to theirs, stepped into the picture.

'Can't you see, she's no damn *blatte*.'

The blonde guy threw the last bite of his hotdog in the rubbish bin, pulled his hand through his greasy back slick and discreetly wiped his hands on his big down jacket while he looked at his reflection in the window. Then he turned toward them, sneered with greased lips.

'She's a bratty. Can't you see that?'

*

She tested Evelina's conviction at Papa's the next night.

'This thing with the Elite School.'

Papa looked up from the latest issue of the film magazine that was still being sent from Iran every month. He took off his reading glasses and sat up straight on the sofa, hands in his lap.

'Yes, tell me, *dokhtaram*. I'm listening.'

She met his honey look and held it, couldn't understand that it had once housed the monster. Papa. Papa, who now had white streaks in his black hair, and a bald spot where the locks used to be as wild as hers. Papa, who had squeezed his eyes shut in the mail van that had driven them to Factory Town, had squeezed his eyes shut and started dreaming for her instead. Papa, who had taught her how to work hard and driven his bus around and around trusting that she would do her best, make the most of the opportunities. Papa, who needed her to make everything worth it. Papa.

'Well, things are good, with my studies and everything.'

Papa nodded.

'Certainly. Of course things are going well, *baba jan*, everything goes well for you.'

It's not that easy, Papa. She swallowed the words.

'And it's going well with the rest too, I think. Everything related to it. It's hard to explain, but there's the work with the student association and there are the people.' *People.* 'And summer jobs, scholarships ...'

Papa nodded.

'Of course it's going well, *dokhtaram*.' He grew quiet and thought a bit. 'You know, I can't help you that much anymore. I don't know as much about that world as you do. You've taught yourself, you know best. Just don't get too comfortable. Think about the next step. It's easy to think you've done enough. Like: I'm done. But you're not there yet. You're never there, *dokhtaram*.'

The Girl saw the image of the strong, tall president in

front of her. She saw how he had stood at the very front of the lecture hall that first day at the Elite School: his back straight, gaze steady. He had stood there with his voice full of home advantage. The president dictated the system. He was the system. He was the elite.

She thought about Kawa's words. *People don't just give you respect, you have to take it; you have to force them to give it. Your platform has to force people to give you respect.* Kawa's last words. *Don't fail.*

'So, the elections are coming up, for the student association. I'm thinking about running for president.'

'President.' Papa tasted the words, nodded happily.

'But it really isn't something for me. I'm the wrong type for it.'

Handicap. Invisible handicap. There was a dark shadow in Papa's honey look.

'What do you mean "the wrong type"? You aren't the wrong type. You're not inferior to anyone.'

'No, *baba*, I don't mean there's something wrong with me. I just mean that those who are elected president are different in a way. Big guys. Swedish guys. They've completed the elite military training. They're parajumpers and Russian interpreters.'

'Parajumpers and Russian interpreters? You don't want to become James Bond, do you? What does that matter? You're the right person for it! You have what it takes; you have it in you. Run in the election, you'll win.'

Papa returned to his magazine. The discussion was over. For Papa it was a simple matter: you dream, then you work hard. It didn't matter that the revolution was a perfect example of the result being worth less than the sum of the ingredients. It didn't matter that one dream after another had gone to pieces.

Then you have to close your eyes and find a new dream, start working hard for that one instead. Those are the two most important things in life: dreaming and working hard.

She turned on the calculator again. There was nothing more to say. There was nothing more to do.

THE ROWING TEAM

The new flat hadn't become a home yet; she hadn't managed to fill all of that air. There was a double bed in one corner, a red sofa in another and a table with chairs. The wall of mirrors in the hall made the space feel even larger and simultaneously it made her chestcloud cringe for some reason she chose not to remember. She didn't understand what was missing. She sat in the window sometimes and looked out over the parquet floor, listened to the silence and stared at the front door. If only someone would put a key in the lock, but she wasn't expecting anyone. She wondered if a home would ever appear around her. She thought, maybe it was her fate to be homeless.

*

Sophia and Greta were now standing in front of that wall of mirrors. They had spread bags, shoes, and dry-cleaner bags over the floor. It was time for the annual dinner for the Elite School's rowing team. The hall was filled with perfume, powder clips, mascara brushes and hair dryers, pastel colours and push-up bras, smacking lips and fluttering eyelids. It reminded her of moments in Dearest Sister's room, the moments when they had tried to make princesses out of trolls but had gotten caught in some sort of world in-between. But Dearest Sister had disappeared a long time ago—or was she the one who had disappeared? She didn't know. They had become different, that was all she knew. They had grown apart, so far apart that the trunk they had shared couldn't unite them. Dearest Sister wouldn't have fit into her hall now. Her hall smelt of princess, sounded like princess, looked like princess. She saw her own shadow passing by in the wall of mirrors, noticed that she was standing between Sophia and Greta, in the middle of their mist. Saw that she contributed to the mist they were creating, that she was the same as them, or not that far off. She looked in the mirror again, but her shadow was gone.

'You have to start drinking too, I'm working on my third.' Evelina called from the sofa where she was sitting, surrounded by vodka bottles. The Girl put on the black pumps and walked over to Evelina, accepted a very full drink.

'I want to go to the dinner now.' Evelina's eyes and nose were becoming red, her words were slurred. There was no response from the others. Sophia and Greta were busy in front of the mirror. She observed Evelina over the straw: the nylon panties had become wrinkled in the black pumps, clumps of mascara threatened to fall toward her deep blue eyes, her blonde hair lay slack against her head.

She looked at Evelina's pumps again. Their black pumps were identical: the troll's and the princess's. She looked toward the hall; no one was listening to Evelina. She wrinkled her brow and emptied her glass in a few gulps. The

274

system had to be put right. She leaned over Evelina's feet and pulled up the stockings, heard her own voice rise, determined and slightly irritated.

'Guys, Evelina wants to go now.'

'What did you say?'

Sophia and Greta tripped over to her. They sank down in the sofa, then looked at her expecting an answer. The Girl stood there quietly, what were they looking at? She looked urgently in Evelina's direction but Evelina had kicked off her shoes and curled up in the corner of the sofa and closed her eyes. The princess was down for the count.

She heard her own voice rise.

'I want to go now. Let's finish our drinks and go.'

Sophia and Greta each gulped down a glass and then stood up. Sophia pointed at her own feet.

'Look, I've bought ones like you were wearing at the hazing. Not as high, but they're nice, right?'

She looked down at Sophia's feet. She was wearing black platform shoes, platform shoes in real leather, higher than the Girl's pumps. How had the relics from *Blatte*-land found their way here?

'They're really cool!' Her vocal chords indicated that she had been the one talking, but she recognized neither the words nor the tone.

She pulled a blanket over Evelina and then stepped out on to the sidewalk with Sophia and Greta on her heels. She peered at them carefully over her shoulder. When had they started following her lead, when had she become the one leading the way? Two princesses and she suddenly wasn't the extra anymore, hardly even an actress. Had she gotten behind the camera? Who had set out the director's chair?

*

The Elite School's dinners had become run of the mill at this point and she knew them by heart. You showed up at the aperitif, collected and with your hair combed back. Kissed the guys on the cheek and praised the girls' dresses. You waved a bit absentmindedly with your little finger and held the wine glass by the stem, conversed about exam results, about who had made out with whom, who had gotten which job. You nodded when someone sounded serious and giggled when someone started laughing, even if you hadn't been listening to the conversation. You searched for the next person, but thought about your next comment, and hoped for a good seat at the table.

When it was time to sit down to dinner the shoulders could relax, and the groups transformed back from middle-aged to wet behind the ears. First you toasted with the person on your left and then with the person on your right—or was it the other way around? At this point it didn't matter anymore anyway. When the appetizer was served the next stage in the metamorphosis came: no one was an individual any longer. Everyone was a particle in a larger mass that rhythmically swung back and forth in the room. No sound, one voice, all words became part of an impenetrable shout that disappeared out the window, bounced against the round crown of the City Library and strengthened, rushed back between the candle-lit chandeliers in another wave. It wasn't that difficult. The troll sat on her shoulder and smiled.

Just swing along, princess. Just swing along.

*

After dinner she and Sophia leaned out of the windows in the corridor, two dressed-up rowing girls with cigarettes hanging from the corners of their mouths. They were waving at Greta, who had mumbled something about throwing in the towel, giving up, caramel sauce with vanilla ice cream, then stumbled down to the taxi.

'I'm so horny.' Sophia tittered with her head bent over her mobile and her fingers racing across the keys. It peeped in response and Sophia stood up straight.

'I'm going now, kiss kiss, thanks for tonight!'

Sophia stumbled off and she was left standing alone. She flicked the cigarette butt toward the bushes below, then pulled down her skirt and straightened out her blouse. She wished she had had platform shoes on her feet after all, half-a-foot taller, a head more certain. She hesitated a moment, thought about running down the stairs and heading home, hiding behind Evelina who had passed out on her sofa. But the moment passed. *Don't fail.* She wasn't going to fail now.

Taking long strides in her pumps, she walked toward the Prince's Gallery where the rowing guys were sitting leaned back in leather chairs, each with a cognac in their hands, and thick cigars in the corners of their mouths. She stepped forward and stared determinedly at Philip, who was sitting in the centre armchair, until he stood up and offered her the chair.

'Are there any cigars left?' She was still looking at Philip.

'Eh, yes.'

The box was held out, and she drew in the smell of tobacco.

'Does anyone want to show me how it works?'

Philip held out his hand, cut off the top of the cigar, lit it and drew the first heavy smoke.

'What have you done with your girls?'

Nordlund. Nordlund was one of the ones who sat on the right side, one of those who had never said a single word to her. Nordlund straightened out his belt unconsciously, then turned his head discreetly to see if anyone had picked up on and appreciated his comment before he dared try a clucking laugh.

She crossed one leg over the other in a slow movement; she was wearing a short skirt. Nordlund lost his train of thought.

'I have a small piece of news I'd like to share with you.'

They were listening.

'I've decided to run in the elections. President.'

Her head was spinning from the alcohol and she was scratching hard at her scarred wrist to clear her head. She needed to be alert enough to absorb the reactions: eye movements, the slightest of hand movements, the clearing of throats, the sound of designer jeans against the leather surface. Had she crossed the line or was it just right? Who did she think she was, or a shrug of the shoulders? A suppressed laugh, or why not?

Jonathan was quick to get to his feet, gave her a kiss on each cheek.

'Shit that's awesome. You're cool, it's going to be so cool.'

She felt a shiver along her spine.

Nordlund cleared his throat and placed his hand on his belt again.

'Absurd! And what makes you think that…'

Jonathan interrupted him, but she knew the rest of Nordlund's sentence, it was inscribed on her wrist.

'We'll have lunch tomorrow and plan! I want to be the campaign manager.'

She nodded. The idea was living out in space now, the vodka had given it life. The cigar tasted like dry, smoking leaves, but she took a heavy drag to try and keep the troll inside. As if to assure herself that the troll wouldn't start leaking out through her pores.

WIN OR LOSE

Once the thought had been released, she had no choice but to chase it: it was a colourful kite and she was the girlchild holding on to the string. She ran after it, ran with it. She kept a watchful eye on the looks that followed her in the corridors, waited for the protests, the jeers. *Shit, Brillo troll, who the hell do you think you are? Don't forget that you don't have a place here. Don't forget that you actually don't exist.* It would come; it couldn't be so simple, could it? A well-oiled pendulum only has one path: back.

*

'You're going to win.' Jonathan looked her straight in the eye. 'Girl, immigrant—everything you think is bad, is actually in your favour.'

Her liquorice pastilles were ablaze.

'Okay, you've never said that you think it's bad. Hell,

279

you've never said anything indicating you're an immigrant. But I get that you see it as a handicap, I see it in your eyes.'

She clenched her fists.

'Take it easy, I'm trying to say something positive here. Everything you think is negative, is actually positive. It's in your favour. It's going to be an advantage in this election.'

Incomprehension.

'People like an underdog, you know? You're the type who actually shouldn't be here. You're *blatte*, you're a girl; you come from the worst working-class neighbourhood. But people see you hanging out with people who are your exact opposite. They ask around and find out that you're a good student and you're doing well. And then they look at you and think that besides the fact that you're *blatte* and a girl and probably a socialist then you actually don't seem so out of place, even though you should be. And then they think that she's someone they should vote for. Get it?'

She listened carefully, but couldn't get the equation to work. Shook her head.

'Okay, it's like this. Most people who start at the Elite School don't think they fit in. They're so sure of the fact that they don't fit in, they spend all their time here trying to do exactly that. In the end you can't tell who fits in and who doesn't because everybody looks the same. Even the people who from day one act like the Elite School is their backyard know they don't fit in. Not all, but most of them. Those who don't think they fit in always outnumber the ones who think they do. You follow?'

She looked up at his soft fringe, a foot-and-a-half above hers. The sunshine spilling in through the glass window behind his back was blinding. Then a lightbulb came on:

the thought had never struck her.

'People vote for their own aspirations. If someone as "wrong" as you can become president that means that they can become anything.'

She nodded. Someone so wrong. Wanting to become anything. She understood that much.

'Think about it like an equation. You need to get the most votes to win. Those who don't think they fit in will want you to win. The ones who don't think they fit in outnumber those who think they do.' Jonathan shrugged his shoulders. 'So you're going to win.'

*

'You have to win!' Evelina stuck out her tongue to catch the snowflakes that were swirling in the crispy air around their heads. It was election night and they were chain-smoking in the courtyard while they waited for the results. Winning had come to mean everything: not having been mistaken, not having been wrong, or maybe having it wrong, completely wrong.

'You HAVE to win. Not for your own sake but for mine. For the sake of the school. Because that's the way I want the world to be.'

'Of course she's going to win,' Sophia was sitting on her haunches, lost in her Canada Goose. 'Didn't you hear how the girls were shouting when she walked into the heckling. They were shouting as loud as they could. They need her.' The green eyes looked up, as if surprised by a newly hatched insight. 'We need you, do you hear that?'

The Girl felt a sudden impulse to run away, back to Factory Town where trolls knew their place and the system was predetermined, run back to the windowsill at the asylum centre where everything was quiet, white and endless. She wanted to run the whole way back to the land far away and the sheet-covered rooms where none of this would have mattered. Or was that where everything had started? Was everything part of that plan, had the plan been born before her, would it go on living without her, did it have anything to do with her?

She saw through the smoke that Evelina and Sophia were waiting for an answer. Should she already start explaining, defending, comforting? Tell them the story about princesses and trolls? No, instead she put out her cigarette, stamped it out with shaking fingers, her blue nails around a yellowing filter. Her lips were quivering. She opened the door and walked in without saying a word. The end of the story still unwritten.

*

The Girl was pushed to the very front of the pub when the election results were going to be announced, wished she was standing against the wall instead. She tried to ignore all of the looks that were directed at her. *A fine line between invisible and impossible to ignore.* She focused her own gaze on Evelina, who was standing on a table at the very back, watching over the screen in her place. She didn't dare look. *Who the hell do you think you are?* She didn't dare listen. *You have no business here.* She didn't react when they called out her name. *You belong nowhere.* It was as if the name didn't belong to her, as if she should be called something else now.

It wasn't her name she reacted to, it was Evelina's smile that made her jump. The sunshine smile that suddenly broke through the dark light of the pub. The same smile that had stepped in and lit up the Factory Town existence ten years ago.

Just swing along princess, just swing along.

TWINKLE LITTLE STAR

She no longer remembered invisibility, not existing, or a system without a place. Being without a platform. It had happened overnight, and suddenly she was something. She was the Elite School. She spoke like an elite, was invited in like an elite, introduced herself like an elite. She had crawled into a costume that covered her from head-to-toe, like the brightest yellow Ronald McDonald. What was underneath didn't matter. If there wasn't anything there, it didn't matter. The costume slid on as if she were Cinderella, and the shoe that actually couldn't be hers fit perfectly, as if it had been made for her crooked toes. She had never been anything else.

*

The PR department was up first; maybe they were the ones who defined her. It was made up of six tall Amazons with blonde hair in buns and black suits. They chattered invitingly into telephone receivers, held out a chilled glass of champagne at the door, led her to the sofa and leaned forward.

'Congratulations good-looking, this is sooo fantastic. This is absolutely wonderful. Wow, look at her. Such charisma! That hair! Those eyes! S-T-A-R Q-U-A-L-I-T-Y! You're a star. No doubt about it. You scream star. We're going to make you a star.'

Her, me, shit and troll? No, that's it. The Elite School. Her, me, the elite.

The Amazons wanted her to represent the Elite School and she sent out her best players, sent Cheshire grin to the frontlines, and turned herself into two wide rows of white teeth. The Cheshire grin whirled around like Hurricane Katrina's good twin, a suggestion box with lightning-fast reflexes. She petted with one hand and tickled under the chin with the other. The Cheshire grin stepped into the office every morning before 8 a.m. and never wanted to go home. She slept on the sofas in the corridor and longed to wake up. She lived on coffee and finally breathed, defecated revenge. She glanced secretly over her shoulder when she shook hands and kissed cheeks, was she really the one who was shining, was that her for real?

*

'Big Gala,' the Amazons called. 'Best of the best, greatest of the best, chicer than chic. Get your glitter ready, we're heading out! EVERYONE is going to be there, and you're going to be the STAR.'

The troll pulled self-consciously at its tulle skirt, glanced up like the dog Lady from behind long eyelashes.

'We want you to hold the thank you speech, and it should come from your heart. We want you to express how grateful the students are for the support from trade and industry. You are going to show them how FANTASTIC the Elite School students are. We want you to BE the elite.'

Glittering blue eyes were staring at her liquorice pastilles.

'This is the crème de la crème—everyone who matters. The king will be there and you're going to make a name for yourself, in the only right circle.'

The guest list didn't say much to her, but she understood her mission. She was grateful for the chance to express how grateful she was. Because she was so grateful. Truly grateful. Writing-version-after-version-of-the-speech-all-night-long grateful. A-long-silk-dress-with-sequins-and-the-highest-stiletto-heels-bought-with-this-month's-food-money-grateful. Poorly-hidden-terror-under-white-fur-and-steady-steps-on-the-red-carpet grateful. A-dressed-up-donkey-among-show-horses-but-I'll-ignore-it-if-you-will, *please-ignore-it* grateful.

It was time for the twinkling star to burn.

*

The Girl changed in the bathroom at the student association before the gala, washed under her arms and shoved her sweater and pirate breeches into an H&M bag. She touched up her make-up: a thick layer of foundation and far-too-red lips. *Ronald McDonald.* Then she washed everything off, it was too much. She put on just as thick a layer again. *Ronald McDonald.* She shelled out for a taxi, put the last of the things in the bag. She stepped out on the red carpet, glanced at her mobile. She was late. She hurried forward in the white fur jacket and glittery dress, the speech

285

was crumpled up in her silver bag. She held the silver bag close to her chest, her breaths echoing right under her ribs. The guards took a step forward when she drew closer. They leaned their heads back, as far back as they would go without them tipping over.

'Sorry. There is a private event here tonight.'

The Girl almost turned on her heel out of impulse, grateful impulse, but then felt the weight of the invitation in her hand. She held it out against her will, and the guards inspected it carefully. Then they inspected her from the heels all the way up to the Cheshire grin, to the red lips that were no longer hers. The guards didn't seem to understand what they were seeing, but they could do nothing but unhook the ropes, and let her through.

She stumbled past them and into the large hall. She shivered under the golden-yellow lights from the crystal chandeliers, became stuck in the door opening, blinded. *The only right circle.* Dress coats and silk sheath dresses. Low champagne glasses and straight backs. Older faces, adult faces, faces that didn't carry a trace of her features. She unconsciously took a step back, crossed one foot over the other and pressed the silver bag tightly against her stomach. The mildest breeze would have blown her over.

Her gaze travelled over the crowd, searching for a way in. The people were standing in groups, groups with clear boundaries. Everyone knew which group was theirs, which group they wanted to belong to. She saw right away which people were dictating the system, who was the system. They were standing as if elevated, not really seeing whom they were talking to, holding out their hands without being sure who was shaking them. The room moved in currents around these people. The king was standing in the middle of the strongest current, she recognized him. She recognized others from photos in the business paper. There was a woman there, a board member with short hair, a cigarette in a firm grip and a look that didn't falter, eyes that saw. She had an impulse to run over, hide in this woman's shadow. The woman's shadow looked warm to her.

Here and there curious looks were being cast in her direction, questioning looks. She remained standing in the doorway and faced them with the Cheshire grin. *I'm one of you, on my honour, I swear!* She stood in the doorway and allowed the Cheshire grin to have its way while she understood why the room looked so familiar, where she had seen this before. *Groups and alpha roosters.* The crystal chandeliers became the lights from the shop windows of the large department store. Coat tails and leather shoes became Alpha jackets and Buffalo boots. The handshakes a brotherhood without reason or history. *Bro! Bro!* Men who had built a steady platform for themselves, here and there a woman who had done the same. There wasn't much separating this room from *Blatte*-land. Maybe there weren't any knives hiding in waistbands and some had probably been born to their platform, but there weren't many differences: cloned groups, identical. They signalled belonging through that uniformity, that brotherhood. The brotherhood made the elite.

*

A man grabbed her arm and held it tightly. He pulled her into his group.

'Ah, aren't you the exotic new president? The cutest president I've seen, just look at you, young lady. Oh, you are burning a hole in my heart with those heels of yours.'

The light from the chandeliers was reflected in the star Academic's bald head and went straight into her eyes. He peered over the rims of his narrow glasses, and straightened out the handkerchief knot in his bow tie.

'The girl who is playing with the establishment. This I like. Let me get some bubbles for the lady.'

The bald-headed man took her hand in his and she squeezed it a bit too hard in return. She saw a fleeting image of Kawa, but the thought soon passed. The Academic was walking quickly and didn't slow down until they were leaning against the bar and he was holding out a full glass of champagne.

'Down it.'

She gave him a questioning look.

'Let's see what you've got. Down it.'

She allowed the golden pearls to rush down her throat, her diaphragm contracted, the bubbles hardened.

'Good. A tip: always down the first drink.'

He handed her a second glass.

'This one you sip on. Loosen your fingers slightly, your knuckles are turning white. This isn't a life-saver, dear girl.'

He examined her with a deep crease in his forehead.

'Maybe you should down the second glass as well. But no, I'm not going to drink the star of the evening under the table or I'll get a whipping from the PR girls. Hold this carefully now, relax your pinkie … there you go. And now you're going to take things slow. You're going to chat, and every time the conversation feels like it's dying out, you take a small sip. And then it will continue moving all on its own, okay?'

She nodded, then stood up straight, rested her arm on the bar and trained the liquorice pastilles on him.

'Ha! She's a tough one. Okay, my dear. I don't care about your life story or what you want to achieve as president or what you think of the Elite School etcetera, etcetera. You're as cute as a button and wearing heels like a Vegas stripper; that's enough for me. But people are going to have questions, so it's a plus if you're smart—are you? Can you fake it if it goes to hell? Do you have any standard answers? Ah, here is the Finance Executive.'

A thin man stepped in between them, he was facing the star Academic and had one foot on top of hers. She was about to wait, to see what would happen, but the bubbles got the upper hand.

'Excuse me, you're standing on my foot.'

No response.

'Excuse me. You're standing on my foot.'

The man turned around.

'What did you say? We're having a conversation here.'

His voice was nasally and his eyes drowsy. She was a head taller than him in the heels, maybe it was the height that gave her the courage.

'You're standing on my foot.'

'Oh, I see.' He looked down, as if to confirm the statement before dragging his heel off her toes.

'But Mr Executive, aren't you going to say hello? Where are your manners, eh?' The star Academic chuckled.

The Executive examined her over the rims of his glasses.

'And who is this?'

289

'This is the Elite School's new student president. Madam President, meet the Executive.' The Academic smiled expectantly.

The director wasn't smiling back.

'Her? You've got to be joking.'

He looked at her, his eyes expressionless.

'I see. Are you adopted? You must be.'

The Executive didn't wait for an answer, he panned the room with his gaze and then hopped over to the next group. The Academic threw his head back and burst out in a clucking roar of laughter.

'Don't worry, sweetheart. He's probably one of the worst. Most people know to keep their opinions to themselves.'

The Academic bobbed away and the bubbles from the champagne were suddenly spinning in her head at a furious rate. They reminded her of the black stains, the cawing crows. The Girl felt ill. She wanted to rewind the tape: pull on the fur coat, back out onto the red carpet, tear the speech into flying pieces of confetti, trip along via Östermalm to Factory Town, trip over Björn in the hallway, be sucked into the centrifuge between Mama and Papa, slide over the coarse rug, *not everyone fits in*, shit, back to the sheet-covered walls and a hollow sheep's head. *A hollow sheep's head.* Shit, she wasn't going anywhere.

*

She was standing in front of the elite's round table, giving her speech with blind eyes. The words came without her thinking a single thought, she knew them by heart, babbled them without actually being there. The Girl didn't hear her own voice, only her heart echoing in her veins. She wondered what people were seeing when they looked at her under the crystal chandeliers. Wondered if they were seeing the right thing, wondered later what it was that was right. She wondered if they were hearing her words, if they were even listening. When she was finished, she stepped down purposefully from the stage. Her stomach acid was eating away at her gums, the fingers that were grasping the sheets of paper were trembling, then the sheets fell from her grasp. She should have eaten something, when had she eaten last? She bent over to pick the speech up from the floor but tripped over her heels, tripped over herself. Her eyes were blinking, she was trying to see, trying to find an emergency exit. She had to get away from here. Her pupils stopped moving, something was taking shape in front of her eyes. It was the board member with the short hair, the woman with the eyes that saw. The woman came over and laid a hand on her upper arm, steady body weight against her swaying one. The woman laid a hand on her upper arm and leaned over, whispered confidentially, as if to her own niece, 'You are Sweden's future, you know that, right?'

She jumped. *The future.* Suddenly she saw everything so clearly. *You are the future.* The pressure on her ears was gone and she heard the sound, the applause that was still thundering. Applause for her, she was the one they were applauding. She looked out over the smiling faces, the smiling groups everywhere. They were looking at her, smiling at her.

Her, me, shit and troll? No. The Elite School. Her, me, the elite.

The Girl had pulled on a tulle skirt and placed herself in the middle of the menagerie. She was completely blinded, couldn't make out the audience in the strong light. She was balancing on the thinnest of threads with tensed ballerina toes. She was jumping through rings of fire with the manliest of roars, putting on her clown's nose during the break, then straightening out her bow tie and entertaining the audience. There were bearded ladies to the left and one-legged acrobats to the right. She had become a real one-man-circus, practising new tricks in her basement, putting make-up over beads of sweat under bare lightbulbs. She ran through the programme with meticulous devotion, roved about as a ticket seller during the lunch break. When the audience was sleeping she loosened her limbs, warmed up her voice, practised backward somersaults. The train was moving so quickly. She made a fire in the coal stove with one hand and blew the whistle with the other.

She was on her way, already there.

*

The morning after the gala the business paper called. The business paper with its pink pages. The business paper that Papa had stuck under her nose. The business paper that was filled with photos of princes and princesses, photos of the future.

She greeted the reporter on the steps to the school wearing a red bow tie, stood there proud as a rooster, ready as a marine, as elite as the diplomat Wallenberg himself. She showed him around with a newly awoken and unexpected maternal feeling. The Girl served coffee, crossed her legs and opened her notebook. Talked about the Elite School, described the unmatched driving force of the students, their potential and their future prospects. She supported the reasoning with data, weighed every word; she was a missionary on a mission of love. The reporter nodded expectantly, wrote down a main point or two. It wasn't until she finally leaned back contentedly in her chair that the reporter woke up and leaned forward, his fingers tightly clutching his pen.

'But hey, as an immigrant, how did this happen? I mean, how did you get elected? Isn't it, like, really difficult? How do they treat you here? How do you deal with it?'

Immigrant girl? It had escaped her short-term memory. The Girl glanced at her reflection in the glass door. Ronald McDonald was grinning back. She had trumped that hand, that card was out of the game, but no, there it was, blinking back in the reporter's expectant eyes.

What did people see?

*

The first letter came the same day she adorned the whole middle section of the business paper, wearing a red uniform and the broadest Cheshire grin you could imagine. The letter came in the evening, was pushed under the door to the student association in an unstamped typewritten envelope. She picked it up in passing, laid it next to the keyboard, then forgot about it until long after midnight when her eyes were tired and her empty stomach was burning from the last cup of coffee. She leaned back in the chair and picked up the envelope, tore it open as she listened to the messages on her mobile phone. She had to read the short text twice before she understood the message.

Hey there you Arab Bitch, the school smells like shit and they say that it's coming from the immigrants, the Muslims and negroes. We Swedes think that you and all the damned sand niggers should leave our country immediately because Sweden is for the Swedes./On behalf of Keep Sweden Swedish, Jonas.

Who is Arab Bitch, did she know any Arab Bitch? Was it the wrong address? What smells like shit? Fuck, is there something wrong with the toilets, is there room in the budget for repairs? Then she gave a start. She was the one who was the Arab Bitch, she was the one who smelt like shit. *Damn shit.* She folded up the letter and put it back in the envelope. *Sweden is for the Swedes.* She suddenly remembered the Torn Sunbeam's words: *You're Swedish, don't you understand? One doesn't become more Swedish than this. You won't become more Swedish than this.* She placed the letter against the computer screen, then kicked off her shoes and lay down on the sofa, crawled under the blanket out of habit, adjusted her body to the limited space. *Sweden is for the Swedes.* Sleep had started spreading in her nervous system when something echoed in the corridor outside. She jumped up, locked the office door and grabbed hold of the letter opener. She glanced at the curtainless window. It was pitch-black outside, and all she could see was her own silhouette in the pale light from the desk lamp. She suspected that Jonas was standing outside, that he was looking straight in, straight at her. Sweden is for the Swedes. She wondered what Jonas saw. Then she stood up straight, with her feet close together and her arms hanging at her sides. She stared straight back, even though she couldn't see what she was looking at.

＊

Once the first article was published phone calls from other journalists came one after another.

Some of them wandered around her flat. They examined the pictures of New York on the walls, the bare parquet floor, and the porcelain Höganäs coffee cups. The business paper that was lying on the doormat. They laughed, uncertain, and a bit dissatisfied.

'I thought … It doesn't look the way I thought it would. I hadn't expected this. I thought you would have leather sofas and Persian rugs hanging from wall to wall. And knick-knacks in a glass cabinet. This looks like an ordinary Swedish flat.'

Other journalists rested their chins in their hands and leaned forward over the coffee cups.

'So, what does your father think of all this? Do you have any brothers? Do you have problems at home?'

Someone asked the photographer to zoom in on her shoes.

'I had expected you to be more … masculine. You know, button-down shirt, short hair, no make-up. I had pictured something completely different.'

She sat there and listened to them describing what they saw, spent more and more energy trying to explain that she was someone else.

'No, I don't think about the fact that I'm an immigrant during my daily work. No one at school finds it strange and I've never received any negative comments about it. It wasn't a drawback for me during the election. I'm surrounded by smart, driven individuals. There are more similarities than differences between us. It's not about what you look like or where you come from, but about how you perform.'

What was so difficult to understand?

'Being an immigrant is only one part of my life, the other aspects have had more influence on me being elected. If I were a blonde sailing boy from posh Lidingö, the result would have been the same. Demographics alone don't determine how much or how little a person can achieve, or how much responsibility you're given. It can certainly have a signal value, and in an antiquated world be a hygiene factor. Focusing on that one issue is, in my opinion, ignorant as well as unprogressive, and don't take this personally, a tad dense.'

Sometimes she cringed at hearing her own answers, at how certain they sounded. She would look at her reflection in the window behind the reporter and wonder who was sitting there gesticulating and articulating and was so certain about everything, when she was sitting there hunched over, wondering what those words meant, the words she had just said.

*

A letter came after every article, pushed through the crack under the door the same day.

Damn Arab bitch, Sweden smells like shit and it's because of people like you. Leave our country and do it soon otherwise we'll throw you out. Sweden is for the Swedes./On behalf of Keep Sweden Swedish, Jonas.

The Girl asked around but no one had seen anyone at her door. No one understood why someone would call her Arab Bitch, no one seemed to see what Jonas saw so very clearly. She tried to get used to it, tried to collect the letters in a pile without opening them, but the envelopes screamed at her with their typewritten text. She felt forced to read every word, she read every word over and over again.

Shut your mouth you damn Arab Bitch, who the hell do you think you are? You don't belong in our country and if you don't figure it out yourself we'll pound it into your head. Sweden is for the Swedes./On behalf of Keep Sweden Swedish, Jonas.

She moved the pile of letters out of sight, then placed it in front of her again. She looked at it as though she were a minesweeper in a war zone: which wire should she cut to deactivate the bomb, make it so that it had never existed?

*

All of the newspaper articles were posted on the noticeboard in the corridor. She didn't know who put them up, but she wished they would stop. She passed that bulletin board several times a day. Back and forth she walked, and out of the corner of her eye she saw the photo of the red uniform, the Cheshire grin and the Elite School's doors grow, but didn't know what they represented. She never looked straight at the noticeboard, avoided it with the same determination she used when she avoided looking at her own reflection. She sometimes wondered what image would form if Jonas pinned his letters next to the articles. What would people think? Would they see something else then, when they looked at the Cheshire grin and the red uniform?

ARE YOU SERIOUS?

The summer stillness was echoing in the corridors when it came time for the interview with the journalist Murberg. Murberg leaned back in the Chesterfield armchair across from her desk, examined the books on her desk and took notes. He looked at the framed headline on the wall and read out loud: 'We were like a flock of shaved monkeys ... Yes, I remember that. Is that what the parties at the Elite School are like? Half-naked girls and sexual harassment?'

She smiled in response. She knew the answer to that question, no doubt about it.

'No, absolutely not. A great deal has changed. It is hanging there as a reminder ... of how wrong things can go.'

Murberg nodded.

'What has changed then? Are you part of that change? A girl with non-Swedish roots isn't exactly the obvious public face for the Elite School.'

She clenched her fists and prepared herself, displayed the Cheshire grin and allowed the now so familiar words to flow. She commented on how interesting that question was. *One doesn't become more Swedish than this. I won't become more Swedish than this.* But Murberg wasn't like the other journalists. Murberg didn't nod, didn't look at her with an admiring and slightly nervous look. Murberg met her tough façade with granite, feinted an open goal before she even had time to assess the playing field.

'Do you really mean that? You mean you don't see any problems? You've never encountered racism? Or wondered if you have control over your future in Sweden? Has it never struck you that you can work as hard as you want, and still not reach your goals, simply because you're a woman and an immigrant? You must have read about what the labour market is like, the discrimination and the glass ceiling? You must know other immigrants, and seen how difficult it can be? Your relatives, how do they relate to the Swedishness? Your father, how is he treated? You talk about your childhood, but how easy can it have been to be an immigrant in Factory Town?'

She stared down at her feet that were dangling in the air, a schoolgirl in a denim skirt.

'It's different here. It's different now.'

Murberg glanced at her wrists. The scars were poking out from under the long-sleeved blouse.

'I don't understand what makes you think that.'

*

Personally she would prefer to talk about what she is achieving. At the same time there is the dilemma—an impossible dilemma.

She was sitting in the park with the newspaper spread out in front of her, reading about herself as seen through Murberg's eyes. The words placed troll in front of princess, and sawed Ronald McDonald into pieces.

She says several times, to the point of annoyance, that the image of the Elite School as a snobby, male-dominated school for only Swedish students is wrong, that the reality is something else.

We could stop there, assume the uncomplicated view of things.

It sounds as easy as pie.

Didn't you find it difficult?

Rolled around in shit …

She pulls at her mini-skirt, remembers what she thought she had forgotten.

She grabbed the newspaper and started tearing. First she tore her face in half, then she tore it into four pieces, and further into insect-sized pieces that her fingers couldn't get a grip on. Then she started tearing at the words, tore them into smaller and smaller pieces until they no longer existed. They flew away, those pieces of paper, whirled away in the wind spreading like white snowflakes over the green grass. She watched the shards of Murberg's words until they had spread so far apart over the grass that no one would suspect they belonged together. Then she tied her shawl around her neck and walked home on the gravel paths.

The quiet street that ran outside her window was deserted in the July sun. It was empty of parked cars, empty of people; they had fled the city. The sound of her sandals on the pavement echoed between the walls. *She pulls at her mini-skirt, remembers what she thought she had forgotten.* She pulled at the hem of the short skirt trying to shield herself, but it was as if Murberg had pulled off all her clothes.

She walked completely naked along the street.

She almost walked past her own windows without noticing anything, but a slow movement fluttered out of the corner of her eye. She stopped. Sticky fluid was dripping down her windows, down, down with gravity. White eggshells were swimming in hardening yellow yolks. The eggs had only just been smashed, hadn't had time to go far. She looked at the end of the street. It was quiet.

She hurried inside the building, put her key in the lock and threw open the door. Then she ran to the kitchen and grabbed the washing-up liquid and a roll of kitchen towels. She wanted to wipe it up, clean it, before anyone had time to see. On the way out she stepped on the envelope. There was typewritten text on the outside: Arab Bitch. No address. She tore the envelope open.

Damn shit. Sweden is for the Swedes./On behalf of Keep Sweden Swedish, Jonas.

Jonas.

Jonas.

Jonas.

She closed the door again carefully, put the bottle of washing-up liquid and the kitchen towels in the kitchen. She left the envelope on the kitchen counter, took the kitchen knife out of the cabinet, pulled down all of the shades and lay down in the bed and crawled far down under the covers with the knife close to her. The sharp point of the knife was close to her thin skin, the thinnest skin.

One doesn't become more Swedish than this.

The autumn term had started and yet another new batch of students arrived at the Elite School. She had greeted them at the stairs, shaken their hands with the firmest of handshakes. They had stood up for her in the lecture hall and she had proclaimed the system, explained that they were here to be born again, become something else, something better than they ever could have imagined. She had explained that they were nothing, nothing without each other. That it was the people who made the Elite School. *People*. Then they had stood up for her again and she passed between them, and left the lecture hall with determined steps, her back straight, liquorice pastilles boiling. She knew that a letter would be waiting on the floor of the office a few hours later, and there was.

Hey there Arab Bitch. You don't belong here. Sweden is for the Swedes./On behalf of Keep Sweden Swedish, Jonas.

Now she was sitting in the cafeteria with the budget folders in front of her, making herself available to the newcomers. She was prepared to provide further instructions, clarify the manual, assure them that it would work out, and that they would blend in before they knew it. They would all become the same. It was lunch hour and the stream of people was thick. She sat behind her folders in the Elite School cafeteria just like she had sat behind her books at high school, but she wasn't invisible here. Here they were looking at her, every single person who walked by. Some of them smiled, and received the Cheshire grin in return. But most of them looked at her and then quickly looked away. Then they looked again in secret, not wanting to make it obvious that they were staring. So she sat there behind her folders in the cafeteria being impossible to ignore. She sat behind her folders and there was no real difference.

She was focusing intently on the numbers when someone pulled out the chair across from her. She looked up and saw shining liquorice pastilles. *Dearest Sister.* No. A girl with black hair in a tight bun, wearing a white blouse, her wide eyebrows arched, like a whip that was being raised and lowered.

'I'm Ella,' a hand was held out. The Girl took it, sat up straight. She was ready to listen, ready to represent.

'Do you have a moment? I don't want to disturb you ...'

'No, no, you aren't bothering me at all. Please sit down.'

The broadest Cheshire grin as Ella sank down in the chair across from her.

'How's it going, are you getting on well? Have you started feeling at home?'

Ella shrugged her shoulders.

'I just wanted to say that it's cool, what you're doing. You're cool.'

Shining Cheshire grin in response.

'You're the reason I applied here. I mean, what you've done and what you say in all of those articles. That being *blatte* isn't all that bad, and that you barely notice and that you don't need to be an outsider just because of it...'

She nodded, waited for the question she had gotten so many times already.

'I want it to be like that, the way you say. But, I don't know ... There are so many situations you know, like when you're talking to a professor or a recruiter from those business presentations. And it's like ... they aren't listening.

You're standing in front of them, and you're talking directly to them and they … just aren't listening. They answer everybody else's questions, shake hands with everybody else, smile and nod … at everybody else. Then you turn around and leave and it's like you were never there. You know? Like you're invisible.'

The Girl's memory is blank, but she knows that something used to be there. Ella's burnt liquorice pastilles strike a chord somewhere in the layer under the circus acts and the budget discussions, somewhere under Ronald McDonald. But it's the faintest rhythm, a dying heartbeat.

'Okay, so. I don't know … I thought I'd ask you, about how you do it. What do you do to keep that from happening, make it not matter?'

Ella leans back in her chair and waits. She waits for an answer, waits for a manual. The Girl clears her throat.

'I don't think it's like that, that it needs to be like that.'

Ella nods.

'You're only invisible if you feel invisible. You're the only person who decides if you're invisible.' She raised her voice. 'You're the only one who decides who you are. Or who you're going to be. You need to decide what you want to be.'

Ella arches her eyebrows again, tenses her lips and crosses her arms. The Girl pretends not to see anything through the mask, and continues with that voice which is someone else's voice.

'You decide what you want to be, then you work hard to become that. As long as you work hard, it doesn't matter…'

'I'm sorry, but it's not like that.' Ella interrupted. 'I've worked harder than everybody else combined, otherwise I wouldn't have ended up here. You know that. But, it hasn't changed anything. I'm not the one who decides what I want to be, I am what I am. It's like I am what people see. How do I change that? You can't change that.'

Ella gets flashing liquorice pastilles in response. She wants to tell Ella about the transformation, that everything can become something else, that everything already is. But she doesn't say anything, just flashes with her eyes. Ella continues.

'Just because you've decided you're Swedish and that you belong to come kind of pretend upper-class doesn't mean you are … Why would people be wandering around in the projects if it were that easy?'

Ella has clenched her fists and raised her voice. The cafeteria glances in their direction. Princess and troll, they are filling out each other's contours.

'That's your answer? That you can become one of them just because you decide to be? It's not like that at all. You'll never be like them. You walk around in those cardigans and those pumps, and talk with that Snob-Swedish you run with. But you'll never be one of them.'

Ella reacted to the volume in her own voice. She looked around and leaned forward even more, hissing with her jaws clenched together.

'I don't give a shit how much you hang out with them or how many of them are trailing after you, or how many of them think you're some kind of new Swedish princess. You aren't Swedish. You aren't everything you think you are— you aren't. You can't just wake up and be something else one day, it doesn't work like that.'

Ella got up and straightened out her blouse under her belt.

'You don't get to decide who you are—you never will. You are what people choose to see. *They* decide, not you. They see exactly what they want to see. They see what they think they see. The only thing you can do is beat them anyway. But you can't become someone else. You can't.'

Ella walked into the crowd taking long steps, then disappeared. The Girl glanced around, and smiled at all the eyes that were steadfastly aimed in her direction.

People, they don't know what they're seeing.

DAMN SAND NIGGER

She didn't even notice when the snow started falling that winter. She didn't notice until her pumps loudly splashed on the red carpet of the lunch restaurant. It was the kind of restaurant where she still couldn't pass by unnoticed, where the guests looked one extra time when she stepped through the door. The kind of restaurant where someone who was supposed to be invisible was impossible to ignore. The kind of restaurant that could rouse the slumbering troll, make her look around causing the golden earrings to strike her throat, and for her to search for wrinkled brows, a sneer or two? But the princess was directing with a firmer and firmer hand. The Girl straightened her back, boiled the liquorice pastilles. There were no trolls—there had never been any.

The pumps splashed on the red carpet of the lunch restaurant, and the Girl realized that she needed to get away to buy winter shoes. She went through her schedule, there were no gaps, everything was full. There was no time, there was never any time. Her thoughts moved to Little Brother, she never had time for Little Brother. He didn't fit in the boxes. She realized that Little Brother could buy the shoes and bring them to the office. Time is money. She sent him a text on the way back to the office and asked. Little Brother answered right away, of course he would come.

*

Little Brother knocked on the door to the office, she didn't know if it was a few hours later or a week later, she wasn't conscious of time's passing. She had the feeling that it was passing too quickly, that she could have done more had she known everything from the beginning, that she could have been better had she been allowed to start earlier. She dreamt about dying and being born again, being reborn in the tailor-made uniform. Then she was struck by the fact that that was exactly what had happened.

Little Brother opened the door and stepped in. He held up a shoebox and pulled out a pair of black boots.

'I wasn't sure how high of a heel you wanted and stuff. Will these work?'

Three inches, exactly within the Elite School's guidelines. She nodded. Little Brother understood, he had always understood, better than anyone else. She waved him in and accepted the shoes, pulled them on.

Little Brother sat down in the armchair in front of the desk, set the sports bag in his lap and leaned back. He watched her as her hands flew over the keyboard and she answered her mobile. She fired off a Cheshire grin.

'Yes, I am. Of course. Absolutely. I'll take care of it. Thank you! Yes, goodbye.'

The Cheshire grin disappeared. She was focusing on the screen again.

Little Brother grinned, and he allowed his eyes to wander over the evening gowns that were hanging from the bookshelf ready to be worn, over the safe at her feet and the president's gavel that was lying next to the keyboard.

'This is a pretty big deal.'

She jumped, had forgotten that he was sitting there.

There was a knock at the door before she had a chance to answer. The Cheshire grin was back; someone stepped in. She stood at attention, answered questions, accepted a pile of paper, nodded eagerly. The door closed and she remained standing. The Girl felt Little Brother's breaths between her own, but she didn't dare ask what he meant, what he saw. Little Brother had looked down at her on that bench in Factory Town. He had seen her numbers and looked away. She had decided that it would never happen again. She would bring Little Brother's gaze back up; he would look up. He had to see that everything could be worth it, that nothing had been lost and that they had everything to gain, Little Brother and her. She didn't dare look at him now. She didn't dare find out in which direction his gaze was moving, didn't want to see that he was looking straight through her.

'It's actually a little creepy ... I don't know,' Little Brother continued, not bothered by her silence. 'People out in the corridors kind of look hungry. Their eyes are roaming ... almost like they've lost something and now they're searching desperately to find it. They don't seem to know what they're looking for.'

Little Brother wrinkled his brow, stared at the cracks in the concrete walls.

Or maybe they haven't lost something … Maybe they're looking for something they never had … I don't know.' She was looking at the computer screen again, standing at attention, her head bent over the keyboard. She didn't look up, but she was listening, listening intently.

'It doesn't matter, there's no doubt about them being in the right place, all of them. This is definitely the right place.'

She glanced up. Little Brother was looking up at her from his sunken spot in the leather armchair, surrounded by the Elite School's fibres.

'You can probably get almost anywhere from here. You can feel it in the air.' Little Brother nodded to himself. The words weren't directed at her, he assumed that she already knew, that that was why she was here.

'It's cool. You should be proud.' Little Brother reached across the desk, placed his large papa-hand over her long, thin fingers.

'There's a tennis tournament this weekend, did I tell you? Come by and watch if you have time. It'll be fun. It's been a long time since you watched me play a match.'

She isn't listening anymore, she doesn't hear anything. Proud. A shiver runs up her leg, along her lower back and goes all the way to her neck. She is busy shivering. Little Brother has understood. Little Brother understands, he sees that it's worth it. She touches the president's gavel unconsciously. It's worth it; she's made it worth it.

Little Brother let his hand rest on hers and she caught sight of the blood red lines on her wrist, right next to Little Brother's thumb. Little Brother wasn't allowed to see. She pulled away, put her hands under her bottom and dangled her legs from the office chair. Little Brother backed up in the armchair, unsettled.

'Okay … I won't keep you any longer. The receipt is in the bag. You can pay me next time we see each other, no worries.' Little Brother threw the sports bag over his shoulder and stood up. 'It was cool seeing what it's like here. I … Come this weekend, if you can. I'd like that.'

She nodded and thought about the bleachers in the sports hall, and Little Brother waving his floorball stick in farewell. She was always leaving, always disappearing.

*

She sank down in the armchair where Little Brother had been sitting earlier that day, with a package of cottage cheese on her lap. The corridors outside were midnight-empty. Something was hanging from her feet, hitting the floor. She looked down and studied the loose soles for a moment before she remembered. Little Brother and the new winter shoes, shoes that had fallen apart after only a few hours. Little Brother. She ran the palm of her hand along the brown leather of the armchair. Little Brother's warmth had escaped the surface. Little Brother. A quiver shot through her chestcloud. She kicked off the shoes, pulled up her knees and was just about to fall asleep when an envelope was shoved in under the door. Typewritten text. She jumped out of the armchair and backed up against the wall, breathing heavily. Then she picked up the tall golden staff that was standing, leaning in one corner. It was the same golden staff the guy with the sunglasses had struck the floor with that first Elite School day when the ruling system was going to be revealed. With the staff in a steady grip, she ran to the door. She unlocked it carefully, then threw the door open and ran out into the long corridor. A glimpse of him could be seen at the end, a black shadow, a black shadow that started running. And she started running after it, dragging the heavy staff so she could run faster. She heard the heavy doors being opened, and was able to make it there before they closed again. She grabbed hold of the handle, then stopped. She heard the footsteps striking the asphalt on the outside, heard the steps disappearing. Jonas existed. He was real. She closed the door cautiously, walked back to her office and carefully locked the door behind her, pulled hard on the door to make sure it couldn't be opened. She picked up the letter and crawled into the armchair.

You damn Arab Bitch. We don't want any more immigrants, negroes and Muslims. Bring another one here and you're dead./ On behalf of Keep Sweden Swedish, Jonas.

She dropped the letter on the floor, then looked around for the golden staff, and realized that it was lying out in the corridor. She thought about running out and getting it, but then thought about Jonas's black shadow, how it might be standing on the other side of the door, breathing as carefully as she was stopped her. So she kicked off the broken shoes and pulled the blanket over her legs, tried to disappear under the coarse fabric.

*

The day after came and went. Evelina came into the office around dusk and looked at her with a frown on her face.

The Girl was standing at the desk and didn't look up.

'Have you looked at yourself in the mirror today?'

Evelina was knocking on the window between body and mind, and was able to catch her fleeting attention. The princess looked at the troll in the mirror: a blazer, button-down shirt, a close-fitting skirt and pink gym-shoes, the last of which she had found in a dusty corner of her sports bag. The broken shoes were lying packed in the shoebox.

'The dinner is starting in half an hour. You can't go like that.'

The Girl was tearing at the scabs on the inside of her forearm with her nails, realized what she was doing and stopped. Her head was full, there was no room left to identify the problem, and the solution was even farther away.

'You have to go to that shoe store. File a complaint about the shoes and get a new pair, okay? Take the shoe box with you and go. We'll go for some drinks first if you're late.'

The Girl nodded, got ready and half-ran at the jogging tempo that had become her daily rhythm. Warm and out of breath, she wriggled out of her coat on the escalator heading down to the basement level of the Galleria. Her thoughts sailed between the boxes in the schedule, from the board meeting to the account system, from the speech she was going to give during the evening's dinner to the plumbing problems at the pub. She was doing everything possible to keep her thoughts inside the boxes, to keep them from fluttering away to Little Brother in the recliner or to Jonas. Her thoughts were still running between the boxes when it was her turn at the register at the shoe store.

'Hi there, my brother bought these shoes here yesterday and both of the soles have already come off. I would like to return them and get a new pair.' The Cheshire grin was burning out of habit. Cheshire grin seasoned with a trace of *can we hurry this up, I really don't have any time, this doesn't fit in the schedule.*

A woman in her fifties was standing behind the counter, her greyish-blonde hair was pulled back in a loose ponytail, cigarette smoke and too much sun had prematurely aged her skin. The woman didn't look up, so the Girl opened the shoe box and pushed it across the counter, ready to sign, get a new box and jog back, keep running. But the woman pushed the box back.

'Uh-uh. Don't you come here and try this. What the hell have you done with the shoes, huh? You won't get any new ones from us.'

The Girl wrinkled her nose at the sour smell that filled the air between them. It smelt like cigarette smoke and peppermints, with a sour touch of afternoon coffee. It smelt like preschool workers and Factory Town. Then a memory started taking shape, and she imagined the silhouette of a Brillo troll, but the woman's words forced their way through, paused the image.

'How can you have the guts to come here with these shoes? Damn sand niggers, you think you can get away with anything.'

The buzz in the shop grew quiet. The Cheshire grin died on the spot. She tried to get the back-up generator started, but there was a power failure, a nuclear meltdown. The Cheshire grin was on strike.

'You can turn around and go, you hear! People like you have no business here!'

Someone giggled. A man in his thirties shook his head

and left the store. The Girl tried to stop staring in surprise. Shit, ugly troll, no: fucking princess.

'May I please speak to your supervisor?' Her voice sounded shrill.

'Well, it won't make any difference! You damned liar.'

The woman was clenching her fists so tightly around the cash register that the liver spots on her hands expanded. The woman's look made the Girl turn away in shame. *You're mistaking me for the troll,* she wanted to scream. *I don't know what you see, but she isn't me. She isn't me.*

She saw a door open out of the corner of her eye, a man stepped up to the counter.

'What's happening here?' he asked with a stern look.

She straightened out the tulle, sought protection behind the princess.

'Well, these shoes were purchased here yesterday. Here is the receipt. I've only used them one day and both of the soles have loosened. I would like to exchange them for a new pair.'

The man took the shoes and looked at the receipt carefully.

'You've forged this. Shoes don't look like this after one day.'

'No, shoes shouldn't look like this after one day, that's why I would like to return them.' Didn't they see the uniform for Christ's sake. The red grin, the stylish bow tie.

People, they're seeing the wrong thing.

'Tell the truth instead you damned sand nigger. What have you done? Did you ride your motorbike and drag your feet along the ground?' The woman was standing right behind the man, shaking with rage. She saw fluttering shadows in the woman's eyes and looked away. She knew all about the connection between fluttering shadows and raised voices, and had no desire to get to know this woman's demons. She tried to hold on to Ronald with her sweaty hands, squeezed the uniform between her warm thighs. The costume was threatening to fall off, but that couldn't happen, what did a naked troll's defence sound like?

'I think it's time for you to go,' said the man. He closed the shoe box and shoved it over the counter in her direction.

The Girl said something about the National Board for Consumer Complaints, took a business number and handed them her business card. She left the store, forgetting the shoes, then stood outside not knowing in which direction she should go. The drinks at the Elite School had been going on for a while now. They were probably waiting for her; they wouldn't sit down to dinner until she had welcomed everyone. There was a place at the short end of the dinner table where her name was listed on a place card, but she had nowhere to go.

People, they don't know what they're seeing.

Her mobile rang. It was Mama. She answered for once, she answered and shared the story. Mama hung up, and called a little while later. The Girl was still standing in the same place trying to get it together. Everything had fallen off: the red tie was lying to the left, the tulle skirt to the right, and the mask was lying in a thousand pieces on the concrete floor.

'Go back to the shop. Right now.'

'No. It's fine.'

'Go now. I've talked to him. He's going to apologize.'

'I don't want to.'

'This isn't about you. You're going back now!'

She obeyed. Mama didn't give orders very often. The man was standing outside the shop staring at her business card, twisting and turning it. *Right, well,* his eyes said when he looked up.

'Well, I've spoken to your mother. She told me about you, and I can see it here on your card, and well ... We've read about you and seen you on TV, I think, so of course ... If you're the student president of the Elite School then you don't come here and lie about a pair of shoes. I understand that. But you must understand that so many immigrants come here with stories, and if we went along with it every time we wouldn't stay in business. So it's not our fault, I guess you could say. It's those immigrants who should be blamed. You understand, of course.'

She stared at him with big eyes, but his eyes were on safari, wandering back and forth over the stream of passers-by.

'Sorry it had to be like this.' His gaze returned to her business card. Now he was bending it, as if to see if it would break in two, go up in smoke.

'Well, we can't replace the shoes just like that, you'll have to contact the National Board for Consumer Complaints instead. But it will be difficult for you to prove anything, you understand.'

The man looked up. The troll wanted to launch herself at him, pound on his chest with her fists and tear at his face with its long nails. The princess held her back. She turned around and walked away, walked away with the proudest steps the pink gym shoes would allow. She didn't look back, knew that the man was still trying to decipher the information on her business card.

At the top of the escalator she took a deep breath and exhaled with force, as if to rid herself of what had forced its way down inside her. Then she slid over to the first plastic bench she saw. She felt a draft and a chill on the bare surfaces of her skin that the uniform was supposed to protect. She was marching completely naked. A group of guys from the projects saw her, they saw her look. The alpha male gestured and they respectfully made room for her. The troll jumped up on her right shoulder, forgetting its shame for a moment, it was following the scent instead. The alpha smelt of Kawa.

The princess cried hush; there was no Kawa. What was Kawa? Kawa had passed by long ago. She looked at them cynically; they had made a mistake. They had looked at her and thought they were seeing themselves. They were seeing the wrong thing, everyone was.

What people think is unimportant.

THE STEPS AND THE STRIKES

She took a taxi back to the Elite School, pulled her compact out of her pocket and covered up what had fallen off. She stepped into the Prince's gallery with the Cheshire grin splashed across her entire face. She stretched her feet out in the pink sneakers and said something. It must have been a joke, she heard loud laughter. She was laughing the loudest of all. She avoided Evelina's eyes, she knew that Evelina wasn't laughing. She gave the welcome speech, said

317

cheers and downed the glass of champagne in three gulps, then said something that must have been a joke again. She took her place at the table's short end, between two men in polished suits. She heard herself telling them about the shoe store and felt Halland's elderberry schnapps burn her throat, then heard herself laugh. Her voice had made the incident into a joke, describing the shoe shop assistants like characters in a hilariously funny skit. The men in suits laughed along and shook their heads lightly, then they filled her wine glass and she took a big sip. She heard her voice take over again, heard it talk about Jonas from Keep Sweden Swedish and say Arab Bitch, repeating it several times. She heard how the murmur around the table disappeared and saw how everyone was looking at her; how they jumped in their chairs when she said that Sweden was for the Swedes. She saw how Evelina's sunshine look shadowed. Then her voice calmed down, she said something else in a lighter tone of voice. The man to her right leaned back and laughed, and the rest of the table took the hint and laughed along. Evelina smiled, and started a new conversation with the woman across from her.

Her voice had saved the day. She glanced at her mobile. It was after midnight again. She excused herself, blaming her exit on 'an early morning', and on the Nobel dinner the following evening. She wanted to go home, go home and crawl as far under the covers as possible. She wanted to disappear. She pushed her chair back, stopped for a moment to find her balance, then left the room on hurried feet.

*

She hears the footsteps when she reaches the sidewalk, exactly as the echo from the heavy oak doors slinks back through the side streets and peters out. She hears them because they are following her rhythm, her rhythm with a slight hesitation. She doesn't turn around; she doesn't want to see. She hurries, looks for a taxi, but the street is empty, empty except for her and the footsteps. She wonders if she should start running, but knows she won't have a chance. If she starts running then the footsteps will start running, and then it will happen, then the blow will come. She slows down instead thinking that if she creeps maybe the time will creep with her. If she creeps maybe it won't happen.

She steers her steps onto the gravel paths of the park. She thinks that she can hide in the shadows of the trees, maybe find a hole to fall into, fall like Alice in Wonderland. She creeps toward the trees and their shadows, gropes with the flat soles of her shoes after an emptiness that wants to swallow her. The footsteps are right on her heels. They aren't searching for emptiness, no, the footsteps are quick. They aren't following her rhythm any longer, they are getting closer. She breathes in, deep and abruptly. The cold midnight air burns her throat. Then she hears it, hears the bat being lifted, hears the friction between the compact wood and the icy air molecules. She doesn't want to look, but her head still turns. A shadow dressed in black is standing behind her, right behind her with a scarf wound tightly around the frozen face and the hat pulled down low over the eyes.

'Damn Arab Bitch!'

The words are heavy, as compact as the bat, which is being raised above her head. She looks up, sees yellow wood against a clear sky, yellow wood in the fog of steamy breaths. The bat falls, the bat falls and she falls, straight down into the snowdrifts in the park she falls.

When she opens her eyes everything is quiet. She draws in the scentless cold and cocks her ears: no breathing except for hers. She relaxes her shoulders and remains lying on her back, twists her lower body and pulls up her knees, crosses her arms over her chest. She looks at the stars as if that is why she's lying there, as if that is why she lay down, to look at the stars. *An invisible star doesn't twinkle.*

The bat had been swung and all she had felt was the wind. She raises her hand to her face, runs her fingertips along the bridge of her nose, over the contours of her lips, over her cheekbones and the frozen eyelashes. Everything is intact; she is the one she has always been. The blow hadn't come. Had someone really been following her? She turns her head. The park is quiet, the snow has smothered all sound, the cold has frozen the movement. Jonas isn't there. She's about to lay back down and turn her eyes toward the stars when she sees the tracks out of the corner of her eye, tracks from heavy boots, tracks from heavy boots that followed her and then ran away. She sits down on her haunches and holds out her hand, feels the tracks in the snow in order to assure herself that someone had actually been there. She keeps her hand there until the tracks melt, until they disappear under the warmth from her hands.

THE FIRM

Climb, climb! Up, up! Dance little doll, turn sweet doll, It's when you stop that you fall, you fall when you stand still.

She wants to get away from the world where the blows threaten to come, where the gazes see shit and troll, see everything she isn't, everything she doesn't want to be. That world, that real world will never see that everything has changed. It doesn't understand strength, it has chosen weakness. The world outside doesn't see. It looks at her but is blinded by its own filter, sees her through its own grid. It looks, but doesn't see what she is. It looks only to dictate its own system. She can never dictate the system in the world outside. She'll never be the one to dictate the system out there.

But in here she is impossible to ignore. In here she is the star, the striker who scores in the corner of the goal. In here it's about hard work, dreams and hard work. Here people see numbers and CVs. They see hours, marks and achievements. In here people have another filter in front of their eyes, a grid that matches her shape. A grid she can squeeze herself into, she who has hard work instead of blood in her veins. The system in here houses the plan—the system was created for people with a plan. For those who live for a plan.

In here is where she needs to stay, to climb and climb. She needs to climb higher up, get deeper inside. Get a good grip in the stirrups on the carousel horse. Not slip, not slide down, fall or fly off.

Climb, climb! Up, up! Dance little doll, turn sweet doll, It's when you stop that you fall, you fall when you stand still.

She has no place outside here.

TERMINUS

The students at the Elite School dreamt about the Firm; the dream about the Firm defined the elite. The Firm was a separate class, an own breed. The breed that trumped all other breeds. She was going to get inside the Firm, it was inside the world of the Firm she was going to stay.

The Firm couldn't say no to her. She had done everything right, done more than enough. She had done so much it hardly fit on paper, so much that it shouldn't have fit in the time span. She had topped her CV, just like she had topped the marks. She had turned herself into her CV. She had become the system, dictated the system. She had become impossible to ignore.

The Firm had selected her, had picked her out. It had called her in and leaned back in its chair with arms crossed, examined her inside and out. It had assessed the quality of her blue-and-white-striped cotton shirt, searched for her sore toes with its fingertips. Then came the numbers. The Firm asked her to calculate, and the tulle-troll was the ringmaster. She calculated like no one had ever calculated before, calculated as though her life depended on it. The Firm's doctored strands of hair flew backward in the tailwind of her calculating: forward and backward, thousandth parts and raised into squares. The Firm nodded approvingly.

The numbers don't lie.

The numbers say everything.
What people think is unimportant.

*

With beads of sweat on her forehead she walked into the last of the five interviews. The Firm understood, who wouldn't be nervous? But it wasn't nervousness that was shining on her forehead, she had nothing to be nervous about: she was already there. She wasn't going anywhere else, had nowhere else to go. It was the compressed air that was condensing on her forehead.

Gustaf, a partner, was waiting for her in the conference room. He shook her hand and pointed at the chair across from him.

'Your results.' He pushed the folder across the table. He had circled the exam results from the statistics courses with a yellow highlighter.

'98 per cent. I have no questions about that. It's obvious you can do maths.' Gustaf winked. 'Nothing you say or do during this hour is going to detract from your analytical skills.'

She relaxed her shoulders, the numbers say everything.

'But numbers aren't everything.'

Her chestcloud fluttered, and she clenched her fists, waited.

'I'm more concerned about the rest: your CV, the formulations in the letter here. Let's focus on that.'

She wrinkled her damp brow and pressed her lips together firmly, then held her breath as if to hinder the compressed air from hissing out through her pores, keep it from filling the room with her steam.

'I would like to get to know you.'

She peered over the conference table. Gustaf caught her gaze and tried to hold on to it, but she looked away. What was there to know? Everything was listed on her CV, everything was there in the results. That was all she was. She glanced down at her body. Had the troll caught up with her after all? Was it sitting in the chair? Was Gustaf seeing a troll? But no. She ran her hand over her hair, it was shiny and straight, ran in a straight line along her shoulders. The troll no longer existed. She was sitting there, princess and dragonfly, the one who had travelled so far. She had already arrived. She cleared her throat.

'Is something wrong?'

'I wouldn't say wrong, no. Well, yes. Wrong depends on how you see it. Or who you ask.'

Gustaf pulled a snuff can from his pocket, held it across the table.

'Pinch?'

She didn't hesitate, picked up some and weighed it in her hand.

'You're the first one to ask.'

'Ha! I can imagine. I don't want to hear any crap about the guys and the girls being treated differently here. We're all one of the boys. Or is it wrong to say that?'

Cheshire grin.

'Definitely not. I'm always one of the boys.'

Gustaf chuckled and she held the Cheshire grin on her lips. She placed the pinch of snuff next to the notepad on the table, thought intensely. What did he want to hear? What else did he need to know?

Gustaf poured a cup of coffee and leaned back in his chair.

'Okay, this is what I think. Your letter and your CV here, you've distinguished yourself. We've sent your papers around the office, and people are impressed.'

Cheshire grin.

'But to me … the tone you use. The pressure makes me take a step back.'

She jumped, and discreetly ran the back of her hand along the bridge of her nose, catching a few drops of condensation. What did he know about her compressed air?

'Don't take it as a criticism, because it's not. You know you're as good as they get. You have a driving force for a whole army. And we only accept the best. But for me this is almost too much. Everything you've done, the jobs, the awards, and then your marks. It makes me wonder. Do you have a private life: friends, hobbies, boyfriend? What about your family? I think probably not. And that makes me think some more. It makes me wonder why. I'm not going to sit here and jump to conclusions, absolutely not. But now that you're sitting in front of me, and don't get me wrong, but you're so skinny, and that raises even more questions. Well, it answers some questions and raises others.'

She knew that people were mistaken; they were the disgusting ones.

'The simple fact that you were elected president of the Elite School … That requires a lot of hunger, especially for someone like you: a woman and an immigrant. I don't think we would have elected a girl with an immigrant background in my time … An extreme hunger.'

People, she was tired of them.

'And then I think ... Well, what do you want the Firm to do for you? What made you apply here? What drives you?'

Her eyes were glassy, but not from tears. They were just blank. She wasn't there.

People. They don't know what they're seeing.

A ten-second silence followed. Gustaf was sitting quietly in his chair, and she was straightening out the notepad and the pen on the table. Straight lines. Then the princess pushed the rag doll away and took over the control column. She knows this system, she has fucking dictated it.

What drives me? What doesn't drive me? I drive everything—are you screwing with me?

*

When the Girl exited through the revolving doors, she was breathing heavily. She leaned against the glass wall of the skyscraper and rubbed her temples with the sleeve of her blazer, then opened the plastic folder and took out the contract that Gustaf had asked his secretary to draw up immediately. There was nothing to discuss. She saw her name in the Firm's carefully calculated plan: salary scheme, bonus schedule, career plan, pension plan. Everything was listed in black and white, everything was stated in clear numbers.

She had signed the Firm's copy immediately and pushed it across the table. Then she had wriggled into her blazer and almost run out, so they wouldn't have time to change their minds and pull back the bundle of paper. She didn't want to run the risk of them checking again, more carefully this time, and glimpse the troll in front of the princess, sense something that lay outside their shared grid.

Salary scheme, bonus schedule, career plan, pension plan. Everything listed in black and white. Everything stated in clear numbers. The Girl stood there leaning against the concrete wall and stared at the contract while her heart pounded. She inhaled the air from the heavily trafficked street, heard nothing except for her own heart, her own heart and the faint echo of someone else's heartbeat.

This is when it had counted.

People.

The ones who had called out her end time before she had even started.

People, they had seen the wrong thing.

Briefcase, blazer and rainy office nights, colourful balloons that were lifting her house. The Firm honoured the dream about Ally.

People, they hadn't known what they were seeing.

WORTH IT

The Girl was sitting in front of the screen, leaning forward with serious wrinkles on her forehead. She was copying numbers from an Excel sheet, pasting them into a Power-Point slide. The silence rested lightly and naturally over the team room. Everyone was sitting with their heads down: counting, calculating, copying and pasting. No one wanted to be bothered. Promise too much and over deliver, that was the Firm's business plan. Promise too much and over deliver. There was no time to look up, no time for distraction.

A few hours after dusk Johan, the team leader, looked up drowsily.

'Dinner time, eh? You'll sort it? Great!'

She looked up. Johan had spoken to Lisen. Lisen was the most junior member on the team, most junior except for her, but she was so new she hardly had a position in the hierarchy.

Lisen hummed something in response, continued striking the keyboard hard.

Johan looked bothered.

'It would be great if you could go now. Would you?'

Lisen looked up drowsily, then stood up without saying a word and nodded. The Girl reluctantly pulled her eyes from the screen as well and got to her feet. While Lisen ran to the bathroom she called for the elevator, closed her eyes and tried to stifle a yawn, glanced at her watch: 7.00 p.m.. They had at least eight hours left before they could even think about going home.

'How's it going?' Lisen pushed her into the elevator and pressed hard on the button that closes the doors.

The Girl stared at Lisen with a numb and frozen look, then caught herself and opened her eyes wide: bright-eyed and bushy-tailed! She nodded eagerly.

'It's great! Awesome!'

Lisen straightened out her tight ponytail, smoothed out a wrinkle in the somewhat too-tight blazer and looked at the Girl in silence.

'Short skirts won't earn you any points,' Lisen raised her eyebrows meaningfully.

The Girl pulled at her skirt, then turned away to put her hair up in a tight ponytail.

Lisen made eye contact with her in the mirror.

'Are you single?'

The Girl nodded again.

'Lucky for you. Not the best combo, this job and a love life. Or a family or friends for that matter. That's why so few girls end up staying.'

The Girl responded with an expressionless look on her face, she had hardly registered the statement. She had no specific need to be a girl. She could just as well be one of the boys.

'My first project was in the mining industry,' Lisen continued as they walked down the street. 'We were stationed in a tragically small town in Northern Sweden, and had an understaffed team just like here. And we ate the whole time. I gained 15 kilos, in four months. Do you know how hard it is to lose 15 kilos?' Lisen stopped in front of the pizzeria, pushed the door open and shouted inside.

'One Capricciosa pizza and two chicken salads. No pasta! No dressing!'

Lisen pulled a pack of cigarettes out of her jacket pocket, lit up and took a heavy drag.

'We might as well stand here and breathe a bit. There's no way of telling when we'll finish tonight … So, my boyfriend broke up with me the same day the project ended. His bags were packed when I came home. Charming, eh?'

The smoke hissed out between Lisen's teeth and settled in a veil over her wrinkled brow, accenting the lines around her green eyes.

'Okay, rules. Never eat carbohydrates during office hours: no pizza, no pasta, no cookies, no sweets, no soda. Stay away from the coffee as well if you can. I have green tea with me.' Lisen pulled out a freezer bag filled with tea leaves from her jacket pocket.

The Girl tensed her heels, rocked on her shoes. She wasn't interested in Lisen's rules, she already knew all of the rules; she knew them by heart.

Lisen opened the door to the restaurant a crack, held out the credit card and lit a new cigarette.

'Will you go in and take care of it?'

She took the card from Lisen's hand and walked in, but stopped in the door opening. The warm air from the oven, the red-chequered table cloths on the table, yellowing spots on the menus, Lisen's cloud of smoke outside: the image was so familiar. The pizzeria on Nelson's Hill. The meeting place for single mothers and drunks, Lelle, Alberto. She had been here before. But no, that was Factory Town. She had left Factory Town behind. She was at the Firm, she was as far in as you could get.

'She's unpleasant, that friend of yours.'

The pizza baker blew holes in her thoughts, and they disappeared. She had never been here.

'You come in, you say hi, you say thank you. Who is she, huh? Yelling from the door?'

She nodded.

'I'm sorry. She's just really stressed.'

'She's always stressed, always pushes the door open and screams.'

He pulled the pizzas out of the oven and watched her while he put them in boxes. The smell of melted cheese was overpowering. The chicken salad paled in comparison.

'What is it you work with, the two of you?'

'Uh, we're consultants.'

'Consultants? What, you mean with computers and stuff?'

'No. We help companies. To earn more money, like…'

'You do that, the two of you? What do you know about earning money?' The Pizza baker stared at her. 'Have you run a business?'

'No. We … We're educated for this.'

'To earn money?'

The pizza baker laughed and she pulled the bags of food toward her, turned on her heel.

'Help me earn money if you can!' he called after her.

She was no longer there.

*

Around nine o'clock she heard her mobile phone vibrating next to the computer, but she let it blink. She glanced quickly, it stopped then started again soon after. She turned off the vibrator, continued pecking at the keyboard and chewing on the inside of her bottom lip. The mobile started blinking again. She picked it up: Papa. It was Papa. Johan and Lisen looked up, looked at her but said nothing. She didn't pick up, let her fingers travel over the keyboard. Copy, paste. The mobile kept blinking, there was a text message.

I'm outside.

Her heart skipped a beat. Papa was here, Papa was standing outside. She pulled the earphones out of her ears, then smiled apologetically and sneaked out of the conference room.

Papa was pacing back and forth in front of the Firm's revolving doors. He looked up expectantly when he saw her rush out.

'How's it going, *dokhtaram*? You don't answer when I call. I want to hear about the job. Tell me!'

Papa's honey eyes against her liquorice pastilles, stars were twinkling in Papa's eyes. Maybe she was the one who was twinkling in his gaze. But no, there was nothing about her that was twinkling, not tonight. She wasn't there, she was in the Excel document. She had to return to the Excel document, not get kicked out. The Girl needed to focus, to keep herself there. She balanced on tensed calves, and tapped her fingernails together. She tried to look away but her gaze had gotten stuck in Papa's honey.

Then she saw it, it was Papa who was standing outside the Firm's revolving doors twinkling. This was Papa's plan, Papa's dreams and hard work. He was the one who had planted and watered the seed. He was the one who should reap the fruits, the fruits belonged to Papa. She blinked her eyes. Ripe fruit was supposed to fall off now, this was what the plan was about: salary scheme, bonus schedule, career plan, pension plan. This was supposed to make everything worth it.

'*Baba jan*, I don't have time now. I have to go back.'

Papa looked at his watch.

'But I can sit somewhere and wait. It's nine o'clock now, what time can you come?'

She tore at the sleeves of her blazer with her nails.

'It won't work Papa. I have to go back.'

'But I'll wait! I'll sit and wait, *dokhtaram*; don't worry.'

She rocked on her heels.

'No, Papa. We'll be working late. I have to go back in. I don't have time.'

Papa interrupted her.

'That won't work! I haven't seen you for a month, *dokhta-ram*. It can't be like this.'

Beads of sweat appeared on her forehead despite the chill autumn air: condensed compressed air. The mobile started vibrating in her pocket. It was Johan.

'I have to go, *baba*.'

She reached out with her hand and ran it over the sleeve of Papa's jacket, but she didn't look at him. She didn't see that the twinkling stars faded when she turned and left, didn't see that they went out when she was sucked into the revolving doors and disappeared.

RESONANCE

The numbers were the foundation of everything the Firm did: numbers in the right equation, numbers that indicated the answer to the problem the Firm had been hired to solve. The Firm's task was to figure out which numbers would lead to the solution, and then construct the Excel equation that would calculate the numbers in such a way as to give the clients the best answers. The last step was to copy the strongest numbers from the Excel file and paste them into a clear PowerPoint presentation that would be presented to the clients as argument for the solutions that were being suggested. Numbers in, numbers out. Copy and paste.

Lisen's task was to construct the complicated Excel equation that would give the team the output, which the whole job was riding on. Lisen couldn't tear herself away from that Excel file. The input was complicated and it wasn't clear how to get the numbers that would match the recommendation the Firm wanted to give the clients. As the months passed, the Excel file became too large to be portable. A stationary computer was installed at Lisen's desk: three screens and two keyboards. That became the place where Lisen sat, wearing a suit on weekdays and tracksuit pants and a sports bra on the weekends. Lisen was constantly on her way to the gym without ever getting there. As the Excel file grew so did the size of Lisen's portions. The lunches were transformed from hummus with cucumber to pasta salad to the same beef and sliced potatoes as the guys. In the evenings, the pile of sweet wrappers and packages from pre-packaged pastries grew around the Excel file. The weekend training outfit was soon replaced by a thick sweater and jeans. Lisen didn't say very much anymore, she preferred not to move her green eyes from the screen. Lisen's squinted, as if they were trying to see all the way to the other side of a tunnel.

'We make sure that everyone is standing on point. You should always stand on point!' Johan explained in the elevator one early morning as they left Lisen behind at the office. 'She has to stand on point in order to climb the ladder, and she has to climb the ladder in order to be allowed to stay. There isn't room for someone who stands still. You always work toward your next promotion, that's how it is for everyone.'

The Girl tensed her calves unaware of what she was doing, then caught herself and looked down at the bent toes of her pumps. She was already balancing on her toes, she always had. She rocked on her heels, tapped her nails together, let down her hair, then pulled it into a tight ponytail again. She understood exactly. She had never stood still, she wasn't someone who stood still. She would climb higher and higher, go deeper and deeper inside. She put a piece of chewing gum in her mouth and chewed frenetically, held out the package of chewing gum to Johan. She stared in past his rows of teeth. He was chewing just as frenetically as she was.

*

At night she glided with her heels over the soft wall-to-wall carpet, sometimes stumbled over her foot that had fallen asleep without her noticing it. It was as quiet as a hospital at the Firm. The deft fingers racing over metallic keyboards didn't break through the silence. They had become part of it, the endless silence. This place was standing still. Here, at the deepest point, everything was standing still. It was like the tape on a security camera had become stuck, so that the same scene played over and over again, night after night. Were they like security guards staring at that screen, thinking the days were passing, that life on the screen was moving forward? Hadn't they noticed that the clock on the wall was always showing the same time: a little past midnight?

She thought there was movement, thought that she was getting deeper and deeper inside when she was gliding with her heels over the soft wall-to-wall carpet. She slid forward in that frozen world thinking that she was moving further inside, she saw herself flying further and further inside. She was moving farther away from the world outside, the one that no longer existed. It couldn't exist, she never saw it. The taxi picked her up at 7.45 a.m. every morning.

There were thick layers of metal between her and the frozen morning traffic outside. She wasn't there. The taxi let her out outside the Firm's skyscraper and then she sat in front of the blue light from the computer screen and allowed her fingers to dance over the keyboard until sometime between midnight and dawn when Johan closed his laptop and put on his wristwatch. She followed his movements like a shadow: copy and paste on order. She glided after him over the wall-to-wall carpet, stepped into the waiting taxi behind his, then went home, and dove in under the covers.

Sometimes she would become startled while walking between the Firm's revolving doors and the taxi, the result of a biting January wind or drizzling rain one night in May. It didn't happen often, but when it did she would stand still for a split second and blink drowsily, as if she was surprised that the world outside was making itself known, surprised by the fact that it was still there.

*

Lisen had been in the ladies' room for a half an hour when Johan tapped the Girl on the shoulder.

'Go and check on her.'

She stood up and glided with her heels over the soft wall-to-wall carpet, stumbling over her foot that had fallen asleep without her noticing it. She knocked on the door to the ladies' room for a long time before Lisen finally opened, and a strong, sour smell drifted out. Lisen was sitting on the floor, her damp hair was plastered to her head and she was hyperventilating.

'Don't say anything,' Lisen said, shaking. 'I have to get

the numbers by tomorrow, don't say anything. I'll be back soon.'

The Girl didn't answer, she just stared. Lisen's light grey blazer was lying wrinkled on the floor, covered in her puke. There were whole chunks of pasty: dirty greyish dough and brown pieces of ground beef. Lisen was staring as well, as if she couldn't understand where the mess had come from. She couldn't understand that it had come from herself, that there had been something inside she hadn't managed to keep there. No, Lisen couldn't even remember that she had eaten that damn pasty, that couldn't be from her. Lisen wasn't there, she was inside the Excel file.

Now Lisen threw up again, but not that much came out, just green saliva, which hung from the corners of her mouth. Lisen didn't wipe it away, she didn't even seem to notice it. The saliva hung there, trembled a bit, but remained hanging there. It refused to drip, refused to fall down toward the floor.

Up, up, dance little doll.

*

Johan was sitting in the conference room, concentrating deeply in the blue light of the screen, his deft fingers moving over the keyboard.

'That took a long time! Where's Lisen?'

The Girl hesitated, rocked on tensed calves.

'Lisen went home.'

Johan looked up, it looked like he had taken a blow to the temple.

'Bloody hell, the analysis needs to be ready tonight!

What do you mean, she went home? Call her! She can't just leave!'

Johan choked on his words.

'What does she think this is, some sort of damn game?'

The Girl shook her head, but didn't answer. She just sat down in front of Lisen's double keyboard and looked up at the screens: numbers squared and endless boxes. This definitely wasn't a game.

'Dammit.' Johan sat down next to her, stretched his arms above his head and popped his fingers. 'Okay then. Let's do this.'

*

She put in the numbers and formulae, then deleted and started again. Johan reasoned, conceptualized. They counted around in circles, one step forward and two steps back, laughed with mouths wide open when they got it to work, chewed on their knuckles when the files got stuck.

It was nearing dawn when it finally happened. Johan was leaning forward, his back was tense and his shirt was stretched over the well-oiled muscles. With stiff fingers he was putting in the numbers to the equation they had constructed together. He swallowed hard when the formula started spitting out the answers they had been looking for. He swallowed hard and started growing in the chair next to hers, inches were literally added to his bald head where small beads of sweat were gleaming, twinkling. Johan was twinkling.

Twinkle little star. Johan wasn't there.

The Girl closed her eyes, and sank down in the chair, ran

her fingers over her stomach, it cramped in response. Then she crossed her arms and rested them against her chest, carefully kicked off her heels and started stretching her legs out under the table, but then a whip cracked. Somewhere a whip cracked, and she reacted instantaneously: tensed her calves, opened her eyes wide, sat up straight. She sat up straight.

Johan also reacted to her, and to the sudden movement. He tore his gaze from the screen and looked straight at her, straight inside her. He nodded at her posture, at her wide-open eyes, then he focused on the screen again.

'This is the stuff I like, you know. I'd prefer to sit undisturbed with a beauty like this all day.'

He stuck his tongue out between his tensed lips.

'I am so damned tired of all the clients and the consults and all the damn talk. All the people.'

His fingers were racing faster and faster over the keys.

'You never know where you are with people. They like you, they hate you, they question you and then change their minds. They lock themselves in the restroom, they go home. They want to eat, sleep, have a lot of needs and complexes and Freudian shit in their baggage...'

Johan shook his head and the beads of sweat started sliding down over his temples. She followed their path with her eyes, resisted the urge to lift her hand and suck up the drops with the dry palm of her hand.

'But an analysis like this, it is what it is, you know?' Johan pointed at the screens with both his hands. 'The numbers aren't wrong. It can take a long time to crack the equation, but it's never the analysis's fault. It's the people.'

She caught herself, took her eyes from Johan's temples.

Resonance. She recognized those words, she knew them. Were they her words? She glanced at Johan, those words, the numbers that are never wrong. People, they are the disgusting ones. Resonance.

Johan and her: both were wearing blue-and-white striped shirts and black dress pants, had combed back hair and shiny shoes. They were identical. She didn't need to look to know that her mobile, clock and laptop were lined up at straight angles just like Johan's. Johan and her. There was nothing that differentiated her from Johan. She was Johan, and Johan was the Firm and the Firm was what she had always been. The Firm was what she had become. She glanced at the glass walls of the conference room, searched for her reflection. All she saw was a head sticking out from behind Johan, a head without a body, without facial features. It was a transferable head, an empty head.

*

The mass email about Lisen's promotion was sent the following morning. The decision had already been made: Lisen had been standing on point long enough, elegantly enough.

Lisen never came back.

A GROWN MAN

The doorbell rang and the Girl sat up straight in bed. She was confused for a moment. Darkness had fallen outside the window, was it night or Monday morning? Was she late, where had the Sunday gone? She hadn't done the laundry, crap, there wouldn't be any clean underwear for at least a week. She groped for her mobile: 5.02 p.m.. Had she been asleep this long, since yesterday? What had she done yesterday? The doorbell rang again, a ring that shot out into the silence. She wasn't expecting anyone. The bell rang again. Shit. She got up, pulled on the black long johns that were lying on the floor, and pulled the Elite School shirt over her head. The Girl stood there staring at the front door before she crawled back in bed. She would wait it out, but then her mobile lit up: Little Brother. Little Brother was calling.

'Are you going to open the door or what?'

She threw off the covers and half-ran to the door. Little Brother!

A grown man was standing outside wearing a black coat, heavy boots and dark red corduroy pants. There was a faint smell of oddkollon. A black coat and the smell of oddkollon. Papa! Papa and the little boy with the knitted cap and the floorball stick. Shopping for Christmas. But no, it was Little Brother. Little Brother who was a grown man. He seemed to be examining her with the same time-travelling look, up and down, but it wasn't entirely clear what he was seeing. Finally her liquorice pastilles made contact with his deep black gaze. Right, we're here and now. Oh, and this is how it turned out.

He stepped inside and walked past her. For a split second their image could be seen in the hall mirror: one large, strong mountain peak and one drowsy troll who was looking up at him wide eyed, asking him to lead the way. They didn't see the image, but were painting it with every breath.

Little Brother sank down in the sofa, and wrapped his coat tightly around his body.

'It's ridiculously cold.'

She looked out into the darkness.

'You haven't been outside today?'

She shook her head. He nodded silently.

'You don't have any food at home, do you?'

She thought for a moment, but knew it really wasn't necessary. Then shook her head.

'Okay, okay...'

Little Brother looked around the room. His gaze moved from the unmade bed, to the empty table surrounded by the symmetrically-placed wooden chairs. From the empty flower pots in the window, to the dry leaves on the floor just below, which bore witness to something having lived and died there. His gaze shifted from the suit dangling soullessly like a skeleton from the hat rack, to the computer bag that was standing by the doormat, and the high heels that were standing right next to it.

The dream about Ally.

'You're never home, are you? It barely looks like someone lives here.'

She sank down in the sofa next to him, sat as close as she dared. She sat close enough to feel the warmth from his body, but left enough distance so that he wouldn't think she was trying to steal it, so he wouldn't back away.

Little Brother didn't wait for an answer. He wasn't expecting one.

'So it's going well for you, right? At work? Papa told me about the salary and stuff, it's sick.'

She smiled at Little Brother, a big salary, a big number. She had a big number in her bank account, even though she never had time to spend any of it, didn't want to spend any money, what would she spend the money on? A big salary, it was just a number, it didn't mean anything. Her own thought startled her involuntarily: a number that means nothing, but she was the numbers, and the numbers never lie. The numbers say everything.

Little Brother stuck his hand in the inside pocket of his coat and pulled out a bag from the 7-Eleven.

'I brought chocolate! The dark kind that you can eat.'

Twinkling, blinking liquorice pastilles. He was a first-rate Little Brother. She accepted the chocolate bar, and allowed her hand to rest on his, her long, cold nails rested against Little Brother's warmth.

'Is it good, then? The job?' He got up and took off his coat, hung it next to her rustling suit in the hall.

'Good?'

'Yeah, you're there day and night. You must like it, right? Why else would you do it?'

She shook her head, indicating that it was the wrong question, that is was being asked the wrong way.

'It's the best job, you know that, everyone wants to work at …'

Little Brother interrupted her.

'That's not what I asked. I couldn't care less about what's best or what everyone else wants. What do you want? Do you like it?' His gaze moved to the empty flowerpots again. 'Do you want to live like this?'

She didn't understand the question at first. Later she understood it perfectly, she had already heard it, had already thought it. Maybe the troll had whispered it in her ear. She pulled the hood of her shirt over her head and groped for her iPod and ear buds. It was a reflex, from an unruly teenager defending herself against pressing questions. But that time had passed without existing. She got up from the sofa, but forgot where she was going and sat down again. What would she do if she didn't work at the Firm? This is what she had worked for. There was nothing better, there was no better way to live, not for her. She would never be more than she was at the Firm, more than she was now.

'There is nothing better.'

'What kind of crap answer is that?'

Little Brother turned toward her on the sofa, looked calmly straight at her.

She sucked in her stomach, and laid her hands on the hips bones, which were sticking out. There was a shiver along her spine again. Little Brother's gaze followed her hands, saw her shiver. He shook his head.

'Are you listening? Listen to me instead of touching yourself.'

Flashing liquorice pastilles and clenched fists. Little Brother saw, then grew quiet. They sat next to each other on the sofa, they sat there in silence until Little Brother couldn't remain silent any longer.

'It's like you've stripped everything away somehow. Like you're uninhabited, just as empty as this flat.'

Her BlackBerry started vibrating. It was an incoming email from Johan with instructions for the coming week. The mobile lay between her and Little Brother. She tried to resist, but her hand reached for it of its own power. She picked it up, the results of an instinct more deeply rooted than thought. It was like a maternal instinct, a survival instinct. Little Brother's hand reached as well, reached with the exact same instinct even though neither of them understood it then. Little Brother tore the mobile from her hand, took out the battery and let the pieces of metal fall toward the layer of dust on the floor.

'I know that he hit.'

The Girl forgot Johan, forgot the mobile. Little Brother. She was supposed to protect Little Brother.

'Papa, that is.'

Little Brother unbuttoned his sleeves and carefully rolled up his shirtsleeves, then looked down at his lap.

'You hid it from me the whole time, I never saw it. But I know. It's crazy because I don't have any memories, not of my own. The only images I have are from your stories. Do you remember the stories, the ones you made up about the monster? You used to say that the monster didn't want to be mean, but that he couldn't help it. That there was a fire-works living inside him that exploded sometimes, and that he couldn't do anything to stop it. You said that it wasn't his fault. When I think about all that shit I only think about your stories. I like think about a shaggy monster and fire-works and it's like the rest never happened.'

She was lying curled up in the corner of the sofa now, listening to Little Brother as if he were the one telling the stories.

'You did it all the time, made up stories that made every-thing easier in some way. It was like you didn't want to take reality for what it was. I've been thinking about that a lot. You refuse to live in the now. This damned anorexic crap! It's the same thing.'

Little Brother got up and opened the window, let in the icy December air.

'You think you need to change everything all the time,

that you need to change yourself. That everything will get better if you work to become something else.'

Little Brother grew quiet and looked at her, but she was still lying curled up, listening. She was listening like Little Brother was telling stories.

'You're like a shark, you know. You swim and swim so you won't sink.' He peered at her, as if he was seeing her for the first time. He was thinking intensely, wanted to say the right thing. He wanted to do the right thing, put everything right.

Now he was gone, that big strong grown man. It was a little brother who sank down in her sofa, yearning for someone who could lead the way. If she couldn't protect she could at least lead the cursed way. Why did he have to do it?

Little Brother grows quiet and she looks up. The steady mountain peak is looking down at the moving river, longs for movement. The river is staring up at the mountain peak, just wanting to stand still.

She disappears in the hood of her pullover, as if backing up into it. The Girl wants to close the door, slam the door in the face of all the people. But this is Little Brother. He is pure and innocent, the mountain peak who will lead the way. His words find a hook inside her, his nut-brown eyes reel in her wavering liquorice pastilles. She jumps, sees something flutter past, behind Little Brother's pupils. She is struck by the seed of a thought, by the suspicion that Little Brother might not be as innocent as she thought, as innocent as she hoped he would remain. She suspects that his words, his always so grand words, are proof that he isn't undestroyed, proof that she hadn't protected him at all.

One insight is worse, but it is too big to slither in between the small crack in her thoughts. Instead it sinks down heavily against her wonderland, and pinches her chestcloud on the way. She grimaces, may never understand: she is one of the shadows fluttering behind Little Brother's nut-brown eyes, just like Mama and Papa are moving behind her own pupils. The same way the heavy soldier's boots have been stomping around in Papa's honey look as long as she can remember.

She wanted to protect him. Now she is one of the ones who has destroyed Little Brother.

CLICK

She heard a click in her pituitary gland as she followed Little Brother's figure with her eyes, this time along the snow-covered street, the shadow of a grown man between the streetlights. The kind of man who leads the way even when he doesn't have the strength himself, who only does it automatically because it was to that purpose he was once born.

The click came from Little Brother and from Lisen who had been so shamefully torn from her Excelbox, and from Johan who had sung her song, but mainly it clicked because something had loosened. Maybe it was the corner of a casing that had covered so much so well that she hadn't noticed it before, like a thick layer of expensive foundation. Or like a duvet that had been filled and quilted, concealing the emptiness, like cotton balls in a lacy red bra. She had no idea what it was, all she heard was a click, a corner coming loose. She didn't want to hear it.

The Girl put on her headphones and sank down in the sofa, drowned out the sound inside with tones from Mama's crackling cassette tapes, with the rhythm she knew so well that it vibrated at the same tempo as her heart. The rhythm helped her heart beat, made it easier to breathe.

Her hands grabbed the chocolate bar Little Brother had left behind. Her mouth nibbled, first small small pieces, then two large bites. She ate the entire chocolate bar. She swallowed it so quickly it got stuck in her throat, it didn't have time to run down to her stomach before she stuck her finger down her throat and emptied it in the toilet. She sat on the bathroom tiles with her knees bent, leaned against the side of the bathtub and stared at her own wrists, her frayed wrists. Her right hand groped after something sharp, but she stopped it, then she laced up her running shoes and ran out into the snow. Around and around she ran to divert her thoughts, keep them away from the enzymes that make fat thighs out of chocolate crumbs, from hands that carved in her skin. She ran until her legs started shaking from the lactic acid and winged insects darkened her vision, ran until she could no longer see or move. She ran to make the time go faster, to make it 7.45 a.m. Monday morning when the taxi would pick her up at the door and transport her to the security of the Firm. She ran to forget that those hours were passing, that they passed without having existed.

*

There had been a click. Something had loosened, and they squeezed through the gap: small insects with the sharpest of claws. They crawled around right under her skin, bit at her cells, tried to bite their way inside her. She sat up straight in bed, awake night after night and could hear how they were rattling. Hear how they were forcing their way further and further in, her chestcloud was their destination. They bit and rattled and she sat awake and wondered why the time didn't want to pass, why it didn't want to go and set her free.

A week passed or a month, or several months. She didn't know because time was standing still, refusing to move. She listened and waited, and in the end she got up and hurried over to the clock on the wall. She squinted and stared at the hands. They were moving slower and slower, were slowing down in front of her eyes. The batteries, it must be the batteries. A minute has never taken that many seconds. She pulled on her hooded sweatshirt and rushed to the 7-Eleven. She found batteries and placed them on the counter and paid. Then she got a package of cottage cheese, and paid. Asked for four cinnamon rolls. Paid. She wolfed down the rolls in big bites on the way home, tried to swallow carefully, hold the lump of dough where she could feel it, where she had control, where she could get at it and force it up again. She fell down in front of the toilet as soon as she came in, stuck her fingers down her throat, but it wasn't moving. Beads of sweat popped out on her forehead, condensed compressed air. Her stomach had to move, it wasn't allowed to stand still. She pushed her fingers even further down, scratched against her throat with her nails. She wanted to press and tear, but she wasn't getting any air. She pulled out her fingers and took a deep, empty breath. No air came. She felt the lump of dough sliding down with gravity. That's the wrong way! Up, it had to go up. She stuck her fingers down again, pressed and found the right nerve, felt the cramps spreading from her throat to her stomach. She felt her insides getting a grip on the sinking lump of dough, and then how it stopped, turned. She sat with her body tensed over the toilet, her eyes open. Her whole face was dripping with sweat, but she didn't know which drip was what. The lump left her body and she collapsed on the tiles.

*

One early winter morning as dawn was about to knock on the window, she carefully took the clock down from the wall. She placed it on the empty table and then stared. The time wasn't going any faster. She took the kitchen knife from the bed, and crushed the face of the clock with the blade of the knife. She carefully picked the shards away and set fire to the minute hand, it burned quickly and pungently. The flames quickly swallowed the thin second hand, then the stubby hour hand. Soon the whole plastic box was in flames. The fire alarm in the hall was sounding. She stuck her finger in the fire, inhaled the smell of burnt plastic with deep breaths. Her hearing was numbed, without warning the insects had disappeared from under her skin. They were finished with their task. She felt nothing. She felt, listened, checked. But she felt nothing.

Once it has clicked there is no turning back. It's like squeezing toothpaste out of a tube: you're stuck with a big sticky mess and there's no way back. What has come loose must come off.

The Girl didn't understand it, so she resisted. She allowed the hours to pass without them actually existing, worked hard and worked late. She ravaged her refrigerator, stuck her fingers down her throat, ran mile after mile. And she waited, thought about waiting out what was happening. She was stronger than gravity.

But what had loosened was spreading in her mind like an infection. She stopped understanding the essence of key priority, didn't care about the secret in confidential, no longer believed in the truth of the numbers. She glanced around the Firm, like a more cowardly version of the boy in *The Emperor's New Clothes*. She wanted to raise her hand, but had neither questions nor answers.

Something had clicked and she wasn't gliding over the thick wall-to-wall carpet anymore. No, the friction had taken hold of her heels, and her feet didn't want to move. She had to look down instead of straight ahead, try and communicate with the tips of her toes: we're going up, higher and higher. Up where people can't reach us. But her feet didn't listen; they didn't want to keep leading the way. She had to leave the screen, push aside the piles of paper, kneel down and whisper, to try and reach them: Aren't we going forward, up, away? Why are you standing still? We can't afford to stand still.

Her feet ignored her; they were receiving instructions

from someone else. Their orders were coming from that click, from up there in her pituitary gland. Someone had taken over the control column, thrown her overboard. She didn't know and she didn't understand, so she went from whispering to screaming when her feet refused to leave the ground during her runs, refused to allow her to burn calories, forced her to fall to her knees in front of the toilet after every meal, where else would the clumps of fat go? She was so preoccupied with snorting and hissing at her incompetent feet that she forgot about Johan, forgot to copy and paste, forgot to follow his movements like a shadow. She felt his looks when her eyes were trained down instead of straight ahead. His gaze was crawling like insects under her skin, biting her where she was the most sensitive. She wasn't focus, she wasn't control; she wasn't the numbers. She had to be focus. She had to be control. She had to be the numbers. What the hell else would she be?

IT'S BEGINNING TO LOOK A LOT LIKE CHRISTMAS

The day before the day before the day. It was the darkest Swedish winter, it was Advent: the windows were filled with light, the streets were glittering, there was the stress of buying Christmas presents and the mulled wine hangovers. It was the brightest Swedish winter.

The air was light and thin when she stepped into the Firm. The projects had been placed on hold: the Christmas party was being held tonight. There were smiles, greetings, and happy cheers. She backed up and looked for a hiding place, but they were everywhere.

People. She didn't want to see herself in their eyes.

The lace edging of her nightgown was sticking out from underneath Mama's old sweater. The dress pants were hanging loosely, she tried pulling them up with her left hand. These were the only clothes that didn't smell like she hadn't done her laundry in a month. She hadn't washed her hair either, couldn't remember when she had washed it last. There wasn't that much left to wash anyway, it was better to pull a hat over her head, far down over her head. She caught her reflection in an office window and looked away. She didn't want to see.

She sneaked into the nearest restroom and locked the door after her. She didn't turn on the light, took off the sweater and spread it out on the floor, then lay down with her head on her computer bag. She could have slept here but her mobile started vibrating next to her head before she had time to close her eyes. Shit! Stefan, appeared on the screen. Shit! Stefan was supposed to gather appraisals and decide if she had been standing on point well enough, and if it was time for her to be promoted to the next level. He would decide if she was going to be allowed to continue climbing. Higher and higher up, further and further in.

She answered on the fourth ring, her voice light and thin: camera, action.

'Hiii Stefan, how nice to hear from you!'

*

He was on the phone when she stepped in. She had taken off the lace nightgown and buttoned the sweater over her bare breasts, squeezed the hat into her bag and pulled her fingers through her hair. She hoped that he saw a smile on her face. The circles under her eyes couldn't be covered up with make-up, not that she had tried. She had to squint in order to keep her eyes from closing.

Curtain.

She had played the cards well with Stefan. She had scheduled lunches on a regular basis, picked carefully at poached salmon and shared one Elite School memory after another, assuring both herself and Stefan that they had much in common, that they were the same kind. She assured them both that the similarities were greater than the differences, and Stefan appeared to agree. He kept an eye on his BlackBerry but chuckled at the right details in her stories, concluded that not much had changed in the ten years since he had graduated.

'You won't have any problems here at the Firm,' Stefan had determined early on, then raised his espresso cup and left her at the coffee machine. She had remained standing there, had felt her stomach cramp. She had held her chin high and nodded, looked at Stefan's turned back with a twinkling Cheshire grin.

Stefan had made up his mind then and there, she knew that. He had spent more and more time on her and less and less on his BlackBerry during the lunches. After about a year, he started asking her about her views on selected application letters and CVs.

'Is this the Firm?' he had asked her with raised eyebrows and then dropped plastic folder after plastic folder on the table. 'Is it the right profile? You have fresher eyes after all.'

She hadn't allowed herself to hesitate a single moment before lifting the first folder and flipping through the bundle of paper, where she read through a perfectly balanced CV, in which all of the Elite School's instructions had been followed to a "T". She had read with wrinkled brow, as if she knew exactly what she was looking for. As if she, personally, knew what she was.

With her heart pounding she stepped into Stefan's office. He was sitting with his feet resting on the table, looking out over the twinkling Christmas lights through the glass walls. She stepped in front of Stefan and waited without expectation.

She knew that Stefan had decided early that she was the right kind of person, but she no longer knew what that meant. She didn't know if he still saw the right kind of person when he looked at her, because she changed form so often that she might as well have shifted from what he had seen last.

She hoped that people weren't seeing the right thing, that they didn't know what they were seeing. She hoped that they wouldn't see that the mask had fallen off, and that she didn't have a clue as to what had materialized in its place.

Stefan finished the phone call then turned toward her, smiling. His eyes were smiling. That should be positive, but what was positive? Was positive being allowed to stay, being allowed to get further and further inside? Or was it gliding back and forth over the thick wall-to-wall carpet, and wading through time that was standing still? Positive meant being able to call Papa and explain that the plan was guaranteed, had been carried out, was exalted in squares! Positive meant salary scheme, bonus schedule, career plan, pension plan and pre-determined short cuts. Positive meant numbers on a piece of paper, numbers in a bank

357

account, large numbers, a stamp on her forehead. She had arrived and gone beyond, further than expected. She was stuck inside a bubble that was floating above the soil of Factory Town.

'Hi, hello!' Stefan got up and she took a deep breath. Filming.

'Hii Stefan, how are things?'

Smile. Smile. Grin.

'Good, hey, good. And you've done pretty well if I understand correctly.'

Grin. Papa. Grin. Grin.

'Performed beyond expectation.' Stefan blinked. 'Just as expected.'

The plan, Papa, the opportunities. She had arrived and gone beyond, further than expected.

'You're being promoted! That's six months faster than the average, and you're getting the highest bonus quota. There's nothing to discuss. I've already printed the new contract. Here it is.'

Stefan sat down on the edge of the desk and held out a plastic folder. She was standing still, whispering to her unmoving feet. They were standing still. Stefan arched his eyebrows and looked at her, he looked up and down. She held her breath and followed his gaze. She didn't see anything, but wondered what he saw. She was silently screaming at her feet, but they weren't moving. Stefan got up and stepped forward, lifted her right arm and placed the folder between her tensed fingers. She stared emptily at the bundle of paper, her mind was blank: work hard, dream and work hard, plans and opportunities. Echo. Papa. That's right. Grin.

Stefan cleared his throat.

'Hey! It can't have come as a surprise, or? You've worked hard. Hard work always pays off.'

She heard her voice rise—that voice which belonged to someone else.

'I'm completely speechless. Of course I had hoped, but to actually have it happen … It's great! Really great.' She held up the contract and allowed the Cheshire grin to take over.

Stefan grinned and sat down, put his feet back on the desk again.

'Celebrate properly! Get drunk at the Christmas party. I'd buy you drinks if they weren't free.'

Stefan winked again. Her feet turned and she left the room before the voice had time to reply. The feet went back to the ladies' room. She sat down on the lid of the toilet, pulled out her hat and pulled it down over her eyes. She closed her eyes and tried to make contact with her, with the one who had always known what she wanted, the one who had wanted this. The one whose house had always been carried by colourful balloons, the one who had flown before she had learnt to walk. The dream about Ally? No reception. She pulled out her mobile to call Papa, and tell him about the new contract, the new numbers, further and further in. But her hands put the mobile away, her voice had done its part for today. Instead she took out the folder with the contract and read. She read line after line, read her name in the schedule, in the plan for hard work, plan for someone else's dreams. It was supposed to be worth it now. Worth it. She formed those words in her mouth. Worth it. Were those her words? She whispered the words: worth it.

Something was striking the windows: hard, pounding snowflakes. Or was it wood, compact wood against fragile panes of glass? No, it was a fist that was hitting, pounding. She clenched her fists and prepared to fight. She still hadn't opened her eyes, but she could feel the weight of the pillow over her face. She was hidden, protected; she couldn't possibly be seen from the street even though the shades weren't closed all the way.

Now she heard a voice. She threw back the covers, and pulled the hood from her hair. It was Papa. Papa's voice. Papa was calling her name.

'*Dokhtaram* ... *Baba jan*. Open, *baba jan.*'

Someone had been ringing the doorbell. It was Papa. She placed her right hand over her left wrist, pomegranate-red drops drenched her fingers. There were blood stains in the bed, blood stains and soot from burnt matches. She couldn't let Papa in, not Papa, not here.

'I know you're there *dokhtaram*, I'm not leaving until you open. I want to see you *baba jan.*'

There was something about Papa's voice. Papa sounded scared, hunted. She wondered if the monster had been stirred to life and was coming after Papa. If the monster was chasing Papa. Should she get up, let Papa in and save him? There was a pain in her chestcloud, sharp as a knife. No, she had no control over the monster. She couldn't do anything about the monster. She had tried everything, but nothing she had done had managed to stop the monster.

'I'll smash the window if you don't open!'

Papa's large hands against the fragile panes. She got up.

He would break them, she knew he would.

'*Omadam!*' I'm coming.

I'm coming, Papa.

She picked up the dirty laundry from the floor and threw it over the bed, covering the stains as best she could. She collected the packages of cottage cheese from the sofa, tried to hide them under the other trash in the rubbish bin. There were only packages of cottage cheese. She threw the dirty spoons in the sink. The spoons made an echoing sound, metal against metal, force against counterforce. The sound from the spoons echoed inside her. Papa struck the windowpane again. Maybe Papa was the one echoing inside her, Papa's echo that had always been there.

'Open the door!'

She looked out over the flat, then walked toward the door. There was nothing else she could do to hide, nothing she could do to become something else. The suit was rustling on the hat rack, the computer bag was sitting on the doormat. Dreams and hard work.

She opened the front door a crack, heard Papa punching in the access code and opening the entrance door wide, heard how he grabbed hold of her door handle and pulled. She saw him standing in front of her, breathing heavily. She opened her eyes carefully, her shrivelled liquorice pastilles against his wide-open honey eyes. She could see Papa's chestcloud flutter, how he twisted in the presence of what he saw.

'*Salam, baba.*'

He stepped inside and grabbed her wrists firmly through the sweatshirt. She felt the blood run and ooze. She didn't move a muscle, she didn't look down. She tried to make eye contact with him so that he wouldn't see. Papa pulled her toward him, held her tightly, so tightly she couldn't breathe. She was falling forward, falling toward Papa but then Papa suddenly let go and took a step back. She stumbled and hit the wall.

'What have you done?'

Papa walked past her and stepped into the room.

'What's that smell?'

Papa walked over to the bed, lifted piece after piece of clothing, dug deeper.

'What's this blood? What have you burnt?'

She got up and placed herself between Papa and her home, her mess.

'It's nothing *baba. Chizi nist.*'

The honey eyes looked at her, and saw something she couldn't make out. Papa looked around the room. There were lumps of cottage cheese on the sofa and underwear lying on the floor. A scale stood next to the wall and a fruit knife was lying on the parquet floor, pomegranate-red drops. Papa picked up the knife and threw it across the room. He grabbed her wrists again, dragged her across the floor, pulled her toward the wall of mirrors in the hall. She had time to think: the monster, the monster's back. The monster was back and the monster was going to throw her against the mirrors, and the eight mirrors would be broken into thirty-two pieces. Then they would fall heavily to the floor and be crushed into sixty-four. All the time that had passed, and the monster still had her in its grasp.

'Look at yourself.'

It wasn't the monster who was speaking, it was Papa. She looked in the mirror. Papa's eyes were looking at her, smooth whites without shadows. She looked down at her wrists, at Papa's strong hands. He wasn't holding her that tightly, not really. It was her skin that was aching.

'Look at yourself.'

She met his eyes in the mirror again. She didn't understand.

'I said, look!'

Papa let go of her wrists, he turned her head straight forward. She was still looking at him, wasn't able to look at herself, her gaze didn't want to. Papa's grip tightened, he grabbed hold of the bottom of her college shirt and pulled it over her head in one movement. She tried to stop him, but her strength paled in comparison to his.

Papa had pulled the shirt over her head and she was standing in front of the mirrors, her upper body naked. There was no cover, nothing that was concealing her. She looked at herself, she couldn't keep from looking. Her gaze was drawn in, spinning, as if it was inside a centrifuge. Papa grew quiet and let her go. His right arm was hanging limply at his side. They were both staring at her, Papa and the Girl.

'What have you done to yourself? *Vay dokhtaram*, do you see what you have done?'

She tilted her head to the side and searched for the answer. She stared at herself. The Brillo hair was gone, not gone in the sense that it was hanging straight and soft, but really gone. She had bald spots on her head. The bald spots were covered by the tight ponytail she wore during office hours, and the cap she wore when she was running, they disappeared in the hooded sweatshirt when she was at home. Bald spots where a troll had once lived. She had lost the troll.

But Papa wasn't looking at her head. Her gaze slid down over her bare breasts that looked like chopped-off muffin tops. Mariella, the physics teachers had been right, they really had stopped growing. She resisted the urge to touch her nipples to feel if there really was something there, something that was separated from her breastbone. Then her gaze continued to her ribs. She counted them, they were sticking out almost more than her breasts. She searched for Papa's gaze in the mirror, it was focused further down. Papa wasn't looking at her poking ribs. She followed his honey eyes: they were staring at her stomach, her concave stomach. The cavity was deep, she hadn't eaten anything today. The shadow of a Cheshire grin started spreading across her face, but she caught herself, hid the satisfaction. It wasn't the hollow Papa was looking at, it was the fine lines. The fine lines created with the thin knife blade. The concave stomach was marked. She had carved a grid on her concave stomach, a large grid, with small, immaculate boxes. Some of the lines were pale, others a fiery red. She had added on boxes accordingly, cutting slowly and patiently. She ran her finger along the lines, along the carefully carved system. Her very own system.

Papa was still breathing heavily. She turned the inside of her arms so that they could be seen in the mirror, as if to show him, to assure herself that he wouldn't miss a single inch. The grid continued on the inside of her arms, where the squares were smaller, carved with a greater precision. The inside of her left arm was her masterpiece: perfectly straight, symmetrical lines. There were fresh drops there. She had never shown anyone before, it had nothing to with anyone.

*

Papa doesn't leave her this night. He collects all of the knives, kitchen scissors, and the nail file. He throws them in a shopping bag and puts them in the car. Then he changes her sheets, and puts her under the shower. Later he lies down on the sofa and stands guard, holds the car keys tightly in his hands the whole night.

The alarm clock rings at 5.45 a.m.. She gets up quickly and pulls on her jogging clothes that are lying in a pile next to the bed. She is on her way out the door when Papa wakens and looks up, drowsy and disoriented.

'*Kojah?* Where are you going?'

'For a run.'

'Now?'

'I run every morning.'

She is kneeling on the doormat, lacing up her shoes.

She doesn't look up at Papa.

'You're not going anywhere. It's enough now! I don't want you to run. I don't want you to go to work. I don't want you to be like this. *Nakhastam.*'

Papa is standing in the hall, speaking in a loud, determined voice.

Nakhastam. This isn't what I wanted. Papa's words stab her between her ribs.

'It wasn't supposed to be like this, *dokhtaram.* This wasn't the plan. It's not worth it, what you're doing isn't worth it.'

This wasn't the plan. It isn't worth it. Papa's words pound against her temple with the same force as the bat that had passed her temple in the park.

'There must be another way.'

Papa hits the dangling suit and the suit rattles on the hat rack. She stands up, sends flashing liquorice pastilles in Papa's direction. She clenches her fists, tenses her biceps. The compressed air is pulsating against her temples, pressing against the inside of her forehead. First she takes a small step forward. The compressed air is building, it passes the boiling point. Papa backs up and she moves toward him. Then she flies at him like an elf, strikes his upper body like a monster.

'How dare you say that to me! It's your damned plan. It's your damn fault!'

She strikes Papa's chest with her fists, spits and hisses. She is screaming, something inside her is screaming. She is shaking, her whole body is shaking. She tries to stop hitting Papa but her fists aren't finished.

'What do you know about another way? What have you ever done? What have you personally done?'

Papa has backed up, he wants to step forward but doesn't know how. He doesn't know what to say, he doesn't know what he is seeing. He doesn't see where it's coming from or what is coming. He sees something in front of him that he doesn't understand, that he doesn't recognize. You aren't her, he wants to whisper. Who are you? But Papa stands quietly, doesn't want to feed the flames of the fire that is burning in front of him.

'This is all I can be! This is the best I can become. I won't become better than this Papa! I am the best.'

She is breathing heavily, staring fiercely. She sees that Papa has lost himself in the shadows behind her pupils, wonders if he recognizes them.

She pulls the sweatbands over the grids on her wrists,

keeps Papa at a distance with her gaze. Papa has sunk down on the sofa, such a small Papa in the presence of all the cubic feet of air around him. Her air.

This wasn't the plan.

This doesn't make everything worth it.

She puts her hand on the door handle but can't open the door. She is breathing heavily, but isn't getting any air. She falls down on her knees.

'*Baba!*' She screams and collapses. '*Babaa!*' She moans and Papa's shadow falls over her, Papa is there in an instant. He lifts her in his arms, almost falls over from the light weight. Her frightened liquorice pastilles look at his honey eyes, he hardly dares meet them. Her shirt has travelled up, and he glimpses the barn red-coloured grid pattern on her body, then looks away.

Papa lifts her, holds her in his arms, doesn't move. Papa doesn't know what he should do, what he can do. Papa wants to get help, but doesn't know in which direction he should run.

FREEDOM

She was sleeping deeply, slouching in the front seat. Papa had pulled the hood over her head, as if trying to conceal the bald spots, hide the traces of lost troll. She was sleeping deeply as Papa drove the Volvo 240 through the morning fog. He was driving against the current, away from the city. She was sleeping deeply and dreaming the dreams she dreams every night, dreams she chooses to forget before the dawn.

She was sleeping and there was a knock at the window, someone wanted to come in, or they wanted to get her? It was hard to say. Was it Papa? What did he want, wasn't he satisfied now, wasn't this enough? The future has no head and no tail. It wasn't Papa, was it the teacher from Saltsjö-baden? Not everyone fits in, you don't fit in. You'll never fit in. That was why she had talked to all of those journalists, fired off Cheshire grin to all of the photographers. It was for the sake of the teacher from Saltsjöbaden. So that she could shove newspaper article after newspaper article under the teacher's nose. No, it was so that she could roll up the articles and shove them deep down the teacher's throat; let her suffocate.

*

She opened her eyes suddenly. The red bus towered up out of the fog. Papa and she were driving behind the red bus, they were driving toward Factory Town. Back to Factory Town. She wanted to protest, opened her mouth but couldn't get anything out. She closed her eyes again.

*

The sirens shrieked through the darkness, absorbed the sound of screams and shouts, left behind an image of people running with their mouths open: mute, fleeing people. There was a smell of gasoline and warm, almost melting asphalt. Asphalt that stuck to her feet when she ran with her eyes focused on her red shoes. The shoes flew through the air, hurried forth over the ground. Her whole body was floating; her arms were hanging in the air like a marionette. She looked up. Mama was pulling on her strings, hurrying her along. It was a woman covered in black fabric. Of course it had to be Mama! The Girl couldn't see the face, the woman's face was looking everywhere but down. Suddenly the woman let go of the strings but it was a man's hand that let go, a hand that was large and warm like Papa's. She rolled down the stairs, straight into that room which was filled with the fears of grown-up people. People with large, hollow eyes and quivering bottom lips. Someone was pounding their chest, complaining, asking why. Why, why? She looked around—none of the adults had an answer. She wanted to walk over to the old woman who was hitting and discuss silence, eternity. Talk about spots of colour that travel over untouched snow. Rabbits and holes. But that was when it started, that was when the blow came. Explosions. Concrete that was blown into a hundred pieces, which fell to the ground and were crushed into thousands. The pieces crumbled over her head, filled her open mouth, her mute, open mouth.

*

Papa put his arm around her, jumped when he felt her shoulder blade poking out like a folded wing, but he held it together. He put his other arm behind her neck and lifted carefully, walked with hesitant steps, to the address he knew well but had never been to. He had never been able to make himself come here. A man with brown hair and a pushchair in a firm grasp hurried up to them and opened the door. He held it open for Papa, then gave the Girl a nervous look.

'What the hell happened?'

Her eyelashes fluttered. She hid inside the hood but she saw: it was skinhead-Tommie. Papa walked passed him, probably didn't hear the question. She turned her head and looked over Papa's shoulder. Tommie, another Tommie. The door closed and she closed her eyes again.

*

She is running with Little Brother's hand in hers, running as hard as she can. The woods ahead of them are growing thick, more and more trees are sprouting from the ground, blocking the view. She is holding Little Brother's hand tightly. She is supposed to protect him; she is supposed to lead the way. They are fleeing, she and Little Brother, fleeing even though she doesn't know from what. She glances over her shoulder. They are getting closer! They are on Little Brother's heels. She tries to get Little Brother to hurry, she pulls on Little Brother's strings. Why are there strings attached to Little Brother's neck? She lifts him and his boots fly through the air. He looks up to assure himself that it is her and not someone else who is pulling, but he doesn't seem to recognize her. She wonders what Little Brother sees. She has never understood what it is the people see. Cold metal is cutting into her back and she falls, she falls to the ground with Little Brother next to her. She throws herself over Little Brother, she is supposed to protect him. Alberto steps forward, the mask in one hand, the bat in the other. Damn Arab Bitch. Jonas from Keep Sweden Swedish is standing in front of her. Jonas from Keep Sweden Swedish has beaten up Papa, now he is after Little Brother. Little Brother shrinks like Alice in Wonderland, disappears. She gets down on her knees, and searches, but he isn't just invisible, he is gone.

*

Two familiar voices force their way through her sleep, two familiar voices that haven't spoken to each other in many years, that haven't listened to each other since a mail van drove them to Factory Town. She inhales deeply, the room smells of childhood and Sunday. She burrows her nose into the pillow under her head, it smells like Mama's detergent. She slowly opens her eyes. She is lying in her old bed, in the bed at home at Mama's. One of the voices she hears outside the door is Mama's, the other is Papa's. Her chest-cloud flutters. She listens for the third voice, the monster's voice but there are no undertones, no shadows fluttering in the conversation out there. They are only talking about one thing, one single person. Papa is crying, Mama is comforting. Mama asks him to leave, asks Papa to leave her in Mama's hands.

'That is what I did!'

Papa's voice is sharp, but he regrets it instantly, sucks in the last syllables. It becomes quiet. They aren't looking at each other, she can hear that.

'Go home. You need to sleep. I'll take care of her.' Mama opens the front door.

371

'I'll wait in the car.' Papa still has tears in his voice.

Mama's voice is like a caress.

'What will you wait for? Don't wait. Whatever happens is going to be something different than what you are waiting for.'

*

A door slams shut and there is a knock at the window again, there is someone there, for real, someone is here to get her, or? She has copied the wrong thing, pasted it in the wrong place. No she has counted wrong: 4,589 calories. She has thought wrong; everything has become wrong. 5,432 calories. She couldn't hold it together; she has destroyed it. 6,890. It's over now.

*

She is woken by the sound of a man's raised voice. She expects women's cries, fists against a mother's flesh but it doesn't come. It is only a man's raised voice that is bellowing on uninterrupted.

'What do you mean "it'll be okay"! It won't be okay. It's only getting worse.'

Mama's voice is like a caress, inaudible.

'No, I'm not going to leave. I'm not going to leave her here with you. I'm the only one who can talk to her. I'm the only one who tries.'

Someone grabs the door handle and she closes her eyes tight, doesn't want to see. She knows that Little Brother is standing in the door opening. Little Brother is standing in the door opening looking down at her, looking down at her where she is curled up making herself small, disappearing under the covers. Little Brother sits down on the edge of the bed and lifts the edge of her shirt. He hesitates at first and then places a light hand on her stomach, a careful hand on her grid. He lets his hand remain there, as if he thinks the traces will disappear under the warmth from his hands.

*

She opens her eyes and hears no one talking. There is only silence. Breaths are floating in the silence, breaths that are floating without disturbing anything. First her own, panting breaths, then Mama's deep, heavy, even ones. She throws her legs over the edge of the bed and follows the steady vibrations, the sound of Mama. She pads faster and faster, jogs when she catches sight of Mama's silhouette under the blankets on the sofa. She curls up next to Mama, very close. Her body curls together as Mama, still sleeping, turns toward her with her arms outstretched. She disappears in Mama's arms. The afternoon sun envelops them while she allows Mama's breaths to float into hers. Deep, heavy, even.

It's a perfectly choreographed series of movements, maybe a scene at The Royal Dramatic Theatre that has been too-heavily directed. The two of them look like they have practised every movement in the rhythm: fall, wait, rescue.

*

Mama's raven-black eyes are resting on her when she finally wakes up. Liquorice pastilles. She had never noticed it before, that she has her Mama's eyes.

'I turned it off,' Mama lifted the Girl's mobile out of her pocket to show that it was dead. 'Your colleagues give me a headache.'

Her heart leapt to her throat, evening darkness outside. It was Monday night and she had been lying on Mama's sofa all day. She wasn't at the office; she was in Factory Town. Factory Town. She had slid outside the box. Dance little doll. She was lying on her back. It's when you stop that you fall. She was the one who couldn't stop running. You fall when you stand still. She pushed Mama away and forced her feet over the edge of the sofa. The Girl tried to rush to the front door in order to stop the first taxi, go back to where she had always been, back to far away, further and further in. But she only made it to the hall mirror, where she became stuck looking at herself. She tilted her head to the side and wondered who was staring back at her with such angry black eyes. She ran her fingers along her collarbone, pushed her nails into the thin skin as far as she could. Blue, the skin became blue right away. Blue half-moons on her dry skin, sneering like the teeth of the Cheshire cat in the sky of Wonderland. They sneered at her for not knowing where she came from, for her not knowing where she was going. Sneered even more at her for thinking she could know.

Mama's laughter was bouncing between the walls like pearls from a broken necklace. The Girl tore her gaze from her darkness. Mama had turned on the lights and was sitting among the cushions on the sofa. She was holding the telephone between her ear and her shoulder, painting her nails with her glass of tea in her lap. Mama always had a glass of tea in her lap. There was a resonance in her internal archive, there were so many images the Girl had forgotten, so many images she remembered, but had never seen. She looked toward the bedroom, the one that had been hers. She remembered fifty-square-foot walks, carrot sticks, chemistry books and Excel boxes. She looked away, closed her eyes. There were so many images she wished she had never seen.

Something embraced her from behind, pulled her over the soft carpet. She glided with it, like the marionette with the red shoes, the girl from the dream. Mama pulled out a kitchen chair, placed her on it with steady hands. She sank down with force, almost bounced against the cotton cushion. Mama placed a glass of tea in her hands and she took big sips. Her taste buds shuddered at the sweet taste: sugar, it was sweetened. The alarm system in her chestcloud went off.

Mama placed a plate in front of her with golden yellow grains of rice covered in lamb meat and green herbs: *ghormeh sabzi*. She hadn't even reacted to the strong smell from the stew, it was so deeply rooted in her nostrils. It was a full plate. She looked up at Mama, curious liquorice pastilles against razor sharpness. There was no room for discussion, all the unsaid was said.

Mama sat down across from her, her shoulders were damp from the newly washed hair. She laid her hands on the table, spreading her fingers like fans. Her nails were a shiny red.

'Don't you have to work tonight?'

Mama smiled in response, smiled with those constantly pouting, deep red lips.

'No. I thought we both needed a day off.'

There was a pinch in her chestcloud. A day off. She didn't take a day off, not her. Mama caught her wandering gaze, looked straight at her. She couldn't remember the last time Mama had looked straight at her.

'No. You aren't going anywhere. You're not doing anything else tonight. You're going to sit here with me and let me talk. Tomorrow you can do whatever you want, continue however you want.'

Curious liquorice pastilles against razor blades. Gone was her Mama on the blankets, Mama behind the kiosk, Mama crying in the corner of the kitchen. Instead there were fan-like hands and sharp liquorice pastilles. The transformation had reached Mama as well.

'Those were pretty bad years, eh?' Mama leaned back in her chair, saw the shiver run along the Girl's spine. Mama knew that she knew which years they were talking about.

The Girl nodded and looked down at the plate, the saffron on the steaming rice. She tried to count in her head, but couldn't get the calculator to work. She tried to measure the distance to the bathroom, but couldn't hold the thought. She couldn't remember its cause, or imagine the consequences. She sat quietly for a while and tried, she tried to think, but couldn't. Her chestcloud was screaming. She lifted the fork and took a careful bite.

Mama bent one knee and hugged it.

'I hardly remember it, isn't that strange? It's like a fog in my head. Everything is like a fog. Starting with those last months in Iran, when all of our friends disappeared. You

376

know, it feels like they all disappeared during one night, all of them. It was like someone had put poison on the streets. Or no, poison would have been better.' Mama shook her head.

Razor-sharp liquorice pastilles against clear white eyes. There were no shadows fluttering in Mama's eyes.

'We were fleeing all the time, we started fleeing long before we left Iran. We ran around like rats in a cage and waited for it to be our turn…And in the middle of that you came, and we hardly understood how it had happened.'

She gave Mama a razor-sharp look, stared at the fine lines that had appeared on Mama's face. Evidence that couldn't be erased, traces of dreams and hard work.

'How can a new person come into a world that is in the process of falling apart? It's not natural, you understand? It didn't feel natural.'

The Girl tensed her calves, they wanted to kick. Her calves wanted to pull back and kick Mama down. Mama didn't notice anything. She got up and rummaged in the pantry, then continued talking.

'The escape here, the first few months, everything is a fog. I wasn't able to accept that everything had gone so wrong. That we had left our country to come and live among drunks. I felt so sorry for myself. So sorry for all of us…'

Mama was holding up two shiny candy bars, winking at her.

'I'll never forget the first time, that time when he threw the bag at the mirrors. I wasn't surprised, did you know that?'

Mama sat down across from her again and the Girl nodded in reply. There was a logic to everything, and the monster was the next step. Like a piece in a domino game, a piece that was waiting, that has to fall. Once you've started playing, it's going to fall.

'From the very first moment, you were standing in the middle. I remember it so clearly. When the mirrors broke, I thought, Where is she? Not because I wanted to protect you. No. I wanted you to protect me. Maybe I thought he would be more careful if you were there. Maybe I was counting on the fact that he wanted to protect you. Later, when I understood that it didn't matter … Well, what can I say? It was so clear. It became so clear so quickly that what was happening, was happening to both of us. That we shared it.'

Mama stood up and put away her plate. The Girl had hardly noticed that she had eaten, looked down in surprise at the empty plate. There wasn't a single grain of rice left. The bathroom! But her feet didn't move, her feet needed to hear this.

'No one was protecting you, that's how it was. We had too many scars.'

Mama put the plates in the sink. Her gaze got caught by the falling snowflakes outside the window: the polka dotted black, the darkness stained with light. She turned around slowly and looked at the Girl with warmth in her eyes.

'But you already know that.'

Flashing liquorice pastilles and a darkness that was bubbling in her throat. She wanted to scream at Mama, like she had screamed at the Swedish teacher Nina, like she had screamed at Papa right before dawn that same day. Yes, she knew! She knew and she didn't understand why it had taken so long for them to understand, that it always took so long. She didn't understand why it was so difficult, why it took so much time. She didn't understand how you could let so much time go by before realizing that you couldn't turn it back. She screamed inside, screamed at her feet to get up and run, run to the end of the world and beyond, run to a place where everything started over from the beginning.

Mama was standing at the stove, calmly pouring the saffron red tea from the pot. Mama was acting like they had all the time in the world, like the time that was passing now was just as good as any other. The Girl glanced at the clock on the wall: 7 p.m.. If she got in a car now she would be able to get a few hours of work done before Johan steered his steps toward the taxi home. The Firm, it was as far away as she could get. But her feet weren't moving, were unaffected.

'We didn't know any better, *dokhtaram*.' Mama stroked the Girl's hair and set down the glass of tea. 'I wish we had.'

The Girl lifted the glass of tea, didn't feel it burning her fingertips where there was no fat. She lifted the glass of tea and wanted to throw the hot, deep red liquid on Mama, mark Mama like she had been marked. But her hands resisted. Her hands let go.

'But I do know one thing. I know that we came here for freedom. We fled to Sweden in order to be free. To be able to think, believe, and become what we wanted. But we forgot to free ourselves from what we had left behind.'

Mama kneeled down next to her, carefully rolled up the Girl's shirtsleeves and ran her fingertips along her scars.

'Sometimes you forget about freedom, you forget that

379

you have it. Maybe we haven't even learnt what it means to be free. Or we've gotten used to it, so used to it that we've forgotten we have it.'

Freedom. She tasted the word. The freedom that had drowned between dreams and hard work.

'You reminded me about freedom once, do you remember? When you packed my bags that night. How long ago was that? God, it's been more than ten years now.'

Mama sank down on the kitchen rug with her legs crossed, dipped the candy bar in the still-hot tea.

'You know there are so many ways to take someone's freedom … And so many ways to lose freedom. You can take it from yourself … Often you take it from yourself.'

Mama gently tapped her temple with a red painted nail.

'It starts up here. This is where you need to be free.'

Mama winked with her long, tight eyelashes. She chewed slowly, looked up at the Girl with a searching gaze. Mama saw her thoughts floating, pushing against the banks which were holding them prisoner. Mama nodded with a knowing look in her eyes. Mama knew that compressed air was power, that the steam from the fire that has burnt will last a long time after the embers have been put out.

'Azizam.' My darling. 'It was for freedom we came.'

ECHO

She opens the folder and reads the contract. She reads line after line, reads her own name in the plan, the plan for hard work, the plan for someone else's dreams. Then she starts tearing, first one copy. She tears it in half, then into four pieces, then into insect-size pieces her fingers can't grasp. She flushes them, then looks at the other copy. Her name in the plan, the plan for hard work, the plan for someone else's dreams.

She starts tearing. The troll and the princess slide down the drain with the snowflakes. The balloons loosen their grip on her house. The compressed air breaks through her pores, leaving only emptiness behind. Echo.

It was for freedom we came.

A special thank you to Susanne Klofsten, P-O Söderberg, Abbe Bonnier, Christina Leijonhufvud, Petra Persson and Peter Shire—without you, there would be no book.

And to Gustaf and Korrie, for giving me the future.

All my love to Mama, Papa, and Little Brother.

For more information or to receive our newsletter,
please contact us at: info@worldeditions.org.